SOUTHERN LITERARY CLASSICS SERIES

C. HUGH HOLMAN AND LOUIS D. RUBIN, JR.
GENERAL EDITORS

PREVIOUSLY PUBLISHED

IN PREPARATION

THE KNIGHTS

OF THE

GOLDEN HORSE-SHOE

AN AUTHENTIC GOLDEN HORSE-SHOE?

Obverse of the original,
owned by Mrs. James B. Stone, of Richmond, Virginia

THE KNIGHTS
OF THE
GOLDEN
HORSE-SHOE

A TRADITIONARY TALE
OF THE
COCKED HAT GENTRY
IN THE
OLD DOMINION

BY
WILLIAM ALEXANDER CARUTHERS

WITH AN INTRODUCTION BY
CURTIS CARROLL DAVIS

THE UNIVERSITY OF
NORTH CAROLINA PRESS
CHAPEL HILL

INTRODUCTION

"Enclosed or rather by the same package," wrote William A. Caruthers from Savannah, Georgia, March 8, 1846, to his Whig congressman from the First District, Thomas Butler King, "you will receive a copy of 'the Knights of the Horse Shoe,' which you will do me the favour to enclose to Mr Bancroft, and though I do not expect him to give Gib the acolade, I would be exceedingly obliged to him if he would dub him with the *order* of the Naval School." [1] Caruthers was speaking of that forerunner of the Naval Academy at Annapolis established the previous October by historian George Bancroft, following his appointment by President Polk as secretary of the navy. The physician's second son, Gibson Caruthers, did not win his "order" to the Maryland institution, and what has become of Bancroft's copy of the book (the New Englander already possessed a set of its predecessor, *The Cavaliers of Virginia*) is unknown. In any event its author had less than six months to fret over the matter before tuberculosis carried him off at Marietta, in the Georgia hill country. At least one portion of his career remains in total obscurity; the details of his literary collaboration with the New York novelist, James Kirke Paulding, are an enigma;

1. Quoted from the manuscript in the Thomas Butler King Papers, Part A, Southern Historical Collection, University of North Carolina Library.

no known likeness exists; and not until 1949 was anything substantial published about his third, last, and best novel, one of the antebellum South's more notable historical romances.[2]

Caruthers had been born in 1802 at Lexington, in far western Virginia, fourth of the eleven children of Phebe Alexander and William Caruthers, one of Rockbridge County's most influential citizens—farmer, merchant, local representative for Thomas Jefferson's land holdings, including Natural Bridge. The younger William attended Washington College at Lexington (now Washington and Lee University); took his degree at the University of Pennsylvania Medical School in 1823; married a Georgia heiress, Louisa Catherine Gibson, of Whitemarsh Island off Savannah; and returned to his home town to practice. In 1829 financial misfortunes constrained the couple to try a new start in New York City.

There Caruthers served professionally in the cholera year of 1832; became active in Gotham's literary circles, notably with Paulding; and saw publication by Harper & Brothers in 1834–35 of his intersectional novel, *The Kentuckian in New-York*, and of his widely read romance about Bacon's Rebellion of 1676, *The Cavaliers of Virginia*. Their release established the doctor as the earliest Virginia novelist of importance. Since the appearance of *The Kentuckian* (in June, 1834) followed so closely upon that of *Swallow Barn* (1832) by the Maryland lawyer, John Pendleton Kennedy, and of *Guy Rivers* (1833) by the South Carolina man of letters, William Gilmore Simms, Caruthers may fairly take his stand with them as one of the three earliest Southern novelists of significance to come before the public.

Early in 1835 he and his family (there were eventually three sons and two daughters) returned to Lexington. Caru-

2. Unless otherwise specified, documentation on Caruthers, his family, and his literary career may be found in Curtis Carroll Davis, *Chronicler of the Cavaliers: A Life of the Virginia Novelist, Dr. William A. Caruthers* (Richmond, Va., 1953), which also contains digests of his novels. Therein Chap. VIII, pp. 196–253, treats *The Knights of the Golden Horse-Shoe*. Cf. also note 14 below.

thers had remained interested in the progress of Washington College—whose new president, mathematician Henry Vethake, he was instrumental in placing[3]—but his primary concern now was literature. While not wholly neglecting his medical practice, he was already engaged in research and in field trips down to Tidewater in search of materials for his next novel, which was to be called *The Tramontane Order*. By the spring of 1837 his notes and sketches were complete. Then struck that time-tested nemesis of authors: the Caruthers dwelling burned down, and among the casualties was his manuscript. Perhaps this was one of the inducements that caused the doctor to forsake the Old Dominion and remove to his wife's home town. By April, 1837, the family was settled at Savannah.

During his nine years in that bustling little port city Caruthers became a distinguished resident. He practiced medicine, served as a Whig representative on the Board of Aldermen, and grew active in real estate. He was a charter member of the Georgia Historical Society and local agent for the American Arts Union. He served as second in a duel and lectured against intemperance. He abandoned the Presbyterianism of his ancestors and, with Louisa, embraced the Episcopal faith. He found time to contribute a spate of articles to Georgia periodicals and a single essay to the *Knickerbocker Magazine*, up in New York—his eyewitness account of a Washington College schoolmate's ascent of the Natural Bridge —which evolved into one of American journalism's more long-lived items and led to the gradual transformation of its factual subject into regional legendry.[4]

Caruthers also reworked the data he had assembled for his aborted novel, completed it under a new title, and gave it to a

3. Cf. also Ollinger Crenshaw, *General Lee's College: The Rise and Growth of Washington and Lee University* (New York, 1969), pp. 51–52.

4. See Curtis Carroll Davis, "The First Climber of the Natural Bridge: A Minor American Epic," *Journal of Southern History*, XVI (Aug. 1950), 277–90, and his "That Daring Young Man," *Virginia Cavalcade*, IX (Summer 1959), 11–15.

Savannah magazine, *The Magnolia*, where the story ran serially during 1841 and was favorably commented upon by newspaper reviewers throughout the upper South. He then made the mistake, probably on grounds of sectional pride, of offering the book publication to an Alabama editor (of Virginia origin) who had facilities to print but far fewer facilities than the Brothers Harper to disseminate. As a result only five press notices of *The Knights of the Golden Horse-Shoe* have been uncovered, and of those only one, that in the Charleston *Southern Quarterly Review*, can qualify as a critique. The fact that all were favorable probably did little to console Caruthers' ego.

Released in the same year as dime novels by Timothy S. Arthur and Joseph H. Ingraham, and such other historical romances as James Fenimore Cooper's *Satanstoe* and William Gilmore Simms's *Count Julian*, the Georgia physician's contribution to the period's burgeoning fictional output stands as the earliest extended treatment of one of the most glamorous episodes in the pre-Revolutionary annals of the South and as the first book of any sort concerning the lieutenant governor of the Virginia colony, Major General Alexander Spotswood (1676–1740). It relates an account of the horseback expedition that was led by Spotswood in the late summer of 1716 out of the settled Tidewater area up through the tangled forests of the Piedmont, over the Blue Ridge, and down into the huge and silent Valley of Virginia—a journey undertaken primarily, as Spotswood later put it in his official correspondence, "to satisfye my Self whether it was practicable to come at the Lakes." His administration of twelve strenuous years, 1710–22, lay amid troublous times for the British Crown. Internationally there were wars with France and Spain. For the Virginia colony there was harassment by pirates along its Atlantic coast and Indian marauders bedeviling its southern and western frontiers, not to mention a subtle internal menace from the rapid increase in the Negro birthrate and its potential for slave insurrections.

Of all these possibilities for fictional treatment it was the
first of these situations that Caruthers chose to emphasize:
Spotswood's dogged determination to extend the boundaries
of the Old Dominion irrevocably westward so as to foil the
imperial ambitions of New France vis-à-vis the Great Lakes
and her Mississippi holdings. The first step was to surmount
"the great Apalachee," and the looming shadow of that challenge raises the fictional Spotswood into a pioneer with a
special vision. This "great subject of all his meditations"
(p. 39) renders aught else secondary. As his daughter Kate is
made to declare of her father, ". . . his thoughts soar forever
over those blue mountains, and that very passion will carry
him one day to their summits, and does it not ennoble his
character? Is he not elevated by it; see how pure and guileless
he walks among the poor intriguing politicians who clog his
steps. . . . Is he not the life and soul of the whole Colony?"
(p. 30).

The soldier's modern biographers have confirmed that
Caruthers' early interpretation was a sound one. "The appeal
of a continent had seized the governor's imagination," states
the earliest student of Spotswood's career, "and it was to
kindle the imagination of others that he restricted the right to
wear the golden horseshoe to those who had drunk the royal
health on Mount George." Concurs the latest (taking cog-
nizance of their subject's birth in Tangier): "The life that
began with sunrise over the Straits of Gibraltar ended with
sunset over the Blue Ridge Mountains. He looked westward all
his years."[5]

The 1716 expedition did not, it is true, lead to immediate
settlement of the Valley, and its recognition at the time cannot
be compared to the renown it has earned from posterity. For

5. Respectively, Leonidas Dodson, *Alexander Spotswood: Governor of
Colonial Virginia, 1710–1722* (Philadelphia, Pa., 1932), pp. 239–40, and
Walter Havighurst, *Alexander Spotswood: Portrait of a Governor* (New
York, 1968), p. 106. "Mount George" is probably identical with the present
High Top, bordering Swift Run Gap between the towns of Stanardsville
and Elkton on the Greene and Rockingham County lines.

fate decreed that the happenstance of a born romancer's fascination with a quintessentially romantic theme should deposit that renown, at one stroke, upon Spotswood's threshold. Following the appearance of *The Knights of the Golden Horse-Shoe* in 1841, slim chance remained that the governor and his fellow riders—now glorified as chivalric adventurers—would ever be ignored again.[6]

Besides being something of an historical landmark, *The Knights* stands as Caruthers' best written piece of fiction,[7] repeating and refining a pattern pursued throughout his novels. Owing to its focus on the cross-mountain safari, the plot is more unified than is usual with him. His characters' conversations have been pared down from disquisition to dialogue. The narrative moves more smoothly, with less of his characteristic verbosity, and the over-all tone avoids that almost feminine softness which vitiates the work of Caruthers' immediate successor in Virginia fiction, John Esten Cooke. The *dramatis personae* are identical with that of the earlier novels but more fully developed. All Caruthers' heroines, as is Ellen Evylin here, are small, blonde, and blue-eyed, leading to the surmise that his wife Louisa stood for each of them; and each has a companion of contrasting personality, such as Kate Spotswood. Caruthers' heroes are all Byronic paragons, but Frank Lee of *The Knights* is a shade better done than his predecessors. Here, too, the principals swing the plot door shut with a mass marriage toward the end of the book.

The "westerner" and comic character, Joe Jarvis, though he may well be based on a living person (p. 242n.), is also a fictional descendant of the drover, Montgomery Damon, titular character of *The Kentuckian in New-York*, who in turn was a reflection of the real-life figure of David Crockett, an ac-

6. Latest reference work to carry an entry on the episode is Howard L. Hurwitz, *An Encyclopedic Dictionary of American History* (New York, 1968), p. 378.

7. Concurring is Jay B. Hubbell, *South and Southwest: Literary Essays and Reminiscences* (Durham, N.C., 1965), p. 247. Hubbell also reaffirms that Caruthers was the first American novelist to introduce the Virginia cavalier into fiction (*ibid.*, p. 245).

quaintance of Caruthers' aunt and uncle, Elizabeth and Henry McClung of Lexington. Both characters indulge in that aspect of the day's fiction so titillating to readers, a backwoods dialect letter, but Jarvis' is better turned out. Like Damon, Jarvis embodies his creator's awareness of the significance of the common man, as do the references to the "plebeian ranks" and to the "primitive tobacco planters" (pp. 43, 121), a fact shattering the generalization by some scholars that the antebellum Virginia novelists were concerned solely with upper-class activity.

The doctor's Negro characters are regularly stratified into two types, the house slave and the field hand. In *The Knights* the former type—soon to become stiffened into a stereotype—is represented by Old Essex, major-domo of the Spotswood establishment, who presides over his underlings with the dignity of a landed proprietor and the language of a teacher of elocution. Of these underlings, introduced for comic relief and local color, June, the banjo player, mouths a somewhat better dialect than his forerunners in Caruthers' pages. Though the doctor's efforts in this regard read almost like burlesque today, he was nonetheless one of the earliest American novelists to perceive the literary value of Negro speech. (June is modeled on Caesar, in Cooper's *The Spy* [1821], and on Ben, in the anonymous *Sketches and Eccentricities of Colonel David Crockett, of West Tennessee* [1833].) The most exotic aspect of Caruthers' handling of the slave character is his perduring interest in their transatlantic origin, especially with those who were still professing Mohammedans. In *The Knights* this type is personified by Old Sylvia, the Moor, who had accompanied Governor Spotswood's father all the way from Africa and "was by the negroes called outlandish."[8] Louisa Caruthers had owned at least one black, Bullutah, bearing an

---

8. Pp. 13–14, below, of text. On a Botetourt County plantation only forty miles from Caruthers' home town of Lexington the slaves regularly referred to their African forebears as "the outlandish people." See Letitia M. Burwell, *A Girl's Life in Virginia before the War* (New York, 1895), p. 18. The first edition of this work was published in 1878.

Arabic patronymic, and in *The Kentuckian* her husband had reproduced an excerpt from the Koran in the original.

Although *The Knights of the Golden Horse-Shoe* ostensibly depicts the landscape of the Old Dominion (one generation later than its predecessor, *The Cavaliers of Virginia*), and is indeed dappled with historical coloration, several of the 'isms and 'ologies of Caruthers' own day intrude upon the scene. This is especially true of those associated with the concept labeled "the Sentimental Years"—a mystique distinctly alien to the atmosphere of the era in question. The characters' tendency to give way, male and female alike, to tears is one example. Another is the excoriation of alcohol (pp. 63, 71). A third is Kate Spotswood's instructing her swain upon the undoubted relationship between floriculture and the Deity (p. 72).[9] A fourth is the lecture to which heroine Ellen Evylin subjects hero Frank Lee on the obnoxiousness of the *code duello* (pp. 216–17).

Nor should one overlook Caruthers' employment, more fully here than in his earlier novels, of songs popular at his own time. "Massa is a wealthy man . . ." (p. 14) is a genializing reversal, for purposes of characterization, of lines in the minstrel song, "Come Day, Go Day, or Massa Is a Stingy Man," and stands as one of the earliest reflections thereof in American fiction.[10] The refrain, "Long Time Ago" (p. 61), though its accompanying lyrics may possibly be by Caruthers himself, boasts "an exceptionally curious history," and had been utilized by Kennedy in *Swallow Barn* and by Edgar Poe in "The Haunted Palace" (1839).[11] The lengthiest song in

9. A later governor of Virginia, J. Lindsay Almond, has also drawn the connection. See *Time: The Weekly Newsmagazine*, LXXII (Sept. 22, 1958), 15.

10. The song appeared originally in *The Magnolia*, III (Feb. 1841), 75. Earliest usage cited by Hans Nathan, *Dan Emmett and the Rise of Early Negro Minstrelsy* (Norman, Okla., [1962]), p. 65, is in New York City some time the same year.

11. See Gilbert Chase, *America's Music from the Pilgrims to the Present*, 2nd ed., rev. (New York, 1966), pp. 172, 206, 279, and Thomas O. Mabbott, ed., *Collected Works of Edgar Allan Poe. Volume I: Poems* (Cambridge, Mass., 1969), p. 317n. This "corn song' appears in *The Magnolia*, III (Feb. 1841), 115.

The Knights, commencing "Farewell, Old Beginny" (p. 210), may likewise derive from the doctor's pen, though its refrain had been adumbrated in one William Clifton's dialect composition of 1836 beginning, "O I was born down ole Varginny, Long Time Ago. . . ."[12] "Fire in the Mountains"—which supplies a chapter title and the unremembered lyrics that prompted Caruthers to a footnote commentary (p. 223)—was both a play-party song and fiddle tune reaching back to British origins and, in this country, identified widely in the South and Midwest.[13] Again, Caruthers' reference is among the earliest recorded in fiction.

The attitude from his own day which Caruthers introduces most significantly of all into *The Knights* is voiced recurrently by the novel's central character. It serves not only as a unifying element to the plot but remains the seminal concept of the story. Its quality is at once religious and political, its enunciation romantic. The doctor had first voiced it through the lips of Nathaniel Bacon in *The Cavaliers of Virginia*, which was released in January, 1835. He made it personal in a Savannah lecture of March, 1843. And again he became one of Southern literature's pioneers, for the concept in question, which did not emerge as a graspable phenomenon until the mid-1840s, was the point of view since designated Manifest Destiny.

The novelist never quite uses the phrase, but the ideal of American expansionism as a destiny is what he is talking about. To Governor Spotswood the beckoning lure of those Blue Mountains (pp. 28–29, 220) is a tantalization that—as

12. William Clifton, "Long Time Ago: A Favorite Comic Song and Chorus," entered at Clerk's Office, New York, 1836. Copy in Music Division, Library of Congress. Caruthers' version appears in *The Magnolia*, III (Oct. 1841), 435.

13. Winston Wilkinson, "Virginia Dance Tunes," *Southern Folklore Quarterly*, VI (March 1942), 9, and Ulrich Troubetzkoy, "Music on the Mountain," *Virginia Cavalcade*, XI (Summer 1961), 8. Musical versions may be found in P[atrick] W. Joyce, ed., *Old Irish Music and Songs* . . . (New York, 1965), p. 99, and in Joan Moser, "Instrumental Music of the Southern Appalachians: Traditional Fiddle Tunes," *North Carolina Folklore*, XII (Dec. 1964), 5. The second verse is usually given as "Kitty's in the cream-crock, run, girls, run!" Caruthers' verse and footnote appear in *The Magnolia*, III (Oct. 1841), 444.

Ralph Waldo Emerson would presently suggest in his poem, "The Forerunners"—stands forth as one expression of the romantic in the soul of man. But Spotswood's yearning is also part of a broader national, and irrevocable, impulse before which the Indians, as a race less well endowed to utilize the resources of the continent, must bow. Struck by the magnitude of the westward sweep of farmer and cattleman, stirred by the success of American arms in the war for Texan independence, Caruthers hailed as glorious the victory of the Rockbridge County Virginian, Sam Houston, on the plains of San Jacinto and descried in that victory a symbol of the white man's mastery of his environment in a progression that "we confidently predict will never rest this side of the gates of Mexico." Columbus had given the initial impetus to this movement, but it was Alexander Spotswood who first ensured its onward march. It was he who "was in reality the great pioneer. . . . How vast were the results of this expedition!" (p. 213).

What were the author's sources for *The Knights of the Golden Horse-Shoe*? As are the criteria for academic research today, they were three-fold—books, people, and field investigation. Among the printed sources of help to Caruthers come definitely the following five, in order of their usefulness:

Hugh Jones, *The Present State of Virginia* . . . (London, 1724)

John Oldmixon, *The British Empire in America*, 2nd ed. (London, 1741)

John [Daly] Burk, *The History of Virginia, from Its First Settlement to the Present Day*, I and III (Petersburg, 1804–5)

William Dunlap, *A History of the American Theatre* (New York, 1832)

William Wirt, *Sketches of the Life and Character of Patrick Henry* (Philadelphia, 1817)

The novelist also very probably consulted the following six titles:

Sir William Keith, *The History of the British Plantations in America . . . Part I. Containing the History of Virginia . . .* (London, 1738)

Edmund and Julian C. Ruffin, eds., *The Westover Manuscripts . . .* (Petersburg, 1841)

Robert Beverley, *The History and Present State of Virginia,* 2nd ed. (London, 1722)

William Waller Hening, ed., *The Statutes at Large; Being a Collection of All the Laws of Virginia . . . ,* 13 vols. (Richmond, 1809–23)

Jared Sparks, ed., *The Writings of George Washington,* I [the biography] (Boston, 1837)

John and John B. Burke, *Encyclopaedia of Heraldry . . . ,* 3rd ed. (London, 1844)

Concerning the individuals who, to a greater or lesser extent, assisted the doctor, the identities of nine are known. All of them were types of the "Virginia gentleman" of their day. Easily foremost was a Caruthers family connection, Charles Campbell of Petersburg, Princeton graduate, newspaper editor, and scholar currently on the brink of releasing what would at once be recognized as the first work on its subject of any real importance, his *Introduction to the History of the Colony and Ancient Dominion of Virginia* (Richmond, 1847). Next came a great-grandson of the governor, and former steward of the University of Virginia, George Augustine Washington Spotswood of Springfield, Illinois, who showered Caruthers with "stacks of letters" notable more for their prolixity than their pertinence. Then, of course, there was the estimable quintet to whom *The Knights* is dedicated, all of them prominently associated with the Williamsburg area: John Munford Gregory, Jr., member of the Council of State and future acting governor of Virginia; Colonel Robert McCandlish, judge in the High Court of Chancery at Williamsburg; Thomas (not

Robert, as the novelist has it) Griffin Peachy, M.D., a director
of the Public Hospital for the Insane at Williamsburg; Robert
Saunders, professor of mathematics at and future president of
William and Mary College; and, lastly, an "old friend" of
Caruthers now closing his term as tenth president of the
United States, John Tyler.

An eighth individual lending the doctor at least a modicum
of help was Francis Taliaferro Brooke, judge in the Court of
Appeals of Virginia, whose letter to the novelist concerning
a family Horse-Shoe closes all editions of *The Knights* and
has, over the years, proved to be that romance's most commented upon single feature. In conclusion there was he whom
the doctor eulogizes in passing (p. 86n.)—onetime member
of the Council of State, former United States congressman
from Virginia, Robert Page, of the "North End," Gloucester
County branch. Though Page was never a "Senator," as
Caruthers believed, nor yet the sole lineal descendant of
Governor John Page, his venerable presence serves to introduce the third element the novelist brought to his research:
field investigation. It was with Robert Page, and undoubtedly
with many another like-minded antiquary, that, as Caruthers
avers in his introduction, he explored "the good old classic
ground of Virginia" and sought to salvage her crumbling
tombstones. In so doing, and in publishing his results, was
not this western Virginian taking one of the earliest steps in
that labor of eastern restoration which was to lag for almost a
century after his day and require the wealth of a Rockefeller
to consummate?

In publishing his results, alas, the novelist was misled by his
sources into a constellation of errors—some mere winkers,
some blazing, several to attain the status of fixed stars in
Virginia legendry. Since they have been discussed in detail
elsewhere,[14] it suffices to tick off the more outstanding ones
in summary fashion.

14. See Curtis Carroll Davis, "The Virginia 'Knights' and Their Golden
Horseshoes: Dr. William A. Caruthers and an American Tradition," *Modern
Language Quarterly*, X (Dec. 1949), 490–507.

"Temple Farm," scene of the opening pages of *The Knights*, has no proved connection with Spotswood or any of his family. The cross-mountain expedition occurred in August–September, 1716 (not 1714). It consisted not of Caruthers' "army" of stalwarts but of sixty-three men, seventy-four horses, and some dogs. It endured neither Indian threat nor hunger privation and was not the earliest party to penetrate the Valley of Virginia.[15] Governor Spotswood did not even marry until two years after leaving office, and his burial site (p. 274) remains unlocated, though it is probably near his country place at Germanna—which was never demolished by fire[16]—some twenty miles west of Fredericksburg in present Orange County. His half brother, Major General Roger Elliott, was almost certainly never in North America, nor yet beheaded, but an anonymous portrait of him in all likelihood identical with that described by the novelist (pp. [iii] and 16) hangs in the Governor's Mansion at Richmond. Spotswood's physician, "Dr. Evylin," represents Caruthers' masking, for some reason, of the identity of William Cocke, secretary of the colony and so close a friend that at his funeral Spotswood is said to have burst into tears.[17]

Once back at his palace after the expedition to the Valley, the governor decided upon a gesture which *The Knights of the*

15. See *The Discoveries of John Lederer...*, ed. William P. Cumming (Charlottesville, Va., and Winston-Salem, N.C., 1958), pp. 88–89. For variant interpretations of the subject see Delma R. Carpenter, "The Route Followed by Governor Spotswood in 1716 across the Blue Ridge Mountains," *Virginia Magazine of History and Biography*, LXXIII (Oct. 1965), 405–12, and Randolph W. Church, "Tidewater to Shenandoah Valley: A Cameraman Retraces Spotswood's Famous Expedition," *Virginia Cavalcade*, I (Winter 1951), 19–25.

16. See below, p. 206. For a sketch of the fort, a photograph of the state historical marker, and related data see John W. Wayland, *Germanna: Outpost of Adventure, 1714–1956* (Staunton, Va., 1956), pp. 24, 80, *et passim*.

17. Cocke is identified as the original of "Dr. Evylin" by one W. S. B., "Historic Landmarks in Lower Virginia...," *Southern Field and Fireside*, III (Aug. 24, 1861), 106. The author was probably the Savannah lawyer, William Starr Basinger (1827–1910), who had studied for the bar under Caruthers' acquaintance, John Elliott Ward. The novelist's reference to Cocke's "cenotaph" (p. 5n.) signifies the mural tablet in the Bruton Parish church bearing his epitaph. The inscription is given in full by W. S. B. and by Havighurst, *Alexander Spotswood*, p. 94.

Golden Horse-Shoe has glorified into perhaps the most
chivalric single episode of record by the English in North
America. The novelist's chief published source, the Reverend
Hugh Jones, described that episode succinctly:

> For this Expedition they were obliged to provide a great Quan-
> tity of Horse-Shoes; (Things seldom used in the lower Parts of
> the Country, where there are few Stones:) Upon which Account
> the Governor upon their Return presented each of his Companions
> with a Golden Horse-Shoe, (some of which I have seen studded
> with valuable Stones resembling the Heads of Nails) with this
> Inscription on the one Side: *Sic juvat transcendere montes* ["Thus
> does he rejoice to cross the mountains"]: And on the other is
> written the tramontane Order.

> This he instituted to encourage Gentlemen to venture back-
> wards, and make Discoveries and new Settlements; any Gentle-
> man being entitled to wear this Golden Shoe that can prove his
> having drunk *His Majesty's Health* upon MOUNT GEORGE.[18]

The "full court costume" (p. 244) in which the Governor
makes the presentation—and which Caruthers cites in his
"Introduction"—probably reflects information the novelist
received concerning the Charles Bridges portrait of Spotswood, aged about sixty, hanging in the doctor's time at
"Sedley Lodge," Orange County, home of the subject's great-
grandson, William Spotswood, and now to be viewed in the
Governor's Mansion, Richmond.[19]

18. See Hugh Jones, *The Present State of Virginia* . . . , ed. Richard L.
Morton (Chapel Hill, N.C., 1956), pp. 58–59. Caruthers' note (p. 213) on
this volume should be glossed to the effect that the "Franklin Library" is
now the Library Company of Philadelphia and that "Cambridge" probably
refers to Harvard University. Each institution possesses a copy of *The Present State*, acquired *c.* 1755 and in 1818, respectively. The Georgia Historical Society, Savannah, still has its copy of Oldmixon's *British Empire in
America*, 2nd ed. (1741). Caruthers' couplet (p. 51) is likewise from Jones,
Present State of Virginia, p. 118, but with "the Queen" substituted for
"George" owing to the novelist's misconception that Anne, who died Aug. 1,
1714, was occupying the throne.

19. Reproduced in color in *Virginia Cavalcade*, XVIII (Spring 1969), 28.
A variant rendering by the same artist, now in the Governor's Palace, Wil-
liamsburg, is reproduced in color as frontispiece to Havighurst, *Alexander
Spotswood*. For a discussion of provenance see Henry W. Foote, "Charles
Bridges: 'Sergeant Painter of Virginia,' 1735–1740," *Virginia Magazine of
History and Biography*, LX (Jan. 1952), 30–31.

Whether Spotswood sought or required Crown assent for his gesture, as Caruthers ponders (p. 245n.), is doubtful. If such had been the case, some hint would surely have been recorded in his official correspondence; the decision was probably the governor's own. What is far more doubtful is the number and identity of gentlemen riders graced with the accolade. Caruthers lists no fewer than thirty-one. True, all bear surnames encountered with greater or less prominence in Virginian annals. But only three (Beverley, Brooke, and Taylor) match those of individuals since proposed as members of the expedition, and none of the three carries the correct Christian name. Research,[20] enlarging on John Fontaine's all too casual references in his journal, would seem to qualify the following gentry—and, to date, no others—as authentic "knights":

NAME	IDENTITY
Robert Beverley, Jr. (c. 1673–1722)	Of King and Queen County, planter, author of *The History and Present State of Virginia* . . . (1705; 1722)
Robert Brooke II (1680–1744)	Of Essex County, surveyor of land grants in western Virginia
Capt. Jeremiah Clowder (fl. 1716)	Of King and Queen County, justice of the peace, sheriff
John Fontaine (1693–1722)	Of London, for the years 1715–19 a home seeker in Virginia colony
Stephen Harnsberger (fl. 1716)	Of Rockingham County
Francis Hume (d. 1718)	Spotswood's factor at Germanna

20. Especially that of the state librarian of Virginia, Randolph W. Church, who is completing a study of the expedition's route and membership based on an examination of land grants in the western part of the state.

Col. George Mason III (1690–1735)	Of Stafford County, burgess (father of the Constitutionalist)
Col. Edward Moseley (1661–1736)	Of Princess Anne County, justice of the peace, sheriff
Col. William Robertson (d. 1739)	Of Williamsburg, clerk of the Council of Virginia
Mr., or Dr., Robinson	Either Col. Christopher Robinson (1681–1727), of Middlesex County, naval officer for the Rappahannock River, or his brother John Robinson (1683–1749), of Essex County, future president of the Council
William Russell (1679–1757)	Of Orange and Culpeper Counties, justice of the peace, sheriff (eponym of Russell County)
Capt. Smith (*fl.* 1716)	Unknown
Col. James Taylor, Jr. (1673–1730)	Of Orange County, surveyor, planter (great-grandfather of President Zachary Taylor)
William Todd (d. 1736)	Of King and Queen County, soldier

And the tokens of "knighthood" with which these cavaliers were decorated? To date, not a single fully authenticated specimen has been found—a situation constituting the most glamorous conundrum in Virginia history. Family carelessness and, especially, the exigencies of the Civil War era probably account for that situation. Two conclusions about the Shoes, however, seem settled: they were of no more than pocket-charm size, and the "nail heads" studding them were garnets. A Norfolk poetess has written of their recipients:

> Scant is the praise that scholars yield
> And few their wreathes of fame,
> But still the happy riders live
> In others of their name

Who take the dusty road of men
    With dignity and mirth
While golden horseshoes print again
    The deep Virginia earth.[21]

Traces of those vanishing hoofprints have been glimpsed at least as early as six years following the original investiture. In September, 1722, Spotswood tendered a Shoe to an Iroquois sachem at Albany in New York colony, as a safeguard should the chief wish to travel to Virginia. In the 1840s the governor's great-granddaughter, Mrs. Susan Catharine Bott of Petersburg, stated that she had once seen her ancestor's personal Shoe and that it was small enough to be worn on a watch chain. During this same period somebody lost one of the baubles behind the marble mantelpiece at "Blandfield," the Beverley estate in Essex County.[22] Shortly before his death in 1846 Caruthers himself apparently succeeded in his quest for "one of the curious relics" (p. 247), since the Tarrytown, New York, physician, Horace Caruthers, subsequently featured one, set in garnets, on his watch chain which he said he had inherited as the novelist's eldest son. By at least 1869 another novelist, John Esten Cooke, had examined one at a Virginia home, again set in garnets. A Shoe alleged to have been given by Spotswood to his son-in-law, Bernard Moore (who figures in *The Knights* but was probably not a member of the expedition), remained in the family until the War Between the States, when it was filched from "Chelsea," the Moore place in King William County, by a Federal trooper. After the war a descendant, Leiper Moore Robinson, sketched it from memory, had it reproduced by Tiffany & Company, and presented the replica, set with diamonds and sapphires, to his fiancée Mary Spotswood Campbell (daughter of the his-

21. Frances S. Lankford, "Ballad of the Golden Horseshoes," in her *Signal the Valiant Meaning* (Richmond, Va., 1969), p. 7. Poem first published in 1935.
22. See Virginia Showell, *Essex Sketches* (Baltimore, Md., 1924), p. 69.

torian), by whom it was eventually bequeathed to a close friend in Richmond and is extant to this day.

The Shoe referred to by Judge Brooke, in his letter at the close of *The Knights*, belonged to Edmund Brooke of Georgetown, D.C.—where it was viewed, among others, by the philanthropist William Wilson Corcoran—but later inquirers were advised that it had simply disappeared! From about 1910 rumors of the existence of the tiny charms have been bruited in North Carolina, Georgia, and Alabama. In the 1920s an army officer, Edgar Erskine Hume, "thought I was hot on the trail of one, but the nearest I got was a lady who had six or eight small garnets which she said had been on one of these emblems, but that the gold had been used to make a wedding ring."

Not until the year 1946 did there emerge what may possibly rank as an authentic Golden Horse-Shoe. This one was discovered in a Richmond pawn shop, where it had been abandoned by a noncommittal old gentleman who had evidently seen better days. "About the size of a Phi Beta Kappa key," the bauble was exhibited for two years during the 350th Anniversary Celebration of the founding of Jamestown (1957) and serves as frontispiece to the present edition of *The Knights*.[23]

So much for vestiges of the Shoes themselves. What sparks, if any, have been struck off by the romance celebrating them? When its author asserted that Spotswood and his entourage "had little idea that they were then about to commence a march which would be renewed from generation to generation" (p. 161), he probably had even less idea of the extent to which *The Knights* would leave its imprint on subsequent annals. True, of Caruthers' three known novels it has easily been the most neglected by formal literary critics. But other,

---

23. It has also been reproduced in *Virginia and the Virginia County*, IV (Oct. 1950), 21, and in Davis, *Chronicler of the Cavaliers*, facing p. 252. For a detailed description by the owner see Davis, "The Virginia 'Knights' and Their Golden Horseshoes," p. 505. Militating against authenticity is the presence of the verb form *jurat* ("swears") instead of the correct *juvat*.

broader types of response have been in evidence from the late 1840s up to today. In order of their first stirrings these responses may be grouped into historico-critical and belletristic categories. Writers in the first category were, almost without exception, aware of a specific piece of fiction and Caruthers' authorship thereof. Those in the latter category were, in general, aware of the historical episode, sometimes of a novel featuring it, and, very rarely, of the man who wrote the novel.

In the first category—the earliest to emerge—Charles Campbell called his readers' attention to Caruthers' romance in both the magazine and book versions of his history of Virginia (1847). In the October, 1853, issue of the *North American Review* at Boston, an anonymous writer who was probably editor Andrew P. Peabody compared the "Order" to that of the Society of the Cincinnati. Five months later John Esten Cooke contributed to *Putnam's Magazine* at New York what may be termed the first revival after Caruthers of the Knights' story, his essay "The Cocked-Hat Gentry."[24] In 1887 Justin Winsor, librarian of Harvard College, listed *The Knights* among authorities for his account of the expedition in his *Narrative and Critical History of America*, and in the same year the Baltimore journalist, Edward Ingle, discussed the event as an episode in the Romance of Cathay. In July, 1889, Caruthers' most prominent successor in their special genre, Thomas Nelson Page, declared in an article for *Lippincott's Magazine* at Philadelphia that *The Knights* was "the novel on which his name now rests." Confederate chroniclers such as Thomas C. DeLeon, in *Four Years in Rebel Capitals* (1892), and Dr. Thomas A. Ashby, in *The Valley Campaigns* . . . (1914), envisaged the Spotswood riders as having set the model of valor for those Virginians who resisted Northern aggression during the Civil War. In 1921 Caruthers' romance was cited by the former rector of the University of

24. In John Esten Cooke, *Virginia: A History of the People* (Boston and New York, 1883), p. 495, he asserted that "Virginia fiction may be said to begin" with the publication of *The Cavaliers* and *The Knights*.

Virginia, Armistead C. Gordon, in his speech at the unveiling
of a stone cairn to the expedition erected by the Virginia chapter, Colonial Dames of America, at Swift Run Gap on what is
now the Skyline Drive. For years the most balanced academic
treatment of Caruthers' work as a whole, giving prominent
attention to and excerpts from *The Knights*, was that by the
Ohio-born scholar teaching at the University of Virginia, Carl
Holliday, in the second volume (1908) of the *Library of
Southern Literature*. It remained for a western-Virginia born,
North Carolina—resident professor, Jay B. Hubbell, to provide
the most fully rounded discussion of the romance in *The South
in American Literature* (1954).

The second category of response to the Spotswood story,
the belletristic, was touched off by the opening guns of the
Civil War. The initial item was a three-stanza ballad, "The
Virginians of the Valley" (1861), by the Georgia physician,
Francis O. Ticknor. Frequently anthologized, it remains one
of the ablest creative reactions, and its final stanza reveals
the first stirrings of that symbolic usage to which the riders
would henceforth be put:

> We thought they slept!—the sons who kept
>   The names of noble sires,
> And slumbered while the darkness crept
>   Around their vigil fires;
> But, aye, the "Golden Horseshoe" Knights
>   Their old Dominion keep,
> Whose foes have found enchanted ground
>   But not a knight asleep!

In the September 25, 1869, issue of the New York weekly,
Appleton's Journal, John Esten Cooke published an essay on
the expedition wherein, apparently for the first time, the episode is labeled "A Virginia Legend." So, too, is the only
known dramatic interpretation, a four-act melodrama, *The
Golden Horseshoe* (1876), by the Richmond journalist, W.

Page McCarty, who stated that his play was founded both on the historical evidence "and the Legendary Account by Caruthers."

Poets treating the theme in the wake of Dr. Ticknor have, like him, usually seen its value as symbolic. In "Sir Fontaine's Ride . . . A New Year's Story" (1881) by the widely published Valley of Virginia balladeer and musical journalist, Aldine S. Kieffer, the Knights become ghostly defenders of the Old Dominion against the Indians, with a macabre Civil War fillip at the close. Envisaging Spotswood as the personification of trail blazer are *Knights of the Golden Horseshoe, and Other Lays* (1909) by the Norfolk educator and naval historian, Robert A. Stewart; the free-verse poem beginning, "Twelve men I chose to see the waiting land" (1932) by Gertrude B. Claytor of Staunton, a portion of which was engraved on the commemmorative boulder emplaced at Swift Run Gap in 1934 by the Virginia State Commission on Conservation and Development; and "The Knights of the Golden Horseshoe" (1934) by Margery Howell of Culpeper. The ablest verse treatment of all, Frances S. Lankford's unsentimental "Ballad of the Golden Horseshoes" (1935), for the first time depicts a young Spotswood and views him and his cohorts simply as the embodiment of happy vitality.

Very few novelists have followed in Caruthers' footsteps along the Spotswood trail. In *The Golden Horse Shoe* (1900) the Maryland journalist and travel writer, Stephen Bonsal, touched on the theme of Manifest Destiny by linking the governor and his fellows with the campaign against Spain in the Philippines under Commodore George Dewey. *In the Days of Jefferson: or, the Six Golden Horseshoes . . .* (1900) by the Rhode Island author of boys' stories and editor of *Youth's Companion*, Hezekiah Butterworth, is a foolish, formless juvenile ostensibly designed as a paean to the third president. Likewise a juvenile, but incomparably the finest handling of the theme in fiction, is *The Golden Horseshoe* (1936), by the Buffalo-born poetess and children's author, Elizabeth Coatsworth. Featuring a little Indian girl, this novelist deftly evokes the English atmosphere of the Virginia of that day.

Clearly, those Golden Horse-Shoes have not only left their imprint all over the Old Dominion but have ventured into many an alien realm. The fact that this quintessentially Virginian story was first given to the world in Georgia, and attained its final form in Alabama, only augments its regional status. As chance would have it, the year of book publication also saw the first appearance in print (posthumously) of a painstaking study of the colonial period by a Scots antiquarian who likewise proclaimed the virtues of Alexander Spotswood and roundly affirmed that his fellow colonials "ought to have erected a statue to the memory of a ruler" such as he.[25] The opinion precisely parallels that of the penultimate sentence of *The Knights of the Golden Horse-Shoe:* "Western Virginia should erect some enduring monument to the memory of that far-sighted statesman and gallant soldier who first discovered that noble country." The sentence was penned by a native of "that noble country" but one who was unaware of the fact that he himself had just fashioned the governor's most enduring monument.

Also his own—for William Alexander Caruthers' tombstone, if he ever had one, has yet to be located.

25. See George Chalmers, *An Introduction to the History of the Revolt of the American Colonies* ... (Boston, 1845), II, 78.

A NOTE ON THE TEXT

William A. Caruthers' last novel has enjoyed five appearances in print before the present edition: (1) as "The Knights of the *Golden Horse-Shoe* . . . ," in the Savannah, Georgia, *The Magnolia: or, Southern Monthly*, III, January–October, 1841, inclusive; (2) as *The Knights of the Horse-Shoe* . . . , two volumes in one, from the press of Charles Yancey at Wetumpka, Alabama, 1845; (3) as *The Knights of the Horse Shoe* . . . , Harper's Franklin Square Library #269, three columns to the page, New York, 1882; (4) as *The Knights of the Horseshoe* . . . , with four illustrations by J. Watson Davis, Burt's Library of the World's Best Books, New York, 1909; (5) as the same, in copyright reprint, 1928. The present text reproduces that of the first book appearance, Wetumpka, Alabama, 1845, retailing at seventy-five cents, and its editor has taken the liberty of restoring "Golden" to the title, which was deleted for reasons unknown.

Philip Coleman Pendleton, the young editor of *The Magnolia*, was so proud of having snared *The Knights* for his pages that when the installments were complete, he presented a bound volume of its issues to the author, duly inscribed. This item is now in the University of Georgia Library at Athens. Caruthers himself had another set of copies bound into two volumes and inside the front cover of each wrote,

"W A Caruthers Savannah Georgia April 1844." This unique item reposes in the J. K. Lilly Collection of the Indiana University Library, Bloomington, and is illustrated in the present editor's biography of Caruthers, *Chronicler of the Cavaliers* . . . , facing p. 200.

The novelist's occasional footnotes to the text of the magazine appearance of his romance were carried over into the 1845 book edition, and four additional ones were added. The dedication was inserted. Stylistically the doctor made various minor changes whose effect was to emend his writing toward a greater colloquialism. Volume One, Chapter IX, was misprinted "XI," an error corrected with the succeeding chapter. By contrast the A. L. Burt editions—those most frequently encountered today—are chapter-numbered consecutively throughout, omit the dedication, all the footnotes, and numerous passages of text ranging in length from two or three sentences to all of one chapter and two-thirds of another (Volume One, Chapters XIII and XXV, respectively).

The 1845 edition of Caruthers' novel is a rare book. Copies have been located at just fourteen repositories, all in the United States. Of these, four are institutional libraries: Newberry, Chicago; New York Public (two copies); Peabody, Baltimore; and the Virginia Historical Society, Richmond (two copies). Ten are college or university libraries: Alabama, Columbia, Duke, Harvard, Indiana, University of Pennsylvania, Samford (carrying the bookplate of the Virginia philologist and Confederate naval surgeon, Bennett Wood Green, M.D.), Virginia (two copies), William and Mary (two copies, one bearing the signature of John Millington, professor of chemistry and engineering in the college), and Yale.

THE KNIGHTS
OF THE
GOLDEN HORSE-SHOE

THE KNIGHTS

OF THE

H O R S E - S H O E.

~~~~~~~~~~~~~~~~~~~~~~~~~~~~~~~~~~~~~~~

CHAPTER I.

A VIRGINIA FARM HOUSE.

AT a moderate distance from Yorktown, (since so famous by the surrender of CORNWALLIS,) there stood a plain looking structure, covering a considerable portion of ground, embracing, under one common roof, a long range of buildings of various dimensions, and surrounded with cool looking verandahs, which extended entirely round the lower story of the house; here entirely closing one portion from view, with the extension of green slats, and there throwing open another from the ceiling to the floor, so that the inmates might choose sunshine or shade, as suited their fancy. Besides this main building, there were others of various sizes and shapes, from the kitchen to the coach house, forming, altogether, quite an imposing looking establishment. One side of the dwelling commanded a fine prospect of the Chesapeake Bay, while the other faced a garden, at that day a curiosity in the colony. It extended beyond the reach of the eye landwards, until it was lost in a beautiful green lawn, which fell off abruptly towards a little bubbling brook which wound its way around the extended bluff upon which the mansion stood. This garden was laid out after the prim and rather pragmatical fashion of that day in the old country, and adorned with statues and grotoes, and curiously devised box hedges. In the centre of these, a *jet d'eau* constantly threw up its glittering spray, giving a most inviting air of coolness and repose to the place. The whole establishment was surrounded by a fence, painted white, the entrance to which was through a high arched gate in the fashion of the times.

This was called Temple Farm, from a circumstance which will appear in the course of our narrative, and was one of the country seats of Sir Alexander Spotswood, then Governor of Virginia, and Commander-in-Chief of Her Majesty's forces in the colony.

Further along the shores of the bay, stood a double row of small white cottages, with a narrow street running between, and one large building of two stories, in the centre, surmounted with a small cupola and weathercock; this was the negro quarter. Beyond this, again, stood the overseer's house; still following the same line.

The whole settlement presented a most inviting prospect to the eye of the weary traveller; and from the water was still more imposing; because, on that side, was one unbroken front, giving the idea of quite a village, from the number of the buildings. No one will wonder at the extent, even of this country establishment, when we state from undoubted authority, that his Excellency's income, at that time, exceeded twenty thousand pounds, per annum, independent of his official salary.

It was near sundown of a sultry day in the summer of 1714; the dim blue outlines of Acomac and North Ampton could just be discovered across the misty surface of the bay. Sir Alexander Spotswood was seated in a large arm chair in the front porch of the building, entirely alone, except his dogs, which were snoozing away around his chair in various groups. He had a pipe in his mouth, held from time to time in his fingers, while he blew away the smoke, and cast his eye now and then along the surface of the water. He wore a cocked hat on his head, which was thrown rather to one side, so as to exhibit a profusion of iron-grey hair, done up in the bob wig fashion. His features were large and strong, but not unpleasing, especially when a smile broke over the otherwise bronzed and statue-like countenance. His face, from the brow to the chin, was covered with wrinkles. The sure guarantee that the youth of their possessor had not been passed in inglorious ease and luxury. He had a fine set of white teeth, which greatly redeemed his countenance from a look of premature age, assisted by an eye which, when under excitement, was black and brilliant with the unspent fires of youth or genius. Surmounting this weather-beaten countenance, was a high forehead, falling back at the temple, so as to leave a hollow on each side, and thus to produce what is called, in common parlance, the hatchet face. His limbs were brawny and athletic, showing their possessor capable of extraordinary physical exertion. He wore knee breeches, met by cloth gaiter leggings buttoned close to his well turned limbs, which, truth to say, were Virginia fashion, thrown over the bannisters, in the most careless attitude possible. Over his person he wore a hunting coat, thrown carelessly back from off his shoulders, while near by rested a fowling piece he had apparently just set down, being his almost inseparable companion in his long and celebrated walks.

While his Excellency thus lazily smoked away alone, in the front of his house, the other portions of the building were by no means in the same state of dreamy repose. About the entrance gate there was much bustle and confusion, incident to the departure of some guests and the arrival of others.

His extensive and princely hospitalities were renowned, even in the Old Dominion, and his establishment, whether in town or country, was the centre and focus of all the elite of the colony. Over that portion, he had already swayed a most happy and judicious influence, far better suited in its free and easy grace, to the age of the country, than the stately formalities of his predecessors. Upon occasions of public ceremony, he by no means abated the pomp and parapharnalia of his office. His previous life had been too purely military for that, but that very education of the camp, lent to the privaces of his own home all the careless ease and grace so common to the undress of the camp.

His being thus seated so long and so indolently gazing out upon the slumbering waves, was by no means accidental. Suddenly there appeared a faint flash and a quick report of fire arms in the offing, followed almost instantaneously by two others, so faint and far off as just to be heard and seen. These reports proceeded from small arms, and were very different from those of a vessel in distress, which idea, indeed, the dead calm of the bay itself precluded. Nevertheless, they seemed to rouse the Governor, the pipe was thrown over the bannister, his legs were drawn to the floor, and in the next instant he had snatched a spy glass, and looked long and silently over the water. After he had hurriedly replaced his glass, he seized his gun and fired three charges as rapidly as he could perform the evolutions of loading and firing. He had no sooner done this, than he ordered one of his servants to light a large pine torch, and having manned one of his boats, jumped in, followed by the boy holding aloft his burning brand. They steered out to a considerable distance from the landing, and then again he folded his arms, and looked long and ardently as before over the expanse of waters, the oarsmen resting upon their oars.

While he is thus employed, let us return to the mansion; over the windows of which, various lights are now seen, indicative of some more busy life within, than is usually to be found of summer evenings at an ordinary farm house.

CHAPTER II.

AN OLD FASHIONED FIRESIDE PARTY.

BEFORE we introduce our readers into this drawing room, let us pause at that old fashioned hall door, and read the inscription over the coat of arms, (the plate on which it was inscribed was in existence within the memory of many now living.) we think it reads thus: "PATIOR ET PORTIOR;" the most appropriate that could be conceived for its possessor, it was his life, both previous and subsequent, in an epigraph. Through this large old dining hall we pass into a parlor well lighted up, and furnished with much taste and elegance. The room was nearly full of company; and we shall proceed to introduce such of them as we take a fancy to.

But, before we do so, let us premise, that that drawing-room contained at that moment the future fathers and mothers of some of the most celebrated characters of our country. First, of course, we shall present the lady of the mansion; she was seated with some half dozen others of her own sex at a small table, around which they were working at the needle, busily chatting all the while, sometimes with the gentlemen standing around, and sometimes with other ladies similarly seated and occupied in other parts of the room. Lady Spotswood, notwithstanding the stiff fashion of the female costume and head dress at that time, was the very beau ideal of a rich farmer's wife. She looked quite young in comparison with her husband, and possessed the remains of a beauty that must have been formidable among courtiers of the royal household, from which atmosphere the General had plucked her. How many ladies thus transplanted, would not have carried with them the faded pomps and ceremonies of their former sphere? Not so, however, with lady Spotswood. No one could ever have imagined, that she had figured in her younger days within the cold formalities of a courtly circle, for there was a whole heartedness, a bon hommie of expression, a freedom of conversation in the highest degree enthusiastic sometimes, which we, simple hearted republicans, believe dies within the purlieus of the royal household. She seemed to enjoy her company with the highest relish, and, of course, she entertained them with ease.

At an opposite table sat her two daughters; Ann Catherine, the elder, by the General called Kate, and Dorothea, the younger. The eldest of these was about seventeen, and the other about two years younger. However much we might lament the unromantic sound of their names, we cannot help it, having previously pledged ourselves to adhere to the real ones. Sure we are, that if we cannot interest our readers in them under their real, we could not under fictitious ones. Being familiar with these, (aye, and with their characters,) almost from our youth, we shall use the Governor's privilege, and abbreviate them whenever we please.

Kate, then, was a fair girl in every sense of the word, or, in other words, she was a blonde. Light hair, dress, and every thing light; even her voice and laughter seemed to indicate a light heart, and that is a very important point upon which to assure our readers. But in all this field of white, there were shades of most delicate tints; her eyes, though not white, were light blue, and the lashes over them, fell down so low sometimes as to form a fine shading for those laughing and rather mischievous, we should rather say merry, looking eyes.

It is a dangerous thing, looking too deep into the color and texture of a lady's eyes ; they become very unfathomable, very, and have an aspect of wonderful profundity ; and the longer one looks, the deeper they get, until, like looking down into the deep, deep sea, or the high blue arch above, we begin to wonder at the heighth and depth. It is a kind of star gazing, which may bewilder the brain as well as another.

Occasionally she would drop her needle and work, and clap her hands with the most heartfelt delight at the sallies of the youth standing over her chair. She was dressed with much simplicity, and her hair seemed to follow the pyramidical fashion of the day with great reluctance, for here and there a stray curl wandered down her pure white neck. The expression of her countenance was rather arch, produced by a slight contraction of the outer angle of the eye, and a constant dubiousness about her pouting lips, as if they did not know their own intention, whether to laugh or not. On one side of her, stood Bernard Moore ; and on the other, sat the Rev. Commissary, Blair, who will be described presently. Her changing countenance, as she turned to one or the other, no doubt formed a pleasing study to the youth at least. One while, all quivering with archness and pent up mischief, and the next moment exhibiting the simplicity of childhood, as she caught the words that fell from the lips of the excellent prelate. She was a fine, tall girl, and one who performed whatever was in hand gracefully, it was impossible for her to be awkward; all this did not seem the result of education, but appeared like nature itself.

Dorothea was a full, round, plump little figure, not so tall as her sister, and of a beauty not quite so spiritual, and differing from her in many essentials, both of appearance and manners as well as character. Her hair was brown, her eyes hazel, her cheeks red. She wore an apron with a bunch of keys dangling at her side, giving one an idea of domestic operations, for which she seemed to have a peculiar turn. She was slightly inclined to *embonpoint*, yet a neat, tidy, trim, little figure.

Dorothea assigned to herself an humbler position than that allowed to her more brilliant sister, but the assent to this was by no means universal in the court circles. She was the favorite with many, and was in the habit of saying sometimes very pungent things in her demure way. Not with the ease, grace, and perfect self-possession of her sister, to be sure; but, perhaps, they told better from popping out as unexpectedly to the hearers as the speaker. She was a decided pet of the old gentleman, and was mostly to be found in his wake, when he chose to throw off the cares and toils of official life, for the more heart cheering enjoyments of the social circle. If no one else laughed at her observations upon things and men, as they passed in review in such constant rounds of society, he did ; and it was no uncommon thing to see them sitting quite apart from the company, she chatting away most volubly, and he bursting every now and then into a laugh.

The two brothers were John and Robert—the former and elder of these sat apart from the rest of the company dressed in the green uniform of the Rangers, of which corps he was an officer. His arms were folded and he did not seem to be at his ease. His face had a general resemblance to that of the Governor and might once have been handsome, but it now bore the impress of early dissipation, and consequently of care and sorrow. The family seemed to look upon him with pain and commiseration, if not of smypathy, though it is questionable whether they understood exactly the cause of his general moodishness. The Rangers, of which John was a Captain, were composed of about twenty or thirty men each corps, and stationed at convenient distances along the then circumscribed frontier of the colony. · He seemed to consider his present position what it truly was, one of honorable exile; consequently, he seized every opportunity to visit the capital. His presence at the fireside circle, was by no means a common circumstance. The sort of innocent gaiety that prevailed there at all times, had no charms for him. He was there now in the performance of imperative military duty, which he dared not disobey; he had ridden express to communicate with the Governor and wait his orders concerning frontier matters—which indeed he had done some time, and as it seemed to him without much chance of a speedy gratification of his impatience, for no Governor appeared. Others in that little party began to feel some surprise at his long absence, for the evening was now on the wane.

The Rev. Commissary Blair, as many of our readers know, was then at the head of William and Mary College, which was at that time as much a school for christianizing the savages as for general purposes of education. He was a hale, hearty, red faced old gentleman, dressed entirely in black velvet, with ruffles at his wrists and broad shining silver buckles at his knees and shoes, and much addicted to taking snuff, a box for which he carried often in his hand. He was a lively old gentleman, though grave at times. On the present occasion, he evidently enjoyed the merry sallies of Kate by whose side he sat. Bernard Moore, the youth who stood on the opposite side of her chair, had been but a few years emancipated from his government, consequently he stood rather in awe of his old master, but still fully amenable to the more lively impressions of his fair young friend. He will speak for himself.

The youngest son of the Governor, Robert, w s quite a lad, and therefore to some extent, like all other lads, he was teazing his moodish brother after the most approved fashion, where we will leave him for the present, while we introduce some more of that company to our readers.

There was walking along the room a tall grey headed old man, of uncommonly benevolent countenance and prepossessing appearance. His hair was combed back from his high polished forehead and fell in long white locks upon his coat collar. He was dressed very much after the same style as his friend the Rev. Commissary, and at first sight might readily have been mistaken for some venerable old father of the church. It was Dr. Evylin, the most celebrated Physican of his day in the colony, and the bosom friend of his excellency.* He stooped much in the shoulders, so as to give him the appearance of greater age than he really was. He carried in his hand an ivory headed cane almost as long as himself. Occasionally he stopped to hear a few words of her ladyship, not addressed immediately to him, said a word or two—shook his head perhaps—or smiled assent, and passed on. He was a man of few words but much thought. No one could converse in the room without feeling that he was present.

There were many others present at that snug little country fire-side party—stowed away in one end of that old parlor, but it is needless to bewilder the reader with them at present. The various parties were grouped as we have described, when the door was thrown open by a man in livery and the Governor entered. Nearly every one rose and bowed at his entrance, except his youngest daughter, who, as usual, ran up and threw herself into his arms.

---

* We believe this fact is inscribed upon his cenotaph at Williamsburg.

He however gently put her away and threw himself abruptly into a vacant chair, a proceeding so very unusual with him as to attract the particular attention of every one in the room. It was now observed that his face was of an ashy paleness, and her ladyship, who had approached and laid her hand upon his arm, started back in terror as she observed a spot of blood upon his face.

The whole party now gathered around his chair in the utmost surprise, each one enquiring what was the matter; some to the Governor in person and others to those nearest him. He told them that it was nothing—a mere scratch; but there was excitement, subdued it is true, but deep and intense excitement in the countenance of the veteran, which these words by no means allayed. He heeded them not however, but taking the arm of Dr. Evylin, walked away in the direction of his library.

CHAPTER III.

A NIGHT FUNERAL.

WE left the Governor and his boat in a preceding chapter, quietly reposing upon the bosom of the silent and motionless waves of the Chesapeake. He had not remained long in that position before the stealthy sound of muffled oars were heard approaching. He stood up in his boat and leaned forward with eagerness to catch the sound, which grew more and more distinct until the boat itself hove in sight, which proved to be a yawl manned by sailors, and under the command of the second officer of a ship. This official when the yawl came along side, rose and touched his cap, and enquired if he had the honor to address Gen. Spotswood. He replied in the affirmative, when the mate handed him a sealed packet, which he broke open and glanced over by the light of the torch. W ile he read the letter he trembled, and seemed agitated for one whose nerves had been braced and hardened in the fierce school of contending armies. "Have you the box here," said he at length addressing the same official.

He replied that it was in the yawl.

The boats were run gunnel to gunnel and lashed together, while all hands proceeded to lift a box of about seven feet long and three broad into the Governor's boat, after which he counted out money to the sailor, and departed as he had come, having ordered the slaves to pull for the little inlet formed by the small stream before described. After rowing some half an hour the boat was run aground high and dry, upon his own lands. The box was lifted out and placed upon poles, and the six oarsmen bore it through the garden until they came to the farthest extremity of the lawn, where had recently been erected a small tomb-like building,* with the ground floor bare and a new made grave open in the centre. On one side of this the box was deposited and the negroes ordered to depart.

About half an hour afterwards the Governor returned bearing in one hand a dark lantern, followed by his carpenter, with various tools on his shoulder. The door was again unlocked and the man ordered to open the box, which he proceeded to do, not without fear and trembling. The outer boards being removed, exhibited a leaden coffin; this also he was ordered to cut through. When it was completed, the man was turned out and the Governor left alone. He then proceeded to roll down the lead about two feet; beneath this, were various folds of what once had been white satin, but now sadly stained and

---

* The remains of the temple were still standing a few years ago.

tarnished; this he likewise removed, when a ghastly spectacle exhibited itself. It was the body of a large fine looking man, in the uniform of a General Officer, his head severed entirely from the trunk and all much disfigured with blood. The Governor threw himself upon his knees and hung over this sad spectacle, and wept long and bitterly. Many times he took the last look of the features of that beheaded man, before he finally assumed composure enough to close it again and summon the workman. This he did at length,— and having changed his apparel, appeared in the drawing-room, as we have seen.

About midnight, there sat round the table in the Governor's library, himself, the Rev. Commissary and Dr. Evylin. The countenance of the former exhibited still the same ghastly appearance, and those of the other two gentlemen were not unmoved. We shall break into their conversation at the moment.

"You say truly, your Excellency, that secrecy in this business is of the last importance, not only to the due preservation of your proper authority, but for the interest of the colony itself, as at present situated."

"I differ with you my dear sir," replied the Doctor, "because I conceive that it can neither offend King nor Council, for one, however high in authority, to honor the remains of his own near kinsman with Christian burial."

"You forget, Doctor," rejoined the Commissary, "that that kinsman died the death of a traitor."

"Hell and fury!" shouted the Governor, striking his clenched fist upon the table—"he died a patriot—a martyr—a victim!"

"Softly, softly," said the Rev. gentleman, laying his hand upon the arm of the Governor, "I only spoke the language of common rumor—of the government—of the laws."

"May a thousand furies seize the government—the laws and rumor, all together!"

"Let me explain all this," mildly put in the Doctor. "Thus stands the case. Here is a gentleman, an officer of high rank, who is beheaded in Scotland for the alleged crime of high treason—alleged remember," seeing the Governor again start. "This gentleman who suffered, is the half brother of another military man who has been appointed Governor of one of the colonies under the very government which beheaded his kinsman. This is not all—this government at home had the same suspicious of this very Governor, and many of his friends shrewdly suspect that he was sent hither to keep him out of harm's way—in other words, on account of former brilliant military services—that he was sent hither in a sort of honorable exile. Is it not so?"

"You are right—you are right, Doctor," said the Governor, between his kis teeth, "go on."

"Then the question presented is, shall he clandestinely inter these remains which have arrived here to-night, or shall he bury them openly in his own burying grounds? I think it better to make no mystery of it, and trust to the liberality and good sense of the ministry, should they hear of it. Such a proceeding would be very natural, surely."

"But you forget, Doctor," said the Commissary, "that this thing is to produce a vast effect upon others beside the ministry, and the first effect too. Recollect the state of the colony. Every party at home is exactly represented here. It is useless to conceal from ourselves, that the government of our friend meets with powerful opposition. What is it that prevents him from leading an army now across the mountains into that unknown eldorado beyond, but this very jealousy of his power and popularity; and would this opposition dare, for a moment, to show head, were it not for the more than encouragement they receive at home. Now, what effect would such a funeral have, when the subject of it was proclaimed through the colony?—that is the question."

"There is force in your reasoning," said the Doctor.

"Besides, there is another point upon which we have not touched," said the Commissary. "The Governor will, doubtless, desire to have his friend and kinsman interred with the rights and ceremonies of the church; now, as he is the secular head of that church, and I am the unworthy representative of my lord Bishop, how can we publicly bestow funeral honors upon one who has fallen like this unfortunate gentleman?"

"You have settled the matter, reverend sir," said the Governor, musing, "you have settled the matter; and as every one seems now asleep, let us betake ourselves to our melancholy task."

It was a most strange looking group that, of the two reverend looking old gentlemen: the doctor with his long ivory headed cane, and the reverend Commissary in his surplice, following the Governor to a surreptitious grave, by the dubious light of a dark lanthorn. As they approached the temple, they all bared their heads, and the clergyman taking the lamp, commenced that most solemn and imposing ceremony of the English church. When he came to the appropriate place, the coffin was lowered by the Doctor and Governor, after which the grave was filled up, and they retired as they had come, the Governor leading the way.

The mansion house by this time, and all the surrounding scene, lay wrapped in the most profound repose; not a single light relieved the dark outlines of the now gloomy looking mansion, and even the statues, which in daytime gave a classic air of lightness and grace to the picture, now rather added to the solemn silence and mystic gloom by their shadowy figures. The late occupation of our three adventurers, too, added not a little to the sombre aspect of these dim outlines. There was that magnificent sheet of water, too, beyond, sending up forever its melancholy roar of the distant waves, and heralding the coming morn with its broken fragments of misty drapery, towering up here in huge abutments, and there arching to the horizon. Away towards the ocean, between the dim outlines of Cape Charles and Cape Henry, the bay seemed relieved by a darker outline of clouds piled up against the sky like a chain of mountains.

CHAPTER IV.

COUNTRY LIFE—ITS DUTIES AND ENJOYMENTS.

THE next morning broke bright and cheerful, emancipated by the morning sun from the mists and clouds of the previous night. Kate Spotswood was up with the lark, brushing the dew from the grass and flowers with an elastic foot, which seemed made on purpose only to bound over nature's brightest and freshest beauties, so fawn-like were her movements. Yet her occupation on this morning seemed of a quite homely and domestic kind. She wore a sun bonnet, and carried a basket on her arm. She took the path leading across the garden and down towards the brook, and in a few minutes ascended the rising ground opposite, leading towards the negro quarter. In the basket were various phials and papers, all labelled in the most careful manner, and arranged so as to be of instant use. She entered the door of one of the white cottages rather apart from, and larger than the others, and called, in plantation language, the sick house. Here, around a pretty extensive and well ventilated room, were arranged sundry cots, upon which lay about one dozen negroes; some tossing in the restless delirium of fever, and others cadaverous with the hues of an ague. She approached their bedsides in succession, followed by an old crone, called the nurse, who scarcely ceased to bless her young mistress even to put a spoon between the teeth of a refractory patient.

"God a mighty, bress miss Kate; poor nigger been dead but for her. She neber forget em! neber!"

She had not been long thus engaged, when a little pale faced white girl, dressed in linsey woolsey, entered the sick house, and stood before the young lady, dropping an awkward curtesy.

"Father begs, ma'm, that you'll come down and see him this morning, he's laid up with the rheumatis, and can't move a hand or foot."

"And who is your father, child?"

"He lives, ma'm, in the small log house on the other side of the overseer's, just beyond the nigger landing."

"Oh! old Jarvis, the fisherman? I remember him now. Run home, and tell your father that I will be there directly."

This fisherman's hut was full half a mile beyond the negro quarter, but she never hesitated. With alacrity she tripped over the damp grass, throwing back her hood as the blood came bounding into her cheeks with the glow of health and exercise, her fair cheeks fanned by the gentle breeze just rippling the bay. Neither ditches nor fences stopped her progress: she bounded over the one and climbed the other, like one accustomed to such obstacles. When she arrived within the fisherman's hut, she found old Jarvis laid up indeed, as his daughter had described, and racked with fever and pain. She felt his pulse long and carefully, looked at his tongue, and made many enquiries as to the manner of contracting his disease.

"I fear, Jarvis," she said at length, "that your case is rather beyond my skill, not that I would fail to try some of my simples to relieve you, but good old Dr. Evylin is at the house, and I will bring him to see you presently."

And then she turned to the old woman, his wife, and made many kind enquiries as to their means of living and present supplies, stroking her hand over the white headed urchins clustering around all the while. She soon after took her leave, promising to send supplies to the old woman as soon as she got home.

A goodly company assembled that morning at breakfast. Dorothea at the head of the table, and lady Spotswood on her right hand, with many other ladies, married and single, occupying the upper, while the gentlemen sat round the Governor at the lower end.

Dorothea seemed to have enjoyed the benefits of exercise, and the consequent glow and bloom of health as well as her sister, but she had been drilling the dairy maids, and marshalling fine pans of new milk, eggs, and butter, and, truth to say, her fair, ruddy face looked as if she enjoyed these good things herself with no little relish. Not that she was at all coarse or vulgar in her appearance, or that there was any thing in these rural occupations, tending that way. We only meant to say, that she looked more like a red cheeked country lass, the daughter of some respectable farmer, than a descendant of an aristocratic stock. She chatted volubly, but with no effort. She laughed heartily whenever she felt like it, and that was not seldom.

"Ha, Miss Catherine," said the Rev. Commissary, as that young lady entered and took her seat at the table, "had you been up with the lark this fine morning, and engaged as I saw your sister, you might have transferred the bloom of that pretty flower in your hair to your fair cheek."

"If your Reverence will but examine that flower," plucking it from her hair and handing it across the table to him, "you will perceive that it is not one to be had by stepping into the garden. I plead guilty to the remissness of dairy duty."

"This is truly a flower," said the old gentleman, examining it with his glass, "which is not to be found among your father's exotics. Is it not so?" handing it to Bernard Moore, "you have just returned from the hot houses and parterres of Europe." Bernard quietly slipped the beautiful little subject of dispute into the button-hole of his vest, before he replied, "That it was a native plant, and scarcely grew within a mile of the house."

Dorothea laughed a low musical chuckle, at the sly way in which Bernard appropriated the flower, and the blush with which her sister watched the proceeding. "I think, Reverend Sir," said she slily, "that the pursuit and capture of that flower has given sister quite as much color as my dairy performances."

The Governor did not seem to enjoy this small talk with his usual relish, for he was wont to encourage these playful sallies of his children, and loved above all things to see them cheerful. But now he sat silent and dispirited; and an occasional glance at his son John, who was beside him, seemed by no means calculated to inspirit him. That youth was so nervous that he could scarcely carry his cup to his head at all, and had not touched any thing to eat. He looked, too, haggard, bloated and sullen. He had once been the Governor's chief hope and delight, and he was equally the favorite of the old clergyman, who sat opposite to him, for his brilliant native abilities, and the highly creditable manner in which he acquitted himself of all his collegiate duties. It is true, that he was known then to be wild, but not viciously so. Now, however, his whole nature was changed. He scarcely noticed his sisters, whose still clinging affection he seemed to loathe. His mother he avoided on all possible occasions, and for these general family meetings in the country he had an especial abhorrence. There was a stealthy, suspicious glance about his eye, as foreign to his former nature as it was inexplicable to his father now, as he, from time to time, cast a sidelong glance at his rapidly depreciating heir.

There was one person at that table who understood the mystery of John Spotswood's peculiar behavior of late, and that was old Dr. Evylin, but he seemed to observe him even less than any other person at the table. Many strange things were told about John by the servants, such as his great precautions at night before he would go to bed; getting up in the night and calling for lights, swearing that some one was under the bed; at other times he would take a notion that some one was locked up in a certain closet. These things the whole family knew; they had been observed at his former visits, and now he was an object of the most undisguised solicitude to the whole of them, and to his father of dread. He thought his mind touched, and that ere long he would lose his reason, if, indeed, he had not partially done so already.

Catherine's brightest smiles were instantly clouded, if poor John happened to come within the range of her vision. At this very breakfast, she sat scarcely listening to the playful, bantering mood of Bernard Moore, so entirely was she abstracted by observing the more than commonly ferocious aspect of her elder brother. She would sit looking at him, lost in abstraction, until the speaker had twice or thrice repeated his words, and then she would reply without seeming entirely conscious of what she said. In short, a settled dejection brooded over the party since John had entered and taken his seat.

As Dr. Evylin was about to leave the table, Kate stepped behind his chair, and whispered a few words into his ear, which brightened up the old man's countenance instantly. "Ha!" said he aloud, catching her hand, and drawing back her retreating figure, "this young lady suffered herself to lie under mistaken imputations, when she ought not to have done so; she has been a mile this morning on foot, before breakfast, to visit a poor sick fisherman."

"Ah!" said the Governor, "is old Jarvis sick?"

"He is," continued the Doctor, "and so ill that my pretty pupil has called a consultation upon his case."

"I owe you an apology, my dear Catherine," said the good Commissary, "and hope whenever I do get in your debt, it may be always for a similar cause, and as happily liquidated. You were right not to divulge the matter;

the right hand should not know what the left doeth.   These are services which God reserves for his own special pleasure of rewarding, and not subject to the poor payment of worldly praise." Kate had broken away and ran before the old Doctor's sermon (as John called it,) was half over.

~~~~~~~~~~~~~~~

CHAPTER V.

AN EXCURSION ON HORSEBACK.

Soon after breakfast a number of horses were brought round to the front entrance of the house, to a gravelled court, separated from the box-bound flower beds before described, so as to admit horses and carriages to the very portico of the mansion.

The horses were of various sorts and degrees; some fine generous animals, others common cobs, while the rear was brought up by ponies and dogs in great abundance.

This was the daily custom of the establishment, at least every fair day. The Governor himself rode a fine imported war-horse, of fine proportions and admirably drilled.   He stood at the porch door with his high erect head, waiting for his master, with as much pride and gaiety as if he had been a thinking animal.   Various were the jokes and rejoinders passed among the grooms and stable boys, as they stood there, each one holding a horse by the bridle.

Any one must have visited a Virginia family party in the country to form any idea what an essential ingredient this morning excursion is in their domestic pleasure, and how highly it is enjoyed by young and old.   We shall perhaps have occasion, before we part with our readers, to trace this and many other customs, which have survived the revolution to our British ancestry. At length the party issued from the house.   Every one at liberty to consult his own fancy as to his company, unless some previous expedition had been such as a visit to some natural curiosity, or to church on Sunday.

Accordingly Kate on a fine pacing poney and Dr. Evylin by her side, had already set off in the direction of the fisherman's hut.   The old gentleman was quite gallant, and managed his sensible looking little poney cavalier fashion.

It may seem strange that Bernard Moore should thus suffer the old gentleman to monopolize the attention of a young lady, for whose favors he was generally understood to be paying the most anxious and solicitous court; but the fact is, she herself had sent him off cantering in an opposite direction.   Let our fair readers be not alarmed; he had not already proposed and been rejected..   The case stood thus: Kate had expressed some regret that she could not accompany her brother a mile or two on his way to the capital, owing to her engagement with the Doctor.   Bernard, in the most self-sacrificing and disinterested manner imaginable, proposed to be her substitute, which offer was most thankfully accepted.   He and John were old class-mates and once very intimate, and she desired of all things to see that intimacy renewed, now that Bernard had returned from his foreign tour, acknowledgely one of the first young men in the colony.

Strange to say, the youth was so blinded by his self-doubting mood, as never once to reflect that this was the very highest compliment which she could, in the then position of affairs, pay to him.

He and John had also now cantered off in quite a different style from Kate and her venerable old beau.   They made the fire fly from their horses heels, as they careered, like winged messengers, over the road to Yorktown and Williamsburg. A very few moments ride at that gait brought them to the door of the tavern in the centre of the former, and Bernard was quite surprised to see John alight and give his bridle to the servant, for he knew not that he so purposed on setting out. He was invited to do likewise, which of course he did; not knowing the business which detained his friend. That was soon explained; for John, instantly upon setting foot within the bar-room, ordered a bottle of spirits. It was with no little astonishment that Bernard saw him pour out and gulph down a tumbler of brandy and water, half and half, enough to have staggered any youth at a single blow. But he was still more astonished at the wonderful transformation, which this short and simple process effected. His old friend was himself again: he now chatted cheerfully, rode alongside of his companion without restraint and without effort to leave him; and above all, he appeared the highly intellectual and gifted man he had once known him to be. He spoke freely of European and colonial affairs, and took now an interest in many little things which he seemed not at all to notice before. Moore conversed with him freely, and at length fell into stories of former days and youthful frolics, until the woods rang again with their merriment. Having thus wrought up his subject to a proper key, as he supposed, purely by his own address, he ventured to ask him for an explanation of his late singular and inexplicable mood; but John passed it off in the slightingest manner imaginable; said it was nothing but a fit of the blue-devils—a constitutional infirmity, to which he was subject.

"But how comes it John," said Moore, most innocently, "that you were not subject to these when we were so long and so constantly together. I do not recollect of your being once so afflicted; during those ever happy and memorable school-boy days, you were the life and soul of every party. If any two started together upon an expedition and you were left behind, it was always—'come let's get Spotswood, there's no sport without him.'"

"True—true Bernard, but those happy hours of idleness do not last forever, indeed I presume that the change which you see in me is but the natural one of thoughtless boyhood, into the higher and more care-giving responsibilities of man's estate."

Thus they conversed; Moore pleased and amused at the half playful—half melancholy mood of his old friend, but not more than half convinced, by his reasoning, backed, as it was, by the change of mood itself—then that ungodly drink of brandy—that the son and heir of the Governor of Virginia should alight at a common tavern and thus quaff spirits like a sailor—it was inexplicable to him, but he finally set it down in his own mind to the effect of the military life in which his father was now attempting to train him. He therefore shook hands with his reanimated friend, as he supposed, with scarce concealed impatience, and galloped back to carry news of the pleasing change to Kate. Little did he imagine the real cause of that change and how very short a time it would last, or he would not thus exulting have sought an opportunity of returning his credentials. He met the Governor and Dr. Blair riding along the road at a staid and sober gait, and seemingly engaged in a conversation little less desponding than that from which he supposed he had just rescued poor John. He did not pursue them to see whether they too would be thus suddenly transformed by a glass of brandy and water. He was rather rejoiced than otherwise, for it assured him that his Excellency would not command his attendance, and thus detain him from the point at which he was aiming. Alas! true love never did run smooth; and Mr. Bernard Moore, after all his haste to join Kate and the Doctor, only arrived to find the position he sought already occupied by another young gallant from the capital, not less highly gifted by nature and fortune than himself. It was Mr. Kit Carter, a scion of the genuine aristocratic stock, and heir expectant of the splendid seat of Shirley. Moore was too highly schooled in all the courtesies of conventional breeding to shew chagrin at such an acquisition to the company at the mansion house, as Mr. Carter undoubtedly was; but we may say at once that he was disappointed in not being able to communicate the result of his diplomacy. It would have taken a shrewd and sagacious observer of human nature to have discovered even this, beneath all the courtly grace which they manifested. Carter and he met for the first time since the return of the latter, and that meeting was most warm and cordial. This was magnanimous, certainly, in Bernard; for, from their school days they had been rivals for the favor of Kate. The good old Doctor had not felt pulses so long and not yet be able to see a little into matters as they now stood, accordingly the old gentleman, with a sly smile, reigned in his pony and dropped in the rear, to muse upon one not less lovely and admired than her whose lively chat he had surrendered. Not a lady-love, nor even a wife—for the old gentleman was a widower—it was his lone and only daughter, almost a recluse within the walls of his own house at Williamsburg; yet so young, so highly cultivated, and, withal, so fascinating in every personal grace, she was fast becoming a devotee in religion. The good Doctor did not regret this, but he was naturally one of those calm, cheerful, philosophic minds, that are enabled to appreciate all that is excellent in our holy religion, without surrendering up the choicest blessing of social life—a cheerful and happy spirit. But we anticipate, the Doctor's lone idol will be introduced to the reader in due progress of our story.

In the meantime Kate was like powder between flint and steel; every spark elicited, fell upon her.

An encounter of wits between two highly endowed young men, and paying court to the same lady, is a study to those curious in psychological matters. But we will leave the whole party to dismount and dress for dinner, while we take a peep into other things having relation to the main thread of our narrative; until then, we bid our readers a cheerful and hearty goodnight.

CHAPTER VI.

A KITCHEN FIRE-SIDE IN THE OLD DOMINION.

Imagine to yourself, reader, a fire-place large enough to roast an ox whole, and within which a common wagon load of wood might be absorbed in such a speedy manner as to horrify one of our city economical house wives—though now, it was late in summer and of course no such pile of combustibles enlivened the scene—besides, it was night, and the culinary operations of the day were over. A few blazing fagots of rich pine, however, still threw a lurid glare over the murky atmosphere, and here and there sat the several domestics of the establishment; some nodding until they almost tumbled into the fire, but speedily regaining the perpendicular without ever opening their eyes, or giving any evidence of discomposure, except a loud snort, perhaps, and then dosing away again as comfortably as ever. Others were conversing without exhibiting any symptoms of weariness or drowsiness.

In one corner of the fire-place sat old Sylvia, a Moor, who had accompanied the father of the Governor (a British naval officer) all the way from Africa, the birth place of his Excellency. She had straight hair, which was now white as the driven snow, and hung in long matted locks about her shoulders, not unlike a bunch of candles. She was by the negroes called outlandish, and talked a sort of jargon entirely different from the broken lingo of that race. She was a general scape-goat for the whole plantation, and held in especial dread by the Ethiopian tribe. She was not asleep, nor dozing, but sat rocking her body back and forth, without moving the stool, and humming a most mournful and monotonous ditty, all the while throwing her large stealthy eyes around the room. In the opposite corner sat a regular hanger-on of the establishment, and one of those who kept a greedy eye always directed towards the fleshpots, whenever he kept them open at all. His name was June, and he wore an old cast-off coat of the Governor's, the waist buttons of which just touched his hips, while the skirts hung down to the ground in straight lines, or rather in the rear of the perpendicular, as if afraid of the constant kicking which his heels kept up against them when walking His legs were bandied, and set so much in the middle of the foot, as to render it rather a difficult matter to tell which end went foremost. His face was of the true African stamp: large mouth, flat nose, and a brow, overhung with long, plaited queus, like so many whip cords, cut off short and even all round, and now quite grey. The expression of his countenance was full of mirthfulness and good humor, mixed with just enough of shrewdness to redeem it from utter vacuity. There was a slight degree of cunning twinkled from his small terrapin-looking eye, but wholly swallowed up, by his large mouth, kept constantly on the stretch. He had the run of the kitchen; and, for these perquisites, was expected and required to perform no other labor than running and riding errands to and from the capital; and it is because he will sometimes be thus employed, that we have been so particular in describing him, and because he was the banjo player to all the small fry at Temple Farm. He had his instrument across his lap, on the evening in question, his hands in the very attitude of playing, his eyes closed, and every now and then, as he rose up from a profound inclination to old Somnus, twang, twang, went the strings, accompanied by some negro doggrel, just lazily let slip through his lips in half utterance, such as the following:

> "Massa is a wealthy man, and all de nebor's know it,
> "Keeps good liquors in his house, and always says, here goes it."

The last words were lost in another declination of the head, until cat-gut and voice became merged in a grunt or snort, when he would start up, perhaps strain his eyes wide open, and go on again:

> "Sister Sally's mighty sick, oh what de debil ails her,
> "She used to eat good beef and beans, but now her stomach fails her."

The last words spun out again into a drawl to accompany a monotonous symphony, until all were lost together, by his head being brought in wonderful propinquity to his heels in the ashes.

While old June thus kept up a running accompaniment to Sylvia's Moorish monotony, on the opposite side of the fire; the front of the circle was occupied by more important characters.

Old Essex, the *major domo* of the establishment, sat there in all the panoply of state. He was a tall, dignified old negro, with his hair queued up behind and powdered all over, and not a little of it sprinkled upon the red collar of his otherwise scrupulously clean livery. He wore small clothes and knee-buckles, and was altogether a fine specimen of the gentlemanly old family servant. He felt himself just as much a part and parcel of the Governor's family, as if he had been related to it by blood. The manners of Essex were very far above his mental culture; this, no one could perceive by a slight and superficial observation, because he had acquired a most admirable tact (like some of his betters,) by which he never travelled beyond his depth; added to this, whatever he did say, was in the most appropriate manner, narrowly discerning nice shades of character, and suiting his replies to every one who addressed him. For instance, were a *gentleman* to alight at the Hall door, and meet old Essex, he would instantly receive the attentions due to a gentleman; whereas, were a gentlemanly dressed man to come, who feared that his whole importance might not be impressed upon this important functionary, Essex would instantly elevate his dignity in exact proportion to the fussiness of his visitor. Alas! the days of Essex's class are fast fading away. Many of them survived the Revolution, but the Mississippi fever has nearly made them extinct.

On the present occasion, though presumed to be not upon his dignity, the old Major sat with folded arms and a benignant, but yet contemptuous smile playing upon his features, illumined as they were by the lurid fire light, while Martin, the carpenter, told one of the most marvelous and wonder-stirring stories of the headless corpse, ever heard within those walls, teeming, as they were, with the marvelous. Essex had often heard stories first told over the gentlemens' wine, and then the kitchen version, and of course knew how to estimate them exactly: now that before mentioned incredulous smile began to spread until he was forced to laugh outright as Martin capped the climax of his tale of horror, by some supernatural appearance of blue flames over the grave. Not so the other domestics, male and female, clustering around his chair; they were worked up to the highest pitch of the marvelous. Even old June ceased to twang his banjo, and at length got his eyes wide open, as the carpenter came to the sage conclusion, that the place would be haunted.

It was really wonderful, with what rapidity this same point was arrived at by every negro upon the plantation, numbering more than a hundred; and these having wives and connexions on neighboring plantations, the news that Temple Farm was haunted, became a settled matter for ten miles round, in less than a week, and so it has remained from that day to this.

On the occasion alluded to, the story-teller for the night had worked his audience up to such a pitch of terror, that not one individual dared stir for his life, every one seeming to apprehend an instant apparition. This effect on their terrified imaginations, was not a little heightened by the storm raging without. The distant thunder had been some time reverberating from the shores of the bay, mingling with the angry roar of the waves as they splashed and foamed against the beach, breaking and then retreating for a fresh onset.

It was yet quite early in the evening, and all the white family had gone to the house of one of the neighboring gentry to spend the evening. No one was apprehending their return for some hours, when a thundering clatter of horses and wheels were heard on the gravelled road, followed by several loud peals upon the knocker of the hall door. A lurid glare of lightning at the same instant flashed athwart the sky, tinging every living and inanimate thing, to the farthest corner of the room, with a bluish silver white, and revealing the mansion-house, on the opposite side of the yard, through the window, in magnified proportions like some giant castle looming up for an instant in goblin outlines, and then vanishing amidst a most astounding and overwhelming crash. During this terrible uproar of the elements, and a deluging torrent of rain, the same incessant rattle of the knocker was kept up on the hall door. No one dared to answer it except old Essex, who sat pinioned to the floor by the poor affrighted creatures clinging to his legs, and arms, and neck; his lips moving all the while in threatening pantomine, vainly endeavoring to be heard amidst the screams around him, and the continuous roar overhead. At every pause in the furious storm, rap—rap—rap went the knocker, a signal for the closer gathering of the terrified domestics. At length the storm took breath, allowing a small interval of repose, which old Essex taking advantage of, threw the crowd from him, in despair of getting his subordinate to answer the summons, and rushed across the court and into the back door of the mansion-house himself, and speedily let go the fastenings of the hall door. Stern, and schooled as he was in the outward show of calmness, borrowed from his betters, the old Major's knees knocked a little as he threw open the hall door and let the light of the lamp fall over the portico and gravelled road.

There stood at the threshold of the door, three persons, two males and a female dressed in black, with black silk masks over their faces. The lady was leaning upon the arm of him who appeared the younger of her two companions, while a carriage and four horses stood opposite the door. The elder of the visitors requested leave to enter for a moment's shelter from the furious peltings of the storm. Essex knew the hospitable habits of the place too well to have paused thus long, had he not been confounded by the studious appearance of mystery in his visitors, and apprehension for the safety of his master's goods and chattels; but these impressions lasted only for a moment, when the old fellow again resumed his courtly air and bowed them into the hall with inimitable grace. His unerring tact had already discovered that these, if robbers at all, were not of the common sort, and were of no ordinary address. One attitude, a wave of the hand, the general air, was enough for the practised eye of the major domo, to discover that they were no ruffians; besides, there was a shrinking, a clinging dependence about the lady, which at once interested him. If he was surprised at this singular visit, thus far, how much more so, when he saw them, after entering the hall, walk straight up to the picture of a soldier in armor, hanging against the wall. It was the well-known portrait of Gen. Elliot, half brother to the Governor, and one of the most renowned soldiers, as well as unfortunate men of his day.* Before this picture, the mysterious three stood, the two males conversing in a suppressed voice, while the young lady sobbed audibly and most painfully, and, finally became so much affected that a chair had to be brought her, which, she turned towards the picture, gazing upon it and weeping by turns. Old Essex handed her a glass of wine and water, which she declined. They presently moved opposite to the full length picture of the Governor, in his court dress, and examined it studiously and with some interest, but not of the painful sort with which they had looked at the other. The lady soon returned to her former position, and there she clung, until removed almost by force; one gentleman taking her under each arm.

As they left the hall, the elder of the two threw a sealed packet upon the table, stopping to turn up the direction, and place it in so conspicuous a place as to be sure to attract attention. The steps were put up, the door shut and offering Essex a piece of coin, the whip cracked and the coach and four moved away as it had come, leaving the old Major in sad perplexity, whether the whole occurrences of the night had not been a part of the goblin stories of Old Martin, among the frightened domestics. The sight of the package, was a sure guarantee that it was no such dream of the imagination, and he turned it over and examined it most carefully, seal and surperscription. Not being able to read even the outside, he of course made little progress with its contents, but he examined the coat of arms upon the seal with the eyes of one not entirely unaccustomed to such things—coming to the sage conclusion, that the writer was some body at all events. He did not return to his late affrighted colleagues in the kitchen, but seated himself to wait the return of the family.

The storm was now clearing away, and there was a prospect that he would not long be left to chew the cud of sweet and bitter fancies. He was presently aroused by the sound of horses and carriages, and soon after by the entrance of the whole party, which had by this time received several accessions. These with sundry other matters appertaining thereto, will found in the next chapter.

---

* This incident was related to the author by a descendant of the Governor.

CHAPTER VII.

A FAMILY SCENE.

THE party entered the hall in fine glee, with the exception of the Governor, who still remained dejected, pale, and entirely different from his usually hearty and even gleeful mood. Kate had again been on horseback, in which she delighted, and entered the room with her skirt upon her arm, and a black cap upon her head, full of drooping feathers. She was quite flushed and really looked charming with the excitement of the ride, or that clashing of rival wits, she so well knew how to keep up between her two assiduous attendants, but it was all playful and courteous in the highest degree. It was the daily practice of Carter and Moore to walk off arm in arm, after one of these sprightly encounters for her favor. The fact was that Kate did not perceive as yet, that either of these youths were in that die-away state, usually called being in love. They had all played together for the last five years, except when the young gentlemen were upon their travels and now that they were returned so much improved, she saw no cause of rejecting attentions due to her and which she really enjoyed. Neither of them had approached the threshold of love-making—the Virginia system requires a much longer probation than that, and the good old custom prevails still, thanks to the good sense of our charming lassies, that even this old prescriptive right of their sex is left willed to them by their great grandmothers.

One addition to the party was Mr. Nathaniel Dandrige, a youth just emerging from his teens and his syntax, and a scion of the same class to which the two others belonged. In the language of the times he was a young gentleman of fortune and birth—the former in expectation of course. As he entered Dorothea had his arm, and was carrying on a most desperate juvenile flirtation in which his Excellency seemed only prevented from taking part by his painful reflections, which every now and then came over him; as it was, he hung in their near neighborhood, and gave way to a smile in spite of himself, occasionally, at the perfect good humor and naivette of his favorite.

Old Essex had replaced the letter and was standing in most respectful deference, awaiting the movements of his master.

"Who brought this, Essex?" was his instant enquiry as he broke the seal.

"Two gentlemen and a lady, all in masks, sir."

The Governor threw himself into a chair and commenced the perusal, with not a little interest. The whole party by this time were seated and waiting impatiently for further developments.

"Did the people in masks run away with any of my spoons and cream pots, Essex?" asked Dorothea.

"No, Miss, they were quite of another sort when I came to see them."

"And the lady," said Carter, "was she pretty, and young?"

"I could not see her face, sir, but she was very young."

"Had she a pretty foot and hand?" continued Carter.

"The prettiest I ever saw in my life, sir."

All the young people laughed outright at old Essex's close observation upon points which the gentleman seemed to consider so essential a test.

"And her figure, Essex" asked Carter, "did that correspond with the two beautiful members?"

"Most happily, sir. Very much such a figure as Miss Catherine's."

"Thank you, Essex, for your compliment."

"The Governor, though reading rapidly, lost not a word of all this, trifling though it was, meanwhile he was racking his imagination for some other clue to their identity, than any he found in the letter. As soon as he had finished he handed the epistle to Dr. Blair, and then turned to Essex, but the faithful and discreet old Major, maintained his reserve. He said not a word about pictures, nor the lady's weeping, but dealt entirely in a general account of the visit, the ostensible objects of which were to avoid the storm and leave the letter. No one in the room perceived that the old fellow still held something back, but his master. He knew him so well, that he divined some cause for his reluctance to make a clean breast of it; accordingly he soon after retired to his library, followed by Essex, and there learned the whole affair, as our readers have done likewise.

Dr. Blair seeing nothing in the letter to conceal, and knowing that if there was it would soon become public, commenced reading it aloud, it ran as follows:

LONDON, 1714.

To His Excellency, Alexander Spotswood, Esq.

DEAR SIR—This letter will be handed to you by one of the most unfortunate adherents of the Pretender. Start not my dear Sir—he is but one of the Scottish jacobins, and will in no wise compromise you. The very fact of his seeking your country is evidence enough if it were wanting, that he desires to be at peace from the toils and dangers of political partizanship. These are claims enough for citizenship you may think, but not warrant sufficient to claim your personal friendship. He has these also, for he was one of those unfortunate men who befriended and supported your late kinsman to the last. He protests that he will in no wise compromise your Excellency with the ministry or their adherents on your side of the water, and has begged me not to write, but knowing that you would delight to befriend so staunch an adherent of the unfortunate General, I have insisted on his taking a sealed packet at all events, as it would contain other matters than those relating purely to himself. And now for those matters. He will be accompanied by a great many ruined families of rather a higher class than that from which your immigrants are generally furnished—they, too, are worn out in spirit and in fortune, with the ceaseless struggles between the hereditary claimant of the crown and the present occupant. They see, also, breakers ahead. The Queen's health is far from being stable, and in case of her sudden demise there will be an awful struggle here. Are they not right then to gather up the little remnant of their property and seek an asylum on your peaceful shores?

Your scheme of scaling the mountains, and cutting asunder the French settlements, meets with the hearty approbation of all the military men about the Court, and not a question of the Queen's approbation would remain, were it not for the everlasting squabbles between Bolinbroke and Oxford. Your friend Mr. ———, ceaselessly urges the matter, and contends that now is the very time to strike the blow ; but my dear Sir, there is a desire for peace on the other side of the channel, and I would advise you to have your preparations in readiness to set out upon the first intimation of her Majesty's consent, so that the news of it cannot possibly reach here before your grand scheme is accomplished.

It is a magnificent one, and at any other time would fire the minds, of our young military men. Hold on then, my dear Sir, to the end, and you will be the ultimate means of laying the foundation of a future Empire, greater than all Europe in extent, and pregnant with a vast future which even your experienced and sagacious eye cannot as yet discover.

There is a young lady to accompany this gentleman, but she is even more loth than himself to burden your Excellency with what she calls the taint of the rebel. I know full well, that you will be a father to this poor heart-broken houseless girl, thrown upon our unfeeling world; not only poor, but suffering untold wretchedness, whether she looks to the past or the future. God Almighty have mercy upon her tender years. All her gentle rearing will now be turned into sources of sorrow. Her cup is poisoned forever, where she is known— and where she is not, she will bear with her recollections enough, to over-shadow her future days with a vision so dark, that no' human hand may ever raise the veil. I cannot say more, for I have promised that I would not, but I think that I have said enough to interest you in these most unfortunate stran-gers, and make you cherish them. Your heart has changed since we served together, if I have not directed them to the very man of all the world, and in the very position to most befriend them. There is 'a new world opened to them in more senses of the word than one—let it be as happy as possible.

Your old friend and companion in arms,   G. B. L.

" Dear me," said Kate, " and our visitors were doubtless some of these. Poor girl, she has followed her father and her brother to these wilds—but per-haps the young gentleman was her lover. That would give quite a romantic turn to the affair."

" I think that hard shower of rain, if they were out in it, would drench what little romance out of them the sea voyage left," said Dorothea.

" Poor child," said Dr. Blair, seeming rather to commune with his own charitable thoughts, " I pity her from my soul."

" I do not see," whispered Carter to Kate, " that a lady with such a foot and ankle, is any such object of commiseration after all."

" Perhaps an orphan," said Lady Spotswood, glancing at her own happy little circle with a tear almost starting in her eye.

These various remarks upon the visitors were cut short by the re-entrance of the Governor, who walked to that portion of the room where the young gentlemen were seated, and asked which of them would volunteer to ride to York on such a night, in search of these unhappy visitors? Moore immedi-ately rose to his feet and volunteered his services, as indeed did both the others, but the former being first, the Governor commissioned him to go, and find them out if possible and bring them back as his guests.

Kate seeing how earnest and grave her father seemed, gave her beau a look of gratitude, which he considered ample remuneration for riding half an hour in a wet night.

The party were soon after assembled for family prayers—the young ladies having hastily retired to throw off their riding skirts and hats. A small read-ing desk was placed before Dr. Blair, while Kate ascended a platform erected before an organ, fitting into the recess formed by the projecting abutment of the chimney. Then the servants came filing in one by one and ranged them-selves against the wall on the opposite side of the room. The old Major at their head.

The whole group being composed to a proper and becoming solemnity, the Doctor commenced reading a hymn. When he had finished, the slow and solemn tones of the organ began to ascend in a prelude of great beauty. Kate raised the tune in a fine mellow voice, which, in that high old fashioned apartment, reverberated through its lofty ceilings, mingled with the tones of the organ, so as to attune all their hearts to this befitting close of the scenes of the day. The fine enthusiasm of the young musician's eye and mein, told how earnestly her heart was concerned in what was before her. When she had finished, the whole party by one accord sat breathless and motion-less, evidently desirous to catch the last note as it died away amidst the solemn moan of the waves without. All then bowed the knee to the throne of mercy to follow in humble response the petitions of one of the purest men that ever adorned the church in the Old Dominion, or illustrated his Master's divine system of Heavenly charity, by a life of spotless purity.

What a fitting prelude to the excellent Prelate's solemn reading, was Kate's

musical exaltation of spirit. Surely the voice of ardent and honest supplication ascends all the nearer to Heaven by being heralded in such divine
strains. If there is any inspiration known and felt by the creatures of this
earth, as pure and refined above all earthly pollution, it is this musical enthusiasm mingling with the sublimations of deeply prayerful and humble hearts.
Surely God looks down upon such scenes on earth, with benignity. It is at
all events the purest earthly feeling—the freest from the dross and corruptions
of this world, of any thing that we know of, and in such an attitude would
we present most of the personages kneeling around that family altar. A
purer and more guileless group of beings has seldom before or since assembled in one room, and ere an all wise Providence scatters them and their
descendants upon a wider and a longer pilgrimage than ever was decreed to
the Israelites, we would fix them in the affections of our readers.

<hr />

CHAPTER VIII.

AMALGAMATION IN THE OLDEN TIME.

Moore returned to breakfast looking rather haggard, after a sleepless night
and a fruitless journey. He said he had traced the coach back to York, but
there it had been dismissed and there in all probability it belonged. There
was a faint clue he said to the supposition that they had gone on to the capital, directly after their return from Temple Farm. Kate, as she entered and
took her seat at the table, welcomed him with a cheerful mood, and asked in
a playful way if he had discovered their Hero and Heroine of the masks.
She looked quite disappointed at the result, and expressed her regret especially that Bernard had not brought the lady back. " It is such an unusual
thing," she said, " people calling at a house in the night with masks on, in a
country like this—and that house too belonging to the Chief Magistrate of the
Colony."

" If you had been in York last night, and seen the crowds of houseless
strangers that I saw," said Moore, " just arrived from England, you could not
have been at a loss to select any sort of character from among them."

" Let us all then ride there this morning?" said Kate, " and see for ourselves."

No objection being made, it was settled that they would make a general
descent upon York, and see one of those human swarms from the European
hives, by which this country was populated. The letter of the previous night
also, added a zest to the general curiosity to see that portion of these said to
be of a higher order than usual.

" Who can that hot headed man be?" said Kate, " whom papa's friend
speaks of in his letter, as having compromised himself by meddling in matters
that did not concern him."

" Our College," said the Reverend Commissary, " will one day or other,
save our young gentry from the temptation of meddling in transatlantic affairs.
Now it is made a mere grammar school—this is all wrong. What say you
Mr. Carter? Mr. Moore?"

" I think, Sir, to speak with frankness," said Moore, " that it will never be
any thing else, while it remains half savage, half civilized."

Both Kate and Dorothea smiled at the rude interpretation which might be
put upon this speech. The Doctor replied:

" I understand, you allude to Mr. Boyle's plan of educating the Indians."

"Exactly, and to the utter impracticability of ever carrying on a literary institution with two such heterogeneous classes as those now in College."

"Why Sir," said Carter, "I have been looking for bloodshed between your Indian hostage pupils and our native young bloods for some time."

"Alas," replied the Doctor, "that the most benevolent intentions, devised with the truest apparent wisdom, are ever thus thwarted by the wickedness of man."

"We grant you the intentions," said Moore, "but for the wisdom of shutting up twenty or thirty wild young Indians, in the same building with an equal number of whites, quite as wild in one sense, we cannot vouch. You must recollect, Doctor, that Carter and myself have been personal witnesses of the experiment, and we can testify to the ceaseless arrogance on the part of the whites, and the consequent deadly enmity of the Indians. They are most of them princes of the blood, too, and may ill brook indignity from mere plebeian youths, even of our color. Why Sir, it was no longer ago than one night last week, being in the capital and hearing a great noise and confusion in the College, I walked up to ascertain the cause. Must I tell it, Doctor?"

"Tell it—tell it," said Kate.

"Tell it," said Dorothea.

"I see the two Doctors and the Governor, hang their heads, but being put upon the stand I must tell the whole truth. Thus, then, you know ladies, that there is a particular wing of the College, devised by Sir Christopher Wren, for the express accommodation of their young savage majesties. Two occupy each room, and for their farther accommodation, there are two cots. Now on the night alluded to, half an hour after the Indian class was dismissed to their quarters, and after prayers, such a yelling was heard from that wing that the people of the town actually thought the College again on fire, and some of the wicked lads in the other end began tolling the bell, which brought also the firemen with their buckets and ladders. In the melee I arrived and found upon enquiring, that the connecting pins from every cot in the Indian wing had been removed, so that each one caught a tumble when he supposed himself only leaping into bed, and that was not all. Every tub and bucket in old Mrs. Stites' kitchen (the Stewardess of the College) had been filled with water, and as far as they would go, placed under the cots, so that many of them got a ducking into the bargain. Such yelling, and screeching, and whooping, never was heard. The savage youngsters were for rushing in a body upon their white assailants, and it required all the authority of the Indian master, backed by the other Professors and citizens who had assembled, to quell the riot. A party of citizens had to patrol the College the whole night, to prevent bad consequences between the two races."

"It is too true," said Dr. Blair, "but that is the fault of our boys, and not of the original design."

"I beg your pardon, Reverend Sir, for controverting your position, said Carter, but the original design to be entitled to the wisdom which you claim for it, should have provided for the liability in boys of one race to play pranks upon another. This is not a solitary instance. Moore and myself could entertain this goodly company till dinner time, with accounts of these disasters."

The Reverend Commissary had risen from the table and was walking along the room back and forth, his hands locked behind him, thrown into painful reflections by the testimony and the arguments of his former pupils. The girls were still laughing over the ridiculous figures which the savages must have cut, but not daring to give full vent to their feelings because they knew that it was a tender subject with all three of the elderly gentlemen.

In this very different state of feeling in the two—the elder and the younger — the breakfast table was soon deserted. The young people to prepare for the contemplated excursion, and the elders to debate that matter gravely, over which the others were still amusing themselves.

CHAPTER XI.

YORKTOWN BEFORE THE REVOLUTION.

It is not known to most of our readers, perhaps, that Yorktown, the closing scene of the Revolution, was once the principal importing mart for all that region of country, now supplied by Baltimore, Richmond and Norfolk. Such was its importance at the date of our story. The roadstead, now occupied by a few miserable fishing smacks, was once occupied by merchant-ships, and a tall forest of masts crowded a quay, now only the mart of the celebrated York River Oysters. Large ware-houses and imposing edifices, both public and private, and brisk business occupied its streets. Such was its appearance as Kate Spotswood cantered up its principal avenue, Moore on one side and Carter on the other, the whole cavalcade following. They rode through the principal streets of the city, until they came to that point, since known as the location of the wind-mill—there on both sides of the angle formed by the entrance of the river into the waters of the bay, in every vacant lot, and even in the unfrequented streets were tents, and camp-fires, many of the latter without the comforts of the former, while the hotels were filled to overflowing with strangers of higher grade. The party rode in among the encamped emigrants, and commenced making enquiries for their mysterious visitors, but there were so many for whom the description would answer, and so many had already set out to the interior, that it was impossible to trace them. Both the young ladies dismounted and walked among the poorer sort, dispensing their charities: they found so many needy applicants and in some instances sufferers, that they promised to send them a wagon with more substantial supplies as soon as they got home. The Governor had alighted at the house of Mr. Diggs, a member of the general assembly, and a personal and political friend, and here again he sent out messengers for the bearer of the letter, but all in vain. While thus occupied a young stranger presented himself as a candidate for employment. He stated that he was one of the emigrants, and without means to prosecute his journey into the interior, and without a single relation among all those who had arrived with him—that he was a classical scholar and desirous of obtaining the situation of private tutor in some gentleman's family, for a short time, in order to obtain means to prosecute his designs in coming over; that his name was Henry Hall—twenty-four years of age, and intended to reside permanently in the colony. The Governor was pleased with the young man, and wanted just such an one to direct Mr. Robert's studies. He told the applicant, therefore, that he would send a horse for him as soon as he arrived at home, and as no credentials or testimonials of qualification had been exhibited, he would place him in the hands of Dr. Blair, who would put him through his syntax, and as for the mathematics, said the veteran, his eyes glistening with delight, and rubbing his hands, I will try you about that myself. "Do you know anything about military engineering, young man, continued he, as he saw him about to depart?"

"Yes, Sir."

"Ha, then, you are just my man, we will make a night of it, depend upon it."

The party soon after returned to Temple Farm without having obtained any clue to the route of those whom they were so anxious to find. The Governor dispatched old June with a horse for the young man who proposed becoming tutor to Robert, as he had promised. Each one now sought out his own amusement until dinner time, some strolled upon the lawn, while others walked upon the beach and gathered shells. Old Dr. Evylin retired into the house to read a letter from his daughter, which the post brought him that morning, in answer to a most pressing invitation from the ladies of the mansion to visit them. As it was characteristic of the lady, and as she is quite an important little personage, we will give it entire:

"WILLIAMSBURG, July, 1714.

" *Dear Father:*

Your note of last night, containing an invitation to Temple Farm, from Kate, has just been received. I will go, but for a reason, among others, which I fear my ever kind friend, Kate, will consider any thing but complimentary—it is because this house is haunted, and I can no longer stay in it. Look not so grave, dear father, 'tis no ghost. I wish it was, or he was, for it is that same tedious, tiresome, persecuting, Harry Lee. I have been most anxiously expecting your return; but, as it seems, you have become a permanent fixture at Temple Farm, it is but right that I should grow along side of the parent stem. The townsfolk are even more anxious for your return than I am. I tell them you ran away from practice, but it seems the more you desire to run away from it, the more they run after you. Few people in this dreary world have been able to effect so much unmixed good as you have, and for that, I thank God. Dear Father, I have no desire to live but for your sake, and that the short time we are to live together may not be diminished by any act of mine, I will be with you presently. Our poor pensioners and invalids are all doing as well as usual, and I leave them in the hands of the Rev. Mr. Jones, who, I know, will care for them as we would. He is surely one of God's chosen instruments for doing good in this world. He has shouldered his cross in earnest, and devoutly does he labor to advance the Redeemer's kingdom.

"The week that you have been absent, dear father, has appeared the longest seven days of my life. I do not know what my flowers and birds will do without me, but I am sure they can better spare my presence than I can yours.

" Ever your affectionate and devoted daughter,

"ELLEN EVYLIN."

Kate was sitting anxiously waiting to hear from the old gentleman what answer his daughter returned, and she saw a tear glistening in his eye, as he handed her the note. She read it over; the old gentleman sitting silent until she had finished and returned it. "Poor Ellen," said she, as she looked up in his face, from which the tears were now stealing down, "but despond not, dear Doctor, the change of scene and air will surely do her good."

" I fear her case is beyond the reach of human aid," replied he.

" Indeed! do you consider it so hopeless?"

" Her's is a crushed spirit, my dear Kate, she has no physical disease except such as is produced by it, and you know it is hard to pluck up the rooted sorrow."

" Never despair, dear Doctor, cheerful company and fresh air on horseback, and long rambling walks among the flowers and green leaves, and the sea-breeze, may do wonders for her. I'll show you that I have not been your disciple for nothing."

They separated; the old man to walk along the beach, and try to relieve his melancholy forebodings by watching the sparkling wave, and the white sails as they spread for that land from which he had brought the mother of his drooping daughter. Let no desponding heart walk upon the sea-shore to cultivate cheerfulness; it is too much like standing on the borders of eternity. The melancholy and monotonous roar of the distant waves is too depressing; they are too much like the great current of human life, forever pouring onwards, regardless of individual suffering.

That evening the Doctor's old family coach came rumbling up to the hall door, at a staid and sober gait, and the whole party in the parlor turned out to receive so unusual a visitor. There stood the gentlemen, old and young, bare headed, and the ladies likewise, surrounding the steps of the carriage, each one anxious to render assistance, but all giving way for the Doctor to receive his daughter in his arms, carrying her, poor old man, to the platform before he suffered her to regain her feet. Fondly she hung upon his neck as they stood there, he within one step of the landing, and she on the top; no one ventured to disturb them, for both were weeping and seemed to have forgotten the presence of any body else.

One hour afterwards she entered the parlor, supported by Kate on one side and Dorothea on the other, to a large arm chair, made soft with shawls. She was rather a *petit* figure, but what was lost in majesty of form was fully compensated for by symmetry of mould, or rather had been, for she was now thin and shadowy. Her face was almost transparent, it was so purely white, and the blue veins upon her temples shone through her wax-like skin, as if the current of life was restrained but by a gossamer texture. Her eyes were large, and of a fine deep blue, so that when they slowly moved over the objects in the room, it almost startled one, so shadow-like was her general appearance. Her hair was of a brown color, but when the rays of light fell upon its rich folds, they played among them, so as to bring out their fine auburn tints—at one moment exhibiting a black shade, and the next a purple. She had no cough, nor any apparent symptoms of physical disease, yet she was evidently wasting away in the very first bloom of her youth and beauty, for beautiful she still was, and in perfect health, must have been a fascinating little fairy. How those two girls tried to entertain her, hanging round her chair, and bringing to her in succession, every object of curiosity or interest about the place! Even little Robert had piled her lap with curious shells, and Kate was turning over some new volumes of Pope's and Swift's poetry, just then in the first novelty of their recent publication; every now and then reading her passages which struck their fancy. How the whole conversation of a room full of company became subdued by the presence of one poor little valetudinarian, instead of chosing the most cheerful and enlivening subjects, the sufferer is sure to be painfully impressed with the fact that he or she, is a drawback to the enjoyment of others; and so it was on the present occasion, for she soon observed it, and spoke of it to Kate.

"You must not let me engross the attention of every one, my dear Kate," said she, in a suppressed voice, " it is painful to me."

The Governor, who was sitting near, heard it, and replied, " Suppose, then, we have in the young tutor, and put him through his facings: Essex tells me he is waiting."

"No, no, papa," said Kate, " it will never do, remember the young man has some feeling, and may not choose to be examined upon his proficiency in a room full of company."

"Poh! poh," said the Governor, "bring him in Essex, we will treat Bob to a scene of his master learning some of his own lessons, before he administers the birch to him."

The boy rubbed his hands with delight at the proposition, and his father sent him off to bring in an armful of Latin and Greek books from the library.

The Reverend Commissary was sent for too, who came, spectacles on nose, just fresh from his books. He, too, objected to the publicity of the examination, but knowing the peculiarities of his friend, his sudden whims and eccentricities, he attempted like a skilful tactitian, to compromise the matter.

"I left the young man in the library," said he, "and I will return and ask him if he has any objection."

"Tell him then," said the Governor, "that I will require these young gentlemen to construe verse about with him, and we will try which has the best of it, Old Oxford or William and Mary."

The youngsters seemed not quite so ready for the exhibition, now that they were to take part in the performance, as they were before, but they acquiesced of course.

The Rev. Commissary returned with the young scholar. He was dressed in black, rather the worse for the wear, but still scrupulously neat and clean. The deep impress of long familiarity with persons of high breeding was in every step and movement.

"Egad, he's a gentleman at all events," said the Governor, as he eyed him coming up the room, and rather abashed himself, that he had proposed such a boyish freak to such a man : such was his way, however, and he attempted to smooth over the matter.

"Mr. Hall, here are two or three young gentlemen, alumni of our Western College, which you have doubtless heard of, and I have proposed that the Rev. Commissary shall play the pedagogue to-night with the the whole of us; what say you, will you be one of the class ?"

"Most willingly, your Excellency ;" seeming to understand the Governor's mood at once.

"Get the books, Bob, the books, the books."

But just at that moment, Kate and her sister ran up to poor Ellen Evylin, who would have fallen had they not caught her, she was almost gone. She had been sitting in her big arm chair, so arranged that she had not seen the proposed tutor. As she recovered a little, she whispered to Kate, upon whose shoulder her head was leaning, "Oh, that voice, it was so like"— then she stopped, and Kate prepared to wheel her into another room, but she strenuously opposed it, and even desired her chair to be turned round, so that she could see the occupants of the other side of the table.

From that moment, her eye seemed absolutely rivetted to the face of the stranger, and whenever it came to his turn to read, Kate felt her whole system thrill and vibrate like one in an ague. This was very strange ; and still more surprised Kate, but she kept these thoughts to herself.

The Governor was once more in high glee with his new class, and was really taking it turn about with the youngsters at the bucolics. Indeed it seemed to afford fine sport for all concerned.

Once or twice the stranger youth raised his eyes above his book and examined the group, now located on the other side of the room.

The new tutor was far from being an an ordinary looking man. To use a common homely saying, he was one who had evidently seen better days. This alone invests one with some interest. The thread-bare garments which he wears, are deprived at once of all their shabbiness and meanness, and invested with a compound interest. A graceful movement, an uncommon expression rivets the eye upon him. We are carried back in imagination to the place and scenes of his birth and naturally our curiosity is excited. Nor was this all in the present instance, there was a desponding sadness in the voice of this young man, a depth in its tones which affected his lady hearers powerfully. They were all more or less interested in him. Then that deep scar across his face ; how came that there ? had he been a soldier ? This question was destined to have some light thrown upon it sooner than they expected. The Governor being satisfied with his classical attainments, in his impatience for his favorite studies, soon had Robert's black board brought in and was figuring away with his chalk at a great rate. He was becoming delighted with his prize, for even Dr. Blair whispered to him that he was a ripe scholar. From mathematics it was an easy transition to their military application, and in less than half an hour his Excellency had one of Marlborough's late battles drawn fully out, and he and his new antagonist engaged in a most animated discussion. The veteran's eye glistened with delight as he listened to the young man's glowing description of the battle. He placed it in an entirely new light, and the Governor now understood some matters which had been puzzling him ever since the accounts were received. He therefore gave up the controversy, which was quite a new thing for him in military matters and no mean compliment to his new adversary. After reposing his eye in a brown study for a few moments on the black board, where the lines of attack and defence still remained, he wheeled suddenly upon his antagonist and exclaimed : " I'll tell you what it is, Mr. Tutor, you must have seen service—none but a true military eye could correct the errors of my lines."

The poor youth was struck dumb, all his late animation and military ardor engendered amidst the clashing of imaginary armies, vanished in a moment. He was confused. His antagonist seeing this, continued: " Never mind young man on which side you took up arms—there shall be no tales out of school here. You are in a freer atmosphere than that which you lately left—where the Dutchess and Mrs. Masham alternately sway the fate of contending armies. I have been a soldier of fortune myself, and it boots little to me in what school you learned your tactics. Sufficient that you are a soldier."

" Gad, Bob, with such a master you will beat John yet, if you only spur up, my man."

" Your Excellency seems fully informed of the shameful wrangling of the Queen's Ministers," replied Hall modestly.

" Rather say the wrangling of the female gossips of the Court, and you would come nearer the mark. It is no longer Oxford and Bolinbroke, and that was bad enough, but it is now a fair fight of petticoat against petticoat. The instructions which I receive by one packet are countermanded by the next. If this state of things continue I must divide my papers into two packages and label one, ' despatches from her grace of Marlborough,' and the other ' from her high Mightiness, Mrs. Masham.' "

" Any further news from home, Governor?" asked Carter, " concerning the grand expedition across the mountains."

" Not one syllable. I have been twice ordered to prepare my little army, and twice has it been countermanded, ere I could cleverly commence operations. The council, damn them—I beg your Reverences pardon as being of them—is too much like the Queen's privy council, they are under petticoat government too, and thus far have most effectually thwarted me."

By this time he had become quite excited, and was walking with immense strides across the floor and talked on, almost in a continuous strain. " They hope to unhorse me before I can set out, but upon the very first intimation from the ministry that my measures are approved, I will set out—then arrest me who can. Curse the block-heads of the council."

" Softly, softly, your Excellency," said the Commissary, " you should not denounce these men, because they cannot think exactly with us. The General Assembly were fully as much to blame, for they refused to vote the necessary funds. They could not see with our eyes."

" See with our eyes!" replied the Governor, contemptuously, " nor with any other, damn them, they cannot see an inch from from their noses. What do they know about military matters?" turning to Henry Hall, as he continued vehemently—" you see, Sir, those rascally Frenchmen are hemming us in, in every direction. They are gradually approximating their military settlements up the branches of the Mississippi, on the one hand, and down the lakes on the other, until they are just about to meet on the other side of the mountains. Now I propose to march an expedition across these mountains and by force, if necessary, seize the strip of land lying between their settlements. No military eye could look upon the thing for one single moment, without being struck with the magnificence of the conception. I have written to the ministry, sent maps of the rivers and mountains, and urged them before it is too late,—but while they are carrying on their cursed squabbles between the rival factions of two old wives, our enemies will have already seized upon the ground."

While he spoke thus, he had seized the chalk, and was rapidly sketching the course of the principal rivers, having their sources most directly among the mountains, and the Blue Ridge, and beyond that again, the sources of the Mississippi, running South and South-west, and the rivers on the North emptying into the great lakes. He was a fine draughtsman, and a military engineer of the highest repute in that day, and when he had finished his handy work, really presented a field for a martial enterprise, calculated to fire up the enthusiasm of much tamer spirits than those he addressed. Hall especially, entered into his views with an ardor and a zeal which captivated the old veteran at once. His practised eye ran over the plan of the campaign with the rapidity of intuition, and in less than half an hour, he had mastered all the then known geography of the country, together with the forces, position and number of the French settlements. It is true, that they knew not of the double chain of mountains, and had never heard of the great valley of Virginia,—that garden spot of the land,—but with that exception, these plans were wonderfully correct, and into that mistake they were purposely betrayed, as will be seen as we progress.

They supposed that the head waters of the Mississippi, had their source immediately beyond the mountains, which could be just faintly discovered from the then frontier settlements of the Colony.

The table was soon strewed with papers and maps, giving an exact detail of the militia and regular force of the Colony, and all the known Geography of Virginia.

"I see," remarked Hall, "that your population numbers an hundred thousand, your militia nine thousand five hundred and twenty two, of which two thousand three hundred and sixty-three are light horse, and seven thousand one hundred and fifty-nine are foot and dragoons."

"Exactly," said the Governor, "and yet these craven hearted delegates and councillors contend that I want to strip the colony of its military protection, to go upon some wild Quixotic expedition beyond the borders of civilization, from whence we will never return, and if we do, to find them all butchered at home. Was any thing ever heard so supremely ridiculous?"

"Can you not raise an entirely new force for the transmontaine expedition?" asked Hall.

"As how?" said his Excellency, eagerly.

"Suppose you issue a proclamation, calling upon all the young gentry of the colony to come forward, with each so many followers of his own enlisting, or chosing. Say three hundred gentlemen, with each fifty followers. If you take possession of this fine country beyond the mountains in her Majesty's name, surely her Ministers will make liberal grants to those who thus conquer or acquire it."

"A glorious conception, by Heavens," hugging the new tutor actually in his arms, and giving way to other evidences of delight.

"I'll tell you what it is, Harry Hall, you shall draw up that proclamation this very night. I'll read it before I go to bed."

"No, no papa," said Kate, interfering, "Mr. Hall is already fatigued with his day's toil, and is besides just from the confinement of a ship, he has already been wearying himself reading at least a bushel of your dry papers."

"Dry papers!" replied the father, "they are far more interesting than the gingling nonsense which Bernard has been reading to you young ladies the last half hour."

"Fie, fie papa, to call Mr. Pope's beautiful pastorals gingling nonsense.

appeal to Dr. Blair, whether there is not food in them to satisfy minds of even masculine vigor."

"Right, right my Kate," said the old prelate, " in both cases. The young man is doubtless fatigued and the poetry is good."

" I am not the least weary, your Excellency, and will draft your proclamation on the spot, if you say so."

" No, no, the general voice is against me, and we will adjourn the subject until after breakfast in the morning, especially as I see Bob is coming already for his first lesson."

The youngster had been standing some time leaning upon a pair of foils, and now approaching bashfully, asked Hall if he could give him lessons with these also.

" Oh yes," said he. taking one of the instruments out of his hand, and telling Robert to put on his basket, while he laid his own on the table, and placed himself bare-headed in a posture of defence. He suffered the boy to make a few passes at him, and then disarmed him so handsomely and so easily that he threw the foil entirely over, end for end, and caught it in his own hand.

" A trick of the Continental army, by Heavens !" exclaimed the Governor. " Come here, Moore, this gentleman needs a more formidable competitor, than Bob. Here, Mr. Hall, is one of my holiday pupils ; toast him a little for the amusement of these girls."

At it they went in fine style, both evidently playing shy until they should see a little into the others fence, and both giving and parrying with caution and dexterity. Neither had much advantage in length of limb, and both were practised swordsmen, but Moore rather undervaluing his plebeian adversary, began to push at him pretty fiercely; instantly his foil was seen turning pirouetts in the air.

" Ha," said the old veteran, rising and rubbing his hands, " have I found an antagonist at last ? Now for it, Mr. Hall."

Even the ladies began to take some interest in the game, for they were quite accustomed to such scenes, and did not usually turn even to notice so ordinary an affair; but now when two such extraordinary swordsmen encountered, every one was looking on with pleased interest. Long and dexterously did they thrust and parry, advancing and retreating, until they were so worn down that the two blades lay against each other in close pressure, neither willing or daring to renew the encounter.

" Come, come," said Dr. Blair, " that's enough—you are both satisfied." Like two boys tired out with fighting, they were willing enough to desist.

The tutor was soon after shewn to his own room. When he had gone, the Governor was loud in his praise, and pronounced him a most extraordinary young man, and the finest swordsman that he had encountered since he left the army.

" I'll tell you what it is, Governor—I have been thinking what an acquisition that young man would be to our College," said the Commissary.

" The College may go a begging this time, Dr. Blair, I intend that Henry Hall shall see the highest blue peak of the Apelachian mountains before I am done with him. Providence has doubtless sent him to me with some such design, and when I have caught the bird in my net, you come and open your cage, and say, let him fly in here. No, no—I have engaged Mr. Hall for Bob, and your College must get along without him, I assure you."

" Well, well, it will be time enough for us when you return from the mountains, if indeed you don't leave the bones of the fine youth bleaching upon their highest peaks."

Rather an unkind cut of the old Doctor, and which set the Governor to thinking for a moment ere he replied.

" Just as sure as the sun shines to-morrow, I tell you, Dr. Blair, that I will lead an expedition over yonder blue mountains, and I will triumph over the French—the Indians, and the Devil, if he chooses to join forces with them."

"No doubt of it—no doubt of it. I did not question the result at all, I only meant to allude to the mishaps inevitable from all human undertakings, and against these, even your great military experience cannot guarantee this youth."

The evening closed as previous ones had done, with family prayer, after which the party separated for the night.

CHAPTER X.

LOVE'S YOUNG DREAM.

THE morning broke still and serene over the shores of the Chesapeake, now in the full fruition of their summer glories, and the flowers clustering with a rich harvest of beauties o'er hill and dale, garden and lawn. meadow and brook. The sun was just scattering his ruddy rays over the eastern shores, and lighting up the sleepy waters of that glorious inland sea, like a burnished mirror clearing itself from the taint of human breath. The marine birds soared in lazy flights along the surface, admiring their own graceful shadows, perhaps, while out toward the ocean, they seemed like white feathers floating lazily in the sun beams. It was a morning to give wings to the imagination, yet the picture cannot be embodied perfectly to the mind of another, it must be felt as well as seen. The accessaries of temperature, health, position, and, above all, the true mood must be present to insure its perfect enjoyment. To exist, to breathe, is then a positive enjoyment.

Kate Spotswood was of a temperament to enjoy all these summer glories, with a relish only known to nature's poets and painters. She was not disposed to indulge in the dreamy mood alone, however, for at the first peep of dawn she was in Ellen Evylin's room, and had roused up the valetudinarian. That wakeful child of sorrow lay with her eyes as preternaturally bright as they were the night before, and Kate saw that they had been very differently employed than in sleeping, for her pillow was yet moist with tears. She begged her friend to leave her to her thoughts; but no, Kate said, "she was her physician, that her father had put her under her care, and she was now about to administer the first prescription;" she drew the curtain from the window, and pointed to the glorious scene without, stretching away in the distance, until it was lost in the misty junction of the watery horizon. "Look, dear Ellen. at those long blue pennants sweeping out towards Cape Charles, did you ever see any thing more beautiful? see how they contrast with the lighter blue of the sky, and now how the sun, rolling up behind, tips their edges with crimson. Get up, dear Ellen, God never made these morning glories to be seen in bed; it is the salutation of Heaven to Earth; nature is just drawing the first curtain from before his altar, and we of the earth should not reject the proffered boon."

"Dear Kate, what an enthusiast you are?" said poor Ellen, still longing to be alone.

"Enthusiast, Ellen? indeed I am an enthusiast, God loves enthusiasts, and the wicked only hate them. They chime not with gross and grovelling pursuits; they are of Heaven, not of Earth. All that is bright and lovely and beneficent on Earth, is born of enthusiasm. Enthusiasm first discovered this glorious land; it fired the hearts of the Crusaders; and if they recovered not the Holy Land, did far more, for they exalted our sex to their true position and dignity. My father, too, he is called an enthusiast by the cold-blooded common sense men; look at him, dear Ellen, his thoughts soar forever over those blue mountains, and that very passion will carry him one day to their summits, and does it not ennoble his character? Is he not elevated by it; see how pure and guileless he walks among the poor intriguing politicians who clog his steps, and yet cannot advance one of their own. Is he not the life and soul of the whole Colony?"

"Kate, you bear down all opposition, I give up to enthusiasm; only bring me back to its brilliant hopes and aspirations, and you will earn your title of Doctress, indeed!"

"That will I, my poor scared bird; you have been caged so long, that you have forgotten how to flutter, much less fly; but come, soar along with me among the bright wings that surround us without, and your pinions will come back again. You were never made, dear Ellen, to grovel, and pine, and die among the tamer duties and every day drudgeries of life."

"I have substituted duty, for enthusiasm, Kate."

"Duty! well, come Mrs. Duty, only give me your hand and I will trip you over field and flower, and brae and brake, and moor and lawn, until we shall accomplish all Mrs. Duty's task, and far more besides. I tell you, Ellen, that duty is none the worse for a little of the genuine fire, she goes lame without wings, and even hobbles on crutches, but clap the pinions to her, and she soars aloft, and sips the very beauties which God created to be met half way by such a spirit. Heaven itself is but one continued scene of enthusiasm; we cannot form a conception of its glories without bidding good-day to Earth."

"And leave poor old Duty behind."

"There you are wrong, dear Ellen, to separate them; I would only clothe the dame in brilliant hues, while you want to murder her with rags and poverty."

"Oh, Kate, how you do run away with the argument."

"Not at all, Ellen, I only want to convince you that there are more ways than one to do right, and that even doing right in in a peculiar way, is very near a-kin to doing wrong."

"Why, Kate, one would think to hear you talk, that I had been doing something very wrong."

"It is not exactly that, dear Ellen, but I wish to c nvince you that there are higher and nobler duties than those, with the performance of which you satisfy your conscience."

"You surprise me exceedingly! tell me what those high duties are?"

"A cheerful spirit is the first and greatest thing which you lack," seeing the poor valetudinarian burst into tears, she pushed away her woman and threw her arms round her, while she continued:

"Nay, nay, nay, Ellen, I would not wound you for the world; I wished rather to coax than scold you from your settled dejection."

"Kate, you know not what I suffer, you cannot, no one can know."

"There is the very point dearest—try it with me, no mother ever listened to daughter with the same indulgence that I will listen to you. If your imagination magnifies trifles into matters of importance, it is enough for me that they are so to you, and I will look at them with your eyes. Dear Ellen, I seek your confidence with the most sincere desire to befriend you—I promise you I will feel too much as you feel—I will weep when you weep, and if you cannot laugh when I laugh, why, we will e'en cry together. Dear Ellen, throw me not off, I love you like my own, own Sister."

"I cannot withstand your appeal, Kate, you have made a child of me, and you must put up with my childishness."

By this time Kate had her arm round the waist of the invalid, and was urging her through the garden, to the grove beyond.

"Here is a lovely seat," said she, "and we can sit here at the foot of this old tree and talk till we are tired—or rather till you are tired, for when that comes, then I will talk to you. The birds you see are warbling their pretty stories among the fresh green leaves. See that mocking bird, how it chatters to its mate, that is me, Ellen, and the silent one represents you, only I'm sure I cannot discourse such sweet music as my prototype."

" Dear Kate, the very sound of your voice, cheers my heart,—before I left home, I had not walked this far, for many, many months."

" Oh how I rejoice, that you are come at last,—you don't know how I have longed to have you here, just as now, your whole confidence mine."

" I shall be so, Kate, and I have often wished for such a confident, but my whole being shrinks from disclosing the weaknesses of earlier days."

" One to-hear you talk, would suppose you fifty at the least."

" I may appear staid and sober enough, but I have not always been so. Do you not recollect when we first met at the Capital, what a thoughtless rattlebrain I was ?"

" I recollect only that you took me captive, heart and soul, little girls as we were, and if I remember right, I was not the only one."

" Oh, Kate! what memories your words recall—what happiness—what weaknesses! those of childhood, to be sure,—but is not the sturdy oak bent when it is a twig, and grows it not so forever ? You know it is so Kate, with our sex at least. The world is all wrong in supposing that we wait to come out into the world to prepare for the world. Those things which fix— irretrievably fix our destiny, are the legitimate fruits of childhood—they are matters of feeling, not of judgment. I am almost wicked enough to repine sometimes when I think that my destiny for this life was cast and lost before I was perfectly a responsible being, but it was doubtless so designed by an All-Wise Providence, to teach me that this is not my true home."

" There now, Ellen, we might begin the argument again, were I disposed to interrupt you, but I am not. You were speaking at the time when we first met."

" Or rather Kate, when I first met Frank Lee. You see I can even call his name now, which my poor fond father would no more do in my presence, than he would explode a petard at my feet. Poor Frank was left a ward of my father's, you know. Papa attended old Mr. Lee in his last illness, he was unprepared to die—no will made. Papa wrote his will and agreed to accept the trust of his two sons, Francis and Henry. He brought them from Westmoreland with him and they went to College from our house. Oh, what happy, joyous, frolicksome days were those of the first year. I saw no difference in the boys, they were both my seniors, and both as brothers to me. Those happy, happy evenings during the long winter nights, when my father used to sit and talk to us about the structure of the earth—its revolutions, and those of the other planets, and then of the innumerable worlds beyond— and sometimes he would perform chemical experiments for our amusement— in short he became a child among children, in order that they might become men. But I went hand in hand in all their studies, aye, and plays too—they almost made a little Amazon of me, and I really believe they would have taken me out gunning with them, if papa had not put his veto upon it. This he could not do however with all the unfeminine amusements into which they forced me. You recollect my little sorrel poney, and how we three cantered over the neighborhood of Williamsburg Not an old fish or oyster negro, but knew us a mile off. Oh, how merry Frank was—so full of buoyant spirits— so exhiliarated with hope—so cheerful—so kind to every body, so obliging— so repentant when he did wrong, so stern and steady when right. I think I can see his pouting lip now maintaining his boyish rights.

" Do you know Kate, that I saw a fearful resemblance to the expression of his mouth in that strange tutor last night. I know it was only a chance resemblance, wholly accidental, but it has interested me in that young man. When I saw him throw his eyes to the floor and become lost in a reverie, until they had to jog him quite rudely, when it came to his turn to read, I would have given any thing in this world to have travelled with his thoughts to his distant home, and proscribed friends. Perhaps thought I, he too has been left an orphan like poor Frank, and wandered as he did, from the happy scenes of his childhood, and is now calling them up one by one, in painful pictures of the past. I longed to compare notes with him, I know it was very foolish, but it was all conjured up by that smile.

"Oh such an expression, never but one youth before had. It told a history—there were years of association with it, long years of memory lent their shadows, and that bright smile was like the dimples round a stone thrown at random into the river, slowly receding and vanishing—leaving the shores and their histories as if the stone had never been thrown. But where was I? Oh! up to this time, I had never perceived any difference between the brother's, or never analyzed it if I had. Frank being the elder, seemed very naturally to take the lead in everything. One circumstance I did remark, by the by—whenever he went away to spend a day or a week, with some neighboring youth among the gentry, we were all moped to death. Father and Harry were as much rejoiced to see him return as I was, but this was attributed by me at the time, to the breaking up of our little family party. I knew not but it would have been the same if any other one had gone. I perceived not that he was the very life and soul of our little meetings. Neither had I perceived up to this time, that Frank was at all different from other youths of his age, he appeared just like them to me—he dressed like the rest of the young gentry—rode like them—talked like them. No, not exactly either—he did not talk like common boys, for there was a winning gentleness about him mingled with the manliness of riper years, which the old negroes used to say betokened an early death. Alas, how true those forebodings were. You see I cannot keep up the history of the two boys together, I so runaway with the memory of Frank. There was no perceptible difference in their attainments at school, more than could easily be accounted for by disparity of years. This was not great, but two or three years is greater I believe in mental than physical growth.

"As I began to approach my fourteenth year, now five years ago, I marked the distinctive identity of my father's wards. I observed little things, but not great ones—those on the surface, but nothing deeply. Henry was the more silent of the two, more cautious, prouder and more given to the pomps and vanities of his station. He loved to affect the gentleman even thus early, would seldom ride out without a servant, and loved to be waited upon for show and ceremony's sake, as well as from convenience or actual necessity. He could not bear a joke, or playfulness of any sort at his own expense, while he was very willing to be amused at the expense of others; yet, when he laughed or played, it was never with his whole heart and soul, like his brother. You see, dear Kate, I am answering your oft repeated appeals in behalf of Henry Lee, in giving his history.

"Henry, to tell the truth, loved self too much, and regarded others too little, while his brother was the very reverse in every respect. Frank, you know, by the laws of the land, inherited the bulk of his father's property, which had been in no way disturbed by the will, except to give Harry his mother's share, which was amply sufficient, I am told, to have made him independent, and better off than younger brothers generally are. Yet there was, now evidently growing up a jealousy of his brother's great possessions. Though the younger he would sneer at his brother's position, as the head of the family—bow to him when rebuked, in mock humility,

" In all their College squabbles with other boys, Harry was sure to be the aggressor in the quarrel, and Frank was sure to do the fighting; not that Harry was a coward at all, but his brother was so much more of a generous and chivalrous nature. I have seen him come home all bloody from fighting Harry's battles, and cannot remember an instance of the latter becoming the champion of the other."

" He was the younger," said Kate.

" True, but he was the stouter and stronger too, I believe. However, give him all the advantages of his position; I would not detract one iota from his claims, of any kind. These distinctive marks in their character began to develope themselves more and more every day, until the very servants plainly showed their partiality for Frank. My father, too, impartial, calm and temperate, as you know him to be in his feelings, could not help showing his greater fondness for the elder brother, and this brings me to the relation of a fact, a small one it is true, but these develope character. Harry perceived this growing partiality of my father—if that may be called partiality, which was nothing more than the love of good and generous actions, and was not long in telling him of it. Not only did he charge him with it, but he alleged that it was the result of interested motives, and grew entirely out of his desire to secure Frank and his fortune for his daughter. We were all present, and I am very sure that I shall never forget the scene which succeeded. My venerable old father was terribly shocked, as you may suppose, and he rebuked Harry, as I never heard him rebuke any one before. If Harry had possessed any genuine feeling, he would have shrunk into nothing, at such a withering castigation, from a source usually so mild and gentle. But he was far from feeling remorse on the occasion, and never retracted.

" It was a beautiful moonlight night, and I ran out into the garden, and there, in that old summer house which you have so often chided me for making my home, I had like to have cried my very eyes out, for mortification. I had never had such a thought pass through my mind, any more than if Frank had been my brother. Now that it was distinctly presented, and in such a startling light, too, shall I confess it to you, my dear Kate, my kind confessor, that it was not wholly unpleasant. The mortification was profound, but I fear the poison had sunk equally deep with it. I, of course, at that age, could not enter into a very rigid self-examination; my powers of self-analysis, if I had even been disposed to exercise them, could not be very great, but I can trace my feelings now, and I confess to you, that that charge, a disgraceful one if true, carried with it a surmise that, though wholly untrue on our parts, it might not be so on Frank's. Oh, what a terrible quarrel succeeded between those two young brothers; Frank poured down such a torrent of indignation upon his brother, as no one could have supposed would ever issue from lips usually so mild and gentle; and, must I confess all, it was mingled with such praises of me, as no poor motherless girl of fourteen could hear in safety. I did not eaves-drop, but hearing the quarrel somewhat abate, I essayed to get to my own room, which could only be approached through the one in which they were sitting. I retreated to my seat again. My poor, almost heart broken father, was already locked up in his chamber, and did not again make his appearance that night.

" At length Henry was silenced, but not abashed or repentant, and walked himself off in great state, declaring he would never enter our doors again. He slept that night, truly enough, in College. When he was gone, Frank came in search of me. You, dear Kate, can imagine my feelings; young as I was, I was covered with shame, and must have looked to him like the guilty participator in the interested scheme with which his brother charged me, but it was from a very different cause.

"I was beginning to have a faint idea that the youth before me was indeed dearer to me than a brother; and after what had been said, and feeling as I did, how could I look him in the face? And how could he look at my evident shame and embarrassment, without having a suspicion, at least, that that part was true; but he was a brave, noble, generous boy; his own nature was too bright and pure to suspect others. He seated himself on the grass at my feet, and took both my hands, and then poured out his whole soul to me, boy as he was, with all its generous treasures and lofty aspirations. He, too, it seemed, had been unconscious of the slumbering passion within, until it had been revealed sometime before by a similar scene between him and his brother, when quite alone. Kate, I had to respond to his eloquent, pleading passion, or else give further grounds for suspecting me of some sinister design in future, because I had betrayed too much already to affect concealment now, and I met his confiding nature with a frankness equal to his own.

"Oh, that bright, fair youth! how the true fervor of passion, in its first and brightest dream, gushed from his heart. How brilliantly his graceful and chaste imagination entwined our future lives, through vistas all green and luxuriant with flowers, and from which even the rude blasts were most carefully excluded. He knew little of the real world; he was as guileless and unpractised in wickedness as a babe, and I was quite as inexperienced. Is it surprising, then, that I listened to him with a charmed ear and a willing heart? No, Kate; no girl reared as I had been could anticipate my sad experience; and it springs not up in the mind by intuition. I listened and believed; my faith was laid in the deepest foundations of my being; it was grounded in my very soul. You, Kate, know something of a woman's love, even in its inception; you know that it is not only a part of her being, but it is the whole, at least, the layer upon which all else is built. But I not only had true and unwavering faith in Frank himself, but I believed in his imaginary paradise, which his glowing and delighted imagination had painted for us. I believe that all of our sex spend at least the first quarter of their lives under a similar illusion, if accident or circumstances produce not the youth who is to walk hand in hand with us through these bowers of Eden, imagination furnishes him at once, clothed in the same ideal colors which we throw around the real youth, when he rises up before us. Oh, what a gorgeous dream it is while it lasts! how its hues are thrown around every thing in our little circumscribed world! your beautiful horizon this morning, Kate, crimson lit, as it was, seemed poor and tame compared with these pictures, which memory was even then rearing up over all the past. Can you wonder that when I turn from them, and look into the cold and dreary future, my physical strength, and even my moral courage, should sink under the withering contrast?

Even our little Eden found a tempter, I will not call him a serpent, for you know Harry Lee and respect him, and he is often your father's guest, but I will say that he is by no means exempt from the fierce and deadly passions of our nature. Nay, more, and let this be the answer once for all to his suit, his long and persevering suit, pleaded by so many able advocates. Though so calm and high-bred in all his exterior man, he is but a common man still—all his passions and deadly enmities are only schooled into good behavior; though wreaths and flowers grow upon the surface, serpents slumber beneath.

"He returned to our house next morning, notwithstanding his anathmas of the evening before, and his stealthy and watchful jealousy very soon discovered that there was an understanding between Frank and me, if not approved by my father, and this brings me to the latter's view of the matter. He has always been mother and father both, to me, consequently the most unreserved confidence existed between us, as much so as ever existed between parent and daughter. I went, after a sleepless night, and told him the whole story of our youthful love and its premature revelation; for I can call it nothing else but a discovery, and an accidental one on our parts. He was most deeply moved, aye, and interested too, beyond that which a fond parent might be supposed to feel, for he was struck with the novelty of such a youthful engagement. *I know* that that youthful sentiment, or call it what you will, has interwoven itself into the very essence of my moral existence—it has become purified and chastened, still more, I know, by poor Frank's untimely fate." Here she was interrupted for a while by her tears, but presently proceeded. "I say it has become sublimated until it mingles with my higher sentiments, and has become a part of my religious faith. I know of no aspirations after Heaven and its enjoyments, that are not mixed up with thoughts of his pure spirit."

"And yet, Ellen, you chided my enthusiasm this very morning?"

"Aye, dear Kate, not because I did not understand your feelings—I realized them too vividly, and it brought a shudder over me to think how soon that pure fountain of your own might be poisoned at its source."

"Let me not interrupt you."

"My father, I could see, was pleased in spite of himself, and in spite of Harry's poisonous breath having been blown into our cup of happiness; but he decided at once, that Frank must anticipate his Edinburgh course, before determined upon, and they had a long interview that morning, the result of which was that he was to set out forthwith. Here again, let me say that this very thing constantly rises up in judgment against Harry. It is unjust, perhaps, but I cannot help viewing him as in part the cause of poor Frank's unhappy fate. True, he would have gone some time or other, like all the youth among our gentry, to finish his education in Europe, but he would not have gone then, and might have escaped the entanglement with your unhappy relative's affairs, at any other time. Harry could not conceal his delight at the new arrangement, even under his cold, proud exterior, and positively refused to accompany his brother.

"The parting between Frank and me was at yonder town, and as you may imagine was only supportable from the hope of our soon uniting again. My father accompanied us to the ship, and we lay upon the water in our little boat, waving our handkerchiefs, until that noble vessel had become a speck not much bigger than the boat itself. I could have stayed there forever, or until he came back, for he carried with him my present existence as well as future. The past only is now my own, and its treasures I have been pouring out with a lavish hand to you, my truest and oldest friend. Harry seemed to think that he had the whole game in his own hands, after Frank's departure—he could not conceal his exultation—he attempted to assume his position in our family, and even went so far as to affect his easy, careless ways and winning manners. You know enough of that proud and haughty spirit, to estimate how very unbecoming it appeared in him, but why need I dwell upon that particular assumption of what was not his own—has he not assumed the hues of the chameleon; and above all, has he not taken every thing that was Frank's?"

"There, dear Ellen, I think you are a little unjust, for he, of course, must inherit his brother's property."

"Of course, but it is not just that—it was the indecent haste to step into his shoes in all respects, to which I intended to allude, but perhaps I am unjust to Harry in detailing particulars. I do not wrong him, however, in the spirit which I attribute to him as to his past life. I know the man, Kate, most thoroughly and intimately. Has not our childhood been spent together—and is he not now ever at our house? No, no, Kate, I have not wronged him on the whole—I have drawn a flattering likeness of him, and now contrast poor Frank's personal outlines with his, and you have the two pictures complete." Saying which she drew forth a small picture hanging to a ribbon, and looked at it steadily for a moment as a mother hangs over some memento of her lost one, and then handed it to Kate. It was the miniature of a fair haired youth, yet in his teens, in a crimson velvet dress—the ruffles falling from his very white neck and hands, so as rather to add to the extreme youthfulness of the general air. It was a face to look upon and remember forever—an eye that sparkled with the high impulses of genius as well as the flush of health and ardor of youth.

"No wonder, dear Ellen, that you cannot look upon Henry with favor, when you cherish ever near your person such a rival as this. Oh, 'tis a noble youth!"

"But let us put it by, Kate. It is not well for me to add to my own regrets by hearing him praised by others. You already know all that sad part of his history connected with your uncle's execution. You know that he fell fighting like a hero for his rescue."

"Would it not be well, my Ellen, to lay it out of sight altogether. I would certainly advise the step, as the first preparation to fit you for resuming your proper duties in society."

"Dear Kate, what inconsistent creatures we poor mortals are—but now I had almost taken your place, and become the enthusiast of the morning—and you have almost taken mine, and gone to preaching of duty."

"It is only the different lights in which circumstances place us. We are not so dissimilar by nature as these have made us."

"Oh, Kate, may yours never change so as to render us alike in circumstances, as in nature, if it should so unfortunately turn out, all those brilliant colors and gay flowers in which you are wont to clothe every thing, will be changed to a vision of darkness. • A young girl with hope blotted from the catalogue of her attributes, is like the sky with the lights extinguished—the longer and deeper you look into it, the blacker and more cheerless it looks. In other words, it is despair, so far as this world is concerned. A woman who can re-enact the scenes through which I have gone, must be like a tragedy queen at rehearsal. No, no, Kate, we are formed for but one great trial of this sort, and my probation is over. I long to sleep forever from the feverish dream of this life's false hopes and bitter delusions. Death has no terrors for me; I look at it as a kind friend, and I solemnly believe, that nothing but my duty to the living has inspired me thus far to carry my troubles amongst the joy of others. Yes, Kate, to make my confession the whole truth, without reserve, there is one faint shadow at which I still cling. Do you know, that sometimes, even yet, I cannot believe that Frank is dead? I cannot realize it, you will say, because I was not present at the sad ceremonies. That is something, doubtless, but I cling to things a little more substantial; two circumstances, so slight, that none but the hopeless could grasp at such straws. First, then, we have never been enabled to hear those sad particulars, the last scene I mean; and, secondly, Harry has some such faint notion himself; I will not call it either a fear or a hope, for I cannot name it, but there is such a surmise; and now, to conclude, let me confess further, that I came here with the expectation of having this hope quenched or revived."

"Indeed!" said Kate, truly surprised.

"Yes, Kate, there has been a secret funeral here, of one near and dear to your father, and with whose death Franks was most intimately connected. Your father has received many papers relating to these things, and I am going to commission you sometime soon to be my embassador. Upon that hope I live, Kate.'

"Most willingly will I assist you, for I do believe that something certain in that matter is absolutely necessary for you, and that shall be obtained at all events, now or hereafter; but do tell me, what funeral do you allude to, and how could it be secret?"

"The remains of Gen. Elliot have been clandestinely removed here, whether by your father's orders or by his friends in Europe, I know not, but certainly with the Governor's approbation, for he had the place of their reception prepared before the body arrived."

"How, you astonish me! first at the facts themselves, and next at your obtaining the information before me; but tell me how you know this to be true?"

"I received the intelligence in a letter from my papa, the very same which enclosed your pressing invitation; he told it to me as a secret, however, never supposing for a moment that I could divulge it to anybody, much less that I would be down here almost as soon as the answer; and brought, too, by this news. I obtained his permission to mention all this to you, last night, as he said your father intended to communicate it to the family, the first moment you were all alone."

"This is very strange, but now I recollect, that gloomy looking structure at the foot of the lawn, in the centre of a cluster of trees; and this accounts, too, for papa's strange appearance, the night we saw blood on his face, and his unusually grave demeanor ever since. And this it was that brought you to Temple Farm, a desire to pry further into these matters that made me your confidant, after all."

"Nay, nay, Kate, could I not as well have chosen Dorothea?"

"Yes, and got laughed at for your pains; sister has no more idea of any one wasting away from immaterial afflictions, than she has of alchemy. Ten to one but she would prescribe for your case a bowl of new cream, drank at her dairy before breakfast. Dear, laughing little jade, she will never die the victim of sentiment, depend upon it."

"Thrice happy she," replied Ellen with a deep drawn sigh, "such should be all the daughters of this world, but she has yet to be tried, Kate. You may underrate her susceptibilities."

"I meant no more myself, Ellen—dear good natured laughing little baggage. I am sure I underrate her in nothing. I think this wide, wide world, contains few such. Father lives over his own youth in her; but we are forgetting the business in hand, and while we talk of our plans, let us be moving towards the house slowly, the sun is getting too warm here for you. Now let me know exactly what I am to do."

"Why, you are to seize the first opportunity of having a private interview with your father, at which you are to inform him how far we are already let into his secrets, and then beg as a special favor for me the the perusal of all the papers relating to the trial, death and attempted rescue of General Elliot."

"And will you, my Ellen, go into his library and pour over those piles of musty papers, at the same table with this new private secretary of his, for I understand that he is going to confer that vacant office, also, upon the stranger who has so captivated him?"

"No Kate, no, we must have them in your room, and then we will search them together, you have become interested sufficiently in my story, to take that much interest, or if you dislike the task I will do it alone. No mother ever read an epistle from a sick child with the same avidity that I will pour over those musty papers."

By this time they had reached the house, and seated themselves at the breakfast table.

CHAPTER XI.

MATCH MAKING.

The Governor's guests and family were already seated at breakfast, more' than one messenger having been despatched for the two missing young ladies. They entered at the very moment, when some surprise was being expressed at the unwonted length of Miss Evylin's walk.

" So, so, Doctor," said the Governor, looking in triumph at his worthy old friend, " I told you Kate was the better Doctor of the two, now look at your daughter and tell me if that is not pretty well for the first morning ?"

The Doctor made room near himself, for his daughter, and looked indeed with much interest for the refreshened bloom to which his Excellency alluded: There it was sure enough, two round red spots in her cheeks—whether the result of health or disease he seemed somewhat puzzled to tell.

Be that as it might, the effect upon her beauty was indeed lustrous. Her eyes too, which on the previous night, seemed to move slowly and painfully over objects in the room, were bright as diamonds, with the late excitement. Every one approved of Kate's practice, and the Doctor was free to confess himself out-done, yet he was not so sanguine as others as to the final result. He would rather have seen that red and white blending imperceptibly in her cheeks like Kate's. His professional experience led him to distrust those deceitful heralds of an early grave.   The effect for the present was much the same however, for the triumphant and enthusiastic Kate her-self, had not brought in from the fields and flowers a richer harvest of beauty. Sickness rather lent an interest to, than diminished from, the loveliness of that delicate young creature. In that large company of gay and fashionable peo-ple, she looked like a little nun, just escaped from the gates of a living tomb. Those two, father and daughter, were objects of peculiar solicitude and inter-est—there was a sweet, confidential air between them, quite different from the ordinary manifestations in similar relations, so placed.   They appeared to be all in all to each other—they had of late lived with and for no one else— of course that air of monastic seclusion about the daughter particularly, was far removed from the conventional courtly grace of most of those around her. Not that there was any *gaucherie*, far from it, she was rather elevated above the conventional standard, than fallen below it—so much did that constant, self-sustained spirit and mental endowments of the rarest order, elevate her above any mere temporary rules of propriety. She scarcely seemed to think that she was called upon to bear a part in the general conversation, and yet, when the Governor or Reverend Commissary, addressed any remark to her, she answered in a manner to convince every one, that she had read and reflected' upon most subjects comprehended under the terms of general information, even in the sterner sex.

It had been one of the favorite projects of the Governor, in days gone by, to unite his eldest son and heir to the daughter of his oldest and best friend. There seemed a peculiar propriety in this, on every account. Some persons thought they could perceive a remarkable similarity of mental constitution. John Spotswood was then one of the ablest men within the boundaries of the Old Dominion—of vigorous intellect—learned and subtle in the use of scholas-tic weapons, and with a power of eloquence, when he chose to use it, which a public assembly could rarely withstand.   There seemed then a propriety in the proposed union of these most carefully educated persons, but a greater mutual repugnance sprung up between them than could could have been imagined from the premises stated.   These are matters our fair readers have doubtless discovered ere this, which are not soluble either by mathematical or logical rules. So it seemed in this case. Any one to have become acquainted with the parties, separately, would have declared at once, that they were just made for each other, and yet all things, thus conspiring thereto, the match could not be brought about. We are speaking of John rather as he once was, than as he has been presented to e reader. He was now a walking mystery to his friends—past finding out—perhaps that mystery may be solved ere we progress much farther in our narrative. He paid her several visits, and spent some long evenings with the Doctor, but when his father catechised him in his bantering way upon the progress of the affair, he answered abruptly that she was a prude.

Ellen ran her eyes over the company at the table, in search of the new tutor, anxious to see how he would appear by daylight, and almost afraid to see those lips again that called up so many painful memories—while she was in the very act, a servant entered with an answer to a message, which the Governor had despatched to him previous to her entrance—to the effect, that he would pay his respects to his Excellency and his guests directly.

" Poor fellow," said the Governor, " he doubts his position in our little circle, and was too unpresuming to present himself, but I will soon shew him that if Lady Spotswood marshals her guests to the table in order of their rank, that I range mine in the order of their merit."

Her Ladyship laughed at this sally and replied " That it was the first time in her recollection that she had been charged with too exact an observance of form and ceremony. What says the Commissary ?"

"I think that the papers relating to the Tramontaine expedition might answer that question for his Excellency. Are not three-fourths of the aristocracy of the land ranged against it ?" said he.

" It was not her Ladyship who offended them ; that sin lies upon my shoulders. Indeed I did but jest about the order of precedence."

A cloud came over that hard weather-beaten face, as soon as the great subject of all his meditations were mentioned; and he remained in a thoughtful mood for a while, and then continued: " My first offence was that I, a military man, and nothing else, arrived in the Colony most unexpectedly to take the place of a gentleman who was captured on his way hither by the French. He was expected to espouse the cause of the clique whom I have mortally offended by attending to the real interests of the whole Colony. Instead of being too much of a political partizan, I have not been enough so to please them. In the second place, I have established ware-houses for the inspection of tobacco at convenient places throughout the land, and this touches the pockets of the planting interest. In the third place, I have established a large iron furnace and forge, and this separates me still more from that interest. And fourthly and lastly, I have advocated the establishment of military posts from the frontiers to the head waters of the Mississippi, thus disuniting the grasping French from forming in our rear, and this they say, all the men and tobacco in the Colony could not accomplish. Is it truly put, Mr. Commissary ?"

" Very fairly stated, but you forgot to mention the Indian hostages at the College."

" Oh, aye. They say farther that I am putting a stick into the hands of savages to break our own heads. Now we have the whole case ; was ever a glorious and magnificent scheme of conquering an Empire, thwarted from from such pitiful and contemptible motives. Oh, if I only had some of Marlborough's brave boys here, how I would shame these poor sordid narrow minded creatures. I would plant the British Lion on the most commanding position which it has ever yet occupied. Grand as the enterprise is, in a military point of view, it is far surpassed in importance by its civil and social relations. The discovery of Columbus itself was nothing—the achievements of Smith and Raleigh are nothing if we are to be hemmed in here within a narrow strip of land along the Atlantic coast. Accomplish my design and resources are opened to the west, which the most enthusiastic visionary cannot now foresee."

Kate exchanged a smile with some of the young gentlemen. She had so often heard him dilate upon the same subject, while Dorothea looked up in his face and remarked, "Papa, I have always heard that old soldiers love to fight their battles over again, but you are always fighting them by anticipation."

Patting her on the head, he replied, "Then I am a gasconader, am I?"

Before any reply was uttered, the tutor entered, dressed pretty much as he had been the night before, but looking weary and haggard as if he had spent a sleepless night. Notwithstanding this, his carriage was erect, and he walked to his place and made the salutations of the morning with a grace and ease, more like a courtier just from the saloons of the Queen, than a poor houseless tutor and private secretary. There was nothing extravagant at all in his manners; on the contrary, they were regulated with the best possible taste, with the exception, that he had seemingly not yet schooled himself into the humble deferential air, usually supposed to become one in his position. Before he was seated, the Governor named the ladies to him, and he again bowed to them, bending over very low and gracefully as he saluted Kate and Ellen, but not uttering a syllable. He passed the hour of breakfast very much in the same way, scarcely ever speaking, except when the Governor addressed some questions directly to him, and which he answered like a man possessed of ample information touching all the interesting questions then involved in the subject of the succession.

It was curious to watch the painful sort of interest with which Ellen Evylin's eyes seemed to gloat on his face every now and then, before she would turn away with a dissatisfied air.

His face was one which, like the Governor's, had seen some little vicissitudes of weather, with this difference, that old Boreas had put his marks on the first after the zenith of life had been passed, while in the other, it was scarcely approached. He wore large brown whiskers, overshadowing much of his face, retained no doubt from his military life, and stretching from one of them, the scar of a deep sabre cut ran along his face and down into his very mouth. So that his countenance, when in repose, had rather a ferocious look, from which, however, it was instantly redeemed when lighted up in conversation. He was tall and slender, and not apparently in good health. Altogether, he was a remarkable looking man.

Kate whispered to Ellen, as they were leaving the room, arm in arm, "Our new tutor has quite as aristocratic an air as any person at the table, and more of the camp grace about him than even papa himself."

"Did you ever hear such a deep toned voice, Kate?" said Ellen, "it sounds like the bass pipes of your organ; I could not help fancying him giving commands along a line of soldiers in battle array."

"The very idea, Ellen! there is command in it, aye, and in more than that about him; poor man, he has not always been a tutor, I dare say."

"Kate, I always feel sorry for your broken down gentleman; there is no more melancholy expression in our language, than 'such a one has seen better days,' and how instantly they occur on looking at Mr. Hall. Without the slightest appearance of an attempt to excite sympathy—indeed quite the reverse—every tone and attitude tells of fallen fortunes. Papa seems to have fallen in love with him at first sight; but that big scar over his face would captivate him at any time. He loves a soldier for his own sake, independent of the cause he has been engaged in!"

"And what cause, Kate, did Mr. Hall espouse?"

"I do not know, Ellen, perhaps papa enquired into that; but, as I said just now, it would matter little with him, if his soldiership and personal honor remained unimpeached."

"I would almost be a surety for them myself, so firmly persuaded am I that he is a true man."

"What strange prejudices you do take up, Ellen, and almost at first sight. Here is Mr. Harry Lee, a gentleman of princely fortune, high birth, great personal accomplishments, and a playmate of your childhood, whom you cannot bear the sight of; while on the other hand, you are ready to vouch for the honor and honesty of a poor stanger whom you never saw but once before in your life."

"True, Kate, I believe it is the nature of our sex to judge more by the heart than the head, and I don't know but they err as seldom in their estimates of character as the other. As to the fortune and birth, and all that, which you have tossed into Harry Lee's scale in balancing these two characters. I do not value them at that," (snapping her fingers.) "I would not marry him if he was heir apparent to the throne of England."

"I heard a servant announce to my father, as I left the room, that Mr. Lee would be here to-day."

"Yes, I recognized the livery, and so odious has even the poor servant's badge of office become, that it hurried me from the table."

"Why, my Ellen, I had no idea, that you were such a spiteful, bitter little jade!"

"Did you suppose because out of health, I was a poor tame somebody that said yea and nay, with a drawl, and nasal twang, and that I would be Mr. Lee's humble servant as soon as he laid his fortune at my feet. No, no Kate, you, if placed in my position, without changing characters, would do just as I have done."

"I confess Ellen, that I never admired him myself, even before your sketch, and I cannot say that my estimate has increased since; he is a gentleman for all that."

"Yes, as your holyday world has it—your world that estimates every thing by the surface, he is a gentleman, but oh, Kate, how I have come to despise that hollow, deceitful, average of all men to one common conventional standard. A certain quantity of broad-cloth or velvet—quantum sufficit (as father's prescriptions say) of lace, four silver buckles—or perhaps gold—a pair of pumps and a cocked hat—and there is your gentleman."

"Oh no, Ellen, that is a mere stuffed figure, such as the tailors shew their fine clothes upon."

"Well, what more is your ball room gentleman, just give this figure a motion backwards and forwards, whenever it meets a lady and is spoken to, and is not the picture complete?"

"Oh no, Ellen, it must talk and laugh."

"Yes, Kate, and to be very excruciating, it must weep too, but how much talk will answer, and how small a phial of tears? poh! poh! you know their small talk is nothing—half of it is about the weather, and the vane upon the cupola does that a great deal better, and says nothing."

"Why, Ellen! if the forthcoming shadow of Harry Lee makes you as satirical as that amusing churchman whom I read to you last night, what will his real presence do?"

"Make me as stately and formal as he is, if not so pompous."

"And is he one of your stuffed figures, that talks of the weather and one thing or another—a walking weather-cock, or the clerk of the weather's deputy?"

"No, not just that to give him his due, he has some mind—covered up, beneath all the pomps and vanities of all the Lee's."

"And what is the staple of his conversation?"

"His world material and immaterial, has one common centre, and that is Mr. Harry Lee, member of the house of Burgesses. He is a philosopher too, and has discovered a new theory of the solar system!"

"Indeed, and what is his grand principle?"

"Why, that Henry Lee, Esq., of Westmoreland, is the grand centre of that system, and that the sun revolves around him."

"Oh, Ellen, how we have all been slandering you here, in your absence. One gentleman declared, that you were only prevented from taking the veil, because there was no nunnery convenient. Another that you were going to join the Dissenters, and another the Quakers—and poor John, that you were a man-hater."

"I am sure I never gave your brother any reason to say so. He, I'm certain, can never be ranked with the automaton figures. Neither of us had much fancy I believe for each other, in a matrimonial point of view, but no one can converse with John, for one hour, without respecting his understanding; but do you know Kate, that he has imbibed deeply of Bolingbroke's most dangerous opinions?"

"Ha! and that is the secret then of your sudden disagreement, or rather agreement to disagree?"

"No, no, Kate, I have let you enough into the history of my past life, to convince you, that I can never listen to the addresses of any living being more, and this may explain also, the story of my man-hating; and presbyterianism, and quakerism; but I will not disguise from you, that had those things never happened, I could never love, honor, and obey any man who did not honor and obey our holy religion. That creature, whether male or female, who has lived in this world even no longer than we have, (and God knows I have lived long enough) must be radically wrong in heart, mind, or education, who can suppose that we poor mortals were placed upon this earth to grope our way, without a guide or light of any kind. Look Kate, at the wonderful disproportion in the grasp of our minds and the duration of our lives. We are but beginning to live as rational creatures when we are called upon to die. Father tells me that his mind is maturing every day, and that he is conscious of no diminution of mental vigor, and his head is silvered o'er with age. His mind is actually climbing the steps of knowledge and science, while his body is going fast down the hill of mortality to the grave. Would it not be the bitterest mockery, if this were our only stage of existence. Why should the mind grow brighter and brighter, as the body grows weaker and weaker, if the mind was not to survive the struggle? No, no, Kate, John and I, could never have been more to each other, than the children of old, long tried friends."

"You astonish as well as afflict me, Ellen, by this statement."

"I know it, my dear Kate, but seeing how ignorant you all are, of the dangerous precipice upon which he stands, could I be silent. I have debated the matter with him, to the full extent of my poor capacity, but what can a heart-sick, half educated girl do in an argument with a man like your brother.—his natural endowments of the highest order, and polished by the culture of the schools. Don't you undertake the subject Kate, he will only play with your woman's argument as the fisherman plays with the trout. Your brother is an antagonist, powerful enough for Dr. Blair. Tell him of it, Kate, and let his long tried wisdom select the time and the manner of combatting these pernicious principles. Oh, I do hope he will be rescued before it is too late. I could tell you more about your brother, but I have distressed you enough for one occasion. Come, get ready for church, you are going to York with Dr. Blair, I know. In the mean time, I will seek my own room and think over all these things. Good day, Kate,

CHAPTER XII

GOING TO CHURCH IN THE COUNTRY.

About twelve o'clock, a long cavalcade drove up to Old-York Church. First came the outriders, in livery, then the body guard of the Governor, in full uniform. This corps, numbering about twenty-seven men, consisted mostly of old veterans who had served with the Governor in his continental campaigns, and one old fellow having a wooden leg. They were a martial looking band, and had the appearance of having seen service. The Governor's country establishment had a range of dormitories for these, and stables for their horses, but he never called them out, except on something like public occasions. Next came the family coach, drawn by four horses, and managed by two postillions in livery, and behind which stood two powdered footmen. The coach contained her ladyship and daughters, with the Reverend Commissary in his canonicals. Then came the Governor, flanked on one side by Dr. Evylin, and on the other by little Bob on his poney. The remainder was composed of the carriages of visitors, followed by the young gentlemen: and then again by the family servants, two and two, on horseback, many of them also in livery, and all scrupulously neat and clean.

We have already said, that it was a beautiful Sabbath morning, accordingly the road from Temple Farm to York was lined with neatly dressed people, going to hear the celebrated Divine then at the head of the Episcopal Church in Virginia. Many were on horseback, but many more on foot, and all filed to the right and left to let the cavalcade pass. Scarcely a pedestrian but touched his hat, or bared his head entirely as his Excellency went by, while the negroes did the same, grinning from ear to ear at the same time, at the display made by the grooms in livery, and soldiers in uniform. Many a poor family from the neighborhood of Temple Farm, greeted Kate and Dorothea, with rude courtesy as they passed.

With all the middle and lower ranks the Governor and his family were very popular, perhaps for the very reason, that he was now at deadly feud with some of the largest and most influential families in the land. The time was now rapidly approaching when this very favor of the plebeian ranks stood him in great stead. The favorite scheme of his life—one for which he had perilled his office—his influence—his standing—his fortune, having been accomplished at last much through their means.

The old Church at York, was built like all those of that period in the shape of a cross, and out of perhaps the strangest materials that ever entered into the structure of a sacred edifice, or any other. These are square blocks hewn from fossil shells, deeply imbedded in a basis of sand or marl stone, giving the whole structure much the appearance of a toy house, built entirely of shells, such as is seen often in the shops. Not that there was any thing puerile, or beneath the dignity of a sacred edifice, in the general appearance of the whole, for it was highly imposing, and must have looked grey and venerable, when comparatively of recent structure. It stood on one of the highest points of the town, commanding a prospect of the city of York, then one of the first in importance in the Colony.

The party entered the main aisle, and proceeded to the two large pews set apart for his Excellency's family, with the exception of Kate, who, attended by Bernard Moore, and followed by a servant bearing an armful of music, entered the gallery and took her station at the organ.

She greeted most sweetly the bevy of city damsels, forming the choir, and taking the music from the servant, proceeded to distribute the score of the pieces she was about to play. Moore seated himself at a respectable distance among the masculine voices, but it is questionable, whether his attention was not too much absorbed by the instrumental music to follow the score very closely. Kate seeing the old prelate enter, commenced her prelude. Even the venerable old clergyman seemed lost in a pleasing reverie, while she attuned the hearts of the congregation to a fitting mood to bow before the throne of mercy.

It was a beautiful picture, o see that fair young creature, so full of life, and health, and high hope, bend in such profound humility at the mercy seat, her pure white neck bent over the prayer book, and uttering the responses, with such a heartfelt gratitude, that the words seemed to gush up with the emphasis of her own fervid conceptions.

It was not so much that she felt the responsibility of her own position and example at the head of the young ladies of that great Colony, as her own inborn acknowledgment of the necessity of these stated confessions. A sense of elevated position, and the force of example, are often talked largely of by those in high places, but she knew and felt that these, to be of any avail, must come from the heart: it is then, and only then, they reach the hearts of others.

The preacher chose a subject, in exact accordance not only with her views, but her devotional feelings at the time. It was the sermon on the mount. How it chimed in with Kate's previous thoughts, when the old man read out slowly and solemnly, "Blessed are the poor in spirit, for their's is the Kingdom of Heaven." It seemed as if her very inmost mind had been penetrated by the preacher, and that the words of the text were only embodying her own thoughts in appropriate language.

No better example in all that Church, whether among the gentry or plebeians, could have been found of the very spirit blessed, than that fair daughter of Virginia's aristocracy. She was indeed poor in spirit, as contra-distinguished from mean in spirit. Much of her very grace and beauty, came from that sweet humility, which seemed to be all unconscious of the graces it inspired. A beautiful maiden, without the true Christian graces, is only a beautiful animal at last, from the Venus de Medici to Pocahontas, before her baptism; it requires the finishing touch of the divine spirit upon the heart, before even the person becomes really lovely, in the highest acceptation of the term, and that very grace spoken of by the preacher, she had; that humble, self-condemning, self-sacrificing spirit, which seeks the lowest seat in the synagogue. Kate Spotswood was a Christian; but she was scarcely conscious of it, so truly had she taken to heart the first words of the sermon on the mount. She had never even been confirmed, for the Commissary had not that power, and as to her being a professed disciple, she never even dared to think herself good enough. Often, during that solemn and heart-searching sermon, did the silent tears steal down her unconscious face, and when it was concluded, she looked round like one just waked up from a moving dream, so absorbed had she been.

Bernard Moore, sad, wicked dog, as we fear our readers will consider him, was sitting, leaning his head upon his hand, and gazing at the devout beauty, and tracing the pearly drops that stole from her eyelids with a true sympathy. "How beautiful are the poor in spirit," thought he. He admired religion exceedingly, when the operations upon the heart, and mind, and person, were thus exhibited; and, to do him justice, he had as high reverence for things holy, as most of his order; but he was a gay young man of fortune for all that. We shall see whether Kate proselyted him, as we progress with our narrative.

"What an excellent sermon," said she, as taking Bernard's arm in the gallery to join her family, " it seemed to me, that I could see our Saviour's figure in all its glorious majesty, proclaiming such welcome doctrines to the sons and daughters of affliction on the earth, and such an unwelcome one to the self-sufficient among the great and worldly-minded."

"Excellent, indeed," said he, "I never enjoyed a sermon more in my life, and it was beautifully illustrated."

"Yes, the imagery was grand indeed; that description of the mountain scene must have touched papa upon a tender chord?"

"I did not allude to that exactly," said Moore, slily "I meant rather to say, that it was most happily personified."

"Yes, I agree with you there too: never was precept better borne out by personal example. Dear, good Dr. Blair, I love him almost as well as my own father."

"Still you do not take my meaning, though I agree with you on that point too."

"To whom, then, do you allude?" looking enquiringly into his smiling face, "not to me, surely?"

"Exactly and to no one else."

"That is a far strained compliment, Mr. Moore; too much at variance with truth and honesty for me to accept any part of it. How little you know my heart, if you suppose me poor in spirit, in the true meaning of the preacher. How little do you know its rebellion, its pride, its vanity, its self-deception, its disingeniousness to others—me, poor in spirit, indeed! Why, I was suffering the pains of self-condemnation, during the whole sermon, for lacking that greatest essential in the Christian character, that very poverty of spirit so admirably described.

By this time they had arrived at the door of the carriage, and Moore helped her in, where the other ladies were already seated, and then mounted his own horse, held ready by his servant, and followed on as they had come.

During their return to Temple Farm, the company had an accession of Henry Lee, Esq. He was a tall, elegantly dressed young man, about the same age as Moore and Carter, but with rather more form and ceremony in his address, and rather more studied attention to his toilet, than distinguished either of them. His features were large and sharp, but well formed, and indicative of more than ordinary mental power. His hair was harsh and frizzled, and set close to his head, so as to give it rather a clean cut, statuary look. When he smiled, the man shone out in his own identity. His teeth were very regular, except two projecting tusks at each corner, which gave a harsh expression to his whole physiognomy, so that when he gave himself up to the freest mood of relaxation, he appeared in reality more forbidding, than when his face was in entire repose, for in the former case, there was a classic air of high birth and breeding, under which the other peculiarities were hidden. One single such guest, throws a damper over a whole company, however much disposed to glee and hilarity. It is like a stream of cold air blowing into a warm room, pile on the combustibles as much as you will, and still the same chilling sensation comes over you.

How stately rode the representative of all the Lee's that day, followed by two servants in livery, one bearing a portmanteau strapped to his saddle, as large as a modern travelling appendage of the same sort for a whole family.

"Mama," said Dorothea, her eye still fastened on the pompous young cavalier, his cocked hat perched to its highest elevation upon his head. "Mama, do you think Mr. Henry Lee is very poor in spirit?"

The old Commissary tried to look very grave, so as to suppress a fast coming smile, while Lady Spotswood, looked out of the opposite window of the carriage, so as to get her eye the farthest possibly removed from the person spoken of, and thus smooth down her gravity before she replied.

"You should not apply the sermon just preached, to others, child, but to yourself; do you not recollect the Pharisee?"

"La, mama, you have made the case worse, who could look at that young gentleman now, and not imagine to himself, that he was saying 'Lord I thank thee that I am not as other men.'"

The Commissary was compelled to laugh in spite of himself, in which Kate and her mother now, joined with hearty good will. The picture was too true and too happily applied, to be resisted; it was like a fortunate stroke of a painter's pencil, which completes the likeness, and little Dorothea sat and viewed her work, with a complacency, which nearly upset the prelate every time he turned towards her. Now tossing her head—exactly as the gentleman mentioned, tossed his, and now waving a hand with a majestic air, and presently inserting a thumb under the edge of her stomacher, as he placed his in the arm hole of his vest. So inimitable was her mimicry, that the good Commissary begged her to desist, lest he should arrive at home, in a plight very unbecoming a minister of the gospel, just descended from the sacred desk.

Even after a long silence, there was a flushed appearance of the whole four, when they alighted from the carriage, which excited the curiosity of Moore. He wondered what could have changed their mood so suddenly after he left them. Kate would not, or could not tell, but broke away and ran into the house, referring him to Dorothea for an explanation. Dorothea promised at some other time, that she would go over the whole story, but now she could not, for papa was shaking his finger at her. "Don't you know," she whispered, "that Mr. Lee has a vote in the house of Burgesses." Papa says I must learn to be a politician, or I shall frighten away all his political *friends*.

The party separated to dress for dinner, that great affair of the twenty-four hours in the Old Dominion.

~~~~~~~~~~~~~~~~~~~~~~~~~~~~~~~~

CHAPTER XIII.

MEMORY OF THE PAST.

How silent a large hospitable establishment in the country, seems on Sunday, just after being deserted by a large and gay party? how deserted the halls and chambers? in what profound repose sleep the dogs? and the very insects fly more more lazily and hum more monotonously. The fowls seek the roost, and the geese stand upon one leg, and bury their heads under their wings, while the cattle in the fields gather in clusters under the shade of some umbrageous tree. So overpowering is this general feeling of repose, that children often imagine that there is a Sabbath in nature—a holyday for the heavens and the earth, as well as for man. Such seemed the day to that heart-sick young creature, Ellen Evylin, as she sat in a deep recess at a window of the parlor, the curtains falling down, and totally secluding her, even from the interruption of a chance servant. She held in her hand Milton's Paradise lost, and appropriate as the subject was to her own peculiar feelings, and deeply attuned as they were to harmonize, with the solemn strains of the poet, her hand lay still in her lap with the open book, and her eyes followed the dreamy expanse of waters, stretching out, and farther out, until they filled with tears from mere exhaustion. Why did she thus look ever towards the far off ocean? Why did her eyes attempt to penetrate beyond that long white surf, that came tumbling up as an *avant courier* from the mighty deep beyond, and rolled into the bay, as if glad to reach a haven once more. She pursued the very track of the vessel, which years before, had borne from his native shores, a youth with whose hopes and destinies, her own had been linked in bonds, as durable as life itself. She lived upon the past alone, the

present and the future were almost blotted from the tablets of her mind.   Is it
strange then, that she became what she now was, a pensive dreamer, who loved
to steal from society of the men, and open up there these her only treasures ?
Is it strange that even her appearance should partake of this coloring
of the past, and indifference to the present, and that she should forever seek
the shades of her own sweet little conservatory at home, where she held converse with the silent and sometimes melancholy flowers—those little miniature pictures of a young girl's life—those especially that come " like angel's
visits, few and far between "—that bloom but once in a life-time: or is it any
wonder that she should prefer the solitary house in which she now was, to all
the bustle and confusion, which had distracted her for the last few hours ?
But was she indeed all alone with her own sad thoughts as she supposed ? did
she not hear a step and deep breathing in the room ?   Slowly she drew aside
one corner of the curtain, beneath whose ample folds she might have been
rolled twenty times; why did her heart throb so tumultuously, and her vision
grow dim ?   It was because there was a man in that room, a strange man—
using most strange gestures to a dumb picture.   It was the new tutor, standing before the picture of General Elliott.   What could he know of that unfortunate officer ?   Why should he be gesticulating to a picture he never saw
before a few hours back, and the original of which he never saw at all?   It
was very strange.   More than once she attempted to move towards him and
ask an explanation of his conduct, but as often her courage failed her, until
the man had disappeared as silently as he came, and she was left alone with
her own thoughts and the silent house, and the more solitary ocean beyond.
The tutor gone—the excitement of the moment once calmed—and her nervous irritability stilled, the mystery did not appear so great after all.   The
young man was generally supposed to have been some way connected with
the unfortunate troubles abroad, and thus to have laid the foundation of his
own.   Was it any great stretch of imagination to suppose him to have known
something of one so famous as the original of that picture.   This sufficed
for a time, but alas, how painfully and fearfully excitable are the children of
sorrow.   To such, a spark of the fire exploding, sounds like a cannon—the
sudden slamming too of a door, is the herald of a convulsion of nature; a
black cloud in the horizon, the adumbration of the gathering tornado, and a
tale or a suggestion of horror, meets with too ready a response, and even the
imagination is ever instant with its sombre shadows, to clothe up the skeleton's
of the past in goblin outlines comformable to its wretched experience.   The
ear is ready to start, the eye to dilate with fright, and the wonder working
kaleidescope of the mind, revolves in perpetual revolution, turning up in rapid
succession a gloomy catalogue of spectral images.

Poor Ellen, her imagination was roaming at large over the too certain past,
and the too uncertain future.   Again and again the strange behavior of the
tutor rose up before her, and she would rear up a tale, in connexion with him,
improbable to a perfectly calm mind, until she would almost laugh at the trick
which her imagination was playing her.   One sane and sound suggestion, however, she retained from the dreamy and fitful reveries of the morning,
it was the probability that this individual could throw some light upon that
one subject, ever nearest to her heart, the last hours of poor Frank Lee, and
to ascertain that he was indeed numbered with the dead.   She resolved at
once to seek him.   She wandered through the house in eager pursuit of the
same individual who, but half an hour before had thrown her into such painful excitement; she regretted now, that she had not sought him upon the
instant, for no where was he to be found.   She rang the bell, and called up a
servant, who informed her, that he had walked out into the fields about the
time he must have left the room.

Why appeared the divine poet so tame, so dull that morning, of all others so fitting to discourse of Paradise, and the reader, of all others, to imagine its loss so vividly? When the imagination is at its highest tension, no living or dead author may bridle the unruly power, and tame it to the beaten track. The judgment may be schooled, the heart purified by suffering and affliction, but the wings of the mind, like the wind, goeth where it listeth. The book was again thrown down, and a long reverie wound up that dreamy morning.

She was first roused from her mood by the clatter of the horses hoofs and the carriage wheels of the party returning from church; she made a precipitate retreat to her own room, where she was scarcely seated before Kate came flying in, exclaiming, "Oh, Ellen, you don't know what you have missed by staying away from Church, such a sermon from Dr. Blair! it was worth riding twenty miles to hear. He preached from the Sermon on the Mount, and is going to continue the series through the whole chapter."

"I am sorry I could not go, Kate, but I was really scarcely able, and still less in fitting mood; there is a preparation for going to church in other things besides dress, and I believe it better to stay away, than go with one mind's wandering, like the fool's eyes, to the ends of the earth."

"Oh, I forgot to tell you, Mr. Henry Lee was there; and Dorothea has been apostrophising him as a personification of the true spirit of the text. I m sure I shall never hear of the Pharisee in the parable again, without thinking of him. She says she means to call him henceforth the Pharisee. I need not add that he joined our party, and you may expect to meet him at dinner—I had like to have forgotten it, that was the object of my call, so now you may be prepared to meet him."

"If he is here, I would prefer not going down to dinner."

"But he may here these three weeks, and you cannot avoid him all that time."

"If he stays three weeks I am very sure he will do so without my company, for I will go home."

"No, no, my Ellen, we are not going to part with you so soon, after such difficulty in getting you here. I will dismiss the gentleman myself, with a bee in his bonnet, rather than you should do that."

"That would never do, Kate, what would your father say to such treatment of a gentleman whom he is so anxious to propitiate?"

"Then Dorothea and I will ridicule him off the field. Leave him to be dealt with by us, or surrender him entirely into sister's hands; she will drive him off, depend upon it, and escape under the plea of non-age. It is your gentle ways, Ellen, that keeps the proud man forever dangling at your apron string."

The maid entering to prepare her young mistress's toilet for dinner, the parties separated.

~~~~~~~~~~~~~~~~~~~~~~~~

CHAPTER XIV.

AN OLD FASHIONED DINNER.

It was a fine old Hall, that at Temple Farm, hung with many war-like trophies, and stag-horns, and fox tails, while here and there were some little peculiarities that distinguished the hospitable owner, from others of the Cocked Hat Gentry. Near the centre of the room on one side, hung the General's own martial implements, which he had worn upon the field, and suspended over them in a small silk net was a rusty cannon ball of about three pounds weight. This had struck the veteran himself when it was nearly spent, and he was in the habit of showing it to his guests, when fighting his battles again over his wine. Dorothea used to insist upon it, that the true signal for the departure of the ladies, was the introduction of the cannon ball by her father, instead of the *lead* from Lady Spotswood.

Two immense fire places occupied the best part of each end of the hall, surmounted by curiously carved work, reaching quite to the ceiling, while the side pannels corresponding to these were painted with various scenes, intended to represent the most remarkable military events of the age. The whole appearance of the room, bore rather a military than a feudal or baronial aspect, for all the scenes and trophies were of that sort, and quite recent, even to the antlers.

The dinner was on the table, and such a dinner! The reeking viands would have furnished a French *restaurateur* a stock in trade for a month. A whole surloin of beef formed the chief ornament of one end of the table. It was furnished from the Governor's own stock, upon which he prided himself not a little. At the opposite end was a ham, which if not the real, rivalled the Westphalia in flavor. These were flanked with various dishes of fowls, both wild and tame, not forgetting the canvass back ducks. They were all placed on the table together, after the good old fashion, and the ladies soon after entered in the order of their rank, and placed themselves at the head of the table; Ellen Evylin among the others. Mr. Lee walked really round the table to greet her, which he did in a really warm manner for him, with many compliments upon her improved looks, all which was received with the most freezing courtesy; barely returning his repeated bows, with a single inclination of the head. Dorothea bit her lip till it almost bled, in her itching restlessness, at such temporizing with so obstinately complacent a man. As he returned to his seat, Mr. Hall was entering and met him full face, just as the Governor presented him by name to the new guest. Hall held out his hand in the most frank and open manner, but the other paid him off with one of the cold bows he had just received from Miss Evylin, leaving the poor tutor with his hand awkwardly extended, without a response. Every one seemed to feel for the young man, except him who had inflicted the unnecessary indignity. The subject of it recovered himself with great dignity, after the first awkward moment, and as if fate intended on purpose to revenge him, his chair was found to be next to Ellen Evylin and Kate. His late discomfiture was soon forgotten amidst the lively chat of the two charming girls. Kate bearing the burthen of the entertainment, of course, while her friend threw in a quiet response occasionally. Both the young ladies seemed determined to make amends to the slighted tutor, for the previous repulse, at the same time, perhaps, rejoicing that they saw it rankling in the heart of him who inflicted it. Several times, while Kate eagerly conversed with the tutor, Ellen sat looking up through her long eye lashes, lost in painful reflections. Again she saw the same smile flashing over that otherwise sad and sombre face, as the summer lightning blazes up behind the dark blue clouds of the horizon. The impression was indescribable, so indistinct, so confused with memories of the past; blending so strangely with the personal outlines of others, yet in spite of all improbabilities and obstacles to the contrary, carrying her back to days and scenes long passed by—her days of childhood. She was of course very absent. The tutor seemed desirous to draw her out, and for that purpose would turn a question or reply to her, instead of her friend, but she would frequently have to ask a second time, even the subject of discourse, then join in for a moment quite brilliantly, and glide away again; busy with her memory.

She desired to become better acquainted with Mr. Hall, preparatory to her asking the questions she meditated: yet he was himself the innocent and unconscious cause of her becoming lost, again and again. But absent as she was, and imperfectly as she may have borne her part in the conversation, it was by far the most interesting dinner party that she had been present at for many a long day. She had almost forgotten that such a man lived as Mr. Henry Lee, until he suddenly addressed a question to her across the table.

"Miss Evylin, here is the Rev. Commissary running a tirade against the new Bolingbroke fashion of tying the hair, (he sported it himself with no small complacency,) what say you, is it an improvement or not ?"

"I will turn that grave matter over to my friend Dorothea, if you please, Mr. Lee, I have been so long out of the world of fashion, that I do not feel competent to answer," said Ellen.

"Well, I think," said Dorothea, "that it is far more important what a gentleman has in his head, than how it is tied outside."

Even the Commissary smiled at the home thrust which the little girl had given the inquisitor, while the young ladies exchanged glances of satisfaction.

"I do not like these innovations upon our good old customs," said his Excellency, "with all due deference to you younger gentlemen : they will put aside our old Cocked Hats next, and gentlemen will cease to wear swords."

"The war has commenced already, my good sir," said Dr. Evylin, "for I read in No. 526 of the Spectator, that John Sly, a haberdasher of hats and tobacconist, is directed to take down the names of such country gentlemen as have left the hunting, for the military Cock of the Hat ; and in No. 532, is a letter written in the name of the said John Sly, in which he states, that he is preparing hats for the several kinds of heads that make figures in the realms of Great Britain, with cocks significant of their powers and faculties. His hats for law and physic, do but just turn to give a little life to their sagacity; his military hats, glare full in the face ; and he has proposed a familiar easy cock, for all good companions between the two extremes."

"Capital," said the Commissary, "by and by we shall be enabled, Dorothea, to tell what a man has in his head by the cut of his beaver, so that you see the outside of the head has something to do at last with the inside ; but how are we to divine what lies beneath those ever towering pyramids upon the ladies' heads? I hope they will take a fashion soon, that may indicate the powers beneath."

"They indicate pretty forcibly the powers above now," said Dorothea, "for I heard Kate declare, the other day, that the maid had screwed her's up so tight, that she could not wink her eyes without crying."

"Fie ! fie ! Dorothea," said Kate, laughing, nevertheless.

"Castle-building, you see, Mr. Hall," said she turning to that gentleman, "is now done on the outside of our heads, while our grandmothers, if all tales of them be true, were wont to erect them elsewhere."

"You seem disposed to carry on Mr. Lee's craniological discussion, while that gentleman has dropped out of the debate," replied he, *sotto voce.*

The conversation gradually merged into literary matters, in which the Doctors both of Theology and Physic took a part, as well as the Governor and Mr. Hall. The latter seemed now more at home than he had been, and having but recently arrived from the fountain head, added many new and interesting materials to the common stock, from Newton's latest philosophical discoveries, to Joe Miller's last and best.

"Have you seen any of our native productions, Mr. Hall ?" enquired the Commissary.

"I have not. sir; indeed, I have not yet had an opportunity. I have seen a small newspaper in his Excellency's library, published, I think, in Philadelphia, and that of not very recent date, but nothing in durable shape."

"Well, said Dorothea, "if you will only excuse me for one moment, I will run and fetch you a specimen of native poetry, which, I think, will satisfy you at once, that there is one genius at least, this side of the water."

She rose from the table, notwithstanding that portentous finger of her father, raised in a threatening attitude. The rest of the company being unanimous, he was overruled, and she tripped away to bring it, and soon returned with a narrow strip of paper, and handed it to Mr. Harry Lee, with a request to read it. That gentleman's physiognomy perceptibly lengthened, and his eyes dilated, while running over the two lines, which, as soon as he had finished, he crumpled up and inserted into his pocket, protesting against such a specimen being taken as the standard of the colony. Dorothea declared she must have the paper, that it was a genuine native production, and must be read. All the company being more eager now than ever to see it, he was forced to produce it, and she handed it to Mr. Hall, with a request that he would read it aloud. He had no sooner cast his eyes over the lines, than he burst into a fit of laughter, the first he had indulged in since landing upon the shores of Virginia. When he had wiped the tears from his eyes, and was sufficiently composed, he rose and read, in mock heroic intonations, the following lines :

> " God bless the Church, and the Queen, its defender,
> Convert fanatics, and baulk the Pretender."*

Every one laughed, except the grave Mr. Lee, he seemed to writhe under the infliction, as if his personal peculiarities were the subject of merriment.

" Why, Mr. Lee," said Dorothea, " you take the thing so much to heart, that we shall suspect you of being the author, presently."

" Those memorable lines," said his Excellency, seeing his guest's confusion, " remind me, that we have not yet drank a toast, never neglected at this table, ' Health and long life to the Queen, God bless her.' "

Ladies and gentlemen paid it due homage, with one exception ; Mr. Hall merely raised his glass, as if about to touch it to his lips, but set it down again, his hand trembling violently. Lee observed it, as did the young ladies, who sat near him ; the eye of the former twinkled with gratified feelings of some sort, while the latter were all pained at the young man's embarrassment. The Governor did not notice the affair ; or, if he did, chose to wink at it.

The desert having been removed, Lady Spotswood soon after gave the signal to the ladies, and they retired to the drawing-room, leaving the gentlemen over their wine. Before Kate departed she stepped behind her father's chair, and in a whisper, begged a moment's conversation with him. He rose, led his daughter to the door leading to the library. After they had passed the threshold, she told him of the secret which Ellen had communicated to her, and begged his permission to peruse the papers which he had received with the body of General Elliot. " What," said he, " you and Ellen turn diplomatists and read my state papers. No, no, my child, it would never do—never." But Kate coaxed and intreated until the old gentleman was compelled to give way, and he opened the door and called Mr. Hall, and directed him to gather up those papers that he had been directed to copy, and hand them to his daughter. He soon returned with the bundle and handed them to Kate, and as he did so, she could not help observing, how excessively agitated he was, but she attributed it to the late patriotic toast which he had declined drinking, and knowing that her father was not the man to create a mountain out of that mole hill, she thought she might as well assure him of it at once, and she did so, endeavoring at the same time to reassure the perplexed youth. He made no other reply than an inclination of the head, and thanks for the interest she manifested in him. Having escaped from the dining-room, and supposing that a poor tutor and private secretary would scarcely be missed, he made good his retreat altogether. Kate secured her treasure in her pocket, resolved, however, not to divulge the secret to Ellen, until they had found their own apartments for the night.

* A genuine specimen.

CHAPTER XV.

THE PAPERS.

THAT night those two fair young creatures sat in one of the upper apartments of the house, pouring over a pile of papers strewed over the table, consisting of manuscripts and newspapers, some relating to the trial of Kate's unfortunate relative, all the testimony of which, was there before them; and some of royal proclamations, and paragraphs from the govermental and opposition papers. The clock down stairs struck twelve, and one, and two, in the morning, still they sat in those high-backed gothic chairs, the taper burning dimly beneath the accumulating wick, charred to a black mass, and yet neither of them flagged or faltered. Ellen particularly devoured with eagerness, even the advertisements in the newspapers, which she read from corner to corner, in hopes to find some faint clue upon which to fasten her hopes—for hopes she still had. The only things they could find at all bearing upon the objects of their search, was the newspaper account of General Elliot's execution, and the attempted rescue by a party, supposed to be adherents of the Chevalier St. George, followed by a proclamation offering a reward for the production, dead or alive, of the young officer who had headed the onset. He was described, and his name given in full as Mr. Francis Lee, but no allusion whatever was made to the place of his nativity. He was supposed to have served under the unfortunate officer, for the rescue of whose life he had perilled his own. The accounts went on to say that the party attempting the rescue had been cut to pieces or captured, that the young man was seen to fall early in the affair, that no efforts had been successful in tracing his whereabouts. Little doubt was entertained that he died from the desperate wounds he was known to have received, yet there was nothing absolutely certain, touching the matter. So desperate had been the state of mind of Ellen, that even this afforded comfort. She threw the papers aside, leaned back in her chair, and came at last to the settled conviction that poor Frank yet lived. So strong is youthful hope, even against a powerful array of circumstantial evidence.

From that moment a brighter light shone from her eyes—too bright, as her friends feared, with those feverish fires which are only extinguished in the grave. Kate was really astonished to see, instead of a sad and settled dejection upon her friend, a sort of hopeful composure steal over her features. Her own convictions were stronger than ever, that there was not a vestige of hope for her. Yet she held on to that frail shadow of a shade—so constant, so persevering is the female heart, to hope against all probability of hope. They separated for the night, but not to sleep on the part of her who most needed its balmy and restorative influence. That whole night she paced her silent and solitary chamber, or sat and strained her imagination, vainly endeavoring to penetrate the future. Towards morning she threw her feverish limbs upon the bed, and caught a few hours of unsatisfactory sleep; mingled with fitful dreams. She thought she saw her betrothed standing before her; but that they were in a strange land, and surrounded with strange faces and things; and that he was pale and emaciated, and grown quite grey with pain and sorrow. Then a change came over the spirit of her dream, and the face of the loved youth was gone, and a stranger stood in his place. She was roused from these tantalizing shadows of a distempered imagination, by the maid entering to assist at her morning toilet, where we will leave her, while we glance at some other rooms in that building, and see what the inmates are doing.

The mornings and evenings were now beginning to be a little cool, and heavy damp fogs rose from the surface of the bay, to correct which it is usual to build a brisk blazing fire, to last only until the revivifying effects of the morning sun are felt. Some of the early planters were in the habit of pursuing this plan for three-fourths of the year.

Such a bright fire was blazing in the breakfast parlor, and there sat round it, his Excellency, the two Doctors, Mr. Henry Lee, Bernard Moore, Carter, Dandridge, and Harry Hall. Quite an interesting conversation was going on ; intensely so to some of the party. Mr. Lee finding what a universal favorité the latter was becoming, not only with the Governor but with the whole family, even down to Master Robert, perceptibly softened in his manner towards the young stranger. He came down from his room determined to be very amiable to this new favorite and pet of the eccentric man then at the head of the colony. What his motives were, we leave our readers to imagine, from the position of the various parties. Hall was quite surprised, therefore, to hear himself addressed by the haughty young aristocrat, after the demonstration of the previous day, and however justified he might have been in returning that ill treatment, he took better council of his discretion, and answered quite courteously.

" Mr. Hall," said Lee, " I have some relations of your name, both in this country and in England—on the mother's side, or rather I had in this country, for the last of them recently died, a venerable old grand aunt."

" And I have some in this country of your name, and when I was first presented to you yesterday, it was my intention to have enquired of you about them."

" Indeed ! will you be so good as to mention what family you are off, and their place of residence ?"

The young man appeared not a little embarrassed, but proceeded to name the place of his family residence in Scotland, as well as to describe his living relations and their descent fr m the common stock of the Hall's of ———shire. Not only so, but he traced distinctly the collateral branch which had emigrated to America, some fifty years before, until he arrived at the last remaining female relation, whose death he had not heard of; the very person alluded to by Mr. Lee.

" How very strange !" said Mr. Lee, " and your christian name is Henry ?" Hall nodded assent, but his face flushed a crimson hue.

"And had you received no letters from America, previous to your embarkation ?"

" None concerning my relations whatever."

" What a strange coincidence," said Lee, " I have the pleasure of informing you, that you are the heir to a very snug little property, left by our venerable old friend."

By this time the ladies had entered, and were also gathered round the fire, and every one was listening with the deepest attention, to the singular conversation going on, and every one seemed pleased too, at the unexpected good fortune of the young man, who was supposed to stand in such need of it—all but that young gentleman himself, he was very much embarrassed, so as to attract the attention of every one in the room.

" Of course," continued Mr. Lee, " it will be quite easy for you to establish your identity ; you have brought letters to some persons in this country ?"

" No, sir, I did not; and, I fear, that I shall meet with more difficulty than you seem to imagine, in the matter." Becoming more and more embarrassed, at every turn which the conversation seemed to take, or to be likely to take.

" Perhaps you have letters addressed to you, in England, from some of our common relations ?"

" None with me," replied Hall, " I expect the remainder of my baggage by the next vessel from England, by which time, I may be enabled to produce sufficient testimony to claim the estate."

"Among those expected letters," said Lee, pertinaciously, "there are doubtless, some from our venerable relation, for I see among her papers numerous letters from you?"

Hall was, by this time, almost speechless with vexation and embarrassment and his face flushed to his ears. He merely nodded assent.

The Governor seeing the young man's painful position, and thinking in his own mind, that he, perhaps, knew Hall's difficulty, determined to come to the rescue. He had already had some suspicion that his protogee's expatriation had not been altogether quite voluntary. "Let us adjourn this discussion," said he, "I think I can put Mr. Hall upon a plan of proving his identity, without even waiting for his papers or returns from the other side of the water."

As he pronounced the last words of the sentence, he placed a peculiar emphasis upon them, casting a sly and playful glance at Hall, only remarked by the person for whom they were intended, and perhaps one other very quiet little individual in the room.

"Agreed," said Mr. Lee, "As I am the executor to my Aunt's will, it is, of course, my duty to act in conformity to law; but I assure your Excellency, and your friend, that no unnecessary difficulties shall be thrown in his way by me; on the contrary, all possible facility shall be afforded him, and I will immediately, upon my return to the capital, instruct my attorney, Mr. Clayton, to draw out upon paper for his use, such steps as it will be necessary for him to take. In the mean time, he can draw upon me for such sums as his present necessities may call for, out of the proceeds of the property, which I will advance upon my own responsibility."

"Wonders will never cease," said Dorothea to Ellen, as they moved round to the breakfast table. "Mr. Henry Lee has been doing a generous thing, but Mr. Hall should credit it to the account of Miss Ellen Evylin, and not to Mr. Henry Lee.

"Fie! fie! Dorothea, do give Mr. Lee credit for his good actions such as they are, surely he has done nothing but what the strictest justice would warrant; true, he might have withheld Mr. Hall's rights, but they are his after all, and he could soon establish them as such. If, indeed, he is not prevented by ————." There she stopped suddenly, as if recollecting herself. "If he is not prevented by what Ellen————."

"Hush, Dorothea, not a word of this—another time I will explain it to you—now, it may be a dangerous subject; and one in which more than mere property is involved.

CHAPTER XVI.

A NEW ARRIVAL—A STRANGE VISITOR.

BEFORE the party separated from the breakfast table, a servant threw open the door and announced Chunoluskee. The Governor instantly rose and extended to him his hand, at the same time ordered a chair to be placed for him at the table. Chunoluskee was a young Indian chief, of the Shawneese tribe, whom the Governor had rescued some four years before, while a prisoner with one of the tributary tribes. The tributaries, were those Indian nations, which had either been subdued by force of arms, or were under treaty stipulations by more peaceable means, to pay a nominal tribute yearly to the Governor of Virginia. Nearly all the well known tribes along the eastern borders of the colony, were thus happily situated. The tribute consisted of a few skins and Indian arrows. These tributaries, however, were occasionally at war with other tribes farther removed, thus they sometimes brought home prisoners. The young chief, who has just been introduced to the reader, was one of them. The Governor invariably claimed these, and placed them at one of his primary schools, one of which he had located within the borders of every tributary tribe in the Colony. When they had remained a certain time at these primary schools, say about two years, they were then removed to the Indian department in William and Mary College, in accordance with the benevolent bequest of the Hon. Robert Boyle.

Some of these pupils were first taken as hostages, and were brought the distance of four hundred miles, so that the College was at once a sort of honorable prison, and a school for higher purposes.

Chunoluskee, the chief before us, had been four years at hard study; two in the primary school, and two in the College, and, for his remarkable proficiency in the latter, he received an office from the Governor, that of Interpreter to the Queen. He was the medium of communication between his Excellency and the various deputations of Indians from the tributaries, and those beyond, which were constantly visiting the capital of Virginia. At no time, since the settlement of the Colony, had there been such numerous assemblages of these. The extraordinary exertions of the Governor and the Rev. Commissary among these native sons of the soil, excited curiosity even in these stoics of the forest. They had heard of the Indian schools, which were then in the first tide of experiment throughout the Colony. How far they looked with approbation upon the singular trial, will, perhaps, appear in the course of our narrative. Certainly, in the instance before us, it had been crowned with success, and we take pleasure in presenting before our readers, an educated Indian; a gentleman, who held office under the crown, sat at the Governor's table, and mingled with the social circle that surrounded that hospitable board.

To a perfect stranger from abroad, he must have appeared by far the most imposing character in that room, not excepting the Governor of Virginia; for his dress exceeded that of his Excellency, both in the fineness of its texture, its colors, and the fashion of the wearer, both as to cut and the manner of display.

He was about twenty-one years of age, tall and slender in form, but handsomely proportioned, with a very uncommon face for one of his race. Nearly the whole of the Indian stoicism was wanting; and, instead of neglecting to notice those little things upon which good breeding so much depends, he was scrupulously attentive to the least movement of any one around him. His eye, instead of having the settled rattlesnake glare of his race, was soft and humanized in its expression, and looked as if it *could weep* upon occasion, which all those who have studied the forest specimen know, always seems impossible with them. His hair grew long and straight to his shoulders, and fell down his temples in perfectly straight lines. On his head, he wore a scarlet velvet cap, bound round with gold lace, and surmounted with drooping plumes of red and white, while he held gracefully upon his left arm, the skirts of a robe of the same gaudy color, which fell in loose drapery from his shoulders. He wore dressed buckskin small clothes, and long gaiters to meet them, terminating at the foot in exquisitely worked moccasins, curiously inlaid with beads and porcupine feathers, and covering a foot and ankle which any lady in the room might have envied. Under his scarlet robe, he wore a buff jacket, fitting so exactly to his rounded form, that, at the first glance, a stranger might have supposed it the natural covering of the muscles, so exactly did it display the outlines of his figure.

He had been taken prisoner when desperately fighting to save a blind mother and a sister, the latter then only twelve years of age. They, also, were brought by the Governor to the capital, and the old blind Indian had been a constant pensioner upon the bounty of the Governor and his family, while the young girl had been placed with Mrs. Stith, (the Stewardess of the College,) until very recently, when prudence suggested, that she was now becoming of an age, to require that other quarters should be provided for her.   Accordingly, the Governor had erected for them a suitable house in the suburbs of the capital, and the Interpreter, his sister and his mother, all lived together.

Such was the character and history of the being, who now walked up to meet the Governor, with an air that might have put the blush upon any king in Europe.   He trod those boards with a majestic air, and a grace too, which would have made the fortune of a hero of the buskin; and bowed over the Governor's hand, in which his own was locked long and feelingly, as if he designed to express both homage and gratitude.

"Thank goodness," whispered Dorothea to her sister, "Mr. Lee's nose is put out of joint now."

Strange to say, that Mr. Lee was the least inclined to treat this descendant of our forest kings with respect, of any person in the room.   Such is the *apparent* inconsistency of human nature, when viewed only upon the surface. To an impartial spectator, the two seemed wonderfully alike in mental constitution; that son of a long line of aristocratic progenitors, and the son of an Indian Sachem, alas, now in exile, and doubtless supplanted in his princedom by some more successful young warrior.

The Governor presented him to Mr. Hall, after he had bowed respectfully to the ladies, he being the only person in the room with whom he was unacquainted.   He was then placed at the table, and made his breakfast, observing all the little formalities, which are so much of a second nature to us, that we do not notice them except when wanting.   Hall watched him closely, expecting no doubt, to see him help himself with his hand, and eat with his fingers, but he not only used knife and fork, but helped others to the dishes near him, without the slightest *faux pas* of any kind.   He was rather more modest in conversation, than one would have supposed from his princely carriage.   He had learned the first great lesson in the advancement of the mind; that is, to know his own ignorance; yet, he took part in nearly all the conversation, being appealed to directly by some of the worthies round him.   The fact is, the Rev. Commissary, as well as his Excellency, were proud of their pupil, and they loved to exhibit him, as well to the stranger, as to such scoffers as Moore and Carter, in regard to Indian capabilities.

There was another subject of pride and gratification with his Excellency, he had received many of his views of the tramontaine country from this young Indian, and he loved to hear him dwell upon its glories, and would sit entranced while his tawny young subordinate dilated upon these matters.

"Now for it," whispered Kate to Ellen, as the ladies left the room to the possession of the gentlemen, "papa will soon carry Mr. Hall over the mountains, where he has before marched so many before him, whether with their own free will or not, their own good breeding sayeth not.   Just look back Ellen, and see with what apparent relish Mr. Moore and Mr. Carter are preparing themselves to listen to papa and that noble looking chief."

The Governor, truly enough, only waited for the Interpreter to finish with his knife and fork before he commenced drawing him out.   His maps were spread out before him on the table, and he had called Mr. Hall to his side. Not an individual in that room, but had occupied the same position repeatedly, except himself, and he prepared the way by tracing out with his pencil, the water courses which had their rise in the mountains.

"Now Chunoluskee, here is a gentleman just from the mountains of my own native land, (Scotland,) and glorious mountains they are too, and delightful vales between them, but I want you to shew him that there is a finer country beyond your blue hills, than any even in old Scotia.   What say you my man?"

" The vales beyond those mountains are my native war-paths, your Excellency, and I look back to them with the same sort of pleasure which you remember the scenes of your own childhood."

" Aye, and you shall look forward to them, man. I will lead you back to your native land, and place you in possession of your rights."

"So your Excellency has promised, and it is therefore, that I have come to look upon your proposed enterprise, with nearly as much delight, as your Excellency."

" But is the country worth the trouble. That is the point that touches these lazy Virginians?"

" It is the most glorious land that ever the sun shone upon, there is a valley beyond those mountains, almost a perfect terrestrial paradise, abounding in deer, elk, buffalo, and game of every sort—the land teeming with wild fruits of every kind, and bright with the purest fountains of water that ever gushed from the solid rocks."

" O aye, I know that is your opinion, but it is contradicted by all the French accounts, and all others which we have received, besides you were a mere boy when you left that happy valley, and cannot know exactly its geography."

"Indian boys, your Excellency, do not, it is true, study geography upon paper, but they study it upon a much larger scale ; they learn the original; and what is more, they never forget it. I can take your Excellency to the very spot where I was taken prisoner."

" Well, well, leave the point about the double range of mountains to be decided by the event, and go on with your account."

"Beyond that valley is the range of the real Apalachee, and when you have crossed these, then you open into a new world indeed ; one in which this little Colony might be set down and not observed to enlarge or diminish it. Before you entirely cross all its wonderful width and breadth however, there are natural curiosities so remarkable, that these gentlemen will again laugh at my presumption and your credulity, if I tell of them."

" Tut, man, tut! a fig for Moore and Carter's skepticism ; tell your story as if they were not present."

"I have often told your Excellency of the ever-boiling springs in which you may cook an egg, and others, the medicinal virtues of which are so great, that even the deer and buffalo, visit them constantly. Indian tribes from the mouth of the Mississippi, on the one hand, and the lakes on the other, visit them in the hunting season, bringing there, the lame and the blind, and the halt, just as I have since read was the custom in the Jewish country."

Moore and Carter here laughed outright, and the latter asked the Interpreter, "if he could enumerate the diseases of which the buffalo and the deer were cured, and how they undertook to administer the medicine; whether they had Dr. Buffalo and Dr. Buck, and if they felt pulses and looked at the tongue. What say you to this, Doctor, turning to the old physician ?"

The Interpreter did not give him time to answer, for he was now becoming excited with his subject, and goaded with the repeated taunts and jeers of the youngsters.

" You may laugh, young gentlemen," said he, " as you have often done before, and you may call it romancing, but I tell you and his Excellency, that the half has not been told. There are wonders of the natural world there, which throws in the shade even these medicinal springs ; apocryphal as you consider them," throwing down his knife and fork with which he had been trifling with the remains of his breakfast, he strode once or twice rapidly through the room, and again halted before the group seated at the lower end of the table, and continued : " There are palaces there under ground, far more magnificent than the one inhabited by his Excellency at Williamsburg ; long colonades, that have supported the dome which they now bear since the world began, and galleries with fancy work, which would shame the skill of any of your handy craft-men, and there is also a noble arch of solid rock—extending from mountain to mountain, and beneath which the Governor's round tower at the Capital could stand, without being a greater object to distract the attention, when looking from above, than the binnacle is to the sailor at the mast-head, when he casts his eye upon deck. The sachems who went before me, have a tradition that the great spirit himself, once upon a time was walking upon the earth, and came to the stupendous rent between those two mountains, inaccessible from their perpendicular sides, and that he threw the wonderful arch across, and then walked over upon it. It looks indeed as if it might have been a causeway for the gods, or some colossal race of men, who perhaps inhabited the earth, when animals dwelt upon it tall enough to browse upon the tops of our forest trees."

"Then you have," said Carter, "in that fine valley of yours, medicines to cure all the ills that flesh is heir to, forever pouring in perennial streams from their bright fountains, so that you are free from the pains denounced against the balance of our race ; fruits forever tempting the hand to pluck them ; water heated to your hand ever ready to perform your culinary operations, and yet not content with this paradise, you have now erected a bridge between heaven and earth, over the valley of death, upon which the gods and your people freely interchange visits. Have you not also some springs or trees or herbs, by which the whole curse of earning bread by the sweat of our brow might be dispensed with? Methinks that the great spirit who first made your fine country, would not have stopped half way, but would have remodelled Eden over again, and upon a pattern too, which would have made Old Adam laugh at himself, for being so taken in with that orchard, which proved his ruin."

"I understand your irony, Mr. Carter," said the chief, " but it cannot alter the facts of the case, for the truth of which I will pledge my life. Indeed the half has not been told ; there are springs beyond the great Apalachee, which produce salt, made almost ready to your hands. You have only to boil the water, which spouts out from the ground, and the work is done. In the same neighborhood, is a burning spring ; flames forever wreathing up from the surface of the water. This the natives of the soil are afraid of, and believe that the great spirit of evil dwells there."

"I thought so," rejoined Carter, " you have only now to tell us of that spring from whose fountain flows the life-giving power of perpetual youth, so long sought for by the Spaniards at the other end of the continent, by all the gods and goddesses in the mythology, we will bring back your Excellency so rejuvenated, that Lady Spotswood herself will scarcely know you. By the by, what a place of resort it will be for elderly ladies. I know several that would accompany the expedition upon half the inducements held out by the Chief."

"Poh, poh, Carter, with your nonsense ; Chunoluskee has no motive for deceiving us," said his Excellency, " and if he had, and could succeed, in the matter of the medicine springs, and the subterranean palaces, and the mighty arch, suspended between heaven and earth; we know that the land is there, and that is enough for us. The others will be so much clear gain, if we find them—and if we do not, you and Moore will not be much deceived, at all events."

"I see nothing so very improbable in the herds of deer and buffalo seeking the medicinal springs," said Dr. Evylin. " We know that these creatures, and many far inferior to them, have an instinct by which they seek relief from medicine, even in the vegetable kingdom, and we know moreover, that the sulphur and salt springs commonly called salt licks, are plenty all over the continent, and that the wild animals do seek them at certain seasons of the year. I see no reason to believe that the chief has even colored the impressions of his youth with imaginary drapery—in fact, there is a good deal of internal evidence of truth in his recollection of the country."

" And his recollection of the sources and courses of the rivers this side of the mountains," added the Governor, " have been remarkably accurate, so far as we have been enabled to trace them yet. Take, for instance, the James river, he has always adhered to it, that this stream runs through this wonderful valley, and through the mountains. This, the council at first laughed at, but every succeeding survey only renders it more and more probable. Its source or headwaters have never yet been reached, or any thing like it."

The youths professed to give in to the Governor's views, but walked off nevertheless, indulging their merriment at the extravagant romancing of the interpreter.

The Governor and the two Doctors hung over those maps for hours, tracing out the future course of the expedition; sticking pins along the designated route, and from time to time acquiring new information, as to the face of the country, distances, means of supply, &c., all of which the former required Hall to note down accurately.

The reader must, in order to realize the terra incognita, into which they were about to plunge, remember that Virginia, at that day, consisted of some twenty odd counties, clustering around the Seat of Government, and they only thickly populated along the rich alluvia of the rivers, and the two shores of the bay, and that the population of the colony was just one hundred thousand.

Few more bold, daring, and chivalrous adventures have ever been undertaken, even in this land of wild adventure, than that planned and executed by Governor Spotswood. It must be recollected, too, that his was among the first of the kind; that he was the pioneer, even to Lewis and Clark, and that his ingenuity invented many of those appliances now so common in such adventures. He was going beyond the reach of civilized resources—among savage tribes—over mountains, hitherto considered impassable—and through a trackless wilderness, in the last degree difficult for the transportation of the necessary supplies.

Was it any wonder that it was opposed by most of the old men of the Colony; by nearly all those considered wise and prudent? They confidently predicted that the Governor, and the mad youths whom he might induce to accompany him, would never return, and some exercised their parental authority, so far as to forbid their sons from accompanying the Governor. To such a height had this opposition ran during the preceding winter, that a public meeting was held, and a committee appointed to memorialize the ministry on the subject. If successful, this of course was equivalent to the Governor's removal, and he had been waiting in some anxiety to hear the result. The two factions of Oxford and Bolinbroke, of which the ministry was composed, were too busy fighting their own battles, to heed these petitions from beyond seas. Sir Alexander Spotswood was fully determined to see the other side of the mountains, either as Governor of Virginia, or as the leader of a private expedition, which he was amply able to set on foot. The question of supplies had been brought up also before the House of Burgesses the preceding winter, and rejected by a very close vote. Since that time, he had been exerting no little address to induce young men to come out for the vacant or uncontested seats, especially such as were known to be favorable to his darling project. Two of these we have already seen almost domesticated in his own house, the open hospitalities of which was no mean auxiliary in the great cause, especially when presided over by the elegant kinswoman of the Duke of Ormond, and her not less fascinating daughters. In short, his personal influence, his official sway, his social position, his wealth, and every thing that was his, was thrown into the scale by the Governor. He almost directed Mr. Boyle's benevolent scheme for christianizing the Indians into the same channel, and he had enlisted the Rev. President of the College, warmly in his interests. A new trial was now rapidly approaching—the members for another house of Burgesses had been elected, and were soon to assemble at the capital. Proclamations were sent to every county, calling upon the young gentry to enlist fifty men, and enrol themselves under his banner. The ranks of the Rangers had been filled up, and new officers appointed, wherever opposition was manifested to the expedition, and these were now undergoing daily drill, and performing camp duty along the whole frontier of the colony, as preparatory to the grand tour. The removal of these very corps was one strong ground of opposition by the timid. They had for some time formed the main security of the Colony, against the inroads of the savages. These Rangers were stationed along the whole line of frontier, within communicating distance of each other, and were perhaps the best security ever devised for a colony in the then condition of Virginia. The Governor's son John, was now in command of these, and as rapidly preparing them for field service as possible. The Governor proposed to march the whole of these, as well as a certain portion of militia from each battalion. Here was another cause of opposition; these men did not like the idea of being marched five hundred miles through a trackless wilderness, and over inaccessible mountains, while their families were perhaps starving at home, and their crops totally neglected, as well the preparation for the coming one as the proper curing of that already housed. The Governor's main dependence, however, was upon the young gentry, and such men as they could voluntarily enlist or persuade from among their own adherents. He thought that if he could embody a sufficient number of them with the Rangers, that the forcible objections against the expedition might be removed, as he would no longer attempt to coerce the militia, from whom powerful opposition had arisen. Indeed something like a pledge had been given at the late elections, that such should be the case, and the whole colony was now looking on with anxiety, to see what would be the result. Such of the gentry as had united in the remonstrance to the ministry, despaired of ever receiving assistance from that quarter, so that the great battle had to be fought at home.

In accordance with these views, the Governor on the morning in question, despatched his new protegee to Yorktown to enlist, not only fifty followers for his own share, but as many more of the emigrants as might choose to try their fortunes in the far west. Largesses of land were most liberally promised, besides the pay, rations, and accoutrements of the soldier. Among those who had arrived with Hall, were a large number of Scotch, Irish, and Presbyterians, a hardy, brave, intelligent set of people, as ever lived. These Hall found to listen most readily to his tempting promises of land and a new home, and freedom from religious restraint. The scheme chimed in exactly with their views, and he was therefore not long in making up his complement of fifty men, and enlisting as many more as the Governor might choose to provide for out of his own private purse. These were quartered in the suburbs of York, and were soon busily engaged in preparing to march at a moment's warning.

Governor Spotswood was not long in discovering that his new protegee was exactly the sort of *aid-de-camp* which he had been looking for. He possessed a thorough education, not a little of which had been learned in the school of adversity, and a sufficiency for his purpose, in the camp. He accordingly set to work in earnest, to have all things in readiness to seize upon that most favorable season of the year, now called Indian summer, for the march. Before that could take place, many things had yet to be done, besides the subsidies to be voted by an assembly, whose opinions were still somewhat doubtful. Clothes, ammunition, horses and supplies of every kind, were to be provided, and the latter in such a shape as to admit of their transportation without inconvenience. Camp equipage, such as tents, iron, utensils, &c., &c., were not so easily gathered in that day in the Colony. He had already built a round tower in the public square of the capital, for the reception of arms and ammunition, and was accumulating them silently, but surely.* Both his public and private stables were already crowded with horses, and he was still purchasing more.

The time was now approaching when that happy family party were to leave the delightful summer retreat on the shores of the Chesapeake bay, for the bustle, the gaiety, and even the political intrigues of the capital. The female inmates would willingly have dwelt at Temple Farm forever. They loved the quiet scenery of the place, and the privilege it gave them of, in some measure, selecting their company, but the present busy season of preparation, on the part of the lord of the manor, required that removal, and they acquiesced. His presence was wanted at the capital, and it now began to form the staple subject of conversation among the young people.

Bandboxes were not yet in requisition, but Kate was already paying farewell visits in the neighborhood, and visiting her pensioners for the last time before a long separation. The negroes were already crowding round the doors, whenever a leisure moment allowed them, to look for those never failing little tokens of good will and remembrance dispensed on such occasions. Others, with purer motives, loved to return their humble thanks to their young mistress, for her kindness in sickness. It was indeed a melancholy day among the domestics of Temple Farm, when all that gave it life and cheerfulness were gone. Old June declared to Kate that the very poultry and stock all looked melancholy, when the " white folks" were gone. On the evening of that day, he brought out his old banjoe into the yard, seeing Kate and Ellen promenading the verandah, and was tuning it up preparatory to improvising their departure in most moving and melancholy strains. What Southron is there who has not been moved by the mere tones of these monotonous dog-grels? Even in their liveliest strains, and when the words of the song are ludicrous in the highest degree, these same mournful sounds accompany them: The same may be said of their harvest and boat songs. On the present occasion June muttered something like the following, to one of his corn songs:

" Oh Miss Kate, she's gwine away, g'wine away,
To leave poor nigger on de lone bay ;
The house shut up—the windows closed—
The fire put out—den nigger froze.
   Long time ago, long time ago.

The fine young men dey no more come,
On de prancin horse to our cold home,
To see Miss Kate, the flower of the bay,
So glad, so glad, de live long day.
   Long time ago, &c."

" Oh June," said Kate, " sing of our return, not of our going away. Don't you see that you affect the spirits of Ellen?"

" Oh, misses, it's for poor June's spirits to be 'fected ; specially when he aint had no spirits all de day long."

" And do you think June that a glass of spirits would change the melancholy of your song."

" De spirits make June feel berry happy misses long as he last, but he no bring back Miss Kate, and all de fine young gentlemen, and de ladies, and de carriages, and de hosses."

" Why, what in the world can these things be to you, June ; you eat the same, and wear the same, whether we are here or at the capital?"

"'Oh, Miss Kate, dey all de world to June ; de berry light ob he eye ; when

---

* The remains of this curious tower still stand at Williamsburg.

white folks gone, it is all one long rainy day at de Farm—no banjoe den—frog hab all de fun to heself. and de whoopperwill, he sing so solemn, he make poor nigger cry for true. '

"Why you are quite sentimental, June!"

"Don't know zactly what de sentinel is, but he see one at de arsenal at Williamsburg, walking so lone jist like June, when young missus gone. De birds find out directly when de house shut up—he no fraid ob nigger ; de owl come on that big tree, and he sit and moan all night long oher de empty house, make June tink some of de familey gwine to die ; and de bay! oh, he moan for true so far off, way down to the sea, and den he come back to de house and fine ebery body gone, he go way along the water, sighing and moaning all de way ; but when Miss Kate come back, all de birds sing glad for true!"

"You shall have the spirits June ; tell Essex so ; but no more banjoe to-night, June ; it affects our spirits."

"Good night, and tanky missus, June gwine to broke he eye, cryin till you come back."

CHAPTER XVII.

A GRIM MONSTER.

In. the suburbs of the capital of Virginia, there stood a one story building, containing several rooms. rather neatly, but plainly furnished. This house was separated from one of the back streets by a vegetable garden, of no very tasteful arrangement, and through its centre led a grass walk, opening from the street directly toward the main entrance.

In the only sitting room which it contained, were three persons. One was an aged Indian female, seated in the chimney corner on a low stool, her elbows on her knees and her head resting upon her hands, so that she seemed almost doubled into a knot. as she crouched over a few smoking chips in the hearth, over which an iron kettle was suspended. She was totally blind, and in some measure, helpless. The other two consisted of a male and female; the former was John Spotswood, and the latter an Indian girl, about sixteen years of age. She had the general appearance of her race, so far as color and general outline of features went, but our readers must not suppose that she was an ordinary young squaw, rolled in a blanket, for she had been delicately nurtured, and had learned many of the customs, as well as the language and costume of the whites. Her *Anglicised* name was Wingina, and she was a sister of Chunoluskee the interpreter to the Queen, until lately a sort of companion to Mrs. Stith at the College, and recently removed with her mother and brother to their new house. She was dressed mostly after the European fashion, with however a few remnants of her Indian taste still clinging about her. Instead of shoes and stockings, she wore moccasins, on a pair of the most diminutive feet imaginable ; and over her ankles and wrists, broad silver clasps, and large gold rings in her ears. Her hair was plaited, and usually hung down her back; and round her neck were many strands of gaudy colored beads. She was as perfect in feature as any of that race ever is; preserving nevertheless, all their distinctive characteristics, such as the high cheek bones and wide set eyes. These were softened by a childlike simplicity of expression in her countenance, and a general air of dependence and deference in her manners ; acquired no doubt, from her isolated and forlorn condition, in the midst of the most polished capital in America, without friends of her own race and rank.

Her position was a very peculiar one; while an inmate of Mrs. Stith's household, she was half way between the two races—too elevated to associate with the negroes, and scarcely considered equal to the whites. We have already said, that she had been removed from the College from prudential motives; her age, and accumulated personal attractions, having already subjected her to very doubtful attentions from the gay youths of the capital; but it was too late. In an evil hour, she in her guileless simplicity had listened to professions from the young man before her, as ruinous to her, as they were degrading to him.

John Spotswood was no premeditated seducer. He never for one moment harbored the deliberate intention, indeed until it was too late he had never analyzed his own feelings and intentions. He was as much overcome in an evil hour, as his unfortunate victim; and he was consequently, a victim himself of never ceasing remorse. His visit on the present occasion, was not of his seeking, but had been brought about by the earnest solicitations of Wingina herself. She seized the occasion of her brother's visit to Temple Farm, to hold one more last interview with the youth who had unintentionally wronged her; we say unintentionally, because he was under the influence of wine at the time, and the world scarcely holds him a perfectly free agent, who surrenders his reason into the keeping of such a master. Wingina's circumstances were becoming desperate, and she sought very naturally the council of the only one in all the world acquainted with her secret.

Her brother, the proud and haughty young chief of the Shawnese, she knew would put her to death upon the instant he learned her shame; and shall we reveal the whole weakness of that poor, frail, half-civilized creature?—she dreaded still more his vengeance against the repentant perpetrator of her wrongs. Most willingly would she have plunged headlong into the neighboring river on either side of the city, but would this surely relieve her partner in the transgression? This was one of the questions she wished to solve by the interview. She had wrought up her mind to the necessary point of daring and desperation for the deed, but she doubted the stability of that calmness and stoicism with which young Spotswood might look upon it afterwards; and she feared, instead of healing all difficulties, her death would only plunge those whom she tenderly loved more irretrievably into ruin.

John had more than once generously offered to dare all consequences, and reveal the true state of the case to her brother and his father, but her fears would not suffer her to listen to this plan; besides, it promised nothing by way of relief for their instant difficulties.

Our readers must recollect the aristocratic notions of that day in Virginia, to realize how utterly impracticable was the marriage of the parties, as a remedy. Could the son of the chivalrous Governor of Virginia, take such a wife to the proud home of his father?—could he make her an equal, and an associate, with his innocent and accomplished sisters?—especially after the revelations which a few months would add to his present difficulties. He saw that it was next to impossible; yet, to do him justice, he thought it more feasible than his innocent victim. She scarcely dared imagine such a thing; so far did he appear elevated above her in social rank. The idea of clandestinely making her his wife and then secluding her upon the frontiers, occurred to him, but then the difficulties with which such a step would embarrass his father's preparations for the great campaign, drove it from his thoughts. He knew that the Governor mainly depended upon her brother, as a guide for the expedition.

What was to be done under such distressing circumstances? This was the question which racked the young man's brain, as he walked the floor. Oh, how the stings of fruitless remorse writhed themselves into his innermost heart. There sat the poor heart-stricken little stranger; a pensioner upon the bounty of his family, the holiday pet of his own sisters; ruined, past all help, and by him, who ought and would have perilled life and limb for her safety. Her head hung drooping upon her bosom, and her hands locked immovably upon her lap, while the burning tears fell in a plentiful shower from her eyes. Her plaited hair, curiously interwoven with beads and porcupine feathers, hung on each side of her neck; and all together she presented a moving picture of hopelessness and utter abandonment, even to an indifferent observer, but to John the very sight of her was agony.

Every now and then he extended his walk to a small table in one corner of the room, upon which stood a decanter of wine, and poured out and gulphed down a measure of the liquid. This was the best remedy he knew of, for that utter despondence which overwhelmed him ; he resolved to adjourn the wretchedness of to-day, for the accumulated sufferings of to-morrow ; never thinking, that while he thus drowned his sorrow, he also drowned his reason, and thereby incapacitated himself from seeing clearly his position, and devising the best means of escape.

Whichever way he turned his eyes, they were met by a picture, that might have moved one less sensitive ; the helplessly blind mother, and the scarcely less helpless daughter. It is true, the old woman understood not his language, and was therefore in blissful ignorance ; but that circumstance rather added to than lessened his remorse. He saw that in the day of full revelation before the world, that ruined family of strangers, from a strange land, would create a tale of wrong and outrage which would overwhelm him. He thought of what would have been his own feelings of indignation against the perpetrator of such a deed, and his own hand was almost ready to be raised against himself.

" Fool that I was," muttered he, as wildly striding through that low narrow apartment, " thus, for a momentary gratification, to peril all the brilliant hopes and high aspirations of my life. Another might have committed such a *faux pas*, and nothing have come of it, except, perhaps, a street brawl with a young savage ; but here am I, the man of all the world, in the position to render the affair not only perilous to myself, but falling exceedingly heavy upon my father. He is the great patron of these Indians ; he has taken them as hostages ; they are therefore under trust to him, and to all connected with him or under him. If this one false step could be retrieved, what a millstone would be taken from about my neck? What a cruel fate was that, which precipitated me into this cursed business?—a life blighted forever by one false step; and that step so trifling when taken by others, so overwhelming to me. It does seem as if a cruel and unrelenting destiny was mocking at me! Are there not thousands of totally debased and profligate men, who pursue long careers of wickedness and folly, without being thus overtaken? Oh, it is hard to be borne! Great God! why was I reserved for a miserable and degrading position like this? Was it because I can feel it? That little bigotted twattler Ellen Evelyn, predicted that my sun would set in darkness. Did she foresee the catastrophe? or was it a conclusion from general premises? What is there in my life, my thoughts, my heart, from which any one could predict such ruin? I love all mankind, and would any time rather do an act of kindness than otherwise. I have wronged no one. Yes—I have wronged this poor creature, but it was not a premeditated wrong. Could she draw the conclusion from my scepticism?—what has the ruin of this Indian girl to do with my religious faith?—methinks these questions would puzzle the old moralist at the College. What a mist we live in; how hard to draw clear perceptions of moral obligation, from general providences? If sin were always followed in this world by sharp and sure punishment, we might see the hand of an all-wise and overruling power, but it is your generous-hearted and unwary youths that are entrapped ; your old lecher escapes scot free, while the perpetrator of a single wrong is plunged to ruin. A man who murders a single individual, is most sure to swing for it; while your whole-sale butcher is glorified as a hero. This life is but a mockery surely; a bit-ter jest; we are but laughing stocks for the universe. And yet some people manage to make a beautiful illusion of it! Dr. Blair for instance—Dr. Evy-lin—my father and my sisters—my pure and innocent sisters—the dream of life is really beautiful as illustrated by them. Why has the dark destiny fallen to my lot alone?—can it be, as Ellen Evylin says, that it is our religi-ous faith that shapes our destiny, and that there is indeed an overruling providence which superintends not only the general movement of worlds, but the most minute details, even to the falling of a hair, as the Bible hath it. Can it be possible that it is I who labor under the delusion, and that they are right after all?—absurd! It is nevertheless a pleasing dream; and I would that my stern philosophy would sleep a while and let me become a Goody Two Shoes, to be tied to my lady-mother's apron string, and dole out charities on a pony, by the side of my sisters, and the two old twattlers now at the Farm. Ha, ha, ha, what a ridiculous idea, and where the devil could it have come from in such a scene as this, with ruin and despair staring me in the face. There sits that Indian girl, a picture of wo; she, too, was being reared to join the happy few, who believe in the protective and conservative power of religion; and I, like a mad fool, must pull down what they were so carefully rearing. Curse my ill-starred destiny, that I should be reserved for such a hang-dog fate. What a mystery is it, this fitful dream of life; but, thank fortune, it has one speedy solution within the reach of the feeblest hand. Here within this vest, I carry a small steel talisman which may unriddle the secrets beyond the grave before their time." Saying which, he drew a small glittering dagger, and held it up admiringly to the light, which Wingina no sooner saw, than she rushed towards him, throwing her arms around his neck, and burying her head in his bosom, crying—" Oh, Captain Spotswood, let me be the victim, I alone am to blame!"

" Poh, poh," said the young man, moving her away with his left hand, and holding her at arm's length, " I meditated nothing just now, I but talked to this little silent friend of mine; but tell me, Wingina, have you really no fear of death?—you look desperate enough, indeed, to dare it. Can such a frail, feeble thing brave the king of terrors? Do you yet retain enough of the heroism of your ancestors, to lay down this life when it is a burthen to you?"

" All that I know, Captain Spotswood, of suicide, I have learned from you and your race. The warriors from which I sprung, consider that an act of cowardice, which you have called heroism."

" Aye, aye, here is another school of philosophy; one of nature's teach-ing; let us learn of it also! It seems I am destined always to be schooled of a petticoat, why not this poor Indian girl, as well as her superiors? Perhaps she has drawn some wholesome truths from the Great Book, whose edges are bound by the sea, and gilt by the sun. Tell me, girl, whence come the notions of your race against self-destruction?

" An Indian thinks outside, and a white man inside."

" Ah, I see, I see—their whole thoughts are occupied externally, and the reflective faculties are not cultivated; then their opposition to suicide, is only after all, because they never reflect sufficiently to become desperate."

" Sir!'

" Your race never commits self-murder, because they never feel wretched enough to loathe this life—that is only a result of our boasted civilization."

" Captain Spotswood, it is I only that should make these complaints of your race—you have taught me to suffer, and God knows I have learned little else."

" Poor Wingina, my teaching has been sad indeed.''

" Oh, sir, pity me not; it makes me all a woman again ;— just now I could have rendered up my life, if only to convince you that a poor Indian girl could die as heroically as one of your own proud race. I could dare it yet, but from another motive which you have never understood, I fear."

" And what is that Wingina?"

Laying her hand gently upon his arm, which had now fallen by his side, and looking up winningly and beseechingly in his face, she said softly, " I could die for you."

" You could die for me? poor girl!"

" Aye, and will too; only assure me that my death would remove all these troubles of which you complain so grievously, and the summer flower is not gone more rapidly."

The desperate young man looked long and searchingly in her face, and then suddenly grasped her by the arm, as he said, " And do you indeed love me still Wingina, after all that has passed?"

" Better than the Great Spirit—more than I love that poor blind old mother, and a brother that became a captive for my sake. I would this instant forsake all, if you will follow me to the wigwam of the Indian, and become a great chief among my people."

" But what, if I loved you not in return?"

The poor girl staggered from his side and reeled into her former seat, and there sat with her head drooping as before, and her hands locked in the attitude of despair.

Spotswood saw that the unpremeditated blow had struck home—that despair was in every expression of her eye and countenance, and his own turbulent passions grew fiercer from the contagion. He strode up to where she was sitting, and drew a chair and seated himself so as to bring his lips almost touching her ear, and said in a tremulous whisper, " Wingina, though I love you not well enough to brave the scoffs and jeers of my race, I do love you well enough ; at least, I am struck with admiration enough for you to dare death in your company, what say you ?"

Her hand was instantly clasped in his, with emotion, as of one who desires to close a bargain only held to her option for the moment, exclaiming at the same time, " Oh how cheerfully."

" Enough!" said he, rising to depart, " when all things are ready—when the storm which is now rising in black clouds round the horizon, shall have closed over head, and all is dark whichever way we look, and just ready to burst, then I will come to you to redeem my promise. Consider my faith as pledged to it ; farewell, poor wronged, betrayed Wingina; we will seal the solemn covenant of our marriage, by a ceremony that if the world approves not, it cannot laugh at. Our races were never formed to amalgamate in this world, let us then adjourn our cases to that immortal tribunal, so much talked of." " Surely," said he, as he left the door, and walked musingly toward the street; " surely that great many headed monster will be satisfied with the sacrifice I propose to offer upon its unholy altar ; the perpetual fires of which are lighted by the devil himself."

The sun was by this time sinking behind the horizon, and the shadows of night stealing over the silent and sombre scene, chiming too well with the darker shadows fast gathering over the hopes and fortunes of that once bright youth. As was too often of late the case, he bent his footsteps to the principal tavern of the place, and there met at the threshold Bernard Moore, just from Temple Farm. " Oh Moore!" said John, " by heavens I am glad to see you; it is a long time since we have had a night together ; now we will indeed revive the memory of those good old times, to which you alluded so often on that damned dull morning after I had been moped to death all day and night, between old Dr. Blair on one side, and Dr. Evylin on the other. How come on the old twattlers, and how is my father and the family ?"

"All well, John, but I fear I cannot join in your revelry to-night—I come upon pressing business of the Governor's."

"What's in the wind now?"

"A proclamation calling upon the young gentry of the Colony, to come out in favor of the tramontaine expedition, and to such of them as have succeeded in enlisting fifty followers, to march to the capital forthwith.. It is a fine chance for you now, John. to distinguish yourself, and to grow rich besides."

"O curse the tramontaine expedition; I have breakfasted, dined, and supped on nothing else for the last three hundred and sixty-five days, until I really believe that I have got a young mountain growing up in my stomach, and made of lime too, for it is eternally parched up with thirst; but tell me how I may grow rich by this eternal crossing of the mountains? that's a new maggot in my good dad's knowledge box."

"It is a project of his new private secretary, Mr. Hall—it is to give magnificent donations of land to all who will comply with the proposed terms."

"And who the devil is Mr. Hall? I never heard of him before."

"A very extraordinary young man, I assure you. He arrived at York with the Scotch emigrants, and applied for a tutor's place over master Bob. He has completely captivated the Governor."

"Oh, aye, any body could do that who would affect strongly the mountain frenzy; tell me now, was that not the way the thing was done?"

"I believe you are partly right, but he exhibited some very curious tricks of fence with the small sword too, which finished what the other left undone."

"Some rascally impostor I'll warrant; but he will not impose on me with his mountain enthusiasm, nor his second hand tricks with the small sword either."

"I tell you, John, he is a match for the Governor himself, and toasted me like a roasted goose with the spit run through him. Your father tried him also at mathematics, and the Commissary at the classics, and in all he was their equal."

"And yet you say he is a poor adventurer. How does he dress and behave?"

"His dress is rather seedy, to tell you the truth, but he has the manners of a gentleman."

"It is all very strange, but let me see the proclamation; that too is his handy work, I suppose?"

"Yes—here it is." Handing him a copy of the paper, which John glanced over hastily and contemptuously, and then handed it back and took Moore's arm as he said, "Enough, Bernard, enough—the very thoughts of the mountain expedition has made me as thirsty as a lime kiln—what shall I order up? port, sherry, madeira, or claret—or will you go with me to the palace? I am all alone there, and we can send out and have as fine a set of fellows in half an hour as ever sung a song or told a story; and, by heavens, we will begin upon the oysters to-night."

"No, John, no—I cannot join you at either place to-night, I am on business of importance, and must hurry back in the morning. I have to send an express to some of the remote counties before I start; of course I shall be engaged until late at night, in giving instructions to these messengers, part of whom are already in the house."

"No matter about that, we will make them all gloriously drunk, and then pack them off at cross purposes; ten to one but they all bring up at Temple Farm in the morning, and get put in the stocks for their pains; a capital place, I'm told, to get sober. It keeps the blood upon a dead spirit level, so you see it prevents determination to the head."

"Why, John, I think you must have dined out already—you seem disposed to make merry of everything, from the Governor down."

"Egad you are right—I have been out and have supped upon horrors—the very recollection of which smacks of brimstone, and that's the reason I'm so thirsty now. Come, you shall not escape me, I swear, if I have to sit and hear your instructions to every one of these express riders. I will have you still. Come down to the palace, order these fellows down there, where we can have the whole house to ourselves. I am determined to make a night of it."

Moore seeing that he must either comply or quarrel with his old friend, determined upon the former for many reasons, and therefore set to work in earnest with his business, determined to despatch that before he should be engaged with one so likely to pledge him in deep cups. He was not more than half inclined to join him at all—not that he did not enjoy a carouse to some extent, like other youths, but there was a wildness, a desperation about John, which pained as well as alarmed him.

They were soon seated over their wine in one of the most luxurious rooms of the Governor's palace, each with a pipe in his mouth and servants standing ready to obey the slightest command. It was an evening to enjoy luxuriously a glass of wine, a cheerful fire, and the soothing repose induced by the glorious Virginia weed, and Moore seemed disposed to make the best of his capture and enjoy these good things like a rational creature, using the wine and tobacco rather as mental than physical stimulants, and plying them lazily and luxuriously along as the conversation flagged. Not so with his friend—he was disposed for desperate and deep potations, he was restless and uneasy, and all the luxury in the world could not have produced in him a sensation of calmness and repose. He scarcely seemed fitted for conversation—he wanted roistering companions, and noisy sport, and practical jokes—and nothing prevented him from having them but the declaration of Moore, that he would only spend a social evening with him in the present way and no other. The only thing therefore for John, was to make up in the depth and frequency of his libations for want of more jovial company, with the faint hope at the same time that Moore would soon be brought to that point of excitement, when he, too, would be led to seek stirring adventure.

Still he sat and sipped his wine, or puffed his pipe, his feet cased in slippers, and his legs over the seat of a chair, while his head was thrown back in the attitude of luxurious repose.

"Come Moore," said John, "let's drink a bumper to the success of that expedition which the Governor seems to have innoculated you with, like all others who come within the reach of his influence."

"With all my heart, John, I will drink to its success, but no more bumpers for me. I do not want to look in the morning as if the devil had sent me a case knife to cut my own throat."

"Lord, Moore, you have sung psalms and hymns with old Dr. Blair and Dr. Evylin, until you are becoming, I fear, one of those nice, moral young men, praised by the old ladies, and held up as patterns by our dads, for imitation. You are becoming evangelical, is that not the word?"

"Pshaw, John, you are suffering yourself to fall off too far to the other extreme, you know very well that I am no stickler for propriety and decorum, farther than they are necessary as the barriers between the various orders of society?"

"Oh, damn the barriers of social order. If I had my way, I would cement the whole of them with the hot fumes of wine into one great social circle of democracy—with our joy in common, our property in common; in short, I would revolutionize your social structure: I would wipe out old things, and begin all anew again."

"Why, John, you are a madman!"

"Egad, I have thought that myself sometimes, but that is always in my dark hour."

He moved his chair round near to Moore, and waved his hand to the servants to vanish, and then seeing that they were alone, by a stealthy glance round the room, he whispered in his ear, " *I am pursued by a demon!*"

" Good God! John, you should consult advice—your spectre or demon is altogether in your disordered vision. Let me send now for the Doctor, and see if he does not say that you should loose blood on the spot?"

John laughed before he replied. " Tush, man, there is nothing the matter with me now, any more than there is with you, but sleep in my room to-night, (and here his voice fell to a whisper,) and I will show you whether it is a mind diseased or not. Call in that old negro, and ask him if I do not have one of these nocturnal visitors every night?"

" No, no, there is no need, I will sleep in the same room with you myself, and see this strange visitor of yours; but does he follow you wherever you go?"

" Yes, wherever I am, I see these strange sights—whether I am asleep or or awake, I know not, but the visitor, as you call him, is not always of the same identity."

John soon after began to grow boisterous—then to sing, and then to hiccup, and finally was carried off neck and heels to bed by two of the servants.

Moore occupied a bed in the same room, in which he ordered a light to be left burning, that he might see the dreaded apparition.

About three o'clock in the morning, he was roused from a deep sleep by a strange unnatural noise in the room, and remembering the conversation with John, instantly sprang out of bed and stood beside him. There lay his friend crouched into a knot, the pillow wound tight round his head, just leaving room for his fiery eye balls to gleam through.

" There, Moore," said he in a whisper of mortal terror, " there he stands; don't you see him? Oh! what a hedious monster; his eye balls are like red hot coals of fire, and his tongue forked like that of a serpent; see, see, he moves. Protect me from him, for God's sake. Look, now he goes—he goes—watch him——Ha, ha, ha—he is gone."

" Why, John, this is the very madness of the moon. You should consult advice at once, for Heaven's sake let me send an express for Dr. Evylin."

" No, no," still in a strained, painful and husky whisper, " here they come again, a legion of them, with fiery serpents in their hands—my God, see how they fling them about."

He had now screwed himself up into the smallest possible compass in the further corner of the bed, his eye balls still glaring from beneath the pillow, and every instant schreeching in the most hedious manner, and now darting from one side of the bed to the other, declaring that it was full of these terrible reptiles. Presently he was hard at work tossing them out of the bed, imitating the exact action of a man grasping suddenly at some dangerous reptile, and then tossing it wildly towards the floor. The cold dewy perspiration was standing over his blue cadaverous face, until here and there it was gathering into little streams and trickling from his nose and chin. His breathing was excessively labored, and his eye balls had now become fiery, and rolled in their sockets without the least volition. His teeth were sunk into his lips until the blood gushed from his mouth, while his hands were alternately clutching the reptiles from sinking their fangs into his person, and tossing them aloft in desperation. He leaped and screamed like a wild man. With astonishing agility, and the strength of a lion, he tossed the servants about, who now stood round and attempted to hold him.

Once or twice, by the persuasion of Moore, he was calmed for awhile, and laid down as if to sleep, and the servants were seated and mutely attentive. The stillness of death pervaded the room, nothing but whispers, and they scarcely breathed, were heard. The eyes of the young man were closed, as if by a powerful effort; and his breathing deep and convulsive. His attendants all thought him asleep; but with the velocity of lightning he sprang from the bed and alighted in the middle of the floor, uttering at the same moment a long shrill scream. He was instantly seized by three or four stout servants, and Moore himself assisting, but all together they could not hold him. He doubled and twisted himself into a thousand strange contortions, and dashed one servant to the wall with his foot, and levelled another on the floor with his arm. At last when exhausted, and about to be overpowered by their numbers, and the steady determination of Moore, he lay in a delirious agony of fear. One frightful monster after another raised his hideous form to his astonished and bewildered gaze. No sooner had one been exorcised, than a more hideous spectre occupied its place.

Bernard Moore determined at once to send an express for Dr. Evylin. He had inquired of the servants and learned that this was far the most alarming attack which he had had. Leaving the unfortunate youth in their charge for a few moments, he despatched such a note to the old Doctor, as he knew would bring him; at the same time leaving it to his own discretion, whether to alarm the family or not. Having seen the boy depart on a fleet horse, he resumed his melancholy position by the bedside of his friend.

CHAPTER XVIII.

THE LOVE OF FLOWERS—CHARACTERISTIC OF THE SEXES.

ABOUT ten o'clock next morning, Moore was startled from his position at the bedside, by the rustling sound of a lady's dress in the entry below   He slipped out and ran down, just in time to meet Kate at the foot of the stairs. He took her hand, and led her into a room, where he seated her.

" Oh, Mr. Moore," exclaimed she, almost breathless; " do tell me what all this means—what *is* the matter with John?"

" Tell me first how you knew any thing about it?"

" Oh it matters not, for Heaven's sake do not keep me in suspense; but tell me when was he taken? how is he affected? is he dangerous? and oh, above all, will he recover?"

" My dear Catharine calm yourself, your brother is ill, I will not deceive you about it, but I hope there is nothing dangerous in his disease."

" Well lead me to him at once, let me see and judge for myself, you know that I am not one to faint at the sight of a sick chamber."

" Stop, stop, not yet—I must prepare you before you go, for your brother's state of mind. He is quite delerious, and sometimes frantic."

She waited to hear no more, but threw open the door and ran up stairs herself, and entered the room so silently, that a sleeping infant would scarcely have been disturbed; but there was an ear listening to that soft tread upon the carpet, that would have caught the vibration of a thread, so magnified was its sense of hearing. John had roused himself upon one elbow in spite of three powerful arms, the instant he heard the first foot fall, and was waiting with distended eyes, for the approach of the dread visitor, which his imagination had conjured up. As Kate passed the threshold, he shaded his eyes with his hands, and glared at her with that vacant stare, which betokens a wandering mind. She approached slowly, so as to give him time to recognize her, and hoping every moment to hear him call her name, perhaps coupled with some endearing epithet, but it was all in vain. His eyes distended wider and wider as she came nearer, until the iris looked almost like a ring of fire, as she gently laid her hand upon his arm, and uttered the words, " My brother!" he started as if stung by a scorpion—pushing back and back, until he had planted himself firmly against the wall, and drawn the bed clothes over his head; trembling and quivering, she repeated, "My dear brother, speak to me."

Kate threw herself into a chair, and buried her face in the bed, and wept long and bitterly. During the while, the poor patient several times raised his head from beneath the bed clothes, and listened to her sobs, as the startled stag listens to the approaching huntsman, bending his head forward, and turning one ear foremost in the attitude of one who listens intensely. The sounds seemed at last to soothe him into a gentler mood, and he stretched forth his hand and smoothed down her glossy blond hair, as one who commiserates the object caressed. Kate raised her face towards his, all streaming with tears, gratified in the midst of them that he had at least ceased to dread her presence; but still he did not recognize her; " go home now," said he, " go home to your poor blind mother—that's a good girl, and weep not for me."

Dr. Evylin and Governor Spotswood soon after entered; the latter was terribly shocked, and even the venerable old physician found the case worse than he had expected. He immediately ordered the room darkened, and cleared of all but the necessary attendants, and then poured out a dose of some liquid medicine, and handed it to Moore, "there, give him that," said he, " enough to kill any two of us!" After which, Kate was led out by Mr. Moore to another room.

"Oh Mr. Moore," said she, " this is very dreadful! can you form any idea of the cause of his derangement?"

" It is not ordinary madness, Catharine," (how affliction levels conventional forms, like the grave,) " it is not ordinary madness, but from what I have heard and seen, it is the mania induced by intemperate drinking."

"Is it possible?—and is my brother indeed that degraded thing, a drunkard?"

"Distress not yourself, the case is no worse now, perhaps, than it has been for some time; indeed this very attack may wean him from the wretched thraldom."

Half an hour afterwards, the old Doctor came in, a bright smile breaking upon his features, his pipe in his mouth, and assured Kate that her brother slept"—"a thing," said he, " which I will venture to say he has not done for hours before." He assured her also, that if this sleep continued for some time, he would awake better, and probably in his sound mind.

Kate insisted that she would watch by his bedside, and that the servants might stand at the door within call ; and sure enough, there she posted herself, and remained six long hours. She watched in that dark room, until her eyes at length became accustomed to it ; and she could see her brother's countenance, the corrugated brow, the quivering eyelid, the alternately distended and collapsed nostril, and the compressed lips, the latter sometimes muttering the delerious wanderings of the mind.

Was it any thing wonderful, that Moore's attention, as he occasionally stole to the door and peeped in, was not wholly absorbed by the condition of his friend? Was he not excusable if a stray glance wandered over that fair neck and arm, as they rested upon the table, while their owner gazed upon the unfortunate sufferer? In fact he caught all the changes upon John's distorted features, reflected with beautiful fidelity upon that of his sisters.

About five o'clock in the afternoon her brother waked up to a stupid sort of consciousness, took a little broth, and fell off again into a deep sleep, the first of the kind that he had enjoyed for many, many weeks. After Kate saw her brother thus comfortably disposed, she took a few turns through the garden to see how her flowers had been attended to in her long absence. This garden presented some of the rarest exotics ever then seen in America, and was furnished with conservatories and hot houses upon a large scale.*

---

* The remains of these were still visible at the author's last visit to Williamsburg.

The gardener was now preparing to re-convey many of the tenderest of his silent family to their winter quarters. Kate walked through the box hedges, inquiring into the condition of each old acquaintance, deploring the sickening condition of some, and praising the luxuriance of others, here clipping off a decayed leaf, and there propping up a rickety stem.

Moore was as excessively fond of flowers, as he had been remarkably devout, when Kate read the responses; he went into raptures over the faded beauties of some little foreign stranger, and was really pathetic over the disasters which absence and want of delicate culture had produced upon her favorites. Oh, what a hypocrite! he did not care a fig for the most delicate pink that ever blushed through its green foliage, any more than he did for a red cabbage, i. e. he had none of the true fervor. He loved the flowers, because he was in love with every thing that she loved; but he did not love them for themselves.

This is the way that men generally love flowers, they like to see the ladies of their love fall into raptures over their silent and beautiful little friends, but few of them have that sort of *affection* for flowers, genuine affection, which ladies have.

Kate not only loved her flowers, but there was a sort of secret communion between them. Moore was of a philosophic turn, even in his love, and he desired to penetrate deeper into this connexion.

" Will you tell me," said he, " what this passionate admiration of flowers is like, in your sex?"

" Adoration, would have been the better word, Mr. Moore," replied she, " not that we commit idolatry in our enthusiasm, but we approach the Deity through them, as the Catholic approaches him through the saints."

" Ah, that is a new idea to me altogether; with us it is different, we do not ascend so high in our purest poetical feelings concerning them. We have— I mean the least grovelling of us, have very sweet associations with the memory, as well as the presence of flowers."

" Is that all?" said Kate, looking up from a pale, delicate autumnal flower; " is that all? why, what poor creatures you are! we mix up our love for these gentle, silent things with our higher sentiments. I am sure I never look at one of them without silent adoration to that Great Being, who could so extend his broad cast benevolence, as to create them that they might minister to our pleasures. Did you ever reflect that they were created for a wise purpose? Nothing was ever created in vain, neither were these. Look at this frail and beautiful thing, it has no medicinal properties whatever, and of course must have been created to minister to our pleasures alone. God must delight in these innocent enjoyments of his creatures, or else he never would have strewed them so plentifully along our paths through this world."

" The passion is all very well in your sex—very lovely, very beautiful; but would it not be a little effeminate in ours?"

Kate rose up, and looked him steadily in the face, before she replied. " Effeminate! effeminate, Mr. Moore, take back that word, I pray you. Remember what our Saviour said, ' Consider the lilies of the field, how they grow; they toil not, neither do they spin; and yet I say unto you, that even Solomon in all his glory was not arrayed like one of these.' Ponder upon those beautiful words. All the poets that ever sung, never uttered in such a compass a sentiment so full of innocence, purity, and beauty. Oh, it is almost sublime in its perfect sublimation. Think of that word arrayed—he speaks of these, my little dumb friends, as if the very angels had been employed at their toilet. What an eye for pure and perfect beauty he must have had! The morning robes of the lily surpassed the glory of the most sumptuously clad monarch in the history of the world, in his eyes. What a contrast that was, in the comparatively rude age in which it was uttered! Who, at that day, had ever before comprehended the whole and perfect beauty of that pale and unobtrusive flower? And yet you are afraid of being thought effeminate, if you indulge in enthusiasm like ours."

" No, no, not afraid. I asked if it would not look so to you."

" Well, then, I answer no—certainly not; but tell me truly, is it so, that your sex does not feel these things which I have been describing, as we feel them?"

" To tell you honestly, Miss Catharine, we do not. I see that it will lower us in your estimation, but I have been reflecting upon it, and I'll tell you what I think is the reason, and perhaps that may set us all right again in your favor. We are not pure enough; we mix too much with the business and the anxieties of the world. The Saviour, though in the garb of humanity, was pure and spotless; does not his very capacity for the highest enjoyment of these, old mother nature's pets, seem to favor my idea?"

" There is force in your remark, but I must say at the expense of your sex; I had no idea that it was so debased; but it cannot be true of all men—there must be some exception, some pure enough to relish flowers. I will henceforth, I believe, go through the world looking for one who loves flowers for their own sake."

"He stands before you; do not leave me just yet, your brother sleeps, and do you listen into what a rhapsody I will fall over this little yellow flower,"

Kate laughed at him heartily over her shoulder as she entered the house, and replied, " that the one he had selected was the poorest thing in the garden, but that it would 'do very well to begin with, and by the time he had mounted to a potato blossom, she would be ready to listen to him."

CHAPTER XIX.

THE TUTOR'S NARRATIVE.

DURING Kate's absence, Ellen Evylin wandered over the house like one in a dream—Dorothea tried her rural system upon her one morning, by dragging her to see the dairy-maids perform their manual exercise, but it was all labor in vain. Ellen told her that it required high health and spirits for these things.

" There you are wrong," said Dorothea, " for it is these that bring health and spirits—did you ever see me low-spirited?"

· " No, indeed, my dear Dorothea, I never did, but remember you are just fifteen; the next five years to you may contain the sorrows of twenty."

The little girl laughed and replied, " not unless all the cows take the hollow horn. Do you think I will?" to young Dandridge, looking on.

" No, I am sure if you ever have the blues," replied he, " it will sour all the milk in the dairy."

Ellen sauntered off alone, leaving the healthful and merry young pair to their fun and frolic. She had not wandered long on the banks of the little brook at the foot of the garden, before she discovered Mr. Hall standing opposite to that gloomy structure, before designated as the scene of the night funeral. He was standing with his hands locked behind him and his hat drawn with the corner down over his eyes, and his head bent upon his breast, every now and then raising it, to look at the tomb or vault, and then sinking it as before. Ellen walked within a few feet of him, but he heeded her not. She was determined not to be baffled this time, however, and accordingly took her stand at a few yards distance, to wait the termination of his colloquy with the dead, for she could hear him talking in an under tone, and once or twice he raised his right arm and let it fall listlessly again by his right side. She heard him say, " his last words to me were, we shall meet again! but who could have thought that it would be thus?"

Ellen coughed, so as to arrest his attention; and preclude the suspicion of stealing upon him unawares. He turned round quickly and colored to his ears, but approached her, removing his hat.

He was aware that she sought his presence, and was not a little surprised at it, and approached her with an inquiring anxious look, as he said—" Can I render any possible service to Miss Evylin?"

She seemed puzzled how to communicate her errand, but after a considerable pause replied—" Mr. Hall, it would be useless to attempt to conceal that I hav been for some time seeking this interview."

" Is it possible !"

His surprise startled her, and she was on the point of retreating at last, without accomplishing her end, but she mustered up her courage and came to the charge again. " Yes, I acknowledge that I have sought for it, with a particular object in view, but before I make it known, permit me to state that I was in the room last Sunday, when you approached the picture of General Elliot and apostrophised it, as you were just now doing his tomb."

Hall started, in still greater surprise, and look confused and rather displeased—he waited anxiously for her to go on. She continued :

" It was purely accidental, my being in the room, and but for my surprise and fright, I would have informed you of it. I do not now state these things to obtain any sort of claim upon your confidence, but purely to explain why I suppose you capable of throwing some light upon a dark portion of the history of "—here she stopped short, she did not know how to finish the sentence— but presently added, " of another."

She looked up—the change was indeed surprising—every muscle of his mouth quivered with excitement, as he struggled for an answer, and his eye told of the most intense interest. They were rivetted upon her face as if he would search her very soul.

" Of whom ?" at length he asked.

" Of Frank Lee."

He started as if a bullet had pierced his heart.

" Of Frank Lee !" exclaimed he.

" Aye, did you know him ?" said she tremblingly anxious for his reply.

" Know him—know him !" he drawled out, " too well, too well." Still gazing with a dreamy eye and absent manner upon that beautiful, agitated, downcast face.

Instantly her countenance rose, and she sprung forward with her hands clasped together beseechingly, as she asked, " Oh, tell me, does he live ?"

" Live—live—does he live ? I cannot say."

" Oh, why do you hesitate ?"

This question seemed to rouse him to his full consciousness, and he answered : " The truth is, Miss Evylin, your inquiries have been so sudden and unexpected, and let me add, so embarrassing, that I scarcely know what I say."

" Why are they embarrassing ?"

" Because I cannot tell you all I know of him for whom you inquire, without exposing myself. I have not always been what I now seem."

" Oh, you need have no fears of me—secrets in which he was involved, would be sacred with me at least, and you—could you suppose that I would betray you, if there was anything to betray ?"

" No, I hope not, but there is another embarrassing point, which I know not how to approach without offending you."

" There need be no offence between two straight forward honest people."

" Here, then, is a seat in this arbor ; you look fatigued and exhausted, let me fetch you a glass of water from the fountain."

"No, no—no water; I will take the seat, but I could listen forever while you talk of him."

"You must know that I was more intimate with him than with any living being."

"Oh, tell me all then quickly, and end my suspense."

"I knew your story when I first entered yonder mansion, as well as I do now, but poor Frank labored under a grievous mistake as to your feelings towards him, unless they have lately changed back again into their old channel."

"Changed back again! old channel! what can you mean? the course of that stream has not been half so steady and constant as the current of my very heart's blood, in his favor."

"Before God, I believe you, but there was some gross deception practised upon him some where. Not an hour before he made the desperate and suicidal attempt to rescue the brave officer who lies buried there, he expressed the desperate determination to throw his life away. All this, produced by a letter from this country."

"From whom?" exclaimed she with vehemence, "from whom I pray you?"

"From his own brother."

"From Harry Lee! is it possible! And what could he say to produce so desperate a resolve in Frank?"

"I saw the letter and can speak very positively to that point. He said that he expected to marry you before his brother's return, that he had already obtained her father's consent, and only waited to break down the obstacles which young maidens love to gather round themselves; that they were already giving way, and would soon totally disappear before the warmth of his suit. Those were almost his very words."

"Oh, the base ingrate—there was scarcely a word of truth in the whole—it is true he asked my Father's consent to pay his addresses to me, but he only referred him to me for a decision, telling him at the same time that he would never interfere with my inclinations, so long as the object of my choice was respectable and intelligent; and as to the obstacle, I was really endeavoring to teach myself to look upon him in the light of a brother, until finding my motives entirely misunderstood, I had to put him upon the stately footing which you have seen, and which much better suits him. Now all being explained, tell me what became of Frank after the attempted rescue?"

"There was still another thing which made him believe Harry's letter; your own had ceased for some time, which gave his statements a remarkable coloring of truth."

"Of the cause of that I know nothing, except his frequent change of place after leaving London. I wrote to him regularly."

"I believe you, most sincerely, and now I will tell you what little I know of him. When he first came over, he spent sometime in travelling, and then entered the University at Edinburgh, as was his first intention, and made great progress with his studies, and would really have been distinguished as a scholar, but for an unfortunate circumstance which happened. You will recollect that Gen. Elliot, the half brother of Gov. Spotswood, came to Edinburgh about the time alluded to, and his brow being adorned with the laurels obtained in battle, he was of course a subject of curiosity to all the ardent youths about the city, and especially to those with any aspirations after military honors. Frank sought him out, and their mutual relations to Gov. Spotswood, soon produced an intimacy. Frank was burning with impatience to join the army, but his guardian's instructions were so positive about the necessity of finishing his collegiate course, that he resisted his impulses for the time. The intimacy with the General, however, still continued. The affairs of this country furnished a never failing theme of mutual interest between them, and it was the intention of the General at some future day to emigrate hither. Alas! he little supposed that his removal would be after death. I was in College at the same time, and knew every turn of Frank's mind as well as if he had been my brother. I was actuated by the same motives, and longed for the same chance of distinguishing myself.

"Gen. Elliot at length left the city, but we did not return to our studies with the same ardor after his departure. Our hearts were in the army, and of course the books were soon thrown aside for the foil, and the broadsword, and if we read at all, it was works connected with military science.

"The General was absent some months, and when he returned he was a changed man.

"His fine blithesome and sportive humor had left him, for a settled and perplexed air. He walked about like one in a dream, and we were not long in discovering that the character of his associates had entirely changed. You know that both himself and the Governor were Scotchmen by birth, and in that country there was a strong predilection for the hereditary claimant of the crown, running through all ranks of society, more or less. Even with those who held office and had fought for the existing order of things, their affections were with the young Chevalier. Besides, it was thought that the Queen could not live long, and there was little hope entertained even then, of a direct hereditary descent of the crown. I believe that if the question could have been impartially put to the Scotch people, without fear or favor weighing in either scale, whether the young Stewart or a foreigner should reign, that the former would have obtained seventy-five in every hundred votes. Gen. Elliot in his then recent excursion into one of the counties of England, had (most unfortunately, as it turned out,) encountered the young Pretender himself. He became at once charmed with the youth, and enamored of his cause. This result was brought about, not a little by the disgust which filled his breast against the ministry for their treatment of his patron and commander, the Duke of Marlborough, who was just then beginning to reap that bitter harvest of ingratitude with which his sovereign repaid his noble achievements.

"Gen. Elliot on his second visit to Edinburgh, had come expressly on business connected with another contemplated attempt of the Chevalier, and hence his perplexed air and new associates. His time was now almost wholly taken up with these men, and a very extensive correspondence. We were not long in discovering that something very unusual was in progress, and it was therefore, I suppose, that the General determined to take us into his fatal confidence. It was with no desire to involve us in difficulties, for his own sanguine nature scarcely contemplated defeat; but if he had any misgivings he was not to blame, for he was in some measure compelled to take us into his confidence, owing to Frank's intimacy with him—brought about by his position with regard to this country, and Frank and I, you know, were relations, and very intimate of course. So that we were almost without premeditation, linked in the treasonable affair. Not that we designed to commit treason, or contemplated our acts as such; we had been led to believe that we were espousing the cause of the rightful heir to the crown, and that it was our opponents who were the traitors. It is success you know that re-baptizes these things with new names—rebellion is patriotism when successful; and treason, when defeated.

The better to blind suspicion, we were still nominally attending our Collegiate routine, but in reality hatching a most formidable plot against the occupant of the crown. Gen. Elliot was not a man to go tamely to work in any thing that he undertook; his whole heart and soul were in the enterprise, and we were not less heartily engaged.

He had now taken a house, the better to have complete control over all those around him, and for the purpose of receiving such young gentlemen as were anxious to join our cause. Such neophytes were generally sounded first by my cousin or myself, and if found of the right materials, were then introduced at head-quarters, which the General's house literally was. Over his household, a young lady presided, who I must say was one of the most arch little traitors that ever ran away with the hearts of a set of young gentlemen. My cousin was greatly attracted by her society, as well as myself."

Poor Ellen, she looked aghast at this, which the young man seeing, he quickly added, " But Frank's attentions to this most charming lady, were dictated by the purest brotherly regard, in which you would have joined him, heart and hand, had you been there. Her name is Eugenia Elliot, a relation of the General's. She came to this country in the same vessel with me."

" To this country!" exclaimed Ellen in surprise, " Where is she?"

" Not long ago, she was in that very house."

" Is it possible? I never heard this before."

" Did you hear nothing of the three masks?"

" Ah, then you were one of the three, and this young lady was another, and who was the third?"

" Her father, Humphrey Elliot, Esq., another of those unfortunate gentlemen like my cousin and myself, who were ruined in fortune and reputation."

" And where are they now?"

" Gone to a place called Germana, a frontier settlement, I believe. They have doubtless changed their names ere this, and are happily settled, I hope, in as peaceful and as happy seclusion as their circumstances will permit."

" And why have you kept these things from Governor Spotswood, when you know that he has been making such anxious inquiries for them?"

" Because I pledged myself to Mr. Elliot that I would do so, and I now only reveal them to you to make my story complete, and under the same injunction of secrecy."

" It shall be observed faithfully, but go on with your narrative."

" While our preparations were in such fine train, as we supposed, for the intended enterprise, and just on the eve of accomplishment, the city was one morning astounded with the news that General Elliot had been arrested in his own house, and conveyed to prison. We had scarcely heard the news before my cousin and myself were arrested, and our papers submitted to the most rigid scrutiny. Fortunately there was nothing in them which could in the least compromise us, and we were after a short examination liberated. I need not dwell upon the melancholy particulars of the General's trial, you have doubtless read them in the English newspapers; suffice it to say, that he was convicted of high treason, and sentenced to be beheaded. Before that fatal day came, all of us who had been implicated in fact, but not in law, resolved to make one daring and desperate effort for his rescue. You know, also, the result of the mad attempt. It was led by Frank—he was cut down by the soldiers on duty, and rode over by a troop of dragoons. No one supposed it possible that he could survive. He was carried off by a party of Collegians, who witnessed the affray and recognised him. To the world he has been dead ever since."

" To the world," exclaimed Ellen, seizing his hand entreatingly; " then he yet lives to his friends."

" I will not, cannot say positively ; but I will say, that I saw him after he was reported to be dead."

" Oh God, I thank thee !" exclaimed his auditor, and would have fallen from her seat had he not supported her.

When she had somewhat recovered, he continued : " while he was yet in a state quivering between life and death, he dictated a long letter to you."

" I have never received a line from him since that fatal day, and indeed for some time before."

" I have that letter in my possession."

" Oh then give it to me at once—keep me not in suspense."

" It is in my trunk—if you feel able now to walk to the house, I will hand it to you as soon as we arrive there."

" On the instant, I am as strong as ever I was in my life , I could walk to the capital, if that were necessary."

Toward the house they moved; the invalid, who but a few hours before dragged her steps along, now almost pulled the tutor, so impatient was she, and so buoyant and elastic her step.

When she had received the precious document, she rushed out of the door leading to her apartment never stopping to thank the donor, or make any salutation whatever. There he stood in the middle of the floor, his hands still extended, and his moist eye resting on the place where she last stood. Whether he envied the unfortunate youth all his misfortunes, who was the subject of such an undisguised attachment, we cannot undertake to say. His interest in that pale young creature seemed to have been deeply aroused, but whose would not, under such circumstances.

She never afterwards recollected how she arrived at her room, but the door was locked all the balance of that day. Occasionally she was heard walking about, no one could account for it, except Mr. Hall, and he said nothing. Such things were so common for her, however, that her prolonged absence was passed over. Her father, the Governor, and Kate, were all at Williamsburg.

The letter ran as follows :

DEAR ELLEN:

I still call you so, in spite of all that is passed. Before you receive this letter, I shall be in my grave ; what a termination is this to all those bright and hopeful dreams of youth, which mutually inspired our hearts at our last meeting : but I do not regret it—indeed I have sought an honorable death, as a relief from the deep, deep disappointment of those hopes. Oh, Ellen, you recollect—you must recollect that blessed evening when our young hearts were suddenly and unexpectedly laid bare to each other. Why could not those blissful moments continue forever? Does the curse which has gone forth against our race, interdict the continuance of such happiness as was then ours ? It seems so; our betrothal has but terminated as all other youthful engagements have done before it; but I did hope other and better things of her who was so entwined round my heart, that to tear away her image, would be to unseat my very soul itself ; and so it yet appears to me. I can die, and leave my possessions to my brother; and above all of them, I can resign you to him—for I considered you as much mine as the pupil of my eye ; but I cannot live and see these things. I would scarcely trust myself with the sight of you as another's wife, even if that other were my brother.

I could not have believed that it could come to this ; and would not now believe it, if I had not received it from Harry's own hand, and no one who bears the name of Lee can lie? It was corroborated also by your own mysterious silence. But think not, still ever dear Ellen, that I have propped up my feeble frame on the bed of death to utter reproaches against you, far from it— far, very far from it. I thought it might relieve your burthened memory in after time, if I would, before I died, voluntarily release you with my own hand from all engagements to me. I know that you were very young at the time of our rash promises to each other, and I know that our affections are not always within our own control. Let not the memory, then, of our youthful loves poison those of your maturer years.

May you and Harry glide gently down the vale of life, undisturbed by the trials which have wrecked my peace! May the gentlest dews of heaven moisten your green paths ; and hand in hand may you support each other through whatever afflictions may be thrown in your way—and at last, may we all meet hereafter in a higher and nobler sphere of action.

These wishes are sincere and honest, for they are the products of the bitter and honest hour of death. I could not write them sooner, and it were not safe to defer it longer, for already I feel the damp dews of death gathering upon my brow, and the shadowy visions of the dark valley falling over my eyes—they are covered with mist. Farewell! farewell!   FRANK LEE.

It would be impossible to depict the various and conflicting em.tions which agitated her heart while perusing this letter. She read it over and over again, and walked the room with it in her hand, occasionally referring to it, to note some passages whose meaning she was attempting to understand more clearly. Night came and still she pondered over that single page of writing, though she had learned every word of it by heart. The very punctuation became a matter of moment. A single note of interrogation after the word lie, though placed there in the hurry of agitated composition, or by mistake, seemed to her excited fancy as if poor Frank had intended to ask the question, whether Harry could have falsified her or not. Who is there in this world of trouble, who has not thus dwelt upon a letter containing bad news, vainly endeavoring to draw consolation from some chance word by which the disastrous news might be softened, and torturing the words of the writer into meanings never meant to be conveyed? Though that long day and night were spent in grief and suffering, it was merely over a new aspect given to the old sorrow by the letter. On the whole, her heart was relieved by a review of the story of the Tutor, and she now, with something like reason, nursed the hope on her heart, that she would one day yet meet her long lost lover. In this happy conviction she fell into a deep sleep before morning, from which she was not roused until the sun was high up in his daily rounds.

CHAPTER XX.

VIRGINIA COURTSHIPS.

IN the course of a few days John Spotswood was able to sit up in his chair, and receive the visits and congratulations of his friends. He seemed to have lost all relish for the disgusting poison which had thus carried him to the very brink of the grave, but the same settled despondence still brooded over his young hopes. Kate was ever at his side, not only anticipating every desire, but exerting her powers to the uttermost to entertain and enliven her dejected brother. She read to him, she sang to him, she culled flowers to amuse his solitary hours, and even affected a gaiety which she felt not, to cheer him from his settled melancholy; but all to no purpose—to the books he listened not, to her charming voice he turned a deaf ear, and her flowers he would take in his hand and perhaps snuff their fragrance, and then let them fall listlessly upon the carpet beside him. No subject, no book, no person seemed to possess the least attraction for him, he hardly tolerated the society of his own sister, delightful as that society was. His whole comfort now consisted in his tobacco, which the old Doctor allowed him to whiff occasionally. He would sit for hours with his pale emaciated face thrown up, his head resting upon the back of his couch, and his eyes fastened upon the ceiling, or following the rich volumes of smoke which issued from the fragrant weed, and never utter a syllable.

Kate would steal away into another room and weep and sob as if her heart would break, and then after removing all traces of her distress, glide back again to her position at his side. Many times she was compelled to rush out of the room to hide her emotion, at some remark of her brother's, showing his utter hopelessness and deep despondence; she was not always alone in her duties at her brother's sick couch. Bernard Moore spent a great portion of his time there, and by his lively conversation and playful humor, assisted Kate in her endeavors to pluck the rooted sorrow from John's heart; but it is very questionable, whether he was not much more successful in planting the seeds of it in his own. It is a very dangerous thing for a young gentleman to see a beautiful girl daily and hourly performing those hundred little offices which minister to the wayward fancies of an invalid, especially if those sweet charities are offered with a cheerful spirit and a temper always yielding, even to the impositions of the unreasonable patient. It is not that man in his selfishness is looking forward to the days of his own imbecility, when he may perhaps need a nurse himself—it is not that or any thing like it, that so lays open his heart on such occasions; there is very little in reference to self passing through his mind; 'tis purely because it presents woman in her true sphere; it is because it presents her in the attitude of a ministering angel.

How noiselessly she moves through the room—with what gentle and steady hands she presents the cup to the parched sufferer—how nicely she balances the pillow supporting the throbbing temples, and then lays it down again so softly, that the slumbers of an infant would scarcely be disturbed. There is no impatience—no drowsiness—no yawning—not even talking, when out of place—they endure all things, suffer all things.

Kate was wholly absorbed with her brother's condition; she seemed entirely unconscious that a very assiduous beau was as constant in his attentions to her slightest wants, as she was to those of her brother. Not that she slighted Moore in any degree, nor on the other hand, did she manifest that alarming politeness, which to the discerning lover is the prelude to a dismissal. The most keen-sighted and sagacious observer of the sex would have been sorely puzzled to say, in what estimation she held the youth. The Virginia system, or custom, has always required a long probation of the lover, and during all the while, how admirable is the self-possession of the sly and demure damsel! Not a look, or gesture, or word, or pressure of the fingers betrays the state of the affections. How this admirable result is brought about, we know not; we speak of the performance of the ladies' part, as matter of history. The object is sometimes effected by a playful railery, and affectation of indifference, in other regions; but it is not so in the Old Dominion. The lady preserves a charming degree of naturalness in the midst of the most interesting passages of life. That nature is wholly suppressed, and that there are no little straws floating upon the still stream, by which the current may be detected, we do not mean to say. We only speak of the general habits and manners of the people.

Moore (as all other Virginia lovers do even at this day) doubtless weighed these things, and certainly took encouragement from the examination, as his perseverance evinced, but Carter did the same, and both could not be right. Thus holding two admirers exactly equipoised, will our readers accuse her of coquetry? There was not a particle of that feline propensity in her composition, which plays with a victim and then destroys him. Nature has placed the female sex in the defensive in this matter; they cannot woo, but must wait to be woed; and man in his thousand intricacies of character, and seeming inconsistencies, retreats as she advances; it is therefore the true philosophy of the sex to be utterly non-committal, until the all-important hour arrives, when these conventional barriers are broken down by the other. Then how charmingly the frost work of that long probation melts before the assiduities of the ardent and persevering lover! Before that day arrives, there are a thousand little playful courtships on the part of the gentleman; he often assumes quite a quixotic devotion, and hesitates not to profess his admiration, at which the lady looks on quite smilingly and demurely, but these are the mere skirmishes of the outposts which precede the pitched battle. It was partly on this account that Moore's position was so dangerous ; all this skirmishing and quixotic devotion to the sex was in a great measure dropped in the sick room, and he flattered himself that he had caught sundry little nameless confiding pieces of forgetfulness in Kate. He saw that she looked up to and relied even upon his presence as a comfort in her present position. In other words, the sick room breaks down a small portion of these conventional barriers. They consulted quite confidentially about the varying state of the invalid's health, and the state of his mind. Was he so selfish as to wish John's sickness prolonged ; we hope not ; we know not ; it would have been no inconsistent phase of human nature if he had ; but he was constant in his attentions, and ever instant with his services. Those whispering conversations which they held in the recess of the palace window, while the patient slept, were exceedingly comfortable things to the doubting youth. How he drank in the words that fell from her now all serious and confiding face, and how he loved to see her eye rest upon him for consolation, after a prolonged gaze upon her sleeping brother.

On the evening in question, as they thus sat, after a little playful bantering of Moore's, and several ineffectual attempts to reinstate her in her usual cheerfulness, she thus spoke to him:

" Will you be frank and sincere with me now, and say, if you know the cause of this sad change in my brother?"

" Thus appealed to, most assuredly I will Kate ; but it is a fruitless frankness in this instance, for I am as ignorant as yourself. The day that you sent me in your place to accompany him on the road, I endeavored to draw it out, but he baffled me."

" You know more of human nature, at all events, more of young men's nature, than I do, what do you imagine could cause this dreadful despondence? Place yourself in his situation as near as you can,what would depress you thus?"

" I know not, unless being crossed in love." Kate turned her head slightly from the speaker, and a warm and just perceptible color flashed over her cheeks for an instant, leaving her face rather pale, and her ears very red. He continued : " But I do not know that any such thing has happened to John?"

" No," replied she—" there was a slight effort made by their friends to induce my brother and Ellen to fancy each other, but they very soon discovered that these are feelings which, in their origin at least, must be spontaneous. Neither of them, I believe, were heart-broken by the effort ; I can speak with certainty of the lady."

" And I, of the gentleman—of course, that cannot be the cause. Have you never heard of any other attachment of his?"

Kate made no reply, but seemed busied with some mortifying recollection, and then darted off to perform some little nameless duty about her brother's sick couch. When she returned, she did not seem to think the question still required an answer, and the subject was dropped.

That same night Moore was seated in his room at the Hotel, wrapped in his dressing gown, his feet cased in slippers and thrown over a chair, while volumes of smoke rose up in pyramids over his head, and broke in fanciful festoons for many yards around. A large volume, with plates, was open before him, and his table was strewed with flowers. He did not seem to be studying very attentively, for every now and then he threw his eyes to the ceiling, and was lost in a pleasing reverie. Presently a rap or two was heard at the door, when who should enter but Carter, just from Temple Farm. Moore sprang up and grasped his hand cordially, as he said :

" Oh, Carter, where the treasure is, there will the heart be also."

" True, my fine fellow, how is Kate ?"

" Well, I thank you, but I had supposed you would ask first about her brother."

" You thank me! and who the devil gave you any right to thank me? You speak as if you were already one of the family. Come, come, Moore, fair play; there must be no stealing a march upon me. We are pledged to a fair race, and that it shall not be terminated until we have crossed the mountains."

" Ha, ha, ha," shouted Moore, " Gad, that would be a long track, sure enough; the Governor to hold the stakes, I suppose ?"

" Moore, what a fellow you are, for turning every thing into a joke."

" Aye, Carter, true; but where my tongue *tickles*, your's *stings*."

" But what do you mean by having these flowers upon your table, and that huge book on medicine; are you going to study the art ?"

" This is a book on botany, and these are specimens. Kate is giving me lessons."

" Ha, ha, ha," said Carter, " love makes fools of us all. You know that you have no more of the genuine passion than a savage. If she were to order you upon a pilgrimage to Jerusalem, don't you think you would undertake it ?"

" By Heavens, Carter, we are both going on one little short of it; and if the honest truth were told, it is more the daughter's influence than the father's arguments that leds us over those mountains, as studiously as you may pore over the old veteran's maps. Is it not so ?"

" Right, Moore, right."

" Well, what is the difference now between my courting the daughter with botany, and your courting the old gentleman with geography ?"

" None, except that I fear you have taken the shortest and pleasantest road; but talking of mountains, I understand our expedition is to be no child's play after all; there is terrible work with the Indians along our southern borders. The North Carolinians have had quite a brush with them, and the infection is extending even to some of our tributaries, and to the whole of the South Western Indians. I do not like the idea of that fellow, Chunoluskee, being our guide."

" Nor I—did you ever hear such stuff as that which he palmed off upon those three old gentlemen that morning. He is an arrant hypocrite."

" As ever lived, and yet the Governor will not believe it; he will peril the success of his expedition, if not the whole of our lives, if his eyes be not opened before we set out."

" It must be our business to see to that, but tell me, have you heard from any more of the counties ? Will the young men join us?"

" Yes; I saw the Governor to-night and he is in fine spirits. He says they are pouring into the capital from every quarter."

" What, the gentry, or their recruits?"

" Both; some have brought their men, and mules, and horses, and are now actually ready; while others have been brought here by the proclamation, to see and learn for themselves. I left at least twenty of the latter down stairs as I came through; they are smoking and drinking over the discussion of the subject, even now."

" How talk they—for us or against us ?"

" For us—I think most of them seem to have caught at that new idea of the Tutors, about the immense rewards in lands. Gad, Moore, that's an extraordinary fellow, a clever rogue; but the Governor says he's a soldier, every inch of him."

" Yes, you can see that in his very step; he never turns his head, but he seems as if it were on a pivot."

" But I forgot to tell you the news about him, since you left the Farm; he is desperately smitten with the old Doctor's little nun."

" Is it possible ?—he is presumptuous."

" Yes, it is a fact, and what is still more remarkable, the little prude is quite pleased with his attentions; she seems at last to have found one of our sex whom she can tolerate, and a pretty selection she has made of it. Only to think of her rejecting John Spotswood, and then accepting this desperate adventurer with the seedy garments."

"As to fortune, Carter, I grant you it would be rather a *mesalliance*, but in every other respect he is a match for any man's daughter. I am very much mistaken if he has not always moved in circles of the highest rank. But tell me what induces you to think that there is any thing in the story?"

"Well, I'll tell you; since you left the Farm they have been inseparable. The morning that Kate came away, they spent about half the day together, over that strange vault at the foot of the garden, about which there is so much gossip just now; after which she locked herself up for the remainder of the day and night. Next morning she came out bright as a new guinea, and again they wandered off together, along the bay shore, he talking poetry, and she discoursing of heaven, no doubt. Well, they came into dinner, and there she sat laughing and talking as loud as Dorothea herself. I asked the little *dairy maid* in an under tone, if she did not think her friend was hysterical, for which she slapped me in the face with her fan. It, however, proved to be no hysterics after all, for she has been quite cheerful ever since, and sits out the evening in the parlor, and has taken Kate's place at the organ every evening. There is a great change in her, from some cause or other—others have noticed it, and her bloom is already returning. If I had not engaged in this everlasting race with you over the mountains for the prize of Kate's hand, and if Ellen was not such an intolerable little blue-stocking, I could find it in my heart to fall in love with her myself; she is a bewitching little fairy after all."

"Well, how does the representative of all the Lees bear being choused by a poor Tutor?"

"Oh, there's the sport—Dorothea, I fear, will die with the effort to suppress her delight; she encourages the mutual attraction of the two quiet ones, while Lee struts like a peacock."

"But, Carter, how was it he played the magnanimous to the Tutor, about the property left him, has he taken all that back?"

"Oh, he was in a patronizing mood then, and cannot very well retract, for the Governor actually drew some of the proceeds of the estate out of him before this business commenced. The adventurer carries it off boldly, I assure you, for he treats Harry as if he were the debtor and Hall the creditor."

"Such is the fact, Carter, if his story be true."

"Poh, poh, Moore, will you never learn the world better; I tell you he is some broken down gambler, or attorney, or perhaps a cashiered officer."

"How could he have known all that family history which he detailed to Lee?"

"Learned it for the purpose of swindling, no doubt."

"I cannot believe it; if Hall is an impostor, I'll never trust mankind again."

"Well, we shall see, for depend upon it if he goes on putting his spoon into Lee's dish, as he is doing now, that gentleman will soon bring him to the proofs of his identity. Indeed, I heard him swear before I left the Farm, that he had suffered himself to be imposed upon, and he wrote a long letter by me to Attorney General Clayton, upon this very subject. You will be sure to see a fox chase before the matter is ended. Clayton read the letter in my presence, and questioned me very closely about the young man, He evidently thinks with me, that he is an impostor. He says the question can be placed beyond doubt, in a short time; that there is a man now living in the Colony who came from the neighborhood of these Hall's in Scotland, and who knows the young man Henry Hall to whom the estate was left. He is, moreover, one of the witnesses to this very will, and was consulted, it seems, by the old lady, about his character and habits, and all that; and her selection of him from the rest of his family, was mainly through his instrumentality. His name

is McDonald, and Clayton has written to him to be at the capital by the time
the Governor's family remove thither for the season. So you see we are
likely to have some sport."

" Should this business terminate as you so confidently predict, it will be
another terrible blow to that little sensitive plant of the Doctor's ; that is, if
she is really pleased with his attentions, as you say."

" Tut, tut, Moore, if she can be inveigled from her seclusion by one man,
she can by another. She is no man-hater, take my word for it. It is only
your broken backed girls and old maids seared with the smallpox, that truly
hate the men, and then it is only because they discover the aversion in us
first. I never saw one of your man-haters who was a pretty girl, in my life. I
confess that Miss Evylin came near shaking my faith for a while, but since I
have observed her closely, as she conversed with this man Hall, I have become
more confirmed than ever in my belief. If ever I saw a girl's soul in
her eyes, it was in her's while conversing with that man."

" You astonish me, Carter. Miss Evylin is the last person in the world
whom I would have supposed would be accessible to a stranger at all, but
that the affair has progressed to the length you describe, really astounds
me. As much as I confess myself taken with Mr. Hall, I would have
preferred a longer probation in the case of a lady."

" Kate leads us a different sort of a dance, aye Moore ? I rather suspect you would not object to any precipitancy in that quarter."

" No, Carter, no ; you are a generous rival I must confess, and bear off
our mutual sufferings with a happy grace, but will you excuse me, if I
say that I do not think you are very deeply touched."

" The devil you don't! wherefore do you think so ? Is it because I can
still crack my jokes and be merry over my wine and tobacco ?"

" Your jokes, Carter, as I said before, sometimes sting more than they
tickle."

" Ha, ha, ha, they do, do they ? I thought I had wrung your withers.
Forgive me, Moore, I have no right to rejoice over your greater sufferings, but being a fellow sufferer, I have some right to laugh."

At this time a slight knock was heard upon the door, with sundry scrap-
ings of the feet. Moore smiled as soon as heard them, and cried come
in. In glided old June, wringing his tarnished cocked hat with both hands,
as if he designed rending it in twain—bowing his head at every step as
he approached, and scraping back his right foot with a grating noise upon
the floor.

" Well June," said Moore, " what brings you to the capital ?"

" I come wid Moss Carter, to fetch back letter for Miss."

" Ah, and you are going back to the Farm to-night. Well, what's your
will with me, June ?"

" Glass rum for poor nigger—please God."

Moore ordered the servant to bring it, which June having prefaced with
a long speech, by way of toast, drank off at a single breath, and then
smacked his mouth and wiped his lips, and stood as before, still rolling
or twisting his hat with his hands.

" Well, June, now you have got the rum, what next ? Your tongue is
loosened ; now for the news on the Farm. Have you seen any more ghosts,
since the night of the thunder storm ?"

" No massa, ant seen spirit since, but June dreame last night."

" Oh ! well let us have your dream, what was it ? About your Miss
Catherine and her beaux again ?"

" No, Massa, not dis time. I dreame say, I bin der der trable, trable, trable,
ta-a-ah ! clean wha neber been befo. De keep on trable, trable, so tay ! at
las, I see high fence—look jis like big wall—he white, jis like chork, ony he

bery shine. When I see dat, I walk all about, der try find who lib dere. I walk, I walk—tay I see big gate dey tan wide open. I gin peep dis way, and peep dat way—las, I skin he eye open tight, and I see plenty ob people. Some dey walk about—some dey lay down—some dey eat—some dey drink—some dey sleep, ugh! dey look so happy. Tay, I look gin, and see some of my fellow sarbents dey, aint hab noting 'tall for do. One call me—say, ' broder June, come in, come in, glad for see you, him de look for you long time—me too glad for see you.' I gone in, ugh! de place pirty, for true—I'h! de corn— de tatoe—ebery ting growin dey. All my fellow sarbents dey walk bout in de sunshine. No hab no close 'tall—ebery ting comfort—no spade, no hoe, no plough—nottin 'tall do, but eat and drink, and sleep in de warm sunshine. I walk 'bout, and I eat and drink, and feel too happy. My Lor', feel too happy last night—happy for true—so tay, I gwine haben to look hine de do, ugh! wha you tink I see, mass Moore—wha you tink I see dey ?—Lor', massa, see big red cowskin hang up dey! Kerry, when June see dat, he trable, trable back gin, till he bark shin ginst skillet, and wake up and find he no nigger hebben arter all."

The youngsters burst into a loud laugh, in the midst of which the banjo player, with many quaint bows, departed, as he had done from his negro heaven, and was soon riding at the rate of eight miles an hour in the direction of Temple Farm; thereby verifying the old adage, that a spur in the head is worth two in the heel.

CHAPTER XXI.

HARD WORDS.

WHILE a portion of those in whom we hope our readers take an interest still linger at the capital, let us again revisit the charming shores of the Chesapeake—that choice region, which is daily deserted by its natives for an unknown land of frogs, and vapors, and swamps.

Before another half century rolls round, the borders of this most magnificent of all inland seas will be sought for by travellers in their summer rounds, from both sides of the Atlantic, and its now decaying mansions will be rebuilt, with far more than their former splendor. The little old squat farm houses, with their dormar windows, will be supplanted by elegant villas, and neat cottages and stately castles, and the hundreds and thousands of monuments erected in memory of the dead of a former generation, and now slanting to the horizon, and many of them dilapidated and disjointed, will be eagerly sought out by some old Mortality, and their nearly obliterated insignia restored and redeemed from oblivion. Perhaps the descendants of these very restless emigrants, now miring in the swamps of Mississippi, may return, and hunt out the faded and perishing memorials of their forefathers, and cast their tents beside them, and say, here will we and our posterity dwell forever, in the land given to our fathers. Well would it have been for thousands and tens of thousands had they been content to dwell in this most favored land, endowed by nature as it is with all that should cheer the heart and content the mind of man. We say, that in less than half a century, the tide of emigration will roll backward, and the desolate shores of the Chesapeake yet blossom as the rose. Oh may that day soon come, when Virginians will learn to venerate more and more the land where the bones of their sires lie ; that land consecrated as the burial place of a whole generation of high-hearted patriots, and where yet breathes the purest spirit of enlightened freedom that ever refreshed and purified the earth; that land in which was exhibited that rarest combination of social aristocracy and public equality—where virtue, and talents, and worth alone were consecrated to reverence, through hereditary lines of descent. Many an hour did we toil to replace the fallen cap of some old tomb-stone, of a sire, perhaps, whose descendants were every one gone to a strange land. We were accompanied in our labor of love sometimes by one,* who even then bore about his person the too sure evidence that he, too, would soon sleep with the consecrated dead, whose memories and monuments he loved so well to cherish.

We could not pass through Old York on our way to Temple Farm, without one more glimpse at that melancholy and utterly ruinous grave yard; where the traveller beholds the faded efforts of heraldry, like a cross-bones and death's head, gaping from every tomb-stone. There the stones themselves, erected to perpetuate earthly honors, are fast sinking to the grave, staring and gaping as they fall, and holding aloft their effigied arms, as if in supplication to the passer by to save them from the threatened desecration. That old grave yard is turned out like their old fields, to rejuvenate upon the very carrion which is left from the ceaseless battle that time wages with all things. Oh Virginians! ye noble few who still cling to the hearth-stones of your fore-fathers, rouse up, and preserve these old time-honored monuments—these old tomb stones, that have withstood the storms of the Chesapeake for a hundred and fifty years. When those old grave stones are replaced, and flowers once more bloom over their green and dark forms, then will the regeneration of the Old Dominion commence, and not till then.

Our readers have caught a glimpse of the position of some of the parties at Temple Farm, from the conversation of Kit Carter and Bernard Moore; but there were others at the farm, to whom they were not so amusing. Harry Lee could scarcely believe his own eyes, when he saw the young lady at whose feet he had been casting his princely fortune, and not less princely self, daily wandering along the shores of the bay, and through the garden and the shady groves, and along the banks of the little brook, with one whom he considered as only occupying his present social position by sufferance. He was struck with the fact, that the more Ellen and Hall were together, the more the hatred of the latter was manifested to him. He determined therefore to seek an early opportunity for explanation from both. In the meantime, it seemed to him as if the stay of the old Doctor would be prolonged forever, so impatient was he for his return. He inquired for him at every meal.

On one of these occasions, Dorothea, with a sly smile upon her face, proposed to despatch a messenger for the Doctor, if Mr. Lee was getting much worse, as she said her brother was better, and the Doctor could no doubt be spared in case of emergency.

"I thank you," said Lee, "I am not myself the patient who most needs his valuable services," glancing scornfully at the Tutor.

"I did not know," innocently replied the little girl, "but it might be gout in the stomach, or a disease of the heart, and these things, you know, mama, are so frightful and so insidious; they never have any external signs, I believe."

Ellen on these occasions would look beseechingly at her little friend, while her Ladyship would carry off the conversation upon some other topic, as if Dorothea had not spoken. On one of these mornings, Lee walked into the library, at that hour when he knew the Secretary was at work and alone. He bowed stiffly to Hall. The latter rose hastily, handed him a chair, and at the same time stuck the pen behind his ear, after which he took his own seat, and waited for Mr. Lee to open the conversation, which he did as follows:

*The late Senator Page of Williamsburg—the sole lineal descendant, we believe, of Gover-nor Page. He had the true antiquarian zeal. His was a pure and bright spirit. Peace to his ashes.

" Mr. Hall, in the absence of Governor Spotswood and Dr. Evylin, I have taken upon myself a very unpleasing duty, and one which I fear in its performance may inflict pain upon you."

" I am utterly at a loss to comprehend you."

" You shall not long remain so, sir—I am not one to shrink from the performance of what I consider due to the worthy and honorable gentlemen, whose representative I consider myself, in some measure, in their absence."

" Indeed—I had rather thought that I had been charged by his Excellency with representing him in his absence."

" I thought, sir, that you must be laboring under some strange delusion as to your position here."

" I am still in the dark, sir."

" So I perceive, and it is my intention to enlighten you."

" I will listen with the greatest attention, and all the respect to which your remarks may be entitled."

Lee bit his lip, and elevated his person still more than usual, if possible, as he proceeded :

" You must know, sir, that it is not usual in this country, for one who holds the—the subordinate office of Tutor or Private Secretary, to assume an equal station with gentlemen of birth and fortune."

" I am at a loss to know, Mr. Lee, in what I have transcended the indulgence extended to me by Gov. Spotswood himself. I even abstained from presenting myself at his table, until expressly commanded to do so by himself."

" In that matter he had doubtless a right to do as he pleased ; but you must know that the Governor is a very eccentric man, and somewhat whimsical—he may command you to set at his table to-day, and refuse you to-morrow."

" But, sir, he expressly stated it to me as his desire, that I would set at his table, as one of his family. Am I to understand Mr. Lee, as expressing a contrary desire?"

" By no means—I only alluded to your appearance at table as an example, and because you first alluded to it yourself ; my design was to touch upon other matters—your intimate association with the female inmates of his family."

" Ah ! you allude to my late rambles with Miss Evylin."

" I do, sir, and it is somewhat remarkable that they should have commenced the moment the Governor and the Doctor disappeared."

" With regard to the point of time, I had nothing in the world to do. The interview was sought by the lady. I state this in justification of myself; and only under such circumstances as the present, would I say this much. Further I will not utter a single syllable, unless you can show by what authority you question me in this matter at all."

" I have already said, that I consider myself, in some measure, as the representative of those two gentlemen."

" Yes, sir, but you are the self-elected representative, and have not yet exhibited to me any other authority."

" Then, sir, I have another title to question you in this matter. I have the authority of the lady's father for occupying a very delicate relation towards her."

" And the lady's, also ?"

" About that, sir, you have no right to question, and I consider it rather presumptuous in one in your position to presume as far as you have."

By this time both had risen. Hall replied—" and I consider it equally presumptuous in you, sir, to question me."

Lee looked astounded. " Very well, sir," said he, " I have at least brought this matter to an issue, and I will state the case to the ladies of the family, and they can act as they choose, until the gentlemen return."

" And I, sir, will relate the whole of this conversation, word for word, to Miss Evylin, so that she at least may know how far each of us have presumed."

"Beware, sir, how you mention my name in that quarter. I will hold *your person responsible.*"

"I don't know what you mean by holding my person responsible. If it be that you imagine that you can hold me to any sort of responsibility, in which you will not be equally so held, you have mistaken me, far more than I can have mistaken my position."

"We shall see—we shall see—it will depend upon your success in establishing your claims to bear the name which now you wear. In the event of this unpleasant business proceeding to hostilities between us, you will not find me unwilling to yield you far more, in such a case, than I think you have any right to claim now, in a social position."

"That is, am I to understand that Mr. Lee is willing to grant me to be a gentleman in war, but not in love."

"Beware, sir, how you trifle with me in this matter. It is no proof of either your courage or breeding to taunt me, while your hands are tied."

"There, sir, you spoke the truth, and I honor even an enemy for that. It is indeed too true, my hands are tied, and that I was too precipitate—thus far, I retract, but the main issue between us must continue, until I establish my claims to be your equal. Soon after which Lee left the room, with a rather more polite and respectful air than he had entered it. He neverthless went straightway to the parlor, and despatched a servant for Miss Evylin. While he was kicking his heels in the parlor, we will glance into the Governor's library again, where we left the Tutor. There was no more drawing of military maps that morning—he threw himself into a chair and buried his face in his hands, and if he did not weep, his frame was convulsed mightily like it. This was a poor preparation for a hostile meeting of any sort, but the bitter things of the heart will have vent, when alone, however much we brave them away in the midst of a personal altercation. How many men would see the error of their ways, if they would thus honestly meditate upon all that they have just said and done after such an affair; not that Hall regretted, in the main, any thing he had said.

He threw on his hat and walked abroad into the fields to cool his feverish brow and excited feelings, and to reflect upon what it was best to do, under the accumulating embarrassments of his situation. He had hoped that the tramontaine expedition would set out before his own private affairs might come to a crisis, but that he now foresaw was impossible, and this reflection made him miserable; for he had entered into all the Governor's plans with spirit and enthusiasm, and besides had other private motives, above the ordinary youthful desire for notoriety—to distinguish himself. He was waiting, too, anxiously for news from Europe—alas, he little knew how disastrous would be the first aspect of that news to him—he little imagined that at that very moment a vessel was ploughing her way into the bay, bringing information almost the reverse of what he expected. Without this last drop to his already brimming cup, he found the weight of his troubles sufficient for all his fortitude and patience.

The main subject of his present reflections was the impending personal difficulty with Mr. Lee. He foresaw that a crisis in that affair was inevitable, and that it was surrounded with difficulties which would ruin him, if he seized upon either horn of the dilemma. He could neither fight Lee, nor refuse to fight with honor, according to the prevailing notions of the country and the times, and yet he gathered from some expressions dropped by that young gentleman in their late altercation, that he would force it to such an issue in the last resort. We will leave him, however, to struggle with his own difficulties, while we return to Mr. Lee, who waited a considerable time for Ellen to make her appearance. She dreaded the interview, because she supposed it was like so many that had gone before it, but she resolved that it should be the last. As she descended the stairs, she was pondering the best manner of communicating to the gentleman, not only her utter aversion to him, but also how she might make him comprehend, with his arrogance and great self-esteem, that his persevering suit amounted to persecution. It may be readily conceived that such a train of reflections were not well calculated to prepare her to receive in a very amiable mood the harangue which was to follow.

She saw as she entered the room, that she had mistaken his object for once, and seating herself, kept her eye upon his countenance, with an anxious inquiring look for his object.

" Miss Evylin," he began, " I have sent for you, to have some conversation upon a subject which I fear will be painful, but I felt it to be my duty to do so, in the absence of Governor Spotswood and your father."

" You startle me, sir," she suddenly exclaimed, " will you be so good as to mention the subject, without farther circumlocution ?"

" I am not one given to much circumlocution, Miss Evylin, but on occasions such as the present, when very delicate matters are involved, it is right to prepare the mind for the reception of disagreeable news."

" News !" cried she, " of whom—my father?—has any thing happened to him ?" and she ran up and grasped his arm.

" He is well as you might have divined, from my mentioning his absence as the cause of my having imposed the present disagreeable duty upon myself."

" True," she said, and threw herself into a chair in a listless mood, as if she cared not what else he might say. She was however mistaken there, for she was roused again in an instant, as he proceeded :

" Miss Evylin—Mr. Hall has used your name in a way, which I have every reason to believe was entirely unauthorized by you, and one, too, which I must say it becomes you to authorize me to contradict at once."

" Mr. Hall, use my name ! authorize you to contradict ! why what could Mr. Hall say of me ?"

" Oh, I see that it was all made up for the occasion ; I thought it would turn out so. Why, thus it was. When I took him to task for his presumption in associating so intimately with the ladies of the Governor's family in his absence, and more especially with yourself, he with quite an air boasted that his society had been sought by you, and not yours by him."

Ellen rose to her feet, and walked straight up to Lee, and looked into his face, as she inquired in a slow, almost whispered voice, so deep was her emotion, " Did Mr. Hall use such language of me, and with such a motive, and with such an air ?"

" He did—and I cannot of course speak as to the exact words, but such was precisely the impression left upon my mind."

" Mr. Lee, refresh your memory again—I would have perilled my life upon the truth and honor of that gentleman—have not your own feelings colored his expressions?"

" I have already stated how the conversation happened, and given you the result as near as I am capable of—there can be no mistake, for it happened not half an hour ago, in the Governor's Library."

She threw herself back into a seat, as one who gives up, and said : " Then I have indeed been grossly deceived."

" You have truly, and by as arrant an impostor as ever lived, and as bold a one. This comes of the Governor receiving men into his family, without credentials of any sort ; but I need not say any thing of his Excellency, for this man imposed as bold a piece of clumsy swindling upon me as any one, and is actually now in possession of monies belonging to my aunt's estate."

Ellen rose to take her leave, from which Mr. Lee endeavored to persuade her, saying that he had far more important matters to discuss with her, than the clumsy tricks of an every day impostor ; but she pleaded her deep mortification, and the confused state of her mind, from the perplexing doubts which still crowded upon her, and that she needed repose and that calm reflection which solitude alone could give. As she slowly mounted the stairs, she thought of the letter which Hall had brought her, and from whom, and was on the point of rushing back into the room, and telling Lee that she would rather doubt him than Hall ; but such was his high standing for a man of honor and veracity, that she did not dare thus to brave the pet of public opinion. She resumed her way, the same train of reflections still forcing themselves upon her mind—how could he (Hall) know all the delicate and intricate matters which he had related to her, if he was the gross and vulgar impostor, that Mr. Lee represented him to be. Her reason was almost bewildered by these conflicting views—between the internal evidence of truth in Hall's narrative to her, and Lee's positive testimony as to his gross and ungentlemanly statement with regard to herself. In whatever manner he might have possessed the information alluded to, if Lee's statement was true, he was undoubtedly some low creature.

Any sagacious observer of human nature will readily divine on which side the victory lay. Ellen was all a woman, and of course the heart won the day against the judgment. Nevertheless her indignation every now and then burst out, whenever she thought of the manner in which he had perverted her acts and spoken of them. Whatever might be her heart's leaning to the accused, she resolved that nothing of it should appear in her conduct ; that she would show him that she knew and scorned his assumptions. Such was about the confused and doubtful result arrived at, when her maid entered to prepare her for dinner.

In the mean time Lee had not been idle—he next sent for Lady Spotswood, and to her and Dorothea he related a somewhat similar story, suppressing particulars in Ellen's case, barely referring them to her for proof of base ingratitude, as well as falsehood. He found all the ladies prepossessed in the Tutor's favor, and Dorothea remained so, in spite of all he could say to the contrary. Of course she did not presume to controvert her mother's decision in a grave matter like that, in the absence of her father too, but she left the room tossing her head, and declaring that there was a mistake somewhere.

Lady Spotswood held a long consultation with the accuser with regard to what was to be done until his Excellency returned, and whether it was best to send after him ; and they came to the conclusion to let the business stand just as it was ; only that all intercourse between the ladies of the family and the Tutor was to be cut off, except, of course, at table ; and ladies generally understand full well how to keep improper persons at a distance.

Reader, did'st ever see some poor wight who had fallen under the displeasure of a party in the country, sitting apart ? If you have, you can form some idea of the situation of Hall that day at Temple Farm.

Dorothea encountered young Dandridge as she made her exit from the family council, and to him she related the story of the Tutor's reputed perfidy. Little Bob, too, formed one of the youthful council, and the three came to the unanimous conclusion that he was innocent. How slow is the young heart to believe in the guilt of those for whom they have taken a liking ; and with all of us, even of maturer age, how easy to believe what we wish to believe.

Bob took his hat straightway and followed his Tutor to the fields where he had lately seen him. The young man seemed to understand the warmth of heart which had brought his pupil upon his errand of love, and he silently folded the lad in his arms, while scalding tears trickled from his scarred face. The child was dumb at this sight, his own heart was overflowing, and' had any more been wanting, the finishing stroke was added to his convictions. He took the hand of the Tutor and silently and slowly accompanied him to the house.

Dinner was soon after announced and Hall took his seat as usual, entirely unaware of the extent of the prejudices which had been excited against him. His own countenance exhibited traces of excitement which would have claimed the sympathy of any company not previously set against him. There was inexpressible sadness, almost despair, marked upon every feature; but he had yet to experience a far greater degree of suffering. In that pale and beautiful face in which he hoped to find sympathy and comfort, he encountered nothing but scorn and indignation. Not a word was vouchsafed to him of any sort, and when her eyes met his, it was the cold glance of a distant acquaintance. He turned an inquiring look towards her Ladyship, and there he met the same cold displeasure. The conversation was carried on between her Ladyship, Lee, and Ellen, as if the poor Tutor had been still in Scotland. Not so, however, the youthful three—Dandridge, Dorothea, and Bob, vied with each other in helping their favorite to the choice dishes, but he ate nothing. Altogether it was a very unpleasant meeting. Most of the guests had departed, except those specially named, and among the others the Indian Chief, so that there was no relief to be found in numbers.

The meal concluded, Ellen hurried to her room and burst into tears; she was soon followed by Dorothea, who exclaimed when she saw her weeping, " I'm glad of it, I'm right down glad of it, so I am, you ought to cry your eyes out, so you ought, for treating poor Mr. Hall so naughtily."

" But Dorothea," said Ellen 'midst her sobs, " how could I help it ?"

" Why, slapped Mr. Lee's face and told him to go home about his business. Did'nt he make all this mischief here. Harry Lee will take the house, plantation and all, if papa don't soon come home."

" Fie, fie, Dorothea, Mr. Lee is not to blame for Mr. Hall's faults."

" I tell you, Ellen, it's Mr. Lee who has the beam in his own eye, and he has swallowed one too for what I know, he's so stiff."

The little girl flirted out of the room in the pouts, little imagining that she left behind her, in the heart of the other, a warmer advocate even than herself in favor of the Tutor.

CHAPTER XXII.

WORDS COMING TO BLOWS.

THE same afternoon Hall encountered Ellen as she was passing through the apartment. He followed and begged her to grant him but a few moment's conversation. She stopped and looking at him with an expression which said as plain as words might speak it, it is more in sorrow than in anger that I avoid you.

" Will Miss Evylin deign," he said, " to inform so humble an individual as myself, how he has fallen not only under her displeasure, but also that of the family ?"

She replied, " Mr. Hall, you have so grossly misinterpreted what I have already said and done, that it is hazardous to hold any communication with you."

" I have misinterpreted what you have said ! never ! I have never for one moment of my life harbored any but the kindest and gentlest thoughts towards Miss Evylin, much less spoken disrespectfully of her."

" Then you have been shamefully slandered."

" I thought as much, and it was therefore that I sought this opportunity for an explanation. Will Miss Evylin be so good as to inform me what I was reported to have said of her ? I need not ask by whom."

" You are reported, sir, to have boasted that so far from your having sought my favor, that I had sought yours."

" Miss Evylin, this is one of those ingenious falsehoods, which none but a perverse head or a false heart could have coined out of what I did say."

" Then you acknowledge that there was some foundation for it."

" As stated by you, it is wholly false in coloring, and nearly so in fact; but the world is governed by such falsehoods as these ; what is called public opinion, is made up of these many little streams combined into one great torrent—why should I endeavor to arrest the mighty current with my puny arm?"

" You can at all events set yourself right in my esteem, by a plain statement of facts—do you consider it worthy of the effort ?"

" Hereafter I can only hope to enjoy the good opinion of the choice few, among whom I would gladly rank Miss Evylin. I will state how the offence was given, if offence it be. Mr. Lee undertook to take me to task for pushing myself, a poor Tutor, forward into society, where my presence was not wanted. He went so far as to intimate that I presumed in sitting at the table with the rest of the family, and when I told him I had done so at the express command of his Excellency, he then changed his ground and claimed to catechise me with regard to my attentions to you. I challenged his right to do so, and he then stated that he was an avowed suitor, with your father's approbation. Under these circumstances I thought myself justified in stating the fact, that *the first interview* was sought by you. I stated neither more nor less, without coloring of any sort, and simply to justify myself from his charge of presumption. This is the whole of my offence."

She offered him her hand, as she said, " Mr. Hall, forgive me, but I am not to blame. I was led astray ; I trusted too implicitly to his honor, for though he did not, it seems, tell what the world calls a falsehood, it answered all the purposes of one, and was so ingeniously designed as to mislead me and baffle detection."

" Aye, his conduct in this affair was not unlike another in which you were concerned, Miss Evylin ; I should have thought that would teach you to guard your too confiding nature against him ; but enough for the present, if I am wholly reinstated in your good opinion, I am satisfied."

" You are, and I take shame to myself that even this explanation was necessary."

" Having then judged hastily this time, promise that in future, when circumstances appear to be against me, you will hear my vindication before you decide."

" Most assuredly I will."

" I ask it, Miss Evylin, because I foresee that I may soon be placed in a position from which it may seem impossible to extricate myself. I will not deny to you, that I am surrounded by difficulties, the causes of some of which you know more than any other person. I make it, then, my last solemn request to you, to hear before you judge. Good day."

He had seen Lee passing in front of the verandah, and followed him down the garden, where he soon overtook and addressed him, thus : " You came to me this morning, sir, professing yourself under the painful necessity of communicating something disagreeable, I now address you under precisely similar circumstances."

" I am ready with all patience, sir, to hear you."

" Few words will suffice to convey my meaning, and therefore your patience will not be heavily taxed. You prevaricated, sir, in relating our conversation to Miss Evylin."

" Prevaricated, sir, and this to me !"

" Aye, prevaricated is the word, sir."

" Very well, sir ! very well ! you shall hear from me shortly." And with this he strode off, but presently returned, and said, "Hark you, Sir Tutor, you must establish your claims to be treated as a gentleman, and that right speedily, or I will not only chastise you in a way you will not fancy, but I will take such steps as to guard the community from your becoming heir to any more stray legacies."

Hall's lips curled in disdain as he replied , " choose your own manner and time of redress for the insult which now adheres to you. I shall be ready to repel in whatever way you advance." Lee was again retreating, as Hall continued, "And hark you, in your turn, Sir, beware how you report any more of our conversations. I will not trust your memory." This was said in a bitter sarcastic tone. Lee strode rapidly up to him in a threatening attitude, with his hand upon his sword, his face but a few inches from that of his adversary, and replied, " Do you mean to provoke me to forget that we are the only grown white males upon the place, and that the ladies are under our, or rather my protection ?"

" You should under such circumstances remember the truth, it is peculiarly incumbent on you to do so."

Lee drew his rapier and flashed it in the face of the Tutor, as he exclaimed by heavens another such taunt and I will let out your base churl's blood here upon the walk, in spite of all the restraints upon me. Human nature can stand no more."

Hall wore no sword, but he carried a small rattan in his hand, which he elevated, touching the point almost in his adversary's face, as one who puts himself in the attitude to guard, exclaiming, " Come on, sir, I am more than a match for you, even thus."

Lee scorned his scientific posture and rushed upon him as if he would despatch him at single lunge, but the next moment found his sword twirling in the air, and Hall leaning upon his cane laughing at the foaming and now fruitless anger of his adversary. A few yards distant, among the shrubbery, he saw little Bob's face peeping out in the same mirthful delight, but truth to say, it was blanched white with fear, and the color had not yet returned.

Lee clutched his sword, and hurried from the garden, swearing vengeance against the impostor. He rushed to the house, and after a hasty word or two with Lady Spotswood, ordered his horses and rode post haste to the capital. Not, however, before he had scratched a few words on a slip of paper, and sent them to the young man in the garden. They read as follows : " The first moment, Sir, after you have established your pretended claims to gentle birth and breeding, you shall hear from me. A reasonable time elapsing and this not done, I will chastise you at sight."

Hall's countenance loured as he read this note, and then tore it into fragments and gave them to the wind, but instantly relapsed into the merry mood as Bob ran at him with a stick, exactly imitating Lee's murderous thrust. " He did not see you twist the foil out of Mr. Moore's hand that night, or he would not have ventured his sword even against your rattan," said the boy.

" No, Bob, I am glad he did not, and then we should have met differently, which I assure you I am rejoiced to avoid, more than you can imagine."

" Well, now I must run and tell Nat and Dorothea, they will laugh till their sides ache ; let me see how it was, thus you twitched him that double demisimiquaver. I would give my pony if I could just catch that trick."

" All in good time, Robert, but come here ; you must not mention this unless Mr. Lee communicates it first ; now remember, you will injure instead of befriend me, if you do."

" Well, to be sure, it's a great privation not to be allowed to tell of this. But you will not object if I make them promise not to tell."

" Yes, Bob, I do object ; I have particular reasons for keeping it quiet for the present, and I am sure you would do nothing to injure me willingly."

" No, no," answered the boy, " I would not injure you for any thing, and if telling it would do so, I will keep it though I burst in trying."

Still he kept on playing with his stick, every now and then bursting into a loud laugh, as the Tutor would humor him by twitching it out of his hand.

CHAPTER XXIII.

THE FALL OF THE LEAVES.

TWILIGHT, that witching time between day and night, came; always a pleasant hour of the twenty-four, but in Virginia particularly so. Here the climate, at the season upon which we have arrived, renders it very delightful, the sun just leaves enough of heat lingering with his departing rays, to temper the cool breeze of the evening. It is not to be denied, however, that there is something melancholy in these early autumnal twilights. The leaves of the green trees which have so long delighted and protected us, begin now to put on their variegated dress. First the deep green fades to a lighter shade, and then is tinged with a pale margin of yellow, and finally puts on the russet dress of winter. Here and there, also, those that have clung to the parent stem by a frail tenure, loose their vitality, and are seen floating about in the lazy atmosphere, as if reluctant to mingle with the parent dust.

" The fall of the leaves," said Ellen to Hall, as they wandered along the banks of the little stream which wound through the grounds, " the fall of the leaves in autumn, reminds us too forcibly of the death of a human generation. These pale heralds of the coming death to all their class, are like the sickly, and the feeble, and the old, of our race; do they not produce that impression upon you?"

" Sometimes, but not always. It depends much upon our circumstances at the time. If the country has always been our home, and we have drawn our chief delight from rural pleasures, then the impression is pretty sure to be a melancholy one : but to the city dame, it is the dawn of the gay season, of routs, and parties, and balls—here I mean in our capital. In London the season of pleasure is much later. To the literary man they produce a mixed sensation ; a pleasing melancholy, tinged with the philosophy you have described, and also a cheerful looking forward to long winter nights, and bright blazing fires, and sweet communion with delightful books."

" That indeed, gives a cheerful and warm glow to the wintry picture, which my melancholy imagination scarcely fetches. Your remark has brought to mind a similar one, with which poor Frank rejoiced my heart one night. Oh what a bright and cheerful spirit he was blessed with ! We were sitting listening to the dismal howlings of the wind as it rattled our windows and whistled through the key holes, and the rain and sleet alternately vied for conquest, when I remarked that it was a dismal night and affected my spirits sadly. He took my hand and looked up in my face, (we were alone,) and said cheerfully—' it is from within that the brightest illumination is to be drawn. There, if the heart, and mind, and affections be all right—is an ever-lasting sunshine of the soul—so bright that no night or storm ever comes over it.' Well, Frank, said I, unlock that magic lanthorn of yours, and try its bright rays on the contending storm and darkness, struggling for entrance at all these windows. Look how the contending demons scowl at us from without, now do drive them away, that's a good boy. Straightway his eye dilated, and he commenced a description of a domestic fireside scene of comfort, which really heightened its colors of beauty from the contrast of the darker shadows without. I imperceptibly caught the bright glow, from his more daring imagination."

"Poor Frank," said Hall, musingly, "some of his brightest fancies have been extinguished, I fear—like my own:" added he hastily, as he saw Ellen's eye reading his thoughts.

"No, they are not extinguished," at length replied Ellen, with a sudden flash of enthusiasm, "for if alive, those bright illuminations of genius, like the light of the diamond, but shine the brighter when all that is earthly around is obscured. There is but one thing on this earth that can extinguish that glorious light from within—IT IS CRIME! Let the conscience be clear, and the light of the soul illumines our dreary path—sheds the ray of hope through the valley of death, and is rekindled again at the parent fountain of the ever-living God."

"In this world, man is impelled forward to action amidst the stirring adventures which are gathered around him like the meshes of a plot, until it becomes with his doubtful and doubting reason hard to separate the narrow boundaries which divide crime from errors of judgment. Nay, even when the actions are past, the ever busy monitor you have named, conscience, hangs suspended over the deeds, at a loss whether to strike or be silent."

"For a little while only," replied Ellen quietly, "when time has sobered the tumult of the passions which drove him forward, conscience, though scared away for a while, will come back in the calmer moments of our lives. This very witching hour of twilight is a favorite time for such visits. In the bright and pure morning, our spirits are elastic and cheerful, and few heinous crimes are committed then; in the noon-tide, the storm of human passions rage, and if the intent is deadly and malignant, it is prolonged into the silent watches of the night; but with a large majority of our race, darkness brings repentance for the crimes of the day. What a beneficent provision of the Creator it was, rolling our little planet but one side at a time next the sun, that while one half the world fretted, and stormed, and sinned, the other half might repent and sleep."

"You seem to have observed mankind!"

"Nay, I am only sporting in borrowed feathers, at all events, only a part of them are my own. These very subjects were discussed by poor Frank and myself many a time, before he sailed upon that fatal voyage. So much had we learned to think in common, that it is hard now for me to separate my own ideas from his. Doubtless my constant association with him gave a masculine cast to many of my thoughts, the observation of which no doubt elicited your remark."

"No, no, I cannot say that they are masculine; at all events, they are not unfeminine. Whatever relates to our higher sentiments and our spiritual natures, certainly belongs in common to the sexes, and if man has usurped the whole claim to discuss them, he assuredly has no right to do so. Indeed, your sex is so much purer than ours, that any thing of heavenly philosophy seems to fall with peculiar propriety from their lips. Poor Frank! indeed he little knew how the germs of his young mature philosophy have been treasured in his absence, and into what good ground they had fallen, and to what a rich truition they are even now springing up. Do you know that every boyish dreamer sketches, for his own futurity, the very circumstances which have fallen as a rich inheritance to my friend in his absence?"

"I cannot say that I understand you fully."

"Every youth, in the hey-day of his imagination, sketches out some charming little beau-ideal of a partner for life, and into this beautiful creation of his own he almost performs the part of creator, for he breathes into her such feelings, sentiments, and opinions as he desires she should possess; now here is poor Frank, with the ideal creature reduced to reality; but like all the bright glimpses vouchsafed to our race, no sooner is it perfected ready for him to grasp, than it either eludes his pursuit, or he is himself engulphed in that remorseless and relentless vortex, whither have been hurried so many bright spirits before him."

"I certainly feel flattered, Mr. Hall, that you should consider me worthy to represent Frank's ideal creations, but I fear the drapery with which your own imagination has clothed me would speedily vanish, amidst the stern realities of such a homely world as ours. I am conscious of the fact, however, so far as the mind is concerned; for there is not a day of my life, and scarcely an hour, as you have seen, that I do not detect myself uttering some of his sentiments at second hand. His mental superiority must have been greater than even I gave him credit for, as I can see the impress of his association even upon your own thoughts, as unconscious as you may be of it."

"I grant you that his influence over me was very great, not less than that which was swayed so powerfully over your own days of childhood."

"Nearly every girl that arrives at womanhood has passed through the same schooling of the affections. True, in our cases, there was a constant similarity in training, association, and circumstances, which merged down the dissimilarities of mental character, but in every other case, the experience is the same, even without these. The heart of every girl clings to some image or other, real or imaginary, and they cling to it through life, whether married or single. If married, the idol of the imagination is set up in secret, as one of the household Gods, and this is one reason there is so much matrimonial unhappiness. It was the early observation of these very things which led me so pertinaciously to cling to that prize which I had drawn in the lottery of life; and I shall continue to cling to it, even if it is but shadow, far preferring that to all the real pomps and honors which this world affords."

"The experience of our race seems to be every where the same. Not only was it cursed and condemned to earn its bread by the sweat of the brow, but the sentence extends much farther. All that beautiful poetry of the fresh and pure young hearts' sentiments, which promises such a heavenly harvest of future flowers, before those sentiments become tainted with grosser passions, seem never destined to fruition in this world. We are just allowed to peep into the garden of Eden, and then banished forever amidst the dark by-ways and crowded thoroughfares of busy life. True, we cling fondly to the memory of this poetic dream of youth, and doubtless these bright morning glories continue to throw a mellow but saddened light over all the future. This constitutes the sum and substance of our ideal paradise in this world, the poetry of real life."

"And do you really think there is no exception to the sweeping denunciation? Are there none who ever realize the romantic dreams of youth?"

"Oh, very few indeed. Look into your own experience, Miss Evylin. You are one of the very few who have struggled heroically against this sweeping flood of the busy world, which overwhelms nearly all who oppose it. Where there is one who thus stands out against the decree, hundreds have fallen victims around; some to ambition—some to avarice, and a much larger portion to the mixed motives which interested parents know so well how to ply the young heart with. And even you, are you not daily beset to listen to the voice of the tempter? Comes he not to you, with splendid estates, and gaudy establishments, and tinselled honors, which your sex loves so well?"

"True, true—but I would not give up that one dear, dear dream of my young life, for all the honors of the world."

"And do you know the fate of the pious and noble few of your sex, who thus devote their lives to the perpetuation of life's young dream?"

"No, I have never counted the cost."

"It is a life of single blessedness. Pardon me, Miss Evylin, but you are a candidate for admission into that abused sisterhood ycleped old maids—that slandered and traduced, class—nearly every one of which are living monuments of the infidelity of man—that noble sisterhood, which lives forever upon the memory of the past—keeping up perpetual fires upon the pure and vestal altars, before whose shrines were offered their first, best, and dearest affections."

" Welcome, thrice welcome the lot !" said Ellen, a pure light beaming from her eyes, as she locked her hands with energy, in the earnestness of her invocation. " It has no terrors for me. As you say, I can turn back upon the past, and what is much better, I can even look to the future with hope. Thanks to that divine personification of hope, charity, and mercy, I can look beyond the narrow confines of this world. Believe me, Sir, these disappointments of the young heart's freshest aspirations, are not ordered in vain. If we could here enjoy an uninterrupted paradise, this world would no more be one of probation and trial ; and though I for one am determined never to be merged with the interested throng you have described, I do not therefore repine at, and rebel against, an inevitable destiny. My own course is one of difficulty and self-denial, and perhaps of reproach and odium, and therefore we, old maids I mean, work out our salvation, if successful, by one road, while our more ambitious sisters travel another."

" Oh, I do not mean to class you just yet with the class alluded to—I only pointed out what would be the result, unless you listened to some of these splendid proposals so often laid at your feet."

" I am willing now to take the veil of the sisterhood, and shoulder all the odium and reproach."

" What ! and surrender up the hope of Frank's being alive, and one day returning."

" No, no, not exactly that—I would only take refuge among them, until this short, and fitful, and feverish state of suspense be over."

" And should he even yet return, the fountain of your joys has already been poisoned."

" How ? I pray you."

" Why, he has been carried by the tide of this world far past those beautiful eddies in the stream, overhung with green leaves, and redolent of summer flowers. He has been tossed upon some of life's stormiest billows, and if not actually wrecked and lost, he may be so weather-beaten and pelted by the contending elements, as to be, when he comes, like an ancient mariner, a better subject for repose and repentance, than for a fresh voyage."

" I know he was fashioned somewhat like other youths—impetuous and rash, and perhaps ambitious, but no storms of the world, such as you describe, can ever leave indelible stains or scars upon him. He may be weather-beaten and worn, but he will be my own Frank for all that, and whatever he may be—should even his tender conscience have suffered with the wear and tear almost inevitable in the dreadful conflicts of the thronged, and busy and turbulent world—still let him be welcome ; for better, for worse, come weal, come woe, joy or sorrow, our destinies are linked forever—throughout this life, and I trust a longer and a better hereafter."

Hall's eye fully expressed his unmeasured admiration of the little devoted creature, as she poured out almost her whole heart. Our readers will readily perceive that he had been purposely tampering with the purest and brightest sentiments of her nature, whether in wanton sport or with higher motives, will be developed as our narrative proceeds. He continued :

" Ah, Miss Evylin, the experience of your pure and charming sex is very different from ours. Your views of the world, and your estimate of human nature, are taken through a very clear medium ; and pardon me, I do not wish to flatter, but I must say that Miss Evylin is even exalted above that of her sex."

" No, I am sure it is not—my experience of the world has been short, it is true, computing it in mere years, but it has been long in sorrow, and bitter in disappointment. You yourself have furnished me with some of the evidence upon which my views are based. What can I think of Henry Lee, after his conduct to his brother ?—and in what way can I interpret his late disingenuousness conduct to you, unless very unfavorably to himself and to his kind. I have endeavored to think that the whole proceeded from his blinding passions, and consequent obliquity of moral vision, but I find it hard to make excuses for him."

" And you will find it harder, Miss Evylin, as his character is more fully developed ; but I do not wish to speak touching him—another very unpleasant altercation has since occurred between us, and he has gone off very much enraged."

" I am very sorry for what you state, but I am glad that he is gone."

By this time they had entered the house.

CHAPTER XXIV.

A JOURNEY—THE END UNFORESEEN.

JOHN SPOTSWOOD was soon well enough to ride out with his sister in the carriage, and after several experiments of his strength, and continued improvement from day to day, it was at length determined to remove him for a short time to Temple Farm. His spirits had now become placid if not cheerful, and every one remarked that he began to look, and speak, and act more like his former self, than he had done for many months before. It was a mere farewell family reunion which was proposed to take place, preparatory to the removal of the whole establishment to the capital. That removal could not now longer be delayed, for the House of Burgesses was soon to assemble, besides a general meeting of all those favorable to the great tramontaine expedition. Accordingly, the same principal parties were soon re-established in the country who were there when we first introduced them to the reader, with such additions as had been made from time to time. Henry Lee did not return with the Governor.

It was impossible for his Excellency not to observe that Lady Spotswood was highly offended with the Tutor from some cause or other, and he very soon took occasion to inquire into the matter.

He first heard his lady's reasons for the difficulty, and then summoned Hall to the library to hear his.

" Well, Mr. Hall," said his Excellency as the Tutor entered, " sit down here, and tell me all about this difficulty with Harry Lee and the ladies of my family. For once they seem to have sided with him, and of course are against you."

" Not all of them your Excellency—I have satisfactorily explained the matter to the only one who has afforded me an opportunity, and the one, too, about whom the unpleasant altercation occurred."

" I am very glad to hear it. That is Miss Evylin, I presume."

" Yes, sir, and I am very sure she will be kind enough to set me right with her Ladyship, which she can do so much better than I can."

Hall here related the whole of the conversation with Lee, word for word, as near as he could recollect it. While he progressed, the old veteran's brow at first loured, but presently cleared away again, and by the time Hall had finished. he was laughing quite heartily. When this humor had somewhat spent itself, he wiped the tears from his eyes, and extended his hand to

Hall, saying—" Never mind *him* ; if I had been here, the affair would not have occurred ; and if you had known him as well as I do, you would have given the whole thing the go-by, more especially as it was no more your interest to quarrel with him than it is mine. In your case, there is an estate pending, in which his good opinion is worth cultivating, and in mine, there is a vote in the House of Burgesses ; but I suppose it is too late to mend the matter between you now."

" It is, your Excellency." He did not tell him of the rencounter in the garden—he did not think it necessary.

" But tell me Mr. Hall, is this true that I hear, that you are likely to carry off the Doctor's charming daughter after all, against all these rich and high born rivals ?—you need not blush man, I meant no insinuation against your own parentage. Was Lee's rumpus nothing but a freak of jealousy ?"

" Nothing else, sir, I solemnly believe, not that there was the least foundation for it. I have put in no claim to the lady."

" Aye, claims refers to rights, and these are rights something like squatting upon lands or our corn laws, which you have heard talked of no doubt. Is it so, and have you been squatting upon Lee's lands ? Come man, out with it."

' No your Excellency—my temporary association with Miss Evylin grew entirely out of her solicitude for another. I have no right to bring those matters farther into discussion between us ; but assure you, sir, that our frequent meetings had very little to do with me personally, any more than the reader of an interesting history has to do with the historian."

"Well, well, it is best, perhaps, as it is. Here comes John—I will leave you with him, for I want you to get well acquainted. You will find that he has an ardent thirst for military adventure ; in the meantime, be sure I will set all things straight in the other end of the house."

John came hobbling upon his stick on one side, and leaning on Kate's arm on the other, looking very pale and care worn. His face, which was before full and unnaturally fleshy about its lower features, was now thin—clean cut and intellectual, with perhaps a dash of reckless determination about the thin closely compressed lips. He had evidently taken a prejudice against the Tutor, and notwithstanding Kate's warm encomiums, he received him coldly and rather cavalierly. Hall's late experience had well prepared him for this, and he bore it with patience and even humility. He waited for John to lead the subjects of conversation, and dropped in so gently, and yet threw so much light upon whatever he touched, that John was compelled to respect him, at least. Kate had left them together.

After John had conversed with the Tutor for an hour or two, his prejudices vanished, and he then communicated to him a proposition of his father's, and which he frankly confessed he was unwilling to do, until he had seen a little more of him. It was that Hall should proceed to the capital, taking with him the Scotch Irish recruits from York, and there take the command of the garrison in John's stead, until his health should be entirely restored.

Hall professed the utmost readiness to do so—indeed, he said he would prefer active employment in the present state of his mind, even to teaching master Bob, for whom, he said, he had taken a great liking.

" Well," continued John, " I must prepare you before hand for a motley array which you will find at the garrison. There are ten companies of the rangers, a little over two hundred men—they are old campaigners, and well enough, perhaps ; but if the volunteer militia, who have come in with their homespun clothes, and with the burrs yet in their horses' tails and manes, can be drilled into decent looking dragoons before we set out, I will call you a soldier indeed."

" Never fear, never fear," said Hall, rising at once to make his preparations for the march. " Some of Marlborough's bravest soldiers were doubtless once as raw as your homespun militia."

"Oh the materials are good enough," replied John, "these Virginia yeomanry would fight the devil, or thrice their number of Indians; it is their appearance which I fear will discourage you, but we are getting them equipped as fast as possible. You will find ten Lieutenants of Rangers, these we are distributing among the raw recruits, so that soon we hope to present quite an imposing little army to the good citizens of Williamsburg. The arms and accoutrements you will find in the tower, and at your disposal."

After receiving further instructions from the Governor, Hall was ready to set out for York. When he went to take leave of the ladies, he found Lady Spotswood somewhat mollified but still rather stately. Bob shed tears and begged to be permitted to march over the mountains with Mr. Hall. Dorothea and Kate were warm and unreserved in their good wishes, and old Dr. Blair bid him God speed. Ellen Evylin said little, but seemed to feel keenly that she was about to lose the society of one who had contributed not a little to that renovation of health and bloom spoken of in admiration by all the party just returned.

Hall cantered off, attended by old June, with a portmanteau bearing his baggage strapped behind his saddle. The former had already exchanged his seedy garments for those more becoming the society in which he had been moving, and every time he glanced at his external renovation, it rankled in his heart to think that the money with which they had been purchased, was obtained from Henry Lee, not that it long interrupted his reflections as he cantered down the avenue on his departure from a place where he had enjoyed so many hours of calm and delightful intercourse with its inmates. His thoughts were soon running upon far different matters than cocked hats, and silk hose, and velvet waistcoats. He had sought the Governor's country establishment as a quiet retreat, where he might for the present shun the observation of men, and though he was at first thrown into the company of some of the very persons whom he would have avoided, yet they were now gone, and he could have remained there for the short time still intervening before the departure of the family, without danger of exposure. He was ordered off just at this opportune moment, and into the most conspicuous part of the capital. Little did he imagine how speedily he would be removed from that position and in what manner! But we anticipate. There were other and gentler thoughts which forced themselves upon his attention. Could the image of that fair little blue eyed girl, be so soon obliterated from the memory even of an indifferent observer. But to him who stood sponsor, as it were, for her long lost lover, and with a skilful and gentle hand had led her back over memory's brightest and darkest pages, could he forget her? Was there no impression left upon his heart by an association so dangerous? Let those of our fair readers answer who have poured the tale of their unhappy loves into the willing ear of some very benevolent and sympathizing youth; for our part we question the stoicism of these youthful philosophers, as much as we question the possibility of platonic attachments between opposite sexes. Especially do we question the stoicism of the gentleman, where (as in the present case) the lady is young, lovely, and intelligent. We do not know that Ellen Evylin had a sly design upon the heart of the poor Tutor, but this we know, that he did not leave Temple Farm unscathed. But there were other difficulties gathering over his head, far more formidable than all the wounds of the heart.

CHAPTER XXV.

REFLECTIONS IN PRISON.

When Hall alighted at the Tavern in Williamsburg, after installing the York recruits at the Garrison, and delivering his credentials to the officer in command—he was met immediately by a man who was a stranger to him, but whom Hall soon discovered to have something sinister in the expression of his countenance. The stranger approached with one of those official bows; or, " Have I the pleasure of addressing Mr. Hall ?" said he.

" You have, Sir," replied the gentleman.

" Mr. Henry Hall, late Tutor at Temple Farm ?"

" The same, Sir."

" Will you be so good, Sir, as to cast your eye over that paper and tell me whether it is your signature ?"

Hall took the paper and colored slightly as he read it, and then turned pale as he answered, " It is, Sir."

" I am authorized by the gentleman in whose favor it is drawn, to request the payment."

" To request the payment !" exclaimed Hall, " why, Sir, the debt is not due to him, except nominally—the money was advanced to me voluntarily by him, as part of the proceeds of an estate which he himself informed me that I had fallen heir to, and he told me when that paper was given that it was intended as a mere voucher on the final settlement of the estate, and now he demands payment almost before the warmth of his hands is off the money."

" I am sorry, Sir, but I must do my duty."

" And I am, I suppose, more sincerely sorry—first that I took the money at all—secondly, that I spent it, after it was taken—and, thirdly, that I accepted an obligation at all from such a man."

" Then I am to understand that you cannot pay it."

" Not to-day, Sir—not until I can write to Gov. Spotswood."

" I am sorry again, Sir, but if you will read that paper, you will see that I am required to demand bail."

" What ?"

" Yes Sir, I am compelled to perform a disagreeable duty."

" And suppose I cannot give bail ?"

" Then you must go to jail, I am sorry to say, Sir; but you certainly have some friend who will go bail for your appearance."

" No one in the world—at least none here—let me see, is Dr. Evylin at home ?"

" I cannot say, but I will walk there with you, with pleasure."

Away they walked to the old Doctor's house.

How Hall's heart thumped as the Deputy Sheriff knocked at the door. It seemed to him as if every jolt upon the pannel was re-echoed by his ribs. The servant came, but informed them that the Doctor was out of town. Hall turned away, rather relieved than otherwise, so mortified was he, at the bare thoughts of asking the old gentleman to bail him from jail, the very first hour of his appearance in the capital of Virginia.

There was something inexpressibly sad in his voice and countenance, as he turned to the Sheriff and said : " I am ready now, Sir, to accompany you to jail, lead the way. I have no other acquaintance in the capital."

In half an hour he was sitting at the iron grated windows of the prison—situated in one of the lowest and most disagreeable spots of Williamsburg; but the locality affected him little. Time and place were to him matters of indifference.

He turned away from the window and paced his solitary cell. His thoughts became calmer by the exercise, and once his observation withdrawn from without, they naturally turned within. There all was calm, pure, and bright. He felt that thus far in the drama of life, he had most signally failed in his part, but he was conscious at the same time that he deserved to succeed. Like all the sons of Adam, he knew that he had erred, and of those errors he repented sincerely—but on the whole, his conscience bore good testimony upon the cross examination to which he now subjected it. He rapidly passed the main incidents of his life in review before him, and if he did not grow better from tracing out the causes of his present misfortunes, he certainly became wiser. What a crisis that is in the life of every man, when he thus pauses and contemplates the first failures of his youth. It is then that the arch enemy of mankind is busiest with his infernal sophistry. He even suggests doubts of the beneficence of the Creator, and questions whether we are not, after all, made in mockery and derision—whether our globe is not one grand theatre; mankind the performers; and the universe sitting round in the immensity of space, the audience.

These satanic suggestions find too ready a response in many young hearts, upon the first experience of disappointment. To a sufferer, farce and tragedy, and melo-drama, seem indeed strangely and inextricably mixed up in this life— tragedy treading so closely on the heels of farce, that it is hard to draw the true moral solution of the wonderful mystery of human life.

One of the wisest and wittiest of mankind has boldly called " the world a stage, and all the men and women actors ;" but if it be so, it is the stage reversed—for in real life, the actors lead off in broad farce, and as invariably end in dire tragedy. Oh! if this life is indeed but a frolic for the amusement of the Gods, it is a bitter jest at which angels might weep. If such alone were the aim and object of our existence, it was a cruel mockery to add sensibility to pain, to our capacity for pleasure. Hall had arrived just at that critical period of life where the buffoonery ends. He had for the better part of his days been playing in genteel comedy, and of late had taken a few turns in the tragedy. It was time then to pause and examine the contract, to see whether he was to play as a mountebank or a hero. It is a solemn and important question in the life of every individual, upon its answer depends his weal or wo, throughout his after existence. Oh, happy is that youth, who comes out of the conflict resolved to pursue the cause of right, and justice, and virtue, and religion, leaving the consequences wholly with that great and Almighty Being, who is the author and manager of the mystery which we cannot solve.

That man's heart never was in the right place, or rather it never was enlightened with a spark from the true divinity, who suffers the wrongs of the world to lead and persuade him to desperation.

Not for one moment did Hall's heart waver under the solemn jugglery of the great author of evil, though his meshes were around him everywhere. He felt himself a prisoner. He was resolved to adjourn his case to the keeping of Providence. Oh! what a great and triumphant court that is, even in this world. The retributive court of equity ! Let the triumphant victor in the court below carry off his perishing honors ; there is a silent witness in the busy throng of evil-doers who comes to the stand at last, and rights the injured and the oppressed, by the very hands of the oppressors. When some striking event of retributive providence happens to be revealed to the gaze of men, how they gape and wonder at the moral miracle, as if God who worketh in secret were not always overruling the rulers of this world. Let the inmates of penitentiaries, and the confessions of criminals under the gallows, speak to the point. Trace out the small and almost invisible links of circumstances by which their guilt is at last revealed, and the finger of the Almighty is at the end of it. The gaping crowd of their fellow-sinners calls the immediate cause of the development an accident ; but these things, call them what you will, have lost or won the greatest battles ever fought upon earth. The whole machinery of the world, both moral and physical, is managed by the same Almighty invisible hand, which strikes sparks from these electric chains. None but the good are truly wise—such are the men who surrender up the mysterious management of the universe into the hands to which it truly belongs—such are the men who are content to pursue simple and unostentatious virtue, leaving consequences, which must be so left at last by every one, to the only living and true God—such are the men who become as little children, and are willing to follow where they know that no mortal may lead. Hall felt that he could not extricate himself from the accumulating difficulties which surrounded him, but his heart had been bruised, and torn, and subdued, until he now calmly surrendered the guidance of his destiny into wiser and better hands; he fully trusted and believed in an all-wise and overruling providence—he clearly and unequivocally acknowledged it.

He had weighed *the great* argument of all the wicked of the earth—the arch tempter had already turned his eyes to the apparent triumph of villainy, thrift and fawning, throughout all the walks of life, and consequent depression of honesty and humble virtue, and he deliberately chose the latter as his portion.

When the rain falls and the floods descend, the gathering torrent rushes down the accustomed channels in a noisy turbid stream. To the inexperienced, it looks as if it never would or could become clear again; but presently the pure and limpid mountain stream begins to work its bright way through the centre of the angry current—for a while it is lost and swallowed up in the surrounding filth, but slowly and silently the work of purification goes on, the muddy and turbulent waves are hurried toward the ocean, and their places are supplied by the purified waters from above. So it is with the current of human life; wave after wave of the busy and noisy throng of the corrupt and the vicious are hurried on to the great ocean of eternity, while their places are slowly but surely filling up with brighter and purer races of men. The world is as certainly growing wiser and better, as that its destinies are ruled over by an all-wise and beneficent spirit. The pure and limpid stream of christian truth is forever working its slow and silent course among the turbid waves of sin and pollution, until the whole ocean of humanity shall be purified.

Hall was by no means a perfect man, but he now had the sincere desire to purge his own heart from all those turbulent passions which had thus far brought nothing but misery and wretchedness in their train. He did not, it is true, elongate his visage and whine psalms through his nose, and proclaim to all the world that he was a changed man, but his misfortunes were working their proper office upon his mind and heart. He was truly humbled in spirit—he felt that there was a mightier hand at work with all the intricacies in which he had been successively involved, than the proud and envious young man who was the immediate instrument of his sufferings.

When the sufferer is able to draw this very definition between the correction from on high, and the poor instrument in whose hands it is placed, it is one of the first great lessons in the heart's purification, because he at once learns to look more in sorrow than in anger upon the immediate author of his woes, while he bows in humble humility before that power, against which it is impossible to feel personal malevolence. Happy is that prisoner who first frees his soul from the bondage of death!

We would not present the imprisoned youth as one who had made large strides in the upward and difficult journey which leads by a narrow path and a straight gate, but as one who had learned that the great thoroughfare of mankind leads to death. He was a mere neophyte, and the best evidence that he had a true and sincere desire to turn from his evil ways, was that he felt as a mere child—he surrendered himself wholly to the guidance of that unseen power which had already so wonderfully delivered him. Alas, his trials were not near ended. In the very hour that many such thoughts as we have condensed were passing through his mind, there was one sojourning in the same town busy entangling the web more inextricably around him. In the very hour that Hall sat down to write a short note to Gov. Spotswood, another individual was penning a very different epistle for the same eye, to be conveyed by the same messenger, old June.

~~~~~~~~~~~~~~~~~~~~~~~~~~~~~~~~~~~~~~~

CHAPTER XXVI.

THE LETTERS CONTRASTED.

It was at night, the candles burned brightly, and the fire blazed cheerfully, while the Governor's family and guests were seated in the same room in which we first presented them. A more than usual cheerfulness pervaded the family circle, not only on account of the Governor's brightening prospects, with regard to the great enterprise of his life, but likewise on account of John's returning health. They all thought the mystery now cleared up, and that henceforth his bright career would go on brightening as in days of yore. Essex had already announced June's arrival from the capital, having just learned the fact from a little negro who conveyed the important tidings from the kitchen. He went out to bring in any letters or messages which June might have brought, and soon returned with the two epistles alluded to in the last chapter.

The consternation of the circle may be imagined, when the following letter was read from Hall. They had all before perceived that something therein contained, had moved the Governor greatly. It ran as follows :

"*James City Jail, Williamsburg.*

"To His Excellency, Sir Alexander Spotswood.

"Dear Sir.—You will no doubt be surprised that I date this letter from the county jail, instead of the barracks, but, Sir, so it is—deeply mortifying as it is to me to state the fact. I had scarcely alighted in the capital, after marching the soldiers to the garrison, before I was waited upon by the Deputy Sheriff of the county, with a bail writ, (or whatever that process is called by which the law seizes a man's person,) at the suit of Henry Lee, Esq., and for the very money which your Excellency was mainly instrumental in procuring at his hands for me. You will recollect, no doubt, *that as a mere matter of form,* (so the gentleman expressed it,) I gave him a note of hand for the amount. Unfortunately I paid away part of the sum for my passage money, and the remainder to recruit my dilapidated wardrobe, so that instant payment was out of the question. None of my new and kind friends were in the city. I had, indeed, hoped to find the good Doctor at home, but unfortunately for me he was absent in the country.

" I had no other friend upon whom I dared call—indeed, to confess the truth to your Excellency, I have not a friend left in the whole world, now living, upon whom I have any right to make a demand for such help as my circumstances require. This, my honored Sir, is but a passage in the chapter of accidents which have fallen to my lot in the last few years, and until the storm has spent its fury, it would seem useless to attempt to assist me. I will honestly confess to you, that I came to this country at this time to avoid those very difficulties (or kindred ones) which have assailed me here. A superstitious man might be inclined under such circumstances to imagine himself pursued by some invisible agency, but I have no such idle fears. *I know my persecutors well,* and I can afford, even in my humble lodgings, to pity them. I am very sure that I am a happier man this evening, than he at whose suit I am thus deprived of my liberty.

" I have accidentally heard that he utters very bitter and unwarrantable things against me, and even threatens a prosecution for swindling. My ears tingle as I write the word, but I may as well write that which I may soon be compelled to endure the odium of in a more tangible shape. All that I can say to your Excellency, and to those who have hitherto espoused my humble cause, is, that I rest for the present in the calm and perfect security of an injured and innocent man, trusting that that God who has permitted the snares of the wicked thus to gather round me, will clear them away in his own good time. This, you may think and say, is poor evidence with which to furnish you, against one so rich and powerful as my adversary; but, Sir, it is even so—it is all I have to give at present. Under such circumstances, I shall not be the least surprised to find that you have turned me over to the tender mercies of my creditor. I cannot hope that my unsustained protestations of innocence of the charges that I hear he brings against me, will be sustained. So let it be. I am willing to sojourn even in this dreary prison for a while, well assured that the time will come, when my name will once again be redeemed from reproach—until then, I must be content to subscribe myself your Excellency's obliged humble servant.   HARRY HALL."

A profound silence prevailed while the Governor (spectacles on nose) read over this letter. The letter remained in his hand, and his hand on his knee, while with the other he raised the spectacles upon his forehead, in a thoughtful abstracted mood. The young ladies waited in respectful silence for a few moments, expecting every instant that he would burst out into some vehement exclamation—they could not long suppress their own indignation. Ellen Evylin was the first to give utterance to her excited feelings, which she did in no measured terms. Kate took the same view of the subject—while Lady Spotswood remained entirely silent, watching the changes of her husband's countenance with not a little interest, heightened no doubt by the late circumstances which had happened under her own eye.

Dorothea wanted to know how the Sheriff could take Mr. Hall for borrowing his own money from Mr. Lee.

"A very pertinent question," said her father, with a nod of approbation.

Carter declared the *denouement* was what he had been looking for for some time, and appealed to Moore, whether he had not predicted it when they were last at the capital.

Moore confirmed the fact of the statement, but demurred to the truth of the charges, alleging his still undiminished confidence in Hall, whatever might be the apparent suspicious circumstances against him. "Suppose your Excellency would read Lee's version of the affair—I see his seal upon the letter before you," said he.

"True, true, I had overlooked it, in the first excitement produced by Hall's letter—let us hear the other side." Saying which he broke the seal, and read as follows:

"*Williamsburg.*

"To his Excellency, Sir Alexander Spotswood, Lieutenant Governor of Virginia, and Commander of Her Majesty's forces.

"DEAR SIR: I owe you an apology for the very abrupt manner in which I left your house, where I had been tacitly, as it were, left in charge of the ladies; but the fact is, Sir, that I found the young person whom you had hastily employed as Tutor, presumptuous and impertinent, and that I must either degrade myself by a personal encounter with him, or leave the premises. I chose the latter, and had hoped to have paid my respects to your Excellency before you left the capital, but was detained by unavoidable legal business until you had unfortunately left the city. It is useless now to enter into particulars as to his conduct in your absence; for the evidence is now before me, that he is such a gross impostor and swindler, that it is scarcely worth while to inquire into minor particulars of conduct. While I was in the very act of consulting Attorney General Clayton, (who is also my own legal adviser,) about the steps necessary to be taken in order to repossess the funds out of which I weakly suffer myself to be cheated, I received a ship letter by way of York. Whom does your Excellency suppose that letter was from? Why, sir, from Mr. Henry Hall, my cousin, the real gentleman, whose name and character this base impostor had assumed for the lowest purposes. You will recollect that I had written to the young man before this person appeared at your house, informing him of my aunt's will. This letter which I have received is in answer to that one, and states among other things that the writer would sail in the very first vessel for this country after the one which would bring the letter, so that by the time that this pseudo Mr. Hall manages to release himself from prison, where I have snugly stowed him, the real personage, whose name he has assumed, will be here to confront him. I am delighted that I am thus able to relieve your Excellency from the disagreeable duty of unmasking the impostor; for if your Excellency will permit me to say so, your kindly nature had so far led you astray with regard to this man, that you might have found it rather unpleasant to deal with him. Leave all that to me, Sir—I will give him his deserts, be well assured; and if he escapes with whole ears and a sound skin, he may thank the clemency of the law, and not mine.

" I have the honor to be your Excellency's most obedient, humble servant,
                        "HENRY LEE, of Westmoreland."

The party was truly astonished by these two letters, both conveying such surprising news. The Governor took a few turns hastily through the room, pained and excited. He was very loth to give up one for whom he had taken such a liking, and for whom he intended such an important share in the great enterprise; but the evidence was too plain and palpable to be resisted, and he resolved to let the law take its course. As he came to this conclusion, he threw himself into a chair and exclaimed, " By heavens I would have believed nothing less!" " And I do not believe this," said Ellen vehemently, her eye bright with excitement, and her frame quivering with the thoughts which oppressed her.

The Governor was reclining in his arm chair in an attitude almost of hopelessness, but when Ellen uttered her bold challenge of the truth of Lee's statement, he sat bolt upright, as if his mind would seize upon the slightest pretext to reinstate his favorite. " Why, what reason have you to doubt Harry Lee's veracity, Miss Evylin?" said he.

" The best evidence in the world, Governor Spotswood. He has committed as great mistakes as this before."

" Indeed, do you mean to say that the young gentleman has ever knowingly swerved from the truth."

" I cannot say whether it was knowingly or whether it is his remarkable obliquity of moral vision, but I assert the fact, that he has before wronged others, as much as I believe he now wrongs this unfortunate young gentleman."

"You surprise me exceedingly—do tell me, I pray you, who the person was?"

" Well, Sir, I have no objection to saying that it was myself."

All the gentlemen exclaimed at once, " What, a lady!"

" Further than that," continued Ellen, " I do not say at present."

The Governor seemed very much perplexed to know what to do—he strode rapidly about the room—his lips compressed, and his shaggy brows louring over his eyes, and muttering violent expressions through his clenched teeth. While he was thus swayed by contending emotions, Moore rose hastily, took his hat, and left the room. In a few minutes he was followed by Ellen Evylin, and soon afterwards by Kate. The latter found Ellen in a most earnest conversation with the former in the verandah. She had never seen her friend under such excitement. She was pressing upon Mr. Moore a purse of gold which she held in her extended hand, and which she plead with him to take.

"No, no, no," said Moore, "I will attend to all that—guilty or innocent, he shall have the benefit of the bare doubt. To-morrow morning's sun shall see him a free man. Will that not content you ?"

"No, indeed, Mr. Moore—it will not—I claim to have rights in this matter which you have not. I beg of you not to deny me."

"But my dear young lady, if I take your gold and offer it to him, it will be the very way to make him refuse the assistance ; many a sensitive man will accept aid from his own sex, when he would peremptorily refuse it from one of your's."

"Well, take it and give it, without letting him know from whom it comes. I ask it as a particular favor."

"Do, Mr. Moore," said Kate pleadingly, and with a look which was irresistible.

"By all that's lovely," said Moore gaily, as he pocketed the gold, and threw on his cloak for the night's ride, "I think I will contrive some way to get into jail myself, if it is only to excite the tears of sympathy in so many lovely eyes. Suppose I find myself in the young man's position before morning, do you think I should have a couple of as fair damsels contriving my release ?"

"Indeed you shall," said Kate.

"Good night," said Moore, kissing his hand gallantly, and striking his spurs into his horse at the same moment.

The girls returned to their own apartment, and there Ellen informed Kate of all that had transpired in her absence, but still there were many things wanting, even to them, to unravel the mystery of the two Halls.

A very keen encounter of tongues was going on below meanwhile, between Dorothea and Carter. The latter contended that Hall was a bold bungling impostor, and that he had seen through him at a glance, and that he had no pretensions to gentility whatever."

"How comes it, then, Mr. Carter," asked Dorothea, "that he overmastered so many of you at accomplishments considered quite refined ? How was it at the small sword ?"

"Oh, any French dancing-master may and often does possess such tricks."

"Aye, but French dancing-masters do not often read the classics very elegantly, if at all ; and here is Dr. Blair, who says that Mr. Hall is an elegant scholar."

"Doubtless a schoolmaster, then, some broken down pedagogue."

"But papa says, he is an accomplished and scientific soldier."

"Learned no doubt, while acting as drummer or fifer to some marching regiment—said you not a while ago that he played upon the flute ?"

"Yes," said Dorothea, "he is a musician."

"I'll tell you what it is, Carter," interposed the Governor, "if Hall is a hypocrite and impostor, he is one of the most accomplished swindlers that ever I have met with. It is a rare thing in my experience of human nature— and it has not been confined in its range—to see a man descending in villainy, and elevating himself at the same time in all the elegant courtesies of life. Neither is it common to see men of that stamp cultivating their minds highly."

"Oh I grant you," said Carter, "that he is no common vagabond—he is a very accomplished rogue, if you will, but still a sly rogue for all that."

"I am not so sure about that," replied the Governor. "There may be some mistake, or Harry Lee may have been imposed upon, or his own feelings may have colored the matter too highly."

"What ! your Excellency ? When he has actually received a letter—a foreign letter too—with the European post mark, from his real cousin—could his imagination make facts, stubborn facts, like these? No, no—either Hall is a consummate swindler and impostor, or Harry Lee is an outrageous liar—one or other horn of the dilemma you must take."

"It has an ugly aspect to be sure," said the Governor musingly, and dropping off into a brown study, while Carter turned once more to the playful and amusing combat with his little lady antagonist. But we must follow the main thread of our narrative; while they are thus agreeably employed.

CHAPTER XXVII.

THE WANDERER.

It was a bright moonlight night, and Moore rode merrily on his way, notwithstanding the melancholy nature of his errand. His fancy was busy with the sweet pleading Kate—he remembered only that her eyes had rested upon him, with confidence that her appeal would not be in vain. So busy was his memory with the most delicate shadows of his mistress' countenance, that he was entirely unconscious that he was riding the fine animal which he bestrode at a murderous rate, until his servant made an appeal in behalf of the horse.

His train of reflections were now turning to the other end of the road. He had a disagreeable duty before him, not in liberating Hall, for that was pleasant to his feelings, but he would be constrained to show that his confidence had been a little shaken, far more than he had been willing to acknowledge to the friends whom he had just left.

This business of the two Halls bore an ugly aspect, and he dreaded the laceration of feeling he would suffer in seeing a man of gentlemanly feelings floundering between inextricable tergiversations. Unless Hall came down frankly and explained the difficulty, he was resolved to make short work of his liberation and be done with him. He began to see, moreover, that he was about to interfere in a more delicate affair than he at first imagined. Not that he was a man to shrink from a task he had undertaken because of any displeasure of Harry Lee, on his own account; he was anxious to make fair weather with him because of the Governor's interests.

He rode immediately to the house of the Sheriff whom he well knew, and roused him up. The whole city was buried in slumber, and Hall himself no doubt slept soundly after the wholesome and honest self-examination through which he had put himself. The jailor was next aroused, and together they proceeded to the apartment of the prisoner. He was, indeed, very unromantically sleeping soundly, wrapped up in his old military cloak, and stretched at full length upon a hard straw mattrass. Moore stood and gazed at him for a few moments, and then remarked to the Sheriff, "that man's face in the *honest expression of sleep*, looks as little like that of a swindler, as any man's I have ever seen. It is impossible to look at him thus without being interested in his fate."

"Fact, Sir, said the Sheriff, he has a taking away with him, he has the whole establishment here, jailors, family and all, interested for him already, but it is generally the way with your gentlemanly rogues. I have seen some of them, capital company."

"You think him a swindler then?" asked Moore sadly.

"Certain I do sir. What else can he be when he takes another man's name in order to swindle honest people with it.

Moore paid the money without further words, and had, influenced by the homely common sense of the hard official, determined to slip away without being seen, but just as he was escaping, Hall sprang to his feet, very much startled and surprised by the lights and the persons he saw in the room, rubbing his eyes in perplexity and bewilderment. "Mr. Moore," he at length exclaimed, "I ought to say I am glad to see you, but I cannot do so honestly, under present circumstances."

"Not when I inform you that I come as a friend," inquired Moore.

"It will be a friend indeed who will adhere to me, under present circumstances," said Hall sadly.

Moore made a sign to the officials to withdraw, when they had done so, he drew one of the miserable stools which the place afforded, seated himself, and motioned for Hall to do likewise, which he did upon the edge of his rude couch.

"How far I may adhere to you," said he, "depends upon yourself. I have come to release you from confinement in any event."

"My mere liberation from this place, is a matter of little moment to me at present, not that I would in the smallest degree lessen the obligation which I am under to you for the generous intention, but that I consider my confinement here as a small portion of my embarrassments."

"Explain then to me, the mystery of the other Hall, you have doubtless heard that Mr. Lee has received an answer to his letter addressed to Mr. Hall, which he says, is the real one."

"I have indeed heard such a rumor, but I cannot do more at present than beg those who are disposed to befriend me, to suspend their opinions until the other Mr. Hall arrives. Let us be confronted, and then the mystery may be explained, and not until then."

"But why cannot you explain it all now, and authorize me to satisfy your anxious friends at Temple Farm? Surely this would seem to be the proper course for you to pursue."

"No one, Mr. Moore can judge of my circumstances but myself. No one could be more anxious than I am, to stand fair once more with the dear friends to whom you allude, but I must be content for the present to be suspected. I cannot expect them to take my character upon trust, under such adverse circumstances, and therefore, I do not ask it; all I do request is, for them to suspend their opinions of me if they can. I promise you that the time will come, when they will no longer blush to own me; but if they cannot even do that, and they must condemn me, I will not blame them. They shall not be troubled with my presence again until such time as I may be enabled to vindicate myself fully before the world."

"Well," said Moore rising and evidently chagrined and disappointed, "be it so. I cannot force your confidence; until the time you have mentioned—and for your own sake I hope it may come speedily—I must wait patiently; I at least will suspend my judgment. I am more than half willing to take you upon trust now, but I could not promise to reinstate you in the good opinion of all your friends so easily. You have therefore, I think, decided wisely to seclude yourself until such time as you are ready to clear your name and fame from all aspersions. You are free to go hence when you please, and I would advise it to be as speedily as possible, both from hence and from the capital. Your creditor will find other means to seize upon your person; indeed I have heard that he meditated a criminal prosecution. Excuse me, Sir, but I must be plain with you."

"No apology is necessary to one in my situation, and more especially for an act of kindness. My desperate fortunes have arrived at that pass when it will not do for me to shrink at the bare mention of those things which I may be compelled to experience in the next twenty-four hours."

Seeing Moore about to depart, he followed him to the door, and extended his hand, as he continued, "Farewell, Sir. I shall never forget that you have rode eight miles and perilled a considerable sum of money to befriend one against whom the world is *almost* unanimous in its condemnation."

"No, no, not unanimous, Mr. Hall, there are gentle hearts at 'the Farm' whom any man would feel flattered to have interested as you have—there is a warm interest in your favor there, at least. You don't know how much you are indebted to them for my exertions, which you are so willing to attribute to my generosity alone. You may find out some day that I am not so disinterested after all. Farewell, farewell. I hope we may soon meet under happier auspices."

Saying which he left the prison, leaving Hall standing at the door, wrapt in profound reflection. Recovering from his abstraction, he bundled up what few things he could call his own, tied them up in a pocket handkerchief, and sallied out into the dark wide world, not to seek his fortune, but repose from the turmoil of life, and its fierce passions and bitter enmities, and heartless friendships. His rapid strides soon threw the capital far in his rear. Solitary and disheartened he passed along the dreary road, cut through the tall pines those most melancholy of trees. It was a silent and solemn walk in the moonlight, with no other company, but the grand and gloomy old forest, which had stood there before the soil was ever pressed by the foot of the white man. It is a cheerless occupation to walk alone at night, at all times, but when one sets out, a wanderer from the haunts of men, fleeing from unknown evil, and seeking repose in total seclusion, he is a philosopher or a christian if he does not repine at his lot. Hall had one cheering star of hope still glimmering in his dark horizon, bright eyes and warm hearts still glistened and pulsated in his behalf, as Moore informed him. "Oh woman!" exclaimed he, as he trudged on his otherwise painful journey, "Oh woman! blessed angel of love, and mercy, and charity—this earth were indeed a gloomy and dreary waste without thee—may my lot be indeed what it now promises, if ever I again doubt thee. Oh, blessed one above all her sex, pure and bright and constant as yon polar star, may an omnipotent and overruling Providence guard thee, as it has hitherto done, from the snares of the wicked, untill I may once more resume my proper station in society—and then—!"

THE KNIGHTS

OF THE

H O R S E - S H O E;

A TRADITIONARY TALE

OF THE

COCKED HAT GENTRY

IN THE

OLD DOMINION.

VOLUME II.

CHAPTER I

THE GOVERNOR'S LEVEE.

WILLIAMSBURG, one of the ancient capitals of Virginia, was first laid out in the shape of the letter W, in honor of the Prince after whom it was named, and through whose munificence its principal ornament was first endowed. This strange and even enigmatical plot of the town was, however, soon abandoned for one more consonant with the natural features of its admirable position.

The houses of the gentry were principally built upon one great thoroughfare, and this was then called the Duke of Gloucester street—for shortness, Gloucester street. At one end, and immediately at right angles to it, stood, and yet stands, William and Mary College; and at the other, about three-quarters of a mile distant, the capital.

These two edifices at once gave a character and dignity to the place; and the traveller even now turns his head naturally, first to the one and then to the other, as he enters the ancient city. We have entered the modern Babel of our country, and, like all other neophytes, have been deeply impressed with the tumultuous and thronging ideas and sensations which they produced, but never have we been so deeply impressed as while entering for the first ttme the scene where those old ruinous walls were once vocal with the eloquence of Patrick Henry, on the one hand, and the academic shades on the other, where Jefferson and Madison wandered in the days of their boyhood, and where was concocted the first germ of that rebellion which eventuated in the

most glorious structure of civil liberty which the eye of man has ever yet
looked upon.

Strange, that the thousands who live under its benign influence—and Virginians especially—have no curiosity to visit this ancient cradle of our liber-
ties. It lies gradually mouldering to decay, and only saved from utter demo-
lition, by the noble literary institution, which has survived alike the royal and
republican capital. Long may it rear its noble head above the ruins which
surround it, the great conservator, of all that remains of Virginia's ancient
metropolis, as well as the stern republican principles which first had their
growth beneath its portals.

About the centre of Gloucester-street, two parallel avenues of noble trees
led through a green lawn, near two hundred yards, to the front of the Palace.
A little to the left of this opening, as you faced the Palace, stood the Episcopal Church, then recently built. On the opposite side of the street, its line
was again broken a little nearer to the Capitol, by a public square, in which
were contained the Market-House and the military round tower, already
alluded to as having been erected by Governor Spotswood. Facing this public
square, was a small Theatre,* and nearly opposite to all these again, on the
other side of the street, was the hotel frequented by the gentry and Burgesses,
when the assembly was in session.

The Palace was a large brick building, flanked on the right and left by two
smaller ones, nearly adjoining it, one of which contained, the dormitories and
offices connected with the culinary department, and appropriated exclusively by
the servants—the other contained the Governor's library, official departments,
&c., &c., so the whole of the main building was appropriated to the elegant
and extensive hospitalities, at all times considered as appertaining to the Gubernatorial mansion in Virginia.

It was a few days after Hall's departure from prison, upon his melancholy
pilgrimage, that the well known sound of a trumpet startled the denizens of
the city—many of them from their early dinners. It proceeded from the Governor's body guard, not yet visible in the city, but the enlivening blast of the
bugle could be heard, from time to time, as they wound along the turnings of
the road—the breeze sometimes wafting its mellow sounds to the ear, and, at
others, suffering them to fall faintly in the distance, as it lulled with the breeze.

It was always a glad day to the citizens when the Governor and his family
returned from his summer residence. Joy was visible upon the countenances
of the portly dames and merry urchins, as they crowded round their respec-
tive doors, to welcome back the loved inmates of the Palace. Near the gate
of the mansion, among the trees of the double avenue, stood a long line of little
girls all dressed in white, with flowers in their hands, waiting to strew the
path of the ladies from the carriage to the house. They were pupils of a
female school, of which Lady Spotswood was chief patron.

First came a company of Rangers, which had been detailed to escort the
Governor, followed by the veteran body guard, all in full regimentals. Then
his Excellency, with his staff, and male guests, on horseback—next, the state
coach with the Governor's immediate family, and Dr. Evylin's carriage containing his daughter, alone ; the rear of the cavalcade brought up by the family
servants, in carriages and on horseback, old Essex riding at their head, like a
field-marshal, and June bringing up the extreme rear, awfully carricaturing the
Major's stately equestrianism.

The troops on duty at the capital, consisting mostly of Rangers—under the
command of Duke Holloway, second to John Spotswood—were drawn up on
the green in front of the Palace, and presented arms as the Governor ap-

* We have undoubted authority—both traditional and historical—for the assertion, that a
Theatre existed at the time stated, though overlooked, if not denied, by Dunlap.

proached: the military escort filing to the right and left as they entered the avenues.

Dr. Evylin's carriage drove on to his private residence, which stood a little back from Gloucester street, between the Church and the College, embowered in trees and vines, and presenting to the eye one of the sweetest retreats it was possible to imagine, in the midst of the capital. Every thing about the premises gave evidence of the ministering hand of that gentle and tasteful spirit, which, since the death of the Doctor's lady, had conducted all his household affairs. The good old physician stood at the wicket gate, almost as impatient as a lover, to throw his arms round the neck of his cherished idol. Even before entering the house, they walked hand in hand among the fast fading shrubs and flowers, the old man giving an account of his stewardship, during his daughter's absence, and having a little history ready for each favorite plant. How these gentle and humanising affections, throw a mellow hue over such trifles as these, and how the heart loves to toy with them on the surface, while its depths, like a deep and silent stream, are tossed all the more for the serene calm above. The servants too, loved their young mistress, and came flocking round, dropping their rude curtsies and awkward bows, and asking about her health as if she had crossed the Atlantic. Each one expressed delight at the renovated bloom of their favorite, and the old Doctor himself, seemed so happy at the change, that he became almost as puerile as any of them. Once more seated in their quiet parlor, Ellen's arm thrown affectionately round her father's neck, we will leave her to detail all the transactions of the Governor's country establishment, while we return to the Palace, where the bustle and excitement of the important arrivals still continued.

The city was thronged with visitors, brought together by the proclamations of the Governor, inviting them thither ; and also by the arrival of many of the Burgesses, who came in obedience to the call of his Excellency for the assembling of their body, somewhat in anticipation of their usual time of meeting.

In the evening, a levee was held, where all the gentry, without distinction of party, were expected to call and pay their respects.

The Governor was very much gratified to find that his proclamation, containing the scheme for new conquests of lands, had fired either the cupidity or ambition of most of the young men of the colony ; but while he listened, with sparkling eye and gratified feelings, to the plans of his young friends, he could not resist the feelings of regret which the subject brought with it, for the young Secretary who had originated the scheme. His eye turned anxiously to the door at each successive arrival of guests, but Hall made not his appearance. He had been greatly prepossessed in favor of this young man, and notwithstanding the powerful array of circumstances against him, he was loth to give him up entirely. He still hoped that something would turn up, to prove at least that he was not criminal. In these hopes, he was seconded by most of the females of the family. Kate and Dorothea at all times expressed their most decided convictions, that he would yet turn out to be a gentleman of untarnished name ; and Ellen, before her departure from the country seat, could brook no suspicions of his integrity or honor. She maintained openly, that there were no charges against him, except those brought by Harry Lee, and that she was ready at any time to lay as great ones at his own door, if necessary, and, consequently, that he was not an unimpeached witness.

It was expected by the young ladies that something would turn up during the evening, by which Mr. Lee might understand, that Hall's case was espoused by them, and that they intended to carry the war home to him if he continued his persecutions against their favorite. Only one thing prevented an open rupture between the parties. Lee was a member of the House of

Burgesses, as before stated, and the Governor wanted his vote.   He had consequently warned them against a premature move in the matter.   Those however who are experienced with the world, will understand how difficult it was for him to make the ladies of his establishment understand any thing of political expediency.

Lee was among the earliest arrivals, and it may be well imagined that his movements did not pass unnoticed by any of the parties just mentioned.   His first demonstration however was in quite an unexpected quarter, on encountering Bernard Moore, soon after paying his respects to the Governor and his Lady, he, treated him with the utmost hauteur and disdain.   Not a hand was extended by either party.   Moore was quite taken by surprise, but, in a moment recollected his late interference in Lee's schemes of revenge.   He passed on, after a cold and distant bow, a smile of derision playing about his mouth. Could he have seen Kate's eyes flashing fire and indignation, as she witnessed the interview, he would have been truly flattered and pleased and, perhaps might have sought a renewal of the experiment, but he did not ; he passed on, and joined himself with more congenial spirits than Harry Lee, and soon forgot that young gentleman, amidst the animated discussion going on relative to the tramontane expedition.   Not so with Kate, she followed with her eyes, the haughty young aristocrat's movements wherever he went.   She was moved by strong impulses, which brooked no control from cold political expediency.   She was all a woman in her feelings; and like a woman would she have acted, had the opportunity offered.   Fortunately for her father's interests, no occasion was presented for the execution of the plans of the female trio, those developements were destined to fulfilment in another quarter. Ellen Evylin was not present at the Levee, seeing which, Mr. Lee soon absented himself from the party, and bent his steps toward the Doctor's house. He rejoiced in his own mind, that it was so ; for he now imagined, that he had placed the man who had interfered with his movements in such a light, that Ellen must feel nothing but gratitude towards him for his efforts in the cause. Such were his anticipations as he lifted the knocker of the Doctor's door—he was admitted.   What occurred at the interview will be related in the next chapter.

<center>~~~~~~~~~~~~~~~~~~~~~~</center>

CHAPTER II.

PROPOSALS OF MARRIAGE.

How delightfully fell the impress of all he saw upon the cold nature of Harry Lee ?   How his intense selfishness warmed itself by the cosy fire blazing in the hearth ?   The pictures that hung round the walls, too, delighted him, because they were many of them painted by a hand that he hoped to call his own.   He stood before them in succession, and pleased himself to think, how the same gentle hand would sketch the glorious landscapes presented, in many aspects upon his own thousand acres.   The sweet flowers, too, snugly stowed away from the rude September blasts, in a little glass conservatory, separated from the room in which he was, but by a single step. He walked out into the green artificial summer, the lights of the parlor windows threw their bright rays over and around, revealing a little aviary, high up among the green shrubbery.   Henry Lee knew every nook and corner about the charming little dove's nest which he intended to rob.   He was like a boy climbing a tree in search of such an object—his head grew dizzy, as the prospect of clutching the prize seemed just within his grasp.   He walked back—the nest was still warm, but he had frightened the pretty songster away A score of music was lying open upon the table, which she had evidently just left, in her precipitate retreat, for some of her female parapharnalia was lying beside it. He walked up and read the title of the song—it was in his brother's own hand writing. Hurriedly he closed the book, and wheeled upon his heel to another part of the room. He picked up a book, lying open in a rocking chair, the face turned down, as if it had likewise received a share of the lady's recent attention. He picked it up, and seated himself; the leaves fell over of themselves, as even they acquire habits sometime, and there again was his brother's name as the donor. It seemed as if his ghost was haunting him at every turn. He threw down the book hastily, and strode through the room with his head down, determined to see nothing more which might recall painful memories. At this moment, the old Doctor entered, cloaked up to the neck, a shawl tied over his cocked hat and under his chin, and his thin legs cased in warm cloth spatterdashes, buttoned up close to his knee buckles.

"Ah, good Doctor!" said Lee, advancing to meet him, "still administering to the sufferings of the sick and the afflicted? What a noble calling is yours?"

"Yes," said the Doctor, rather gruffly, as he took the proffered hand, before he seated himself over the blazing pine knots in the hearth. "Yes, it is indeed a noble profession, and all those should earn the crown of martyrdom who practise it."

"You surprise me, sir—I thought, if there was a man in the world satisfied with the lot which had fallen to him, it was Dr. Evylin!"

"And so I am; but that makes the remark I made none the less true. I am content to be a martyr. It is true, that I am sometimes a little chafed, that men look upon our paths as if they were strewed with flowers."

"Well, Doctor, I confess that I am one who looked upon your profession as affording the highest gratification to its followers. You are always relieving the pains and sufferings of others."

"No, not always; we stand by a dying patient powerless, and feeling as nothing before the great Ruler, who holds the destinies of man in his hands. But that is not all; we are forever shouldering the troubles of other people—always looking upon the black shadows of the picture of human life—it is impossible for one of my profession to be uniformly cheerful. Then, its dreadful responsibilities weigh down all those who have any sensibility, and only such are fit to enter a family when the hearts of all its members are laid bare; when the lacerated affections require to be ministered to as well as the physical suffering. One advantage we have over other men: we see less of the hypocrisy of our race than they do; suffering stamps a solemn sincerity upon every countenance around a sick couch. I was called, the other night, to visit one of the comedians of our little Theatre—he was very sick, and his bedside surrounded by his brethren of the sock and buskin in the same dresses which they had just worn upon the stage. Farce and Comedy sunk abashed before the Tragedy of real life. The sufferer himself, though the principal comedian, was one of the most captious and fretful men I ever attended. The scene impressed me powerfully—yet, somewhat of the same thing is presented to me daily. The sick couch disrobes every man of his masquerading dress."

"Yes," said Lee, musing, "you have fine opportunities to study human nature. You see it in its undress."

"Aye," replied the Physician, "we do see it in a state of nudity truly, and the disrobing adds nothing to the beauty and symmetry. One half of our race, at least, is presented in entirely different aspects from what it appears to other men. The male portion appear in new and untried lights on the sick couch."

"Ah! is there then so much difference in the sexes?"

"Aye, truly—women, in civilized countries, are constant inhabitants of the house, and often even of a single room, and sickness makes no such great change in this respect to them, but there are characteristic differences besides those produced by habit and occupation—and all telling in favor of the weaker sex. They are much purer in heart than we are, Mr. Lee, much more elevated in sentiment, more patient and hopeful in suffering, with a much livelier and realizing faith in the power and presence of an overruling Providence. Seeing these thing, it almost looks wrong, to one of my profession, to see them excluded from active participation in more than half of all the concerns of life. They have not yet, with all our boasted refinement and civilization, their due influence."

"That is made up, Sir, by their sway over the hearts of men."

"Ah, that may do very well for a very young man to say, at such an age, it is boasted of and paraded as an excuse for our wrongs, but old men know how long it lasts, especially old Physicians—it lasts a much shorter time than the honey money."

Ellen entered at this moment, and returned Lee's salutation with a cold and formal inclination of the head. Her lips were compressed in a way quite unnatural to them, and giving a rather harsh expression to her usually pensive and mild countenance. Her health seemed still on the mend ; she walked firmly and actively to the seat which her father had just vacated. She threw a beseeching glance at the older gentleman as he left the room, as much as to beg him to remain and support her through the interview ; but he seemed to have a sly suspicion of the subject about to be brought upon the tapis, and he retired—a quizzical, and half humorous smile playing about his mouth as he shut the door, and gave one glance back at his daughter.

The two, thus left alone, sat for some moments without exchanging a word the gentleman, for once in his life, very much embarrassed, and the lady more at her ease. The former, at length, broke the silence. "Your father, Miss Ellen, has just been complimenting your sex in a way, which was quite new to me ; he was giving me, as you entered, his professional testimony in their behalf."

"The best men are the best witnesses in such a cause."

"True, but your father was giving me much higher testimony than ordinary men could give. He need not go far, Miss Evylin, for his sources of inspiration on that subject."

"No," said Ellen, quite unmoved, "only to the bed side of his nearest patient."

"You are invulnerable, Miss Evylin, to those weapons of our sex, usually considered so potent."

"That, now, I consider a real compliment, while your general staple article of the other sort, seems to me to belong to any body that will appropriate them—they are like the wind, or the atmospheric air we breathe, or the water we drink."

"Mine shall not be so wide of the mark, I assure you—the purpose of my visit to night was to renew the highest compliment which a gentleman can pay to a lady. I went to the Governor's country seat for the same purpose, but my object was there frustrated by some unfortunate occurrences, which it is nedless now to allude to more particularly. I hope I shall find you more inclined to listen to me, than I have found you hitherto. Always some unfortunate interruption, either designed or accidental, has prevented me from laying open my whole heart to you. Is this to be the lucky time ?"

"I will not profess to misunderstand you in any particular, Mr. Lee, either with regard to the object of your late and present visit, or the occurrences at Temple Farm. I am, indeed, now ready and willing to listen to you."

Lee was immediately on his knees before her, and made an effort to seize her hand, but she rose up on the instant, and said, "But not in that posture,

Mr. Lee, it does not become the relations which henceforth we must bear to each other. I professed myself willing to hear you, and I expect to have something to say myself; and that you will be equally courteous to me; more than that we can never be to each other."

"You shock me Miss Evylin, inexpressibly, both by the manner and matter of your discourse. I see now that there is displeasure in your eye, but let me hope that I shall by a frank and full explanation of every thing be enabled to remove it." He had again seated himself, as had the lady.

"Every thing Mr. Lee!" exclaimed she, putting particular emphasis upon the words.

"Yes, Miss Evylin, every thing, why do you question me so pointedly?"

"Because I doubted, and still doubt, whether you will be explicit upon every thing which you have said and written concerning this matter."

"The very object of my visit is, to have just such an unreserved conversation with you. I have long seen that it was necessary to rip up those old matters which at first I avoided out of delicacy to you; I have seen that it was necessary, before we could properly understand each other."

"I am all attention, Sir, proceed."

"Since my late visit to the Temple Farm, I am more than ever convinced of it, excuse me therefore, if I touch upon subjects, which I once understood were forbidden in this house."

"If you allude to my engagement to your brother, you are free to speak.

"Lee seemed surprised for a moment, at the prompt and unembarrassed manner in which she spoke of the long forbidden subject, but proceeded: "I will not pretend to conceal from you Miss Evylin, that I rather more than suspected the fact, which you have just acknowledged, at the time of its occurrence. I mean your engagement to my brother, and as long as he lived, you know that I never openly interfered or expressed those feelings which animated me as well as him. (Ellen's eye flashed and she could scarcely restrain an indignant exclamation.) Even had he lived, I cannot even yet see why my claims would not have been equal to his own, unless indeed I were to attribute those mercenary motives to you, from which I know too well, no human being is more free. My attachment was at least coeval with his own, and though he possessed greater powers of address, you know enough of human nature, to be aware that the strongest passions like the deepest rivers, run the most smoothly and silently. I was always firmly persuaded that his love was far less deeply rooted than my own, indeed I might have given way altogether, had I not been so firmly persuaded of the evanescent nature of his. Had you not some evidence of this even before his death?"

"Such as I had, or rather have, you shall see, before we conclude this interview;" replied Ellen, with compressed lips, and struggling to appear calm and unmoved.

"I am sure that such was the fact, I could exhibit evidence of it myself, were it necessary, but we will take it for granted for the present. After the sad affair which deprived me of an only brother, all those impediments which had so long restrained me, were removed. You cannot deny that up to that time, I was governed by a scrupulous delicacy towards you both."

Ellen again became restive, she could no longer restrain herself, and she exclaimed pointedly: "Mr. Lee, recollect yourself! before that time, had you not spoken to my father on the subject?"

"True, true, I had," replied he somewhat embarrassed, "but my offence proceeded no farther; nor was my suit prosecuted afterwards until I supposed your lacerated feelings had entirely recovered from the blow. From the time of my first unsuccessful proposal to you up to the time of my late visit to Temple Farm, I have lived but with a view to prosecute it. I have studied nothing but your pleasure. I have devoted myself to you and followed you like your own shadow ; nothwithstanding the oft repeated partial rebuffs with which my devotion has been rewarded, I have still persevered, in hopes that when the recollection of your first attachment had softened away by time, it would naturally glide into that strange store-house of childish things which every memory contains, and at last give place to the more matured and rational feelings of the woman."

" And your letters to your brother, was there nothing in any of them inconsistent, with what you have just said ?"

" Nothing, so help me heaven, so far as I can recollect."

" Mr. Lee," said Ellen with a severe expression of countenance which he had never before witnessed, "I must refresh your memory : I would not question your veracity, but I cannot suffer you to go farther without convincing you that I am far better informed on this subject than you suppose me to be. You may have forgotten what you wrote then—I hope you have, but you will never forget it again, as long as you live, when you have read that letter." Here she handed him Frank's last letter, and continued. " I hope and pray that it may soften your heart towards your brother, (she hastily corrected herself) towards his memory I mean. You will find there that not a few of his troubles were produced by the very interference, which you have just so emphatically denied. Read it, and reflect upon it. I am sure it will move every generous and feeling impulse within you."

He took the letter with a trembling hand, and drawing the light towards him, commenced its perusal. His eye dilated as he did so, while the cold perspiration gathered upon his brow and lip, and his whole frame shook with ill concealed excitement. Before he had half finished, he turned it over and examined the superscription carefully—he seemed reassured by it, and became rather more composed as he finished the remaining portion.

" Whence did you obtain this letter, and through what conveyance. I see it has no post mark."

" It matters not, Mr. Lee, how I obtained it, it is sufficient for me, and for you too, I suppose, that it is genuine. You will not deny that it is poor Frank's hand writing ?"

" I will not deny that it is admirably imitated, but I must know from whom you obtained it, before I grant that it is genuine."

" Well then, I obtained it from one who had suffered alike with him—from one who received it from his own hands—from one whom you have treated in a manner very poorly calculated to recompense your brother's last and dearest friend."

" From the arch impostor Hall."

" I did receive it from Mr. Hall, but he is no impostor, Mr. Lee."

" He is the veriest impostor and swindler that breathes. He has assumed another man's name, has swindled me, if not others, out of money—and he has forged every word of that letter. There is not one word of truth in it, as I verily believe."

" Mr. Lee, I will not quarrel with you ; it would neither become my sex nor inclination to do so; but I as firmly believe in the genuineness of that letter as in the truth and honor of its bearer, as I believe in my own existence. Indeed I would rather surrender my life than doubt either."

" Very well, Miss Evylin, very well ; the time will speedily come when you will repent this hasty decision. I pledge my word, before many weeks have elapsed to produce such evidence of the falsity of this man at least, that none can doubt. I will not only confront him with the real person whose name he has assumed for the most diabolical purposes, but I will put the matter beyond all question, by the testimony of a disinterested witness who knew the real Hall and all his family in Scotland.'"

" It will be time enough for me to believe it, when you do so, in the mean time, let me at once and forever close the main subject between us. I have already said that I would no longer profess to misunderstand the motives with which you pursue me so constantly. Now, let me undeceive you : If you can establish all that you say, if you can fortify your own honor, so that it will be entirely free, even from suspicion, if you can make out Mr. Hall the swindler that you say you believe him to be, it can make no alteration in my feelings towards yourself. We can never be more towards each other than we are at this moment !"

" Time may work wonders, Miss Evylin, as it has done before ; are you willing to allow me the poor contingencies which it may produce."

" I am not ; because you have already satisfied me that you could not calmly wait its developements, even if there was a possibility of any such contingencies as you suppose—there is none. I tell you frankly, Mr. Lee, that I would not marry you, if there was not another man in her Majesty's Colony. Will you believe, now, that my purpose is fixed ?"

" I am answered,"—taking his hat, and standing in the doorway—" I have only to bid you now a long farewell. I trust, indeed, that you may *fare well* in the hands into which you seem, by some strange and wayward destiny, to have fallen. Should you see me, or hear of me prosecuting, vigorously to punish the man whom you are so unwilling to give up, do me the justice, at least, to believe that I am actuated by no motives of petty revenge against yourself. Farewell—farewell !" Exit Mr. Lee.

" No, no, said Ellen, musingly, but bitterly, as she heard him slam the door, no one could suspect the gentle, amiable, forgiving Mr. Lee, of harboring revenge against any one. Thank God ! my father is no way in his power !" The old gentleman entered as his name passed her lips, having exchanged his spatterdashes for black silk stockings and gold buckles, and all the other corresponding articles of dress befitting his presence at the Levee, late as it was. There was a mischevious smile upon his mouth, as his daughter threw her arms about his neck, and burst into tears ; her bitter and sarcastic mood already gone. The father looked down upon her with untold stores of affection beaming in his eye, but still that playful smile lingered, as he said, "So you have given that proud boy his quietus at last ! I am glad of it, my Ellen, glad of it—indeed I am !"

" How did you know what happened, dear father ?"

" Oh, I knew it from the way he slammed the door, if I had had no other evidence, but your expression about his power over me, as I entered, would have been enough without that."

" Well then, go, dear father, and leave me to myself, while you pay your respects to your friend the Governor."

" And Ellen," he called out, as she left the room, what report shall I make to your young friends, they have doubtless missed Mr. Lee, from the saloon and will know full well his whereabouts."

She came back again, threw her arms round his neck, as she said, beseechingly, "Make no report at all dear father, however much you might be amused at Mr. Lee's pompous absurdities, you cannot exhibit him in a riduculous light without involving me too—and I would like every thing connected with the affair which has terminated to night, forgotten forever. Let Harry Lee be to us, as if he had never been. I do not like to think of him, because I cannot think well of him ; and, for the sake of one, whose memory is dear to me, the next thing is, not to think of him at all. Do impress this upon the dear, mischevious girls at the Palace. I see the smile upon *your* face has already given place to a tear, but let me kiss it away, and then a long adieu to Mr. Harry Lee. Good night, dear father, good night."

" God bless you, my child !—God bless you !"—said the old man, as he drew down his broad cocked hat over his eyes, and took his long ivory headed cane, to trudge his way to the Palace.

CHAPTER III.

MEETING OF THE BURGESSES.

The great day at length arrived—that day, the events of which were to fulfil the highest hopes of *he chivalrous and enterprising Governor of Virginia, or blast them forever. The Burgesses, at the previous session, had refused to vote the necessary supplies; and should the present representatives be governed by the same feelings and opinions, there was forever an end of the great tramontane expedition. Very different means and exertions had been used this year, however, from those which preceded the former election. Though the Governor was not formed by nature so much for a politician as a soldier, he was compelled to learn by experience. His frank and noble nature was coerced to adopt those measures of policy and expediency — always found inseparable from high political station. Governor Spotswood, soon learned, like all others who have trod the devious ways of politics, that human nature must be dealt with, by means suited to its grovelling propensities. Not that we would insinuate, for a moment, that any improper or criminal influences had been used to secure the election of his friends—far from it. Dearly as he desired the fulfilment of that long thought of, and anxiously studied enterprise, he would have sacrificed his highest hopes and aspirations, before he would have stooped to any thing mean or unworthy to accomplish it. But he had taken pains to have the counties actively canvassed; and had, in several places, suggested the most proper persons to be run by his friends, while no means were spared to diffuse correct information among the people. After all those means had been used, however, the Governor was well aware, that the fate of his darling hobby rested with some half dozen grave old planters in whose hands was the balance of power. They were friends and followers of Mr. Bird, the celebrated traveller and journalist, who was, at the time of which we write, a member of council. The Governor had been closeted with him half of the previous night, and, up to the meeting of the House of Burgesses, had received no assurances calculated to ally his anxious fears. The neutrals were known to be under the influence of Mr. Bird; and thus, as it were, he held the fate of the whole expedition in his hands.

It was known that the Governor was to make a speech to the Assembly, and, consequently, the town was thronged at an early hour. Even before daylight, crowds were pouring into the city, insomuch that long before the first meal, the taverns were full. The back streets and lanes in and around the city presented the appearance of a great camp-meeting. Horses were tied to the fences in continuous lines, wherever the eye could reach, while Gloucester street, the Palace, Capitol, and Market Greens, were filled with a dense crowd of men. Of course, not a tithe of these could squeeze within the walls of the Capitol; but it mattered not, it was a great public day, and the Governor was to make a speech, and it was sufficient that they were on the ground. As characteristic of the times, let our readers just cast their eyes over one of these groups collected round the tail of a cart, from which was sold eatables and drinkables. The old planter, at the right extremity of the semi-circle, with a pewter mug in his hand, has on a hat which was perhaps cocked in London, but it now bears indubitable marks of having passed through perils of flood and field, it is of a foxy red color, and the loops by which it was held in shape being all gone, the brim is rolled up on each side, so as to give it the shovel shape in front and rear. His coat is homespun, and of a grey color, the flaps falling almost to his heels, and containing pockets equal to a modern pair of saddle bags. His waistcoat is made of a web with staring figures, as large as our curtain calico, and the pockets covering the hip bones, where it is met by his inexpressibles, made of the same materials as his coat, and terminating at the knee and fastened by huge buckles ; homespun stockings cover the remainder of his legs, and his shoes are fastened with the same sort of buckles as those at the knee.

His wife stands next him, waiting for the pewter mug most patiently ; on her head is a fur hat, exactly such as the male sex wears in our day, with less stiffening. It is kept on her head by a shawl tied over the top and under her chin. Her dress is made of materials which bears a striking resemblance to those of her husband's waistcoat—the same straggling large red figures. The waist terminates just above the hips ; and below, on each side, are pockets to match those in her husband's coat tail. The other parties of the group were dressed very much after the same general fashion, varying somewhat, perhaps, with the taste of the wearer. At every corner and cross street, such a group might be seen. It mattered little to those primitive tobacco planters of the humbler sort, how eloquently the Governor might discourse at the other end of the city—the tail of a gingerbread cart was their exchange, tavern, and reading-room ; there they received all the information they ever acquired.

The next grade above them were seated round tables in the tavern, covered with bottles and glasses, and there the same theme occupied their attention. What strange ideas were then developed of that great country, which now gives character to our land. They thought the mountains inaccessible, in the first place ; and even if crossed, that the French and the Mississippi were both immediately beyond. We would like to stand near, with the reader, and take down a few of their dialogues, but time presses—the Capitol bell is ringing, and the crowd is in motion. Carriages filled with elegantly dressed ladies are sweeping up the Capitol green in one direction, and, after depositing their inmates, pouring out at the other in a continuous line. The young bloods, on fine prancing steeds, are endeavoring to force their way through the dense throng. The police officers are cracking the crowns of the obstreperous lads, trying to force their way in ; while the white teeth of a grinning cuffee or two might be seen shining from every tree in the neighborhood, staring with all their eyes, to see they knew not what.

At length the booming sound of a cannon announces that the Governor has set out from the palace. Immediately the crowd breaks away to the right and left, and soon a troop of cavalry passes through, and file to the right and left on each side of the avenue ; next, the body guard, and then the state coach, with the Governor in full dress, attended by two of the council. There was an expression of anxiety on his countenance as he entered the Capitol, which he could but illy conceal ; he was evidently laboring under apprehensions for the fate of his cherished enterprise ; at the same time, no doubt, reflecting upon what he should say, in order to fire the enthusiasm of his auditors.

The members rose respectfully upon his entrance, and were gracefully saluted by him in turn. He took the seat appropriated to him for a few moments, a profound silence obtaining the while. He rested his head upon his hand, as if he would still its tumultuous throbbing.

The house was packed as tight as it was possible, and at least one half the member's seats given up to the ladies, their gay feathers and brilliant colors contrasting strangely with the grave faces and dresses of the members.

The Governor rose and stepped forward a pace or two, and commenced slowly and under some embarrassment. He related the history of the inception of the undertaking—said that while carrying out the benevolent views of Mr. Boyle, with regard to the Indian scholars in the college, he had been induced to make the effort to accomplish a double purpose, i. e. he had taken the Indian prisoners of the proper age to school, instead of to prison—that some of them had been taken by the tributaries from beyond the mountains, and it was from them that he had obtained his first information of that glorious country. He said that he saw some of those then in the crowd, who were willing and ready to testify, if the Burgesses desired to hear them. The old veteran began to warm as he described the glories of the conquest, and the beauty of that Eldorado, which his imagination constantly presented to his mental vision. Most eloquently did he also present it to the minds of his hearers. He gave a faithful and graphic detail of the then known geography of the continent—passing rapidly from the Northern lakes to the Gulf of Mexico. He declared that nearly every other colony had hitherto done more toward the advancement of the great interests of civilization than Virginia, and that it was peculiarly incumbent on her, the representative in America of the intelligence, the religion, and the liberty of her father-land, to prosecute what Smith and Raleigh had so nobly begun. When he arrived at the military aspect of his subject, the old "war horse" was roused up, as if he smelled the battle afar off. He fired up the ardor and enthusiasm of the most lethargic by his historical and classic allusions, and wound up his address by describing Virginia as holding in her hands the very key to all that rendered the discoveries of Columbus available.

"If we are tamely to fold our hands," said he, "and suffer this mighty inheritance to pass from us, we may as well return at once to Old England. If we are to be content with a sparse settlement along the seacoast, and never make an effort to enlarge our boundaries, I have no hesitation in pronouncing the whole scheme of British colonization in America nothing but a splendid failure. France has already seized upon both ends of the cornucopia, while we are penned up within the horn—too feeble or too inert to strike a blow for our extrication. Shall it be said in after times, that the descendants of the noble cavaliers and gentlemen who conquered and reclaimed this country had become so degenerate as to suffer this great inheritance to pass from us? Oh, never let it be said. Gird on your armor, Virginians, and follow me at least to the mountain's brow. Take one glance over those hitherto impregnable barriers, the great Apalachee, and I will show you a finer country than that promised land which Moses beheld, but never reached. It may be as my enemies predict, that I too must fall by the way side, but if it must be, I trust that God will grant to me as to his servant of old, to view before I depart, that land which my waking and sleeping fancies have so long held before my, I trust, prophetic vision. I ardently desire to see before I die, the western half of this great, glorious and gigantic picture. In the language of our eloquent red brethren, I long to travel towards the setting sun, and behold his golden rays as they reveal the beautiful savannas, and boundless prairies and forest-crowned hills upon which the foot of an European has never yet trod. Is there nothing in this idea to fire the ardor of my young friends whom I see around me? Have they no desire to experience the sensations of Columbus, when first he planted his foot upon the maiden soil? Follow me, all ye who are desirous of new sensations—all ye who would live hereafter in the pages of history, along side of Columbus and Americus—all ye who would grow rich as well as famous—all ye who would carve out that which is greater and better than a deathless name—the future scene of the grandest enterprises yet in the womb of time and destiny. No military or scientific eye can rest for one moment upon the map of Virginia which I hold in my hand, without being struck with the fact, that such an achievement is immediately within our grasp. Look at these noble rivers, forever pouring their rich tributes into the bosom of our loved Chesapeake! shall it be said by our children that their fathers were afraid to seize upon the fountains—the streams and lands of which they already possessed? Does any planter purchase land, the fountain-head of whose springs lies within his neighbor's farm?—and shall we, as a people, be less wise than any one of us would be individually? Shake off the lethargy which oppresses you, and go with me to this great, this boundless country—this future seat of empires. Cast your eyes forward into a probable futurity, and behold the rich resources which your discoveries and conquests may pour into the lap of our loved colony. Behold the rich meadows, and neat farm houses, and the gilded spires as they point towards heaven. Think of the thousands and millions of happy emigrants and their descendants from the crowded marts of the old world for whom you will have carved out homes.

" But there are broader and more profound bearings to this subject than even these, grateful as they are to the philanthropist and christian. We have arrived at a crisis, not only in the affairs of the colony, but of the world. No statesman, no man of enlarged views can cast his eyes over the boundless field which Providence has opened up to the irrepressible energies of our race, without being impressed with the critical position in which we are placed.

" It is needless to disguise that, from this time forward, there is to be a contest for supremacy on this continent, between the French and the English, between the Protestant and Catholic religions. Thus far, the race has been equal, or nearly so; now, however, Virginia holds in her hands the pass, the key, the gates of the mightiest empire ever conceived of by the most towering ambition. Is she to close this entrance of the world to the far West— to suppress the energies of our race—to stifle the great onward enterprises, upon the threshold of which we have barely entered. Rouse ye up, Virginians, and sleep no longer at the portals of the world. It is not merely to explore a few insignificant water-courses, and thread an unknown mountain pass, that I would urge you, but it is to enter upon that grand inheritance which Providence opens to our acceptance. Beyond the mountains, spreads out the most wonderful country ever dreamed of by the most daring imagination. I base this opinion, not alone upon the evidence of the Indian hostages, but upon other and irrefragable testimony within our reach. Compare the distance from the lakes to the Gulf of Mexico—examine the mouths of the vast rivers pouring into that sea. Whence come they? Is it consistent with the known geography of the world, and the philosophy of its construction, to suppose that they burst suddenly from the ground? No, my fellow-subjects, there is a vast unexplored region between us and the mouth of the Mississippi, which it almost beggars the imagination to conceive of. So far from the poor hostages having exaggerated its wonders, I believe that the half has not, and cannot be told—at least by them. Their poor bewildered intellects become numbed and paralyzed, in the vain effort to grasp the outlines. It requires the far-reaching eye of an intelligent and cultivated mind, of a philosopher, a statesman, a philanthropist, a christian—in the largest aceptation of the term—to comprehend these things. I trust there are many such in this enlightened assembly. Certainly the interests of our sovereign and country never required their presence more. Trusting that your deliberations will redound to the honor and interests of both, as well as to your own lasting reputation, I leave the subject with you, to make such response as to you may seem wise and proper. The needful documents will be furnished you in due time."

After the Governor had retired, there was a considerable murmur of applause and some stamping of feet and clapping of hands; more among the spectators, however, than the Burgesses. With the common people, as distinguished from the gentry, as we have before remarked, the proposed expedition was extensively popular, but with the latter, especially with the elders among them, it was not so much so.

The discussion of the response necessary to be made to the Governor's appeal, and which was also a test of the fate of the bill for subsidies, which would follow of course, was long and animated, and enchained the attention of the crowded hall until a late hour of the night.

In this debate, Bernard Moore took a leading and distinguished part. Kate slightly hung her head, and drew down her veil when she saw him rise, and color to his ears and clear his throat, through the awkward exordium of his maiden speech, but it was not a long while before her veil was thrown to one side, and her ringlets parted from her face, which now responded to her lover's eloquence, in the brightest glow of her enthusiastic and ardent temperament. We know not if the young Burgess caught back any of his own fire, so beautifully reflected ; but he might have done so, and probably did. Certainly it was a fair mirror in which to view the effects of his first effort. Her fine eye sparkled most brilliantly, while the young orator descanted upon the glorious achievment before them, and when he turned round and addressed himself to the younger members, in particular, with a power and eloquence which was natural to him ; Kate's eye roamed over the face of each one thus appealed to, with an anxious, enquiring solicitude for the fate of her father's darling project.

Moore felt and spoke as if his own fate hung upon the success of the measure before them.   He had somehow or other, brought himself to consider his own suit as connected with the expedition.   He had so long, jestingly with Carter, put it upon this footing, that he really began to think that there was some sort of mysterious link between the two dissimilar affairs.   No one would have laughed more heartily at this than the Governor, could he have divined the secret thoughts of the young Burgess, but they were confined entirely to his own breast.   And Kate, could she have penetrated those secret thoughts, and felt that Bernard, while he appealed so feelingly to his fellow representatives, was, at the same time, pleading his suit to her ; what would have been her feelings on the already exciting subject.   But she was far too disinterested for that, and too entirely absorbed in her father's interest in the great scheme.   She believed that his assistance was none the less effective on that account.   When he had concluded, there was a breathless silence for many minutes—there was a " counting of noses "—and the Governor's friends trembled for the result.   The opposition, it is true, had already spent its force, and no one seemed disposed again to take the floor in answer to Moore !   But then there was one member absent, who had been calculated upon certainly to vote for, if not advocate the measure—namely, Henry Lee—he was most unaccountably absent.   The Governor's friends, as soon as it was discovered, had sent messenger after messenger for him, but no where was he to be found.

The Governor was sitting in the General Court-room, surrounded by some of his old friends, and members of his Council, and most anxiously canvassing the probable state of the vote, when Moore hastily entered, and whispered to him the disappearance of Lee.   "Damn him," said the old veteran, striking his hand upon the table and speaking in an under tone, through his clenched teeth, " If I had supposed that he could have deserted me at such a moment as this, I might have saved a deal of expensive politeness. Send for him again Moore !"

General Clayton, who was sitting near, and hearing Lee's name pronounced, and suspecting the cause of the Governor's excitement, came up to the latter and told him, that Lee had left town some time before, he believed, in pursuit of some young man who had swindled him.   The Governor and Moore exchanged glances of mutual understanding and indignation ; and the former, exclaimed, rising, and with some vehemence, as he strode about the room, "Go back, Bernard, and let the issue be tried—if it is destined to be disastrous as at former trials, by Heaven, I will march without them and their aid ; keep up your spirits, my lad, I will as surely lead you over the mountains as the sun shines, and that before the world is a month older."

Moore did go back to his place, very much disheartened however, by the untimely desertion of Lee, for he knew that the vote would be a very close ofie, and a single *aye* might be of immense importance. Some stupid proser was concluding as he returned. He walked round among his friends and communicated the disheartening news. Several of the young men had determined to speak against time, until Lee could be found; but the plan was now useless, and they suffered the question to be taken. Respiration almost seemed suspended during the short and exciting period. The audience rose to their feet, and crowded round the Clerk's table so much, that the officers had to be called in to preserve order. The votes were at length counted, and the Speaker announced that there was a tie. So that had Lee been at his post, the victory would have been gained by one vote. His absence was, however, not long a subject of regret, for the speaker gave the casting vote in favor of the measure. There was an instantaneous rush from all parts of the house for the green in front of the Capitol; and when the eager throng without caught the bright glow upon the faces of those who rushed out, and, even before the result could be embodied in words—a loud and deafening shout of applause made the welkin ring again—the boys and the soldiers about town, and all the other idlers took up the peal and echoed it again with interest. All that day, nothing but songs of the mountains were heard, and every popular ballad that could be at all tortured into any thing having the slightest allusion to the subject was sung. It was a great day, also, at the Barracks and the Taverns. Such victories, from time immemorial, require to be moistened with plentiful libations, as if Bacchus alone presided over the contest. Partizans of the same school drink in congratulation; the victors offer the wine cup to the vanquished, at once as a pledge of still enduring good will, at the same time, as a fitting opportunity to meet again on the middle ground of the social board.

There was one, in that thronged assembly, however, who, though feeling as deep an interest as any one in the vote just taken, quietly stole away, without manifest exultation and really feeling the heart's heaviest oppression in the midst of her friends' rejoicing.

Ellen Evylin sought her father's carriage alone, while every one else of the Governor's party mingled in the scene of mutual congratulation. She threw herself back in the carriage, and thought how Frank Lee would have rejoiced to be present. These regrets were far from being selfish; she knew that he would have pressed forward with the young chivalry of Virginia, towards the high prize which was then firing the imaginations of all the youth of the colony. She knew that it was an enterprise exactly suited to his temperament and impetuous impulses; and she could not but regret that his already disastrously spent energies had not been reserved for an occasion so well calculated to develope them with advantage to himself and benefit to his fellow creatures. She had so long interwoven every thought and feeling of her own with his, that it was impossible for her to mingle in any such exciting scenes as she had passed through, without placing him in her imagination as one of the actors. This total absorption of the mind and affections towards one beloved object for any great length of time, bears a striking resemblance, and has not a little affinity to that one featured mania, so much better understood since that time.

CHAPTER IV.

THE LAST MEETING.

THE doors of the Palace, the next day, were thrown open to all the gentry in the city of whatever party, and the Governor received the congratulations of his friends with beaming eyes and outstretched hands. He was now indeed the frank, hearty, joyous old soldier which he had been in former days. The doubts and difficulties which had so long weighed down his spirits, no longer clouded his brow, and his broad jokes and merry laughter were once more heard within the Gubernatorial mansion. Indeed the horizon in every direction seemed brightening to his vision. The ministry no longer interfered with his operations—the faction in the council was silenced—public opinion gathered strength and power from the victory in the house of Burgesses, and above all, his son and heir, seemed now entirely relieved from the dominion of the monster passion, which, as he supposed, had so long thrown that air of mystery and reckless dejection about him.

John entered fully into his father's views, and was eager to plunge into the bustle and business of preparation. There was, it is true, an impetus given to his movements towards the opposite extreme, from his late sudden legarthy and gloomy misanthropy, which an acute observer well versed in the human heart would have distrusted, but his father was too much pleased with his renovated spirits and new born energy, to criticise it closely.

This was the last day which he was to spend in the capital. It had been determined, that he was to proceed at once to the fort at Germana, and there take command of several companies of Rangers, which the Governor had ordered to concentrate at that point, and from thence, he was to join his father on the march.

As he walked out of the Palace gate, and up the avenue toward Gloucester street, he had not proceeded many rods before his steps were arrested by an object directly in his path, It was star light, and he could not see distinctly who it was, and made an effort to pass to the right or left, but still he found the same object in his way. He brought his face close up to the person thus way-laying him, and now discovered that it was Wingina wrapped up in her brother's cloak.

"What, Wingina!" exclaimed he, in a suppressed voice, but hoarse, from excitement, "Do you dog my footsteps? Do you watch me to my father's home. Am I secure from your persecutions nowhere?"

"Oh, Capt. Spotswood! you are very unjust, very cruel. I heard you were going to set out to-night to my own country, and I come to beg you, for God's sake to take me along. I cannot much longer conceal my dreadful secret. Before you get back, it will be not only discovered but I shall be killed; my brother strongly suspects it now."

"But, Wingina, Chunoluskee goes with my father as his guide, and, before he returns, in all probability, your troubles will be over."

"Alas! they will indeed be over; but my life will pass away with them."

"What an inconsistent creature you are, Wingina; but lately, you professed to be willing to court death, and now you whine over its possible occurrence, like some sick child!"

"It is a very different thing to court it, when the resolution is worked up to it, and to be in continual dread of it from an angry brother of whom one has lived in constant dread, and always under his constant authority. You know how arbitrary it is among our race; the male over the female."

"Why, he always appears mild and gentle to me, Wingina?"

"Aye, and so does the fiercest warrior of our tribe when mingling with your race, but in the wigwam it is different. An Indian girl should never be enlightened at all, unless she is to be permanently removed from the tyranny of the wigwam. It was a thorough knowledge of this, which made me fall so easy a prey to—I will not say to you, but my love for you;" and she laid her hand gently upon his arm, and looked up in his face, as if she would fain discover by the doubtful light, whether his mood towards her was softened.

"Hush, Wingina; saw you not a tall shadow pass from behind the trees towards Gloucester street?"

The Indian girl wheeled her head suddenly in that direction, at the same time clinging with both hands to the young officer's arm, as she exclaimed: " It is! it is my brother! Oh, John, I am now lost indeed, unless you save me. I will never return in life to my brother's house."

Spotswood took her arm and hurried her along through the shadows of the trees and across the common, until he arrived at the brick wall of the grave yard, and following this—still keeping close within its protecting shadow, they were soon within its enclosure, and seated upon a low tomb stone.

" Now tell me Wingina—and think and speak quick, for I have not a moment to lose, whether you can ride on horseback ?"

" Oh yes, indeed."

" And if I procure you a suit of boy's clothes, will you wear them and pass for my servant if I take you with me, until I can find some of your people."

At first she hung her head, as if pressed down with hopeless dejection. Spotswood mistook her feelings and supposed that maidenly delicacy prevented her from at once acceding to the plan, but her thoughts were running upon a very different point of the discussion as her next question will show. "And should we happen to meet some of our people, will you go with me and be a great chief among them, as your father is here ?"

" Poh, poh, Wingina, I thought you had given up all that nonsense long ago. How can I go with you, when I am to lead part of this army over the mountains ? Come decide quick about my plan, I am to set out for Germana to night, and if you agree to my plan, I will take you at once to an acquaintance of mine in the suburbs, to wait while I procure the dress and order round the horses."

" I have no choice left, Capt. Spotswood, I am compelled to go with you, I dare not present myself before my brother again."

They were soon hurrying through the cross streets of the capital until they came to a small shanty occupied by an old negro woman. There they entered and John taking the crone to one side, made her understand that she was to observe secrecy about what they were going to do, and that she was to cut off the girl's hair and assist her to put on the clothes which he would bring, so as to have her ready by the time he came with the horses.

In about half an hour he returned and handed in a bundle to the old woman at the door, and again hurried off.

The negro assisted, as she had been ordered, at the strange toilet of Wingina, the first step of which was to cut off her long black hair. When it was completed, it would have been difficult to find in the colony a neater and trimmer little page than she presented. John scarcely knew her himself, when he alighted to see that all was ready, so complete had been the metamorphosis. Still he found her dress not complete, for she had resisted all the old negro's entreaties to exchange her moccasins for a pair of boots. John soon convinced her that, all the other changes were useless, unless she completed it by the change proposed; that her Indian moccasins were the most dangerous mark she could wear about her. At length she complied, but with great reluctance, for she had been partly ruined by flattery addressed to her diminutive foot, and her prettily ornamented moccasins. John understood well what was passing in her mind, and he could not avoid cursing himself, that he had undone such a mere child of nature. The fact was, all his reflections and observations upon her character and peculiarities came too late. A lustful imagination had blinded him to every thing but her personal attractions. These attractions were still the same, yet how powerless now.

We must leave them to pursue their midnight journey, while we turn our attention to the main thread of our narrative.

CHAPTER V.

A FRONTIER SETTLEMENT.

SOME three day's journey from Williamsburg, there stood a settlement which would puzzle an European traveller of our day to tell what it was. It was neither house, barn, stable nor fort—but a compound of the whole, or rather of many of them. It was called in the language of the country, "a block house." There was a strong picket fence running round an open area, and round the inside of these, built in with the fort, were various houses or shantees—some one story and some two; the latter having loop holes to shoot through, and commanding the approach to that side of the pallisade. Out side again, were some twenty straggling huts or cabins, which were all occupied in day time, but closed at night, for the owners slept within the fort.

This was not the great frontier station, Germana, to which more than one of our characters are now wending their way, but had originally been a trading station for similar purposes. It was now a sort of half way house, a convenient protection for travellers as well as the small planters and traders around.

It was about dusk several days after the one alluded to in the last chapter, when a traveller on foot with a bundle of clothes tied up in a handkerchief and thrown over a stick which he carried upon his shoulder, arrived at the settlement. He was weary and wayworn and his shoes covered with the dust of the road. About his face there was a settled dejection, at the same time a winning grace which would have commanded the sympathy of any one not hardened by constantly rubbing against a cold and unfeeling world. The women and children around the block house were driving in their cows and sheep and poultry, for at night the open area was a sort of stock pen. Hall, for it was none other than the late Tutor, took his bundle in his hand and rested upon his cane, watching listlessly the while, the proceedings of the women and children in their rural occupations.

"You need'nt wait for an invitation," said one of the women—"the block house is free to all travellers—the only thing is to get something to eat when you are in there."

"And will you not furnish me, my good woman, either for love or money ?"

"Faith and with that bonny face of yours you may well ask, but I doubt you have been a wild blade in your day, from that same cut across your cheek."

"That, my good woman, was got in no private brawl."

"It matters not to me if it was, you shall have your supper all the same."

Hall was soon seated near one corner of a log fire, with his plate of smoking viands on one end of a rude bench and himself on the other. From the rapidity of his operations he was neither dainty nor fastidious in his appetite, and what was still less romantic, he was very soon after leaning with his head against the logs, and snoring away at a great rate. He had not long been thus occupied, before a loud noise at the entrance announced other arrivals, hearing which, he rose and lifted the rude seat upon which he had been reclining to the farthest and darkest corner of the room, and again seated himself, wrapped up in his cloak, that he might examine unobserved the new comers. The same woman soon after entered, ushering in Capt. Spotswood and the young Indian, followed by his servant bearing his portmanteau. Every one about the place was soon afoot when it was ascertained that the son of the Governor was within the block, and he consequently found no difficulty in obtaining such accommodations as the place afforded. He walked round the enclosure and examined into the condition of the place. He found the lowest state of discipline prevailing, and since the erection of the fort at

Germana, and the general peace with the Indians, that all precautionary measures had been abandoned, and the place literally turned into a fold for cattle, rather than a military post. One of the primary Indian schools was also kept at this place, and this also he found in the most languishing condition. For an hour he was engaged examining the orderly who had charge of the establishment, and the master who had charge of the school, together with such Rangers as were left, their horses, equipments, &c., in order to ascertain if he could press any of them into the service of the expedition. The horses he found to consist of some dozen wretched skeletons, which he declared the ravens were only prevented from carrying off by their poverty. The arms were very little better; the holsters of one soldier carried a single pistol without a flint—another presented his sword rusty and without scabbard or belt, and so on. John swore, that Falstaff's company were veteran soldiers compared to this remnant of the Rangers of the district. While he was laughing alternately over the ridiculous figure which they cut, and cursing the orderly by whose neglect such a state of things had been brought about, a gentleman and his servant rode into the enclosure, without let or hindrance. "Ah, Lee," said John as he recognized that young gentleman, as he came full under the reflection of the pine torches which one of the wiry haired urchins of the forest bore—"just from the capital?"

"No Captain Spotswood, I left the city several days ago, and come now from another direction, but what have you here, is it possible your are marching toward the frontier with such a troop as this!"

"Oh, no, not so bad as that either"—and he laughed immoderately at the idea—"I was only inspecting the condition of the garrison, to see how many troops I could muster into my father's tramontane army. You see he has little dependence in this quarter—ten equestrian skeletons—twelve Rangers, with ragged uniforms—one stupid orderly, (or disorderly,)—five rusty sabres—three pistol barrels—and saddles which it would puzzle a philosopher to tell which would win the victory—they, by cutting the horses in two, or the horses by cutting them in two. If the enemies of the expedition could only have paraded this troop upon the Capitol green, while the subject was under discussion, they would have turned the whole thing into ridicule." Here both the young gentlemen and even the soldiers and servants went off into a merry fit of laughter, in the midst of which the torch light review was adjourned, and the two young gentlemen retired to the same room into which we have already introduced previous arrivals. John cast a hasty glance round the apartment, in order to whisper a few words into the ear of his page, but it was entirely empty, with the exception of Lee and himself. He saw that the sleeping traveller had vanished as well as the person whom he sought, but the circumstance made no impression, and he remarked not upon it— apparently satisfied that his young protegee had discretion enough to keep out of sight of those by whom they were known.

Hall had quietly withdrawn, upon perceiving through the logs of the hut, the new additions to the party. He remained in the shadow of one of the buildings, until he saw the two young men fairly seated at their rude supper, and then without any guide or conductor, entered what appeared to be one of the most remote and retired buildings of the establishment, and threw himself down upon some straw already spread upon the floor, and worn out with fatigue and exhaustion of mind and body, fell into one of those profound slumbers which only those know who inure their bodies to labor and fatigue. Rude as his couch was, he had accidentally stumbled into the best chamber in the establishment, and that one appropriated as the sleeping apartment of the stranger and wayfarer. One by one the other travellers found their way into the same apartment. Each one as he entered rolled his cloak about him and threw himself upon the straw without inquiry as to his bedfellows. Few even of the gentry, at the time of which we write, but had roughed it, after a similar fashion, whenever business or pleasure led them toward the frontier, and though this was by no means on the extreme borders of civilization, yet the settlements were becoming few and far between, and even these were mostly upon the low lands of the rivers. Upon nearly every public road, there was to be found at convenient distances, these military posts, and the traveller through the wilderness did not inquire in the morning before setting out, how many miles to such a tavern, but if it is possible to arrive at such and such a block house before night. His provisions for the noon meal, and often for the day and night, he carried with him.

After all the male portion of our travellers were snugly stowed away upon their straw pallets, and more than one of them giving loud evidence of the sincerity with which they worshipped at the shrine of the drowsy God—Wingina, with the stealthy tread of a cat, entered the same apartment. Spotswood had secretly sought a few words with her ere he retired to rest, and positively ordered the arrangments differently, and the poor, care-worn creature had indeed endeavored to find repose elsewhere, but an undefinable dread of coming evil, which her superstitious nature could neither withstand nor resist, prevented her from sleeping so far away from the only protector which she had in this world, and she surreptitiously entered as we have seen. She paused at the threshold, to listen to the deep breathing and loud snoring of the sleepers to assure herself that they all slept ere she laid herself down to follow their example. A blanket nailed across the entrance, supplied the place of a a door, and neither sentry nor guard was stationed there, or at the great entrance of the block-house, though she had heard Capt. Spotswood positively order the sergeant, that a corporal's guard should do alternate duty at the gate. She had gone the rounds herself, and if any sentry pretended to guard the great entrance, he slept too soundly to be disturbed by her light tread. She walked among the sleepers and stooped to examine their countenances by the star light, until she could find the one she sought.

The first one she examined was Hall, and she gazed upon his face and hastily withdrew to the one who slept next—it was the one she sought. Long and earnestly she gazed upon the sleeping countenance of him she loved, by the doubtful light afforded. She crouched down beside him, and watched over his slumbers for some time, occasionally, however, her eye roaming over the other sleepers. Becoming accustomed to the darkness of the place, she soon discovered the various positions of the parties. Lee slept on the other side of Spotswood, from that occupied by Hall, but at a greater distance; and further still, towards the door, lay the two servants. Folding a cloak about her person, which Spotswood had furnished her for the purpose, she laid herself down immediately across the door way so that should she even fall asleep, she might be the first aroused by any one moving, and thus escape before it was clearly daylight. She, too, was worn out by the fatigues of the long and weary days' journey and though for a while wakeful with her foreboding fancies, nature, or rather matter, obtained the mastery over mind, and she slept as sound as the rest.

CHAPTER VI.

A DARK DEED.

An hour before day-light next morning, Hall rose from his straw couch and bundling up his small stock of clothes, and taking his staff in hand, carefully stole out of the room which he now, to his surprise, discovered, was occupied by other sleepers. It was yet very dark, and a drizzling rain was falling as he walked abroad into the wild dark forest He took the road toward Germana, and travelled along with cheerfulness and alacrity, rejoiced to think how fortunate he had been to escape the observation of his pursuer, for he doubted not, that Henry Lee was seeking him for some purpose or other.

The circumstances of a young man must be unfortunate indeed, and the weather far more unpropitious than that described, if exercise in the early morning does not produce a bright rebound of the spirits. Hall experienced bright and glowing sensations, as he trudged along the muddy road ; having left his enemies far behind, as he supposed, and anticipating great pleasure in once more beholding his friends of the voyage and the masking adventure, and, above all, he pictured to himself, that calm and delightful repose which he thought must surely be found in a settlement so far removed from the scenes of trade, and politics, and intrigue, which he was so rapidly casting behind him. "There," said he, "I will live, in the profound solitudes of nature, where the turbulent passions of men come not to disturb me—where I may hope to escape from the storm which has so long tossed me about at its pleasure. There the consequences of the one great error of my life cannot pursue me—there nature in her primitive simplicity and purity reigns forever; beneath my humble log cabin I may sit and smoke my pipe in peace, until these lowering clouds have passed away. But while we leave him to pursue his onward way through the forest, as well as the train of reflections upon which he struck, we will glance at the block-house once more, which he had just left.

About day-light a shrill scream was heard from the sleeping room alluded to, which roused every inmate within the stockade, even to the drowsy sentinel at the gate.

It was a prolonged and agonized scream, such as is never heard except on occasions of mortal extremity. How quickly the ear detects these heralds of death or disaster. Instantly the shantees and cabins were seen to pour out their tenants as if roused by one simultaneous impulse, all rushing toward the place from whence the sound issued.

Some fifteen or twenty persons in all, were assembled, crowding thickly round some object which lay upon the floor. Among the others stood Harry Lee, gesticulating wildly, and his eye dilated with horror and astonishment. Immediately in the centre of the group lay the body of John Spotswood, wrapped up in the same cloak which he had borrowed from Lee the night before (having lent his own to Wingina) and perfectly dead. He had been killed by a single blow of a dagger driven through his heart, and sent with such force that the long formidable weapon (worn in those days by Indian fighters,) had actually penetrated the floor and pinioned him to the puncheons beneath. As if the attrocity of the deed was not sufficient, an attempt had been made to mutilate his person by a circular incision upon his crown.*

Lee immediately ordered a guard posted at the entrance of the fort, and that, no one should be permitted to escape until he had investigated the matter, about which he immediately set to work. He found that the room had been occupied by two sleepers who had already escaped, and the woman had proceeded no farther in her description of the one who had lain next to the deceased, than the whiskers and the big scar, before Lee called to the orderly and commanded him to divide his corps into two bodies, and pursue the fugitive until he should find him, and bring him back, dead or alive.

The other absentee was described as a small Indian boy, and as having come with the deceased officer himself. Lee was sorely puzzled to imagine who this could be, and Spotswood's servant could give him no information, except

---

* The attrocious circumstances of young Spotswood's murder, have not been at all exaggerated by us.

that he had been picked up in the capital, just before they had set out, and that he had ridden with his master more as a companion than a servant. The woman who had received the travellers on the previous evening, and from whose throat the scream had issued, stated that the boy had slept in another apartment, by Capt. Spotswood's own orders, while one of the servants declared that he had seen him lying across the door-way of that very room, during the night. The instrument with which the deed had been committed, was a silver mounted two edged dagger, highly ornamented, which several recollected, and Lee himself knew to have been worn by the deceased himself.

From this circumstance, some of those present were disposed to believe that the deceased had committed the rash act upon his own person, but this surmise was put entirely at rest, by the gash upon the head, as well as several distinct finger marks upon the throat, showing that whoever had perpetrated it, had held his victim by a powerful grasp, to prevent noise while the blow was inflicted.

Hall had deviated from the great military road to take a near cut by an Indian path, and thus his pursuers passed him. About ten o'clock in the morning he again emerged into the great thoroughfare, (if two wagon ruts through a pine forest could be called such) and was seated, with his bundle open before him, and helping himself to some cold provisions with which he was provided. He ate with great relish and a fine appetite, and seemed to be disturbed by naught under the sun. The drizzling clouds had blown away, and he looked forward to a cheerful and happy day, amidst the almost unexplored beauties of nature, in one of her wildest and grandest phases. His spirit was buoyant with the idea that at last he had cast off the cares of civilized life and above all, that he had broken loose from those entangling meshes, either of designing men, or fortuitous circumstances, under which he had so long suffered. There was a shade of sadness over his face it is true, it could hardly be otherwise with one who had so lately and so severely suffered—he was more cheerful, however, than at any former period when presented to the reader. He rejoiced in the anticipation of soon enjoying the society of two persons who were now situated so much like himself—Mr. Elliot and his charming daughter. He recollected well the wiser determination of the old gentleman, when they last parted, to abandon at once the crowded thoroughfares of life, and the arguments they had held upon the subject, and he now freely confessed, that the elder was the wiser man of the two. But he had objects to accomplish in daring the frowns of that society, which he had offended, and many of those objects he had more than accomplished, while on the other hand his adventure had resulted more disastrously, in some respects, than he could have anticipated. One subject gave him poignant regret; it was the difficulty of his now accompanying the tramontane expedition. His heart had been fixed upon the Governor's grand scheme, and he had forseen that it would be an admirable offset, could he distinguish himself in that enterprise, for the real offence which he had committed against society.

Alas, he little imagined that he was soon about to be brought to the bar of justice, for the commission of a crime far more heinous than any with which he had yet been charged. With all his previous sufferings, he was not fully aware of those strange and mysterious links which observing men have discovered in the chain of successive misfortunes, insomuch that no adage is of more common use than that "misfortunes never come single-handed." It is a most inexplicable law of Providence. There is such a crisis of greater or less magnitude in the life of every man. Doubtless, to brave and noble spirits, these storms are tempered with more severity than those decreed to the "shorn lamb." One thing is certain, that no one ever attains to preeminence in this world, without having passed through this terrible gauntlet. Tamer spirits shrink from them, or succumb at once, while the more daring and heroic natures bare their hearts to the storm, and manfully buffet them to the last.

Hall was still seated at his rude and homely breakfast, when he heard the distant tramp of horses. His eye was first directed down the road towards the stockade which he had left in the morning, seeing nothing in that direction but the long and monotonous road, he turned his eyes to the other end, and soon perceived five or six horsemen galloping towards him. His mind was relieved at once on perceiving that they belonged to his own race, for he had been for a few moments painfully reflecting how defenceless was his condition, should the new comers prove to be Indians with any hostile intent.

The whole guard immediately dismounted and proceeded deliberately to tie their horses to each other, while the sergeant walked up and tapping him upon the shoulder, pronounced him his prisoner. When informed of the death of Capt. Spotswood, and that he was charged with the murder, he was awe-struck. A clap of thunder and a bolt falling at his feet from a cloudless sky, could not have more truly astonished him ; but when informed farther, by the sergeant, that his face was even then sprinkled with the blood of his victim, his whole frame trembled like an aspen, under a superstitious dread of that unseen power which seemed so relentlessly to pursue him.

CHAPTER VII.

RETURN TO THE CAPITAL

HALL was mounted upon one of the trooper's horses, and conveyed back to the stockade. When brought into the room where the diabolical deed had been perpetrated, no one could express more horror and astonishment than the prisoner. Up to that moment a sort of stupefaction had seized upon his faculties—he scarcely seemed to believe that the murder had actually been committed, or if he did, could not fully realize the fact in all its dreadful particulars, until he saw them with his own eyes ; much less could he realize the position in which he stood, and those circumstances tending to induce the belief that he had done it. When he heard the evidence detailed, he was scarcely surprised that others suspected him, for he would have suspected another under similar circumstances. It made him almost superstitious, when his faculties were sufficiently relieved from the astounding blow to contemplate it, that any one could be placed in such a situation. If he had been disposed to fatalism, here was ample materials to fortify his philosophy, but we have seen already how he scouted the tempter under circumstances much less urgent. So overpowering was the first weight of the blow, that the fact of Henry Lee, his chief enemy, appearing as his accuser, witness, and judge, for the time being, scarcely attracted his attention. All these minor affairs were swallowed up in the astounding fact, that he must appear to the world as a murderer. Then there came over him the recollection of all the late disasters from which he had just escaped, but which now, when once brought back before they were cleared up, would appear as so many corroborating circumstances. When asked by Lee to explain the position in which he found himself, he sank into a seat and covered his face with his hands. He was bewildered and confounded. To the spectators, this looked exactly as they supposed he might ; it had a very natural appearance for a murderer, who, if not detected in the very act, was apprehended with the blood of his victim still upon his hands. At length, however, he rallied, and made an effort to tell all that had happened within his knowledge during the previous night.

He stated that he had sought the room in which he slept for the purpose of privacy, and that so far from seeking to have any thing to do with the other travellers, that he had particularly designed to avoid them by going there— that he was entirely unaware that the room was occupied at a later period of the night by others, until he awakened about an hour before the break of day— that as soon as he discovered it, he stepped lightly over the sleepers as he supposed them to be, and pursued his journey straightway. He professed to know nothing of the other traveller who was missing—the young Indian— that he had neither seen him during the night, nor in the morning. He heard no noise in the night, and was, he said, entirely unconscious how the blood came upon his face—that he was as much shocked and surprised to find it there as any one, and was wholly unable to explain it. He called the attention of those around him, however, to the fact, that his cloak, in which he slept, was also stained with blood, which he had discovered since his arrest— that it was impossible for him to have committed the murder, wrapped up as he was—that the stains upon the garment corresponded exactly with the position which he had described as the one in which he slept—and that his hands and not his face would have been stained—his other garments, and not his cloak, had he been the murderer. He stated, also, that there was no ill will between him and Capt. Spotswood—that the last interview between them had been of a friendly nature, and that he had actually left Temple Farm on the Captain's business.

The whole of this statement, and much more which we have omitted, was written down at the time by Henry Lee, and signed by the prisoner; after which, he was secured on horseback—the corpse put into a cart, and with a guard of half dozen troopers, set out upon their return to the capital.

It is much easier to conceive than describe the sensations of Hall, as he thus began to realize the fact that he was a prisoner once more, and for an ignominious offence.

At first, his whole nature shrunk from the disgrace and exposure, and he thought that he never could or would survive its publicity. He could not help contrasting his present situation—riding between two troopers and tied upon his horse, like a petty larceny thief—with his youthful days, when he had travelled surrounded by those willing and anxious to minister to his slightest wish. He thought, too, of his late bold promises to himself, while in jail, and how brave then he thought his spirit. "But merciful heaven, who could have conceived that I should ever be brought to this!" and with this inward exclamation, he wrung his manacled hands, and the scalding tears ran down his manly cheeks. But this melting mood did not last long—the mind under the heaviest depression rebounds exactly in proportion to that depression, just as the spring of a piece of machinery when bent with great force in one direction flies back in the opposite direction with a corresponding force. For a while his heart sunk down and down, until there was a blackness over all the landscape—the sun itself seemed to shine unnaturally—though it had cleared off beautifully since the morning. The ribald jests of the vulgar men at his side sounded ill-timed. It seemed to him as if the world itself was coming to an end, and talking of the things of to-morrow, the greatest absurdity imaginable. There are few people in this world of sorrow and trouble, who have not experienced more or less of this feeling, just as they happen to be endowed with much or little sensibility, and to be tried with heavy or light afflictions.

Black and dreary would be the colors of the landscape in such a case, did not the tender and gentle emotions of the heart glide in to soften it. Hall was speedily approaching a point of recklessness and desperation, which would but poorly have prepared him to fulfil the high and heroic resolves of his prison chamber, until his memory began to wander back along the bright and glowing path of his youthful days. Then it was that the tears burst forth—and they were succeeded by a calm repose and a high settled purpose of endurance and perseverance to the end. He thought that the wheel of fortune—to speak in the language of the world—was now down to its nadir, and must needs soon commence its revolution towards the zenith.

He had ample time to summon up his courage and his energies, for they were nearly three days in making their way back to the capital—very little faster than Hall had walked the same distance.

It is impossible to describe the consternation produced in the city by the news that Hall had murdered the son of the Governor. How it got there no one knew, but such news always seems to be borne ahead by some winged messenger. We have known *rumors* of such facts outstrip any possible earthly conveyance.

The cart conveying the corpse was surrounded by hundreds before it entered even the suburbs of the city, and Hall found himself a spectacle for idle boys and negroes to gaze at, even before he had entered the scene where he had expected it. For this abject humiliation, he was wholly unprepared. He could have met the scorn of gentlemen with scorn, but against the jeers and ribaldry of the mob he had nothing to oppose—he was wholly defenceless. Public opinion was fast gathering head against him—eager gossips picked up the horrid details from the soldiers and negroes who accompanied the corpse, as the more respectable persons drawn thither by the crowd caught a few brief words and an ominous shake of the head or two from Harry Lee. While the cart containing the body rested in the public square, Lee rode on to the Palace, to communicate the heart-rending news. The scene which there presented itself beggars description—the news had preceded him, and the ladies of the mansion were already frantic with grief. His ears were saluted with the wild shrieks of despair, and the Governor was locked up in his room and would not see even him. He sent him a message to take the prisoner before a magistrate, and have him examined.

This was done accordingly, and the same evidence detailed which we have already condensed. Not the slightest hesitation was manifested by the magistrate in making out Hall's commitment, for there appeared no redeeming circumstances whatever, save those thrown into his former statement, which of course passed for nothing, at the present stage of the proceedings.

The unfortunate, or the guilty young man, as the case might be, was loaded with irons, and deposited in the same prison which he had left but a few days before. Very few persons ventured to question his guilt—indeed, the general opinion settled down at once, that Hall had killed young Spotswood, in mistake for Harry Lee; there was very little room for surmise in the matter—there was no one else to suspect—no one else upon whom suspicion could fasten.

There were some mysterious and unexplained circumstances attending the dreadful deed, as there generally is attending all murders, such as the presence of the Indian boy. Public ingenuity was at fault in fastening upon any one whom the description would suit, and that feature of the tragedy was soon overlooked or forgotten in the absorbing horror of the plain, straight forward matters of fact. The previous circumstances connected with the history of the prisoner—such as his reputed change of name—obtaining money under false pretences, with a hundred other things which he had never done—soon accumulated into such a torrent of public indignation, that his personal safety might have been endangered in a large and more populous city. In a few days, however, this all settled down into the undoubted conviction, that John Spotswood, the son of the Governor of Virginia, had been murdered by a young man named Hall, who had found his way into the Governor's family as private tutor.

CHAPTER VIII.

VISIT TO THE PRISONER.

THERE was one strange circumstance almost contemporary with the murder, which ingenious minds endeavored to connect in some way with that mysterious affair.   Three nights before the deed was perpetrated, every Indian pupil in the college absconded, and had not since been heard of.   The interpreter, his mother and sister, were also missing.   If the desertion from the College had taken place a few days earlier, so that any of them could have arrived at the *half way* station, then the presence of the mysterious boy might have been accounted for, but all the testimony tended to prove that Spotswood himself had conveyed the boy there, and it was clearly impossible that any one of " Mr. Boyle's disciples," (as they were called,) could have reached there on the very night of leaving the city.   As the public mind became calmer, all these things were discussed, without however elucidating the dark deed much more than the first investigation had done.

Same few persons maintained Hall's innocence, even under present adverse circumstances, and notwithstanding the cloud of witnesses who were ready to appear against him.   Among the most staunch and active of these, was old Doctor Evylin, who busied himself in his behalf, by setting about a private investigation into the mysterious circumstances attending the murder—those that as yet had no light thrown upon them from the first moment of the occurrence.   Such as the affair of the Indian boy—and the disappearance of the pupils from the College.   The sagacious old man knew that if these two circumstances could be unravelled in all their bearings, that much light would be thrown upon the dark transaction, but all his inquiries were fruitless. Spotswood had taken such precautions, when he left the city, that it was impossible to trace the place from whence he had procured the boy, and all the preparations of the Indian pupils had been conducted with such secrecy, that not a trace of them could be obtained, nor could any cause be imagined for their sudden departure.   There had been no very recent outbreak between the two races in College, indeed there had been for the few days preceding their departure, uncommon quiet and peace.

The Doctor had paid one visit to the prisoner in jail, in order to learn something from which he might persue his investigations more understandingly, but except the plain tale which he had already told he could say nothing. The Doctor found him in rather a strange state of mind, for one of his intelligence,—he seemed to think, that as he had been placed in his present unfortunate position by the unforeseen concurrence of providential circumstances, that his deliverance would come from the same quarter, and by means equally startling and mysterious.   The Doctor endeavored to reason him out of this superstitious looking for of miracles, and to convince him, that the exertions of himself and friends must be in proportion to the strength of the testimony which would be brought against him; but it was to very little purpose, for up to the termination of the interview, the prisoner maintained a state alternating between mental stupor, and that wild dreamy hopefulness already described. The old man left the prison, much affected and deeply pained for the condition in which he found him, he in fact feared mental alineation.   Nevertheless, he went to work as industriously as ever, but with the same results as before. He at length determined to try what a visit from his daughter would do in the way of bringing the prisoner to a plain common sense view of his situation. She had already been struggling in the same unpromising cause, but she was now precluded from her usual resource, of consulting with Kate, as the family at the mansion, were wrapt up in profound grief, and of course could not be expected to take any part in the endeavor to exculpate the supposed author of their afflictions. No one knew what their opinions were, as to his guilt or innocence—indeed, as is usually the case, under such circumstances, they thought very little about the perpetrator of the deed; their thoughts were wholly absorbed by the death of one so near and dear to them, and it mattered little how the sad event had been brought about. The funeral was just over, and they were not visible to any body, except Ellen—she was like one of the family, but of course Hall's name was now one of those dread talismanic words which brought all the horrid tragedy to view in revivified colors, not because of any revengeful feelings towards him—*profound grief is incapable of revenge*—but that the associations of his name alone were painful. Ellen was thus, so far as female council was concerned, thrown upon her own resources, and she naturally turned to her father, that dear confidential friend from whom she concealed no secrets. She found him already actively engaged in the business, and forthwith they united their councils. She was not so ready to adopt the old gentleman's suggestion of a visit to the jail, as he had expected, but when he described the alternate lethargic and wild moods into which the prisoner was plunged, she consented at once.

It was after dark, and they found him sitting upon his wretched three legged stool, and a small taper burning on the table, within reach of the chains which hung down from his hands. His feet were free, and he could walk round a semicircle of four or five feet. On the table was a bible open, and upon it his eyes rested as they entered.

"Oh," said the old Doctor, "I am glad to see you so much more profitably employed than at my last visit; but see here I have brought you a visitor to cheer a solitary hour.'

Ellen was leaning heavily upon her father's arm, her veil still drawn close over her face. Hall made an inclination of the head, and rose and stepped forward as if to seize her hand, but was jerked suddenly back by his chains, his head fell immediately upon his chest, and the scalding tears stole down his cheeks.

All reserve was gone from Ellen at this sight, and she threw back her veil and her ringlets, and advanced and offered him both her hands. He seized and held them for some time; when he raised his face again, it was almost convulsed, so fearful was the working of his spirit, brought to a full consciousness of his position by the presence of one who had once before, as it were, brought him back to life and hope. At length he spoke—" Your presence here, Miss Evylin, is an assurance to me, that at least, there is one of your sex, who believes me innocent of the horrid crime laid to my charge."

"Oh, Mr Hall, we have never for one moment supposed you capable of crime, much less such an one as this."

"Miss Evylin, I have tried to think, but I cannot. My faculties are benumbed by the appalling severity of the blow. I have tried in vain to rally my scattered thoughts, and reflect over my past life, to try and ascertain what I have really done to deserve the afflictions which have fallen in such quick succession upon me."

"The judgments of the Almighty are not always proportioned exactly to our past offences, they have also reference to the future."

"Ah, Miss Evylin, when the poor faculties of the mind are paralyzed as mine have been, it is very difficult to discern nicely, the designs of the great and mysterious power, which rules us. If my sufferings are indeed but the chastening rod, administered in mercy and not in anger, it seems to me that the punishment has been meeted out rather beyond my capacity."

"It is only your sex," replied Ellen quickly, "that runs into these nice hair-splitting questions, ours seize upon the broad lines before us—we see, and see quickly, that this is a world of suffering and not of pleasure—of probation and not of enjoyment. Yours only finds that out in old age, but the heaviest denunciations of the curse falling upon us, we are endowed with quicker perceptions of the uses of this world."

" If it is wholly a world of trial and not of enjoyment, as you say, it appears to me as if there were studied deception about it."

" You astonish me."

" I say it in no irreverent spirit, I merely speak the honest impressions of my mind—your views are somewhat new to me, and I frankly present the difficulties in the way."

" I am impatient to hear them."

" Look at the beauty of the natural world around us—the clear blue sky— the pure air—the solemn and magnificent ocean—the towering mountains— the majestic rivers—the beautiful meadows—the sweet landscapes, and then dot them over with flocks and herds, and scatter here and there a few of man's handy works—a ruinous tower, an old vine clad castle, around which the memories of the past may gather, and tell me if this beautiful, beautiful globe, looks as if it had been made for the grand penitentiary of our race."

" I do not perceive the point at which you aim."

" It is the inconsistency between God's natural and moral governments. If this is indeed but one great prison house for the purification of our race from sin, why is it not clothed in the habiliments of the penitentiary ?"

" Why, Mr Hall ! would you have the heavens hung eternally in black, our mountains dark precipices and beetling crags—our rivers driving torrents ; our beautiful landscapes nothing but dreary wilds, inhabited by howling monsters ? Why this would lead the thoughts down to hell, and not up to heaven. Think of the first glories of the natural world upon your own heart, give scope to your imagination and reinvest the pictures which you have just drawn, and see and feel if they do not point to heaven and tell of God! All the poetry of this life—the real poetry—is nothing more than the overpowering aspirations after still brighter regions and sunnier skies, elicited by the faint sketches which we catch here and there from these beauties which are scattered around us for this very purpose. Poetry is the true language of heaven, and not a breath of inspiration ever fell to man, but was drawn, if not from God, at least from his glorious works."

Hall forgot for the time his sorrows and his chains. He replied, " You overpower my benumbed faculties with your delightful enthusiasm, but still my reason is not wholly convinced. We know that deception is the result of all the beauties of nature of which we have been speaking. Men bow down before these bountiful works of God and forget the maker in that which he has made. Does it not seem to our poor mortal vision, that it would have been better, had the scene of our probation been less seductive ?"

" Why what difference does it make whether the sufferings with which we are surrounded are of a spiritual or a physical nature. Surely there is mercy as well as wisdom in the present arrangement. If we are in a penitentiary, as you call it, it is certainly mercy to us that our prison house is so beautiful, and filled and surrounded with so many comforts. God does not wish to punish but to purify us. Moreover, when our trials are mostly of, a spiritual nature, it enables the great ruler of our destinies to measure out the chastisement to the capacity of the creature. If all nature had been shrouded in gloom and our physical necessities constantly kept on the stretch as the means of purifying us for a better state of existence, then all men must have been afflicted alike, and the poor grovelling unintellectual creatures of our race have suffered unnecessarily. As it is, only those who are highly endowed, ever suffer the afflictions which surround you. You never saw a mere animal man schooled and purified in this manner. There is no truer precept in that holy book, than the one which says, ' whom the Lord loveth he chasten-

'eth.' Rest assured, Sir, that you are reserved for some great purpose yet, even in this world. I have suffered in the same school, and therefore I have presumed to lecture you."

" May God always send me such a teacher !"

The old physician meanwhile, slowly walked the narrow cell, and occasionally as some remark of one or other of the speakers arrested his attention, he leaned his hands upon his cane and his chin upon his hands, raising up his benevolent visage between the speakers, with a beaming smile lightening up the parchment like wrinkles. He was delighted to see how Ellen, with all a woman's tact, succeeded in her errand, so much better than he had done.

" You see, Mr. Hall," said the old man, " that we do not even entertain the question of your guilt or innocence, we take it for granted that you are unfortunate and not criminal, but, my dear Sir, you know enough of the world to be aware that the public is not so easily satisfied, where appearances are against a man. You must now look about you, and take the necessary steps to make your innocence apparent ; and, if possible, ferret out the real criminal. Have you no suspicions of any one?"

" None in the world. I am as ignorant of the person who murdered Spotswood—the manner of its accomplishment—and nearly all the attendant circumstances, as your innocent daughter. I was so shocked and benumbed on the morning of my arrest, that I scarcely noted the wretched details taken down by Henry Lee; and since then I have had less opportunity than others to learn anything of them."

" Have you any suspicion that Lee himself did the deed?" and the old man stopped and looked searchingly into his face, as he waited for his answer.

Hall mused a moment, and then replied, " No, no—he could not be guilty of such a crime, he had no earthly motive. Had it been me, now, that was killed, I am not so sure that he would not be liable to suspicion"—hastily checking himself, he said, " but no, it is too bad, I must do even him the justice to say, that he could not commit murder upon his enemy."

Ellen's beaming eye rewarded him for his magnanimous admission, as she said, " you are right, Mr. Lee, with all his faults, is no murderer ; but think you he will be as generous towards you on the day of trial?"

" I know not, nor does it matter much—luckily, neither my condemnation nor deliverance will come from him. My reliance is upon the discovery of the real criminal."

" Well, Mr. Hall," continued the Doctor, " if you can throw no light upon the murder, at least you can relieve yourself from your doubtful position before that time. I understand from your counsel whom I sent to you, that all suspicious circumstances anterior to the date of the murder become now of immense importance, and—"

Hall waved his hand impatiently—"No more! no more ! my dear Sir. Had this thing not happened, then indeed it might have become me to clear my good name from reproach, and to tell you the truth, I only waited to hear from the other side of the water to do so, but now I must begin the work of purification at the bottom. If I am destined to die the death of a felon, it will make very little difference in what light I stood previously. If, on the other hand, it is the will of Providence to point out the real criminal, so that I may stand forth before all men, free even from a shade of suspicion, then I will indeed resume my station in society."

He was much agitated while touching upon these delicate matters, and walked the length of his chains like a chafed lion in his cage, and when he had concluded, threw himself upon his rude seat, and buried his face in his hands.

The father and daughter seeing his deep distress, approached to take their leave. He rose up, and taking both of Ellen's hands within his, shook them with great feeling, and evidently struggling to maintain his composure, and then wrung the old man's hand, without uttering a word.

As the two left the prison, the former said, "Did you ever see such a man as that, in like circumstances before—such an one charged with a crime so wholly foreign to his whole nature."

"Ah, my Ellen, if you will look through the State Trials of our father-land, you will find gentlemen and noblemen, whose whole lives gave the lie to the charges brought against them, and guilty, too, and for which they suffered. It is not that upon which I found my confidence of his innocence, it is the absence of all motive."

"But they say, he supposed it was Harry Lee, because poor John was wrapped up in his cloak."

"Aye, but did you hear him just now say, that he could not suspect Lee of the deed, and would a man murder another of whose character he was thus tender. No, no, my child, he neither committed it intentionally nor by mistake."

Thus they discussed the subject until a late hour—between them devising the best means they could to assist the prisoner on the morrow, when he was to be brought out for examination before the Grand Inquest of the County, or rather of the Colony, for the General Court had jurisdiction to its utmost limits.

CHAPTER IX.

TRIAL FOR LIFE.

It is sufficient to say, that a true bill was found against the prisoner for the murder of John Spotswood, and as the evidence was pretty much the same as detailed at both trials, we will not fatigue the reader with the long preliminaries of the law's proverbial delay, but convey him at once to the court-room, where Hall was put upon his final trial for life. Some time had intervened since he was last presented to the reader—in that time a good deal of alteration had taken place in his personal appearance. He was very well dressed, but looked thin and pale. Never at any time robust, care, confinement, and excessive wear and tear of mind and body, had reduced him to great attenuation—his large whiskers, and the scar across his face, made him look cadaverous, as he stood up to plead guilty or not guilty to the charge—the latter of which he did in a deep, clear, manly voice, which rung through the court-room with something of the assurance of innocence to those who were interested in his fate. It was impossible for disinterested strangers, or those who were no way pledged against him, to look upon that intellectual forehead—clear sparkling eye—fine chiselled, and new wax-like features—without being interested in his fate. Nevertheless, there was something unnatural about his appearance—his eye was wild and bright, and his mouth was compressed with a solemn compactness, such as often produces a painful impression when looking at fine statuary. Those best acquainted with him were struck with his appearance; and Moore, in the benevolence of his heart, and shaken in his faith by the reputed unanswerable testimony against him, moved round to where he saw old Dr. Evylin sitting, and asked him if he did not think that there was a maniacal look about the prisoner's eyes, which might account for the deed of guilt. The old man gazed long and steadily at him, and then shook his head, and turning to Moore, whispered to him, that "Hall was as innocent of the death of John Spotswood as he was, who was more than a hundred miles distant."

Over this court the Governor usually presided in person, but on the present occasion, the chair was occupied by the venerable Commissary, the senior counsellor, surrounded by his associates. No difficulty was made by Hall whatever to empannelling the jury, notwithstanding the earnest remonstrances of his counsel and the old Doctor, who came across the court-room and seated himself near them.

The room was crowded to suffocation, and not a few of those present, ladies of the first families of the Colony. Ellen Evylin was not there, she could not trust herself, or rather her father would not trust her, but she had delegated her zeal and interest in the issue of the cause to the keeping of her venerable parent. She followed him to the gate issuing into the street, as he was leaving home to come to the court-house, and hung upon his arm, and charged and enjoined upon the old gentleman to leave nothing undone to make Hall's innocence manifest. "Recollect father," said she calling after him, "that it is not enough merely to pronounce such a man not guilty, but he must be raised above suspicion; and remember, too, that if it becomes necessary to show Harry Lee in his true character, I must be summoned. Be sure I will not shrink from the trial in such an extremity."

All eyes were turned towards the prisoner, when he rose as before described to respond to the challenge—seldom, or never before, had such a prisoner stood within that bar. There had, it is true, been interesting trials; for the old Roman at the head of the Colony had just hung in chains six pirates, who had infested the coast during the previous years of his administration, and who had been pursued and caught through his energy alone, but never had there stood such a man charged with such an offence within that bar before. There was a death-like stillness pervading the room, (after the crowd had become once settled down,) showing the absorbing interest of the trial even to the multitude. This multitude, however, was of a higher grade than usually made up the throng of the court-house, for the tramontane army was to set out as soon as the Governor was sufficiently restored to himself to conduct it; and most of the youthful chivalry of the Colony were present—the very men who were soon to march across the great Apalachee.

Hall seemed to feel that far more than life was upon the issue of that trial. It might have been seen in his countenance, that character and standing in society once gone, he would not value mere animal life at a "pin's fee."

The Attorney General rose and stated the case of the crown plainly and succinctly. He lamented that he was called upon by imperative duty to lend his professional efforts to unfold a career of crime almost unexampled on this side of the water, especially among that class which he had understood the prisoner was so well calculated to adorn. He said he had heard of his elegant accomplishments and brilliant abilities, and however much these were calculated to add to our regrets that such a man should so demean himself, and however much they might seize upon our sympathies, those in whose hands was placed the administration of justice, were more bound than usual to prosecute to the utmost extent of the law. He said that no one within the walls of that court-room would rejoice more sincerely that he would, if it should turn out differently from what he supposed; but he expected to prove that the prisoner had landed at Yorktown, with some Scotch Irish emigrants sometime before; that immediately upon his arrival, he had, with other accomplices, taken the usual means of burglars to spy out the condition of the wealthiest houses in the neighborhood; that in the night time, and during a thunder-storm, he had found his way into the Governor's country house, with his features secured behind a mask, as well as his two associates, one a male and the other a female. He was not, he said, absolutely certain that he could prove this link in the chain of testimony by admissible evidence, because the reconnoitre had been undertaken when all the white family were from home. However, from this point, he said the chain of testimony was unbroken—that he had soon after the mask adventure presented himself to the Governor, as a young man anxious for employment—that His Excellency had him then examined by the

Reverend Gentleman then presiding over the court, and finding him competent, had out of the abundance of his benevolence and kind-heartedness, for which he was well known by all present, given him the employment—that he had most shamefully abused the trust reposed in him by his patron—first, in presenting himself under a false name; and, secondly, in using that name to obtain moneys to which he had no earthly claim, and for which he would have been indicted as a swindler, had not the minor offence been swallowed up in the monstrous one with he now stood charged. That he had gone on from step to step, until he had wound up his career of guilt, by murdering the son of his benefactor and patron, if, indeed, the prisoner himself knew who it really was that he had slain. He thought it would appear in evidence, that he harbored deadly malignity against one of the most honorable and respectable young men in the colony, who slept in the same room on the night of the murder, and who was at that very time in pursuit of the prisoner. That the young gentleman in question, Henry Lee, Esq., had lent the deceased his cloak, and that in the dark he had been murdered, in mistake for Mr. Lee; that the prisoner had fled as soon as the dark deed had been perpetrated, and when apprehended, was making his way with the utmost expedition towards the frontier, and had actually left the military road and taken to the woods, until he supposed himself out of the reach of pursuit; that upon his arrest, he had manifested unequivocal symptoms of guilt, and, moreover, that the blood of his victim was still reeking from his clothes and person.

He concluded by assuring the court and jury, that in all his professional experience, he had never been able to present to that court or any other, such an unbroken chain of circumstantial evidence. That though he was not seen in the actual moment of committing the offence, that he would be able to trace him in a career of crime, from the first moment of landing to that of his arrest. That the motive was apparent—the usual steps of criminal graduation were also present, so that the enlightened jury, would feel at no loss to trace in their own minds the whole criminal process, by which this most gifted but criminal individual had reduced himself to his present state of degradation.

The first witness called on the part of the crown was Kit Carter. He was proceeding to relate the adventure of the mask, as he had heard it on his return to Temple Farm on the night of the adventure, but he was stopped by the counsel for the prisoner, and told that he must relate no hearsay evidence.

Hall exclaimed in a loud clear voice, "Let him go on. I was one of those masked visitors!" His counsel assured him that he would throw up the case, unless he entrusted the whole management to him.

Carter then went on to relate what is already well known to the reader, about Hall's introduction as Tutor—his conduct while acting as such, and his general deportment so far as he had observed it. His evidence upon the whole was rather unfavorable to the prisoner.

Moore was next called to the stand, and he related pretty much the same story with the exception of his conduct in prison, and their private intercourse, which had made a rather more favorable impression than the prisoner's conduct had done upon the previous witness. The facts were mostly the same—the general impressions more favorable.

Henry Lee was then called on to give his testimony. There was a general restlessness in the crowd, and a disposition to get nearer and hear better, as this witness was called. It was known that he would bear hard upon the prisoner, and would give nearly the whole of Hall's history since he landed in the country. Nor was this anxiety to hear him, confined to the rude and the vulgar—the mutual acquaintances of the parties, were also curious to hear him relate all the circumstances of their quarrel, for it was generally reported that they had quarrelled. Moore suspected that the quarrel had proceeded to blows, and he knew that there was a deadly enmity on the part of Lee, at least.

The witness stated that on a recent visit to Temple Farm, he found the prisoner acting as Tutor to the Governor's youngest son, and occasionally as his draftsman and private secretary. That he was surprised to find that he was of the same name with a young relation of his in Scotland, to whom he had but recently written—preceding his visit, that one morning he had expressed this surprise to the prisoner, when he immediately stated that he was the very man himself; that he stated to the prisoner that he had written such letters, but he the prisoner, said he had never received them, which seemed reasonable, as there was scarcely time for those letters to have arrived out before the prisoner at the bar must have set sail: that he, (Lee,) was taken by surprise by the prisoner's statement, but backed as he was by Governor Spotswood, had yielded to his ready assent; that he had stated to the prisoner the fact, that he had fallen heir to a snug little property here, and that he, (Lee,) had surrendered into his hands part of the available funds of said estate, without any other voucher or guarantee than the prisoner's note of hand—that money however, had since been repaid by Mr. Bernard Moore. He stated farther, that he had very soon after forming an acquaintance with the prisoner, and after having admitted his claims to relationship, began to suspect him—he did not exactly know why, unless it had been the impression made by his general deportment; that they had several unpleasant altercations before the witness left Temple Farm; that the prisoner had never taken any steps to prove his identity—that he could show no letters from any one, either credentials of character or letters of credit—and moreover could show no letters from his venerable relation deceased, although there were several found among her papers from Henry Hall—the individual whom the prisoner pretended to be. The prisoner evaded this by saying that he would be able to show them when the remainder of his baggage arrived, but so far as he knew, to this day no such letters had ever arrived. He stated that he had lately received answers to those very letters which he had written to Mr. Henry Hall, in Scotland, purporting to be written by Mr. Hall, then in Scotland, so that there were two Henry Halls, if the prisoner at the bar established his claims to the name.

As to the murder, he stated that he had pursued the prisoner, after he had been liberated by Mr. Moore, and must by some accident or other, have passed him on the road, as he was on his return to the capital, when he stopped for the night at the stockade where the deed was committed. He said he had not seen the prisoner on the night of the murder at all, and was entirely unconscious that they had slept in the same room, until the investigation of the next morning had convinced him of the fact. He said he had lent Capt. Spotswood a cloak usually worn by himself, at the request of the Captain, who stated that he had lent his own to a boy who accompanied him, and who had none. Who that boy was, and whence he had come and whither gone, he could form no idea. All search for him had proved fruitless, although troopers had been despatched along both ends of the road at day-light.

He described the position in which the body lay when found at daylight, as well as that occupied by the prisoner during the night—and stated that the prisoner had escaped before any one was stirring—that there were distinct foot-prints in blood on the puncheons of the floor, and on the ground leading to the gate of the stockade—and that these when measured, corresponded exactly with the size and shape of the prisoner's shoes—and, moreover, that when the shoes were taken off to be compared with the foot-prints, blood was still distinctly visible, having deeply stained the leather beneath the mud; that his face and person were also stained with blood, and that he had offered no explanation whatever of all these suspicious circumstances when arrested, except that he had left the block-house about an hour before day light. When asked why he had stolen off without seeing any one, and without even thanking the woman who had furnished him with his supper, he acknowledged that he had done so to avoid observation. The prisoner, he said, wore no weapons about him when arrested. The dagger with which the deed was done belonged to the deceased, and was so driven in when the fatal wound was inflicted, as could only have been conveniently done from the side on which the prisoner lay. Such was about the sum and substance of Lee's testimony, elicited by the questions of the Attorney General. He was then turned over to the prisoner's counsel, who proceeded to cross-question him very minutely, not, however, by any prompting from Hall, who now sat with a solemn serenity upon his features, and scarcely taking an ordinary interest in the details of the evidence. Occasionally he would start as some answer of the witness seemed to surprise him, but speedily relapsed again into his former mood. He declined prompting his counsel altogether in his cross-examination of Lee, and that gentleman was compelled to call Dr. Evylin and Moore, each side of him, in order to learn more accurately the various relations of the parties touched upon by the witness. Moore very soon discovered that this was a conjunction by no means propitious to the objects in view by the Attorney, and he wrote as much on a slip of paper ; soon after which, he whispered to the old Doctor, who retired for a while. When he was gone, the cross-examination commenced.

Question. Did you form a bad opinion of the prisoner upon your first acquaintance ?

Answer. I cannot say that I formed any very definite opinion of him. He occupied at that time very little of my thoughts. I thought him rather out of place in the society in which I found him.

Question. Did you, Mr. Lee, see anything wrong in the prisoner, until you discovered him to be your rival for the favor of a very estimable young lady, to whom it is generally understood you were paying your address ?

[Lee curled his lips with high disdain, and at first seemed to think of declining a reply, but the counsel insisted upon an answer.]

Answer. However presumptuous I might have thought the prisoner, I scarcely esteemed him a very formidable rival, if one at all.

Question. Will you tell the court and jury in what way he was presumptuous ?

Answer. By intruding himself into society where he had no claims whatever. It is not usual, I believe, for tutors to associate on terms of equality with the female members of his employer's family, and more especially when that employer occupies the exalted station of Governor of the Colony.

Question. Was it, Mr. Lee, so much the prisoner's forcing himself into the society of the ladies of the Governor's immediate family, which gave you offence, as into that of the young lady before alluded to ?

[The witness refused to answer, until ordered to do so by the court.]

Answer. It was not.

Question. Did his presence seem offensive to that lady ?

Answer. Not until after I had informed her of the ungrateful return which the prisoner made of her kindness, by representing her as having sought him.

Question. Was there not a quarrel between the prisoner and yourself which grew out of that very representation which you made to the lady ?

Answer. He was rather insolent to me, Sir, and I threatened to chastise him, and perhaps in the heat of anger, I made a pass at him with my sword.

Question. What did the prisoner do then—did he tamely submit ?

Answer. By an accidental and fortunate use of his walking cane he disarmed me for the moment.

Question. For the moment, Mr. Lee ! Were you not completely at his mercy, and did he not act with the greatest magnanimity towards you ?

Answer. I was perhaps somewhat in his power; but the matter was adjourned, not concluded.

Question. Well, Sir, the prisoner seems to have been victorious in war—who triumphed in love?

The witness appealed to the court for protection against the trifling and impertinence of counsel.

The counsel hereupon stated that he considered it a very important question—that he wished to show by it, that the witness had every earthly reason for cherishing deadly hostility against the prisoner, having been triumphed over by him in two most tender points.

The court ruled, that if within the witness's knowledge, he must answer the question.

Answer. I know nothing as to the result of the prisoner's love affairs, if he had any.

Question. Has not your own terminated disastrously, since the prisoner's acquaintance with the lady?

Answer. It has, Sir.

Here there was a general titter throughout the court room.

Many other questions were put to this witness and answered, but mostly touching points already made known to the reader, we shall therefore intermit them and pass on to the next, who was Mr. McDonald, a man originally from Scotland, and who lived in the neighborhood of the deceased lady who had willed her property to Henry Hall. He was asked if he knew the individual to whom that property was intended to be given? He said, he had known him almost from his infancy! He was then asked to look upon the prisoner, and say whether he was the individual named Henry Hall?

"There was an intense interest manifested to hear the old man's reply, as he turned his head and gazed long and searchingly at the prisoner. Once or twice he turned his head away as if satisfied, and then turned his eyes upon him again, evidently baffled and perplexed.

The Attorney-General put the queston to him again: "Is this man—the prisoner at the bar—the Mr. Henry Hall you knew in Scotland?"

For his life, he said, he said he could not tell, "at times when he looked at him, he thought it was, and then again when he moved his head, he thought it was not. He is certainly very much like, if it is not the man himself." He said further, that he had not seen him for some years, and in a young man, doubtless great changes might have taken place.

Lee was confounded—he now sat near the Attorney-General, and consulted with him anxiously,—he had supposed that McDonald would not hesitate, and that Hall would stand forth before all men, not only a convicted murderer, but one who had run a long career of deception and guilt. He had no doubt of McDonald's honesty, from the Attorney-General's character of him, and he was utterly at a loss to account for his hesitation.

General Clayton next asked the witness, "if Mr. Hall, when he knew him had that large scar across his face."

"No; he had not."

"Was the color of the hair and eyes the same?"

"Yes; precisely."

"Did Mr. Hall, when you knew him, wear whiskers?"

"No; he did not."

"Did the height of the two correspond exactly?"

"No; the prisoner was taller by several inches, but then he might have grown that much."

"Were they about the same weight?"

"No; this gentleman is broader in his shoulders, and a larger frame."

"Then, except the hair and eyes, they were totally dissimilar?"

" He could not say what it was about this man that reminded him of the one he had known, but there was something—whether it was in the features, or the expression, he could not tell, but still he would not swear that this was not Mr. Hall."

There was a grim smile of some sort of gratification playing about the corners of the prisoner's mouth during the whole of this examination. He looked straight at the witness, and his eye never quailed for an instant. It was the only time during the whole trial that he conferred with his lawyer, and seemed to take an interest in what was going on.

The witness being now turned over to the prisoner's counsel, several questions were asked which evidently came from the prisoner himself.

" Did you not know of Henry Hall's having met with an accident—a fall from his horse—by which one of his arms was dislocated ?"

" Yes ; I remember it well."

" Is not the mansion house of the Hall's, one of peculiar structure, one that a man would not easily learn from mere description ?"

" It is very peculiar, and it would be almost impossible for one to learn its localities from paper."

" Was there not a picture of a celebrated battle hung just between the windows of the gallery facing to the east ?"

" There was."

" Had not the frame of that picture been penetrated by a ball from a pistol discharged by accident from the hands of this young man himself ?"

" I must believe it to be so, for no one could well know those things but himself."

The witness sat down. His testimony had evidently a little shaken that fickle thing, popular opinion, and in a much greater degree re-assured the old Doctor and Moore, and such other friends of the unfortunate prisoner at the bar, as dared to adhere to him.

The witnesses of the stockade were now called in—the woman who had waited upon the prisoner—the soldier who had seen him on the fatal night as well as those who arrested him. By these pretty much the same testimony was given as had been already given by Lee, or else made known to the reader at previous investigations. Very few were called in on the part of the prisoner, few indeed knew him, except those who had already testified against him, Old Doctor Evylin, was the chief one relied upon.

He stated, "that he had known the prisoner almost from the moment of his landing in the country—that he had felt great interest in him from the very first—partly, he supposed, from the circumstances of his being an elegant scholar, and a polished gentleman in every respect, and from his friendless condition when he had made his acquaintance. He saw from the first, that he was in a false position—that his circumstances at some period of his life must have been far higher. He drew this opinion, from certain habits of thought as well as actions, from deep and inherent tastes, not as he believed, the growth ever of one generation. He expressed the opinion unhesitatingly, when questioned—that the prisoner himself, was not only a gentleman of the highest toned feelings and instincts, but that his fathers before him had been, and that he was utterly incapable of a mean or dishonorable action, much more of a cold blooded and deliberate murder. There was a general smile throughout the court-house, at the old Doctor's warmth of feeling, more than at his thorough and inbred aristocratic notions. The evidence having been all gone through on both sides, and it now being quite dark, the court was adjourned until the next day at 10 o'clock, and the jury handed over to the care of the Sheriff. The remainder of the proceedings, will be treated of in the next chapter.

CHAPTER X.

THE DEFENCE.

PUNCTUAL to the hour, the court assembled, and along with it, even a greater crowd of anxious spectators than had attended on the previous day. This was partly occasioned by the previous appointment of this very day, for the meeting of the young gentry at the capital in order to make arrangements for the immediate marching of the tramontane expedition. But even the great enterprise itself, was forgotten in the intense interest manifested by all classes in the trial going on.

The prisoner was again placed at the bar. The court in their judical wigs and robes, and the jury in the box. Old Dr. Evylin and Bernard Moore sat together in melancholy silence—the excitement produced by their exertions in behalf of the prisoner as long as it could avail anything, served to stimulate them, but now it had died away and left them sad and dispirited, and with a gloomy foreboding as to the fate of the unfortunate young man. Except these, there was a very general feeling of indignation against him. Amidst all these discouraging circumstances, the counsel for the prisoner rose and commenced a most labored and ingenious defence. He argued that there was not one particle of positive testimony against the prisoner, and none that would not equally lie against the very witnesses who had most strongly testified against him. Indeed, he said there was more impelling motives urging Mr. Lee himself to the deed than him, not that he would insinuate so foul a charge against that gentleman—he only pointed the minds of the jury to the possibilities of the case—aye, and to the probabilities—in order to show that the matter was still shrouded in the profoundest mystery—that one of the persons in that room was as liable to have done it as another—that no more probable motives for the diabolical deed had been traced to the prisoner than to any of the others.

Indeed, that a motive might be imagined on the part of one of the witnesses, but none in the world on that of the prisoner. As to the miserable story about his mistaking young Spotswood for Lee, it was not worth one moment's consideration. Could the prisoner, who was in the habit of daily association with the two gentlemen, mistake the arms of a Ranger, constantly worn by John Spotswood, and with which the deed was done—as well as mistake his gold laced uniform? It was in evidence that the deceased had been throttled by a powerful adversary—could the prisoner have approached him in such an attitude, without discovering who it really was, if he had been laboring under a mistake—and above all, could that feeble and almost consumptive figure grapple in the death struggle with such a man as Spotswood was known to be—nearly, if not entirely restored to health?—it was absurd and ridiculous.

"I say then, again," continued he, "that there is just as much evidence that Lee committed the murder as that Hall committed it. If it is a groundless assumption in the one case, it was in the other also. I see the Attorney General smile; but, sir, let me suppose a case which I think quite as probable as the one he has made out. It is known that there was a deadly enmity existing between the prisoner and Mr. Lee—they were rivals—the former, whatever he was in reality, supposed to be the successful one. They meet in a dark room at a frontier settlement, the latter finds an opportunity of throwing the odium of the blackest offence known to our laws upon his rival. Circumstances so turn out that the prisoner from his position in that room must be suspected, let who may have committed the deed. Now, is this hypothetical case more improbable than that made out by the Attorney General? I merely make it—not to cast suspicion upon the young gentleman who has been the principal witness in this case, but to show that the matter is still so much involved in obscurity, that it is capable of being laid at this, and that man's skirts. This it could not be, if the evidence was sufficient to warrant conviction." He went into a long legal discussion to show that the law compelled the jury to acquit the prisoner, when there were grounds of reasonable doubt, and that there was ground in this case, and they were therefore bound to give the prisoner the benefit of those doubts ; and finally wound up by a manly and thrilling appeal to the feelings of the jury.

Several times during the delivery of this speech, of which we have merely given a rude synopsis—the prisoner caught his counsel by the coat tail and tugged at it, as if he would have him desist; at which the legal gentleman would turn round, almost in a passion, and beg in a whispered voice not to be interrupted. So troublesome did his client become at last, that he was compelled to request Mr. Moore to set by him, and prevent the unreasonable interruption.

The Attorney General then summed up in behalf of the crown. He linked together most ably all the circumstances which we have already detailed to the reader, from the landing of the prisoner to the night of the murder, not forgetting the prisoner's admission as to the mask scene at Temple Farm. He did not for a moment contend that he had murdered young Spotswood knowingly, but that he had perpetrated a cold-blooded and deliberate murder, and it made no difference in the eye of the law, that the object or the party had been changed in the meantime or mistaken. He laid down the law and called upon the court to bear him out in it, that the crime was precisely the same. He even went farther, and contended that if the blow had been feloniously aimed at his victim's dog or his horse, and had killed him instead, the law still held him guilty, not only of the homicide, but of the malice *prepense*. He lamented that he was called upon to perform so irksome a task as the prosecution of one, who, from the testimony, was so well calculated to adorn the highest circles in the land ; but at the same time contended that exactly in proportion as he was pre-eminent for abilities, or distinguished for accomplishments, were the court and the jury bound to protect their fellow-subjects from such dangerous weapons in such unprincipled hands. He knew, said he, the ingenuity and the eloquence of his legal adversary, and that he would attempt to excite the sympathies of the jury in behalf of the friendless and accomplished stranger ; but he advised them to turn their sympathies into another channel—to look at the cold corpse of his noble and gifted victim, cut off in the first bloom of youth, without a moment's preparation, with all his sins upon his head ; and then to turn their eyes to the distinguished family, and listen there to the wailing and weeping which ascended constantly to heaven from that bereaved house. He concluded by a judicious and high wrought invocation in behalf of the injured laws of the country, and called upon the jury to pronounce that verdict of condemnation which he could see public opinion had already awarded to him, and which he solemnly believed he so well merited.

This speech had considerable effect in rather confirming, than changing the opinions of the court and jury, and indeed of the public generally, for there were scarcely two opinions in the court-house, as to his guilt or innocence.

The lawyers having concluded on both sides, that awful moment of suspense arrived, when the court paused, previous to summing up the evidence and charging the jury.

It fell to the lot of the Reverend Commissary to perform this unpleasant duty, from which, however, whatever might have been his feelings, he did not shrink. He summed up the testimony in the most lucid manner, and charged the jury to suffer no ingenuity of the prisoner's counsel, nor affecting appeals to their sympathies, to swerve them from the strong and irrefutable circumstances of the case, and from performing their duty to the crown and the country, however disagreeable.

The jury brought in a verdict of "guilty of wilful murder," without leaving the box; and as was usual in Virginia, the prisoner was immediately arraigned to receive sentence. A death-like silence reigned throughout the crowded court-room, when he was asked if he had aught to say, why sentence should not be pronounced against him. He clapped his hand to his forehead for a moment, ere he arose to his feet. He stood at length in the full dignity of his height, and in one moment had thrown all agitation to the winds. There was something attractive about the man, even to that indignant court and audience—the deathly paleness of his visage—his bright, but serene eye and that solemn voice, when it first thrilled high over the heads of the people—altogether, had no ordinary fascination in them.

Every eye was bent upon the prisoner, and every ear strained, as he exclaimed, "Have I anything to say, why sentence of death should not be pronounced upon me? I have not—too much has been said already; but I call the court and these good people to witness that it was not with my consent or approbation. God is my witness, that I crave not the poor boon of mere animal life, when it has been stripped of all that distinguishes it from grovelling natures. By the strangest concurrence of circumstances that, I solemnly believe, ever befel an individual before, I have been stripped, one by one, of the ties which bound me to life—the sweet charities—the domestic affections—the warm friendships—the noble aims—the bright aspirations—the daring enterprises—have all been struck down. Every fibre of my heart has been rudely torn asunder, and trampled upon by this cruel array of circumstances. Why should I desire to live longer, when in living thus long I have met nothing but disaster. I shudder with superstitious dread when I look back to the days of my young and bright hopes, and see how they have been fulfilled. Oh! those gorgeous dreams of youth are but too bitter delusions? Who could have foreseen then that the brilliant promise of such a sunrise, would so soon set in utter darkness. 'Tis not that I fear death; on the contrary, I court it, in an honorable field—but my whole mental organization shrinks from the reproach and the odium which has already been, and will still more be cast upon my memory. Great God! the wildest fears of my diseased imagination during the delirium of fever, never dared approach the gibbet—neither sleeping or waking have I thought such a thing within the range of possibility. But to live, after what has passed, is even worse than a disgraceful death. One is a short and sudden pang; and the fitful and feverish dream of life is o'er--its painful illusions, its hollow friendships, and its fleeting and deceitful pleasures; but the other is a living and breathing death—a walking target for the shafts of slander and calumny. What man is there within this vast throng, reared at the feet of a sweet and angel mother, to all the softest and tenderest sympathies of a gentle nature, (here he dashed a tear hastily from his eyes, and proceeded,) and all the instincts of the gentleman—who could have the stamp of Cain officially branded upon his forehead, and then walk the earth, as God created it, with his face towards Heaven. Oh, it is too much! This seat of the passions and affections which throbs so tumultuously within me, will surely burst the barriers of its prison, before the final seal is put to this legal wrong. Not that I would insinuate aught against the purity or impartiality of court or jury, both have done every thing that the poor means within their reach permitted. The offended majesty of the laws, *according to its forms*, demand my death, and most willingly is life offered up to those bald and barren forms.

"But be assured that the death of the victim will only keep up the cruel mistake for a brief while; the time will surely come, when the real murderer of the Governor's son will stand revealed to the world. For a while, the unfortunate train of circumstances which compassed me about on that fatal night, must appear stronger than the poor, tame truth. No one who has lived long in this world of cheating and deception, but must have discovered that truth generally lies far beneath the surface in the ordinary current of its affairs. I shall not undertake the now useless task of showing where the really wonderful body of circumstantial evidence brought to bear against me fails, and where a single link of the real truth would point the whole in another direction, because, as I have already intimated, the truth would appear almost ridiculous, when brought into comparison with the splendid logical conclusions of the Attorney General. Sufficient for me here, in the presence of this court and this good people, to call Heaven to witness my entire innocence. I am not only innocent of the special crime laid to my charge, but may the lightning of Heaven strike me dead where I stand, if such a conception as murder ever entered my heart. I cannot realize it—I cannot imagine how any one could commit a murder ; and yet I am convicted by the laws of my country, after a patient and laborious investigation, of that crime—of the foullest crime known to those laws. It all seems to me, even now, like some fearful dream ! That I, whose whole soul has been fired almost from infancy with longing aspirations after some legitimate means to benefit my fellow-men—that I, who have aimed at and struggled after unattainable perfection, whose ambition soared to none but lofty eminences, and to whom, for a long time, the honest and every day occupations of men appeared poor, and tame, and mean—should at last fall to such a degradation—so low as this. Oh ! 'tis overwhelming. It is hard to die a violent death at all times, doubtless ; but it is doubly hard to fall thus, with the unjust execrations of all men ringing in my ears. But surveying the whole ground as impartially and as calmly as I can, I can see no false step of mine since I arrived in the Colony, by which I could have avoided my present position. I have done and suffered every thing which a mere human agent could do, and I leave the result in the hands of that righteous Judge to whose decrees I bow with resignation.

"Now, with my hopes blasted—my aspirations crushed—all the sweet charities of life trampled upon and outraged—my affections blighted—no, thank God, they are enshrined beyond the reach of evil ———."

At this point, there was great confusion near the door, and the officers in vain endeavored to keep silence. At first, some supposed a rescue was to be attempted ; and the court directed the sheriff to the prisoner, who had sat down and was calmly waiting with others to see what had produced the disturbance. Presently a servant of Dr. Evylin was seen forcing his way among the crowd, holding a letter as a sort of passport for his intrusion. Some one seeing the superscription plucked it from his hand, and conveyed it at once to the old man. He tore it open and read it hastily—great drops of perspiration still standing upon his brow and lip from the painful excitement of the trial ; but he had no sooner ran his eye along the lines, than his eyes brightened, and the whole man was instantly transformed. He sprang upon one of the benches with the activity of a boy, and leaning his chin upon the bannister surrounding the platform on which the court sat, motioned to the judge that he had something to communicate. That venerable functionary moved his chair, so as to bring his ear near enough to hear, alone, what the old Doctor had to say. The first words whispered by the latter startled him, and they were instantly engaged in the most earnest conversation—a few moments after which, he took the letter handed by the Doctor, and read it himself. He consulted a few moments with his colleagues, and then rose—standing, however, many minutes, before the confusion incident to so unusual an interruption could be subdued. He stated to the lawyers, on both sides, that a most providential revelation had come to light—that he held in his hand a note from a lady, who could have no motive in deceiving them, stating that a most important witness had that moment arrived in the capital—one who was present at the murder, and had seen the very act committed. " Of course," said the old man, " no mere forms of law, to whatever lengths we may have gone, can prevent us from retracing our steps, if we have unknowingly done injustice. The note does not state who the witness is who saw the murder committed—but I presume from the eagerness with which the writer demands that her witness may be heard, that some other person must have committed it than the prisoner at the bar. God grant that it may be so—for though still a human being has done the foul deed, it would be difficult to find within the Colony one to whom it would attach with the same moral turpitude as the prisoner ; and let me add, as a necessary consequence, that my joy at the prospect of his deliverance is proportionably great. I would not willingly have condemned such a man to a felon's death."

The eager crowd was now busy with the startling news. Groups were gathering here and there, wondering who the witness could be, and the prisoner was heard to exclaim, " My God, I thank thee."

Bernard Moore grasped his hand cordially, and congratulated him upon his prospect of deliverance. Hall motioned for him to be seated beside him, and then said in a low tone, " Moore, should I live a hundred years, I will never forget that you dared befriend a stranger, when the whole current of public opinion was setting strong against him. Any man may have mere physical courage, but *that* is what I call true moral courage ; and the good old Doctor stood by me manfully to the last, and he would have followed me to the gibbet, if all the world hooted at him. Such are the materials, Moore, of which true friendships are formed. A man passes through the trials of life, and they all drop off but one or two—those that are left are the ones to cling to. In a few days, perhaps, should I ride through those streets in my carriage, how vastly enthusiastic this now indignant mob will be. They would shout long life to Harry Hall ! But listen—they already shout something ; what is it ?

Moore pushed his way to the door and looked down Gloucester street, and saw the Governor's carriage approaching the Capitol, surrounded by the mob, endeavoring to see some one inside, but apparently without success, for the old guard rode in front and rear, and kept them at a respectful distance.

Arriving at the Capitol green, the Governor first descended, clad in deep mourning, and much bowed down with grief since we last presented him to the reader—then came Ellen Evylin—and lastly an Indian girl, whom the reader has already devined to be Wingina. She had doffed her male garments and now appeared uncommonly well dressed, for she had been furnished from Ellen's own wardrobe, and dressed out by her own hands for the occasion.

The Governor did not take his seat upon the bench, or rather with the court, but sat apart with the two females. Hall's lawyer now approached and conversed earnestly with them for a few moments in an under tone. He was apparently remonstrating with Ellen about something and did not prevail until her father joined them. She then gave way, and placing her hand in her father's, walked with him to the witness stand.

After being sworn, she stated that during the morning a strange looking Indian, very much wearied and worn, rode into her father's grounds and demanded instant speech of him, and upon being informed that he was gone to the court-house and could not be disturbed on any account, he wrung his hands and appeared greatly distressed. Supposing that some one was very ill and that my father's professional services were required, I begged him to make his wants known to me. I was very much surprised at his calling me by name and demanding that we must be alone—tor the servants were standing around—before he could communicate his errand.   At first I refused this, as there is more or less suspicion attaches to the race, but I was then informed that the business was urgent and connected with the trial then going on at the court house.

I hesitated no longer, but led the witness into the house. The head was then uncovered, and she announced herself to me as Wingina, the sister of the Interpreter—that she was present at the murder and had stolen away from her brother and his friends, and been on horseback almost constantly for three days and good part of the nights. I immediately despatched a note to my father, and sat about preparing her to appear here. The rest, she can tell, herself, better than I can.

Such was about the amount of her testimony, condensed into a small compass. During the whole of its delivery she never once cast her eyes towards the prisoner. Not so with him, however—his eye was rivetted upon her face. He leaned forward with the most intense interest, as if he would gladly hear his name, and fame vindicated by such lips. He had not manifested such an interest in any part of the trial, and seemed disappointed when she moved away and was led out to the carriage by her father.

Wingina was now called to the witness stand and closely questioned as to her belief in a future state of rewards and punishments, and her knowledge as to the nature of an oath. The court were satisfied on both points, and ordered her to be sworn, The first part of her testimony related to the interview with John Spotswood, on the night he left the city under the trees of the avenue in front of the Palace, and their having been watched by some one. She then went on to detail circumstances sufficiently well known to the reader; many of which, however, were drawn from her with great reluctance on her part. It was almost impossible to understand her testimony, or why Chunoluskie should watch her and young Spotswood; and why she should fly with him, unless she told all, and that all, neither age nor sex ever deters lawyers from obtaining; and they succeded on the present occasion in worming from the witness the whole story of her shame and ruin. Woman like, however, she took the whole blame upon herself, and almost wholly exonerated her deceased lover; for whose memory she wept bitterly many times during the delivery of her evidence. Having revealed all this part of her sad tale, she arrived in her narrative to the fatal night at the stockade. She confirmed what had already been stated by one of the witnesses, that she had not slept in the place assigned to her by Capt. Spotswood, but had risen in the night and laid herself down across the door of the apartment where the young gentleman and their servants slept. That sometime after midnight as she supposed, she was awakened by the grasp of a powerful hand upon her throat and another over her mouth—that she was held in this posture by a young Indian whom she named, (and who was well known as one of Mr. Boyle's disciples, and who had for a long time been paying unsuccessful court to Wingina,) that while she was thus held her brother repeatedly flourished a drawn dagger over her, plainly imitating that if she raised her voice or her hands, he would strike her dead—that the young Indian mentioned held her firmly, while Chunoluskie examined the sleepers. She stated that he was at first baffled by Spotswood's having slept in Lee's cloak, but that he was not long in ascertaining the one he sought; which he had no sooner done, than he seized him by the throat and stabbed him at the same moment; that he had also attempted to scalp him, but the convulsive efforts of his victim hurried them off. She stated that the area of the stockade was filled with young Indians, many of whom she had seen about the College and knew. After the murder was completed, she said some one of them were for setting fire to the premises, but her brother, who appeared to be in command, would not permit it, as he said it would put the Governer too soon upon his trail, and before he had done other work which was before them. She said she was placed on a horse before her brother, and the whole of them set off at full speed for Germana, where they arrived the next night, only pausing once to refresh themselves and their horses.

She said the military discipline of the stockade at the latter place, though superior to that of the first mentioned, was by no means active and vigilant—that the Indians dismounted in the forest, when they came in sight, and approached stealthily on foot, that her brother sprang upon the sentinel on duty and dispatched him, (as he had previously done Captain Spotswood,) without the slightest alarm being communicated to the garrison; that the whole band, except, the one who held her, then rushed in and slaughtered the sleeping soldiers and inmates, with the exeception of a single person—a young lady, whom they carried off, as they said, to supply her place, as a wife, to the young chief for whom her brother had intended her. This was about the amount of her testimony, except that she had made her escape while they caroused on a certain night, and that she had left the young lady still their prisoner. When asked why did she not assist her to escape, she said she looked so delicate, she knew it would be impossible for her to escape their pursuers, that she had taken one of their horses, and rode for life and death to communicate the tidings—thinking that the surest way to afford her relief. That she had heard, when she approached the city, of the trial going on, and for some time her whole attention had been absorbed by the act of injustice which she feared would be perpetrated. The Governor and the prisoner were much affected by the appalling news just detailed. The trial itself, and all interest attached to it, seemed swallowed up by the startling account of the massacre.

The court consulted together for a few moments, and after calling the Attorney General into their councils, ordered the prisoner set at liberty. His appearance on the green seemed to revive the public interest in him for a while, and the mob set up a shout of triumph. Poor Hall had almost forgotten already that he was lately all but a convicted murderer, so greatly was he suffering for the death of his friend, Humphrey Elliot, and the captivity of his daughter.

CHAPTER XI.

PREPARATIONS FOR THE MEETING OF "THE TRAMONTANE ORDER."

No sooner was Wingina released from the witness' stand, than she went straightway to Dr. Evylin's, as she had promised his daughter.

"Now, Wingina," said Ellen, as the former re-entered her room, "now we have succeeded in releasing Mr. Hall, for one of the servants tells me he is already at liberty, you can tell me of the captive lady, and the message she sent by you to this strange and unaccountable Mr. Hall."

"You must know, Miss Ellen, that we were closely watched, and that it was only as chance occasions offered, that I could hold even five minutes conversation with her, and therefore I may not have caught her meaning exactly."

"Well, well, tell me what you did learn from her, and perhaps I may understand it better than you can."

"As I was about to tell you, on one of those stolen interviews of a moment, she asked me if a young man, by the name of Hall, had arrived in the Colony? I told her yes—that I had seen such a young gentleman I believed, and had heard a great deal more about him—that he had been living with the Governor's family, and, I believed, teaching his youngest son. She said it must be the same ; but she could not see why he should undertake the business of teaching—but she told me, if I succeeded in escaping, to go straight to this Mr. Hall, as soon as I arrived at the capital, and tell him that Eugenia Elliot is a captive in the hands of the Indians, and her father murdered, and if he indeed loves me, to save me from a fate worse than death !"

" Did she say that?" exclaimed Ellen, pacing the room.

" As near her words as I can recollect, and that was the reason that I discovered the situation of Mr. Hall as soon as I did.   The first person I met, as I approached the city, I asked if he knew whether Mr. Hall was in the capital—' yes,' said he, ' snug enough, they're trying him for his life.'   From the next, I received almost the same answer, and then I knew there was something wrong, and thinking over the position in which he slept at the stockade, and how little any one here could know of the real circumstances of the murder, I hurried on to you. Now, that we have succeeded, must I still seek him out, and deliver the captive lady's message ?"

" By all means, Wingina, and hark you, be sure and tell him that you have told all she said to me, and haste back here, and tell me what he says, when you have done."

Wingina went immediately in pursuit of Hall, and after hunting over most of the town, found him again at his old quarters, the Governor's, who had insisted on taking him to the Palace at once.

"Oh my little deliverer," said Hall, as he saw her approaching him, "I would have sought you out, had I known where to find you, not only to return you my sincere thanks for your heroic exertions in my behalf—for I understand you have traversed a wild wilderness to save me—but to make farther inquiries, concerning the fate of some dear friends whom you mentioned in your testimony."

" That, is the very business which induced me to disturb you now."

" Oh ! Miss Elliot! tell how I can best undertake to deliver her from her cruel captors."

" We were fellow prisoners and almost the last words she uttered to me, was a charge to find you out, and tell of her sad state ; she told me moreover, of the near and dear ties which bound you together, and said she trusted her whole hopes of deliverance upon you."

" She told you this ! poor girl, her misfortunes have surely touched her brain, nevertheless I will exert myself to the uttermost to restore her to her friends."

" Poor young lady, she said she had no friends in the world except yourself."

" She has many, the Governor himself among the number, and when I received your message we were even then discussing the question whether an expedition to set out immediately, would be of any avail ; but here he comes to speak for himself.   I was just mentioning the subject of our conversation, your Excellency, to my little deliverer here, and asking her about the prospect of success ? "

The Governor appeared greatly moved at the sight of Wingina, and took her hand and turned his head away to hide a tear, but quickly dashed it away and joined in the conversation.

" You can, indeed, tell us Wingina, whether an expedition to set out this night, would have any prospect of overtaking your brother and his mad companions."

" That depends entirely upon the question, whether they have returned in pursuit of me, or have pursued their way to the mountains.   I think they have gone on to the mountains, at least the main body of them, because they intend to oppose your passage over the Apalachee, and as they knew nothing of the causes of the delay of the expedition here, they would be expecting you to have set out by this time. My brother, may indeed be even now on the look out for me round the city, but if it is even so, the young lady has gone on with his friends."

"What!" exclaimed the Governor, "do they hope to oppose my passage with a handful of raw pupils from College—tut, tut, I will cut them to pieces with my old guard."

"Oh no, Sir, they hope no such thing—they intend to rouse up every Indian on the frontier. I heard them discussing the matter, and each one is to visit his own people—for you know they are all of different tribes—stir up their wrath against your Excellency, and meet you hand to hand at the mountain pass.".

"They will meet me at Philippi, will they, damn their impudence, if it were not for the poor girl in the case, I would wish no better sport than teaching my little army how to flesh their maiden swords!" and here the old veteran strode about at a magnificent rate, almost forgetting the urgency of the case he came to consult about, in the fire of his military ardor, he had even began to hum a martial air, but checked himself suddenly, and was again seated near the other two.

"Well, Hall," said he, what think you, will you take the troop I offer, and and a trusty guide, and precede us to the scene of massacre, or will you wait for the rest of the expedition ?"

"I leave the case entirely with your Excellency, if you think I would stand the slightest chance of overtaking the crafty murderers by preceding you, I will set out this very afternoon."

"I do not think you would, said the Governor promptly, nor do I think I ought to let you go—you have no experience with these red men, they would, even if you should overtake them, lead you into an ambush, and perhaps scalp you all before we could come to the rescue—nay, nay, no impatience, my lad, it is no impeachment of either your soldiership or discretion. Moreover, you know that there is to be a meeting of the young gentry in the Capitol to night, at which I am particularly anxious you should be present." Here the Gover-nor placed his finger upon his lip, and then called a servant to whom he con-signed Wingina, telling him to lead her to his daughters. When she was out of hearing, he resumed. I am particularly anxious that you should be there, for I understand that Harry Lee intends to object to your name being enrolled among the young chivalry of the Colony."

"Ah! upon what new tack is he now ?"

"He says, I hear, that you have only cleared your name from one of the charges with which it is blackened, and that he for one will not be of the ex-pedition, if you are permitted to be. He says that the other Hall has arrived and he has sent an express to York for him."

Hall appeared a good deal agitated at this news and walked the floor with some perturbation—the Governor eyeing him the while in any thing but a satisfactory manner, he would rather have heard him speak out promptly and manfully to the challenge of his enemy. At length Hall discerned what was passing in the frank old veteran's mind, and he approached him and said, "Governor Spotswood, I have too long taxed the patience and credulity of you and your friends. I acknowledge that there has been a mystery about my movements, but not one played off in any idle prank, nor yet for sinister pur-poses. I have merely acted hitherto, from the necessity of case. I must ask you to forbear with me only until to-night. I must indeed attend this meeting, and if I do not then and there put the blush of shame and deep morti-fication upon my enemies, then you are fully at liberty to set me down for all they would represent me to be."

"Well, my man, no one can, after what has happened to-day, shake my confidence in you, but yourself. I grant you that I was a little shaken just now by your hesitation, but that is all over, and I will wait patiently, and in full faith until the time you name ; and by the by, when you and Harry come to hard words, don't forget to throw into his teeth his shameful desertion from the House of Burgesses, when, for all he knew to the contrary, the whole enterprise hung upon his vote."

" Never fear, Sir, never fear, I will give him something harder to swallow than that ; but before this meeting takes place, I have a great favor to ask of you, it is that you will furnish me with a fleet horse and a trusty messenger, for a couple of hours."

"Certainly—certainly ! but for what object ? "

" I must contrive some means, to slip a note into the hand of this new Mr. Hall, before they produce him at the capital to confront me."

The Governor was taken all aback again, and did not pretend to disguise his doubts and gathering indignation. His eye rested upon the young man as if he would penetrate his very soul, but he quailed not beneath the prolonged examination. The old veteran lowered his grey shaggy eyebrows, into an awful frown of gathering wrath, and every instant Hall expected to see the storm burst, but he had lately been through various ordeals, well calculated to steady his nerves, and he stood up under the gathering storm in a way at once so meek, and yet so dignified, that the old soldier was partially satisfied, and characteristically exclaimed, " Damn me, if there is another man in the Colony, who would have dared to ask me to be a party to such a scheme, and yet you brave it out, as if there was nothing in it."

"Nor is there any thing in it, your Excelleny, except a little innocent counterplotting, an ambuscade perhaps—nothing more, I assure you."

"Is it so indeed, and no more of these infernal mysteries after all. Forgive me, my boy, here is my hand upon it, you shall have my assistance, but the fact is, you have been so long wrapt up in the clouds that I did not know but this was some new freak of yours to mystify us all again."

" And so it is, your Excellency, but only for a few hours, you shall yourself be witness to the explanation, and I think, you will say it was well done."

"Well, well, there is my hand upon it, I will trust to your honor and discretion, you have come out so well thus far, that you must be knave as well as fool, to sacrifice all now to a silly manœuvre."

" Trust me, General Spotswood, that I am the last man in the Colony (to use your own words in part,) who would ask you to be a party in the smallest degree to any scheme which would sully those laurels which you have so nobly won and so nobly wear."

" Tut, tut, man, I am ambitious of no laurels except those which grow upon the highest peaks of the great Apalachee, I would rather wear a sprig of that in my cocked hat, legitimately earned, than wear the honors of Marlborough himself. By the by, did you ever see this scar which I wear here to match that one of your own, (bareing his breast, and exhibiting a wound which must indeed have put his life in imminent peril) that was received as I led a charge at the battle of Hockstadt,* right under the glorious old veteran's eye. He had me carried from the field himself, and actually shed a tear over my bier, as he supposed it to be. No one thought I could survive for twenty-four hours. This is a mere scratch to many others which, you see, has marked me with a premature old age ; but it is only the outside, my boy— the fire burns as brightly within as if these old locks were not decked out in their frosty garb, and I will yet show an ungrateful ministry, that I am a better servant to our royal mistress, than they are, with there old wives' factions.

* Usually spelled Hochstet, and by the English, called the battle of Blenheim, from the village of that name three miles off.

But we have no time to lose, you must prepare for the meeting, and so must I—remember, now, that you are pledged to clear up all this mystery—you will have a glorious opportunity—for your enemies, and they are numerous and powerful, will make a combined attack upon you, and I have even received an intimation that it will be extended to me, and that I may yet peril the expedition, unless I throw you overboard."

"I trust, your Excellency, that I may be enabled to right myself in the eyes of all men; at all events you shall not suffer by me, nor shall any of my short comings attach their odium to your enterprise. Either I enter upon it as a gentleman of untarnished name and lineage, or I enter it not at all. Such, I understand, indeed are the pre-requisitions to enter your chivalrous band. I will not say, that my past life has not been fruitful of errors, but there is no personal stain in all the sad retrospect, at least none that I think your Excellency will consider as such; but I will not anticipate the work of the evening, by recounting to you the only thing which could be tortured into matter for my exclusion. I will make a clean breast of it, when we meet—it may produce a stormy meeting and that far, I regret the necessity on your Excellency's account."

"Pooh, pooh. I have heard thunder too long to be frightened at a few pop guns let off by some run-mad boys in the Capitol. I was once as mad as any of them, and I have not forgotten it, nor do I mean ever to forget it. I love the wild spirit of the untamed colt, provided it is only the impetuous impulses of young life, and nothing vicious in it. I shall keep my eye upon one youngster, who will doubtless figure largely there to-night, however. I have hitherto found it impossible to decide, whether he was of the true metal or not, and only spoiled in the training, or whether he has innate deviltry so deeply imbedded in the texture of his composition, that the ups and downs, even of a campaign, will not wear it out."

"I think I know to whom your Excellency alludes, and without presumption I think I know him better than you do. You allude to Mr. Henry Lee! Be under no apprehension for the harmony of your expedition, at least for any disturbance that he may create on my account; for I predict now most confidently that one or the other of us will withdraw entirely from the enterprise. It is next to impossible that we can unite in any undertaking of the sort, after what must necessarily come to light at the meeting. He has hitherto had the whole game in his own hands and I have suffered him full swing, but the time has now arrived for me to assert my just rights in this community, so that you may possibly see a double unmasking."

"Well, well, only do as well as you talk, my boy, and I assure you there is no one who will be more gratified than myself. I have seen for some time that you were in a false position, and that he maintained some unaccountable power over you, and I thought indeed that you had given him full swing sure enough. I rejoice to hear you say that it is now about to end. I cannot tell you how many remonstrances I have had addressed to me on your account. Some hinted one thing and some another, but all thought it unseemly in me to countenance you without credentials of any sort. So, you see, it is full time to unmask, as you say. By the by, did I not hear that you were one of the masking party at my country house?"

"No more, your Excellency, no more; have patience only until one telling of my tale may answer."

"Well, good day, and remember what is before you!" and with these words Hall was left alone. There was no need to remind him that he had an arducus task to perform—he well knew it, and felt it keenly. He knew that he was in a delicate position—that he was a mark, as well for the shafts of envy and malice, as for the eager eyes of all men.

He retired to prepare the note for the Governor's trusty messenger, which he did in a few minutes.

CHAPTER XII

LAST EVENING AT THE CAPITAL.

SINCE we last presented the Governor's daughters to our readers, they had suffered the first great affliction of their lives. 'Tis an era in the life of every one, and by its results may be marked the forming character of either sex.

Kate's life hitherto had been unusually brilliant and happy, not a cloud obscured her serene horizon—every thing was seen *couleur de rose*, and the native enthusiasm of her character had burst into full fruition, unchecked by the frowns of fortune or misadventures of a tenderer sort. If we have suc-ceeded in presenting her properly before our readers, they have seen in the records of her young, and innocent, and happy life, almost a perfect contrast to the melancholy and heart-stricken experience of her intimate friend. Happy was she, that such a one was near her, and that she knew what mis-fortunes were, or the blow would have been more dreadful than it really was. For a brief space, they had almost changed places, and while Ellen's pros-pects brightened, she became the constant comforter of her sanguine and enthusiastic friend. True, their trials were somewhat different—the one bemoaned an absent lover, but not entirely without hope, and the other mourned a brother. It may be well imagined, then, that the first sight of Wingina, ushered into Kate's presence without notice or warning, was anything but soothing to the lacerated feelings of the poor girl. She hid her face and wept afresh, when she saw her—for she had heard the whole of the sad story of her shame—indeed her appearance began now to put secrecy any longer out of the question. It was impossible for Kate to allude to the melan-choly affair, and she could only weep and wring the hand of the poor forlorn creature. Kate looked and expressed in pantomime a thousand promises of sym-pathy and protection, but she could do no more. Dorothea left the room, she could not look upon the sister of her brother's murderer with the same Christian forbearance as her sister. She expressed no feelings of hatred or indignation, but obeyed her youthful impulses, and left the room upon the instant. Poor Wingina could not fully understand all this—she could not appreciate the feelings of either sister; for though brought up in many of the outward and conventional forms of civilized life, her education had been very defective in all that touches the heart, either through the ministrations of religion, or even the refinement which *may* be acquired without them. There was no senti-mentality about her. It is true, indeed, that a rude and savage heart may be touched by an influence from above, which softens and humanizes the char-acter, but even then, there is something still wanting in the point we have alluded to. We have never seen an Indian, converted or not, possessing this delicacy of feeling. But Wingina could not comprehend the full measure of her disgrace. Her previous distraction was made up of fear of her brother, and dread of being separated from the one she loved, and but for her subdued and meek natural deportment, might have been considered brazen-faced and shameless. She could not comprehend her fallen position in the eyes of those around her; she felt bereaved, but much in the way she would have done had she lost a husband, after the aboriginal manners and customs. All through the house she met the silent tear and the averted face, and per-haps the patronising air of pity and commiseration. Lady Spotswood could not see her at all. This was all very different from her former reception in the same place and from the same people, and she was about to make a speedy retreat; but Kate seeing the nature of the case, begged her to wait a few moments, and she sat down and wrote a note by her to Ellen. As this note was somewhat characteristic, and at the same time expressed better than we can do the state of feeling we have attempted to describe, we shall transcribe it. It ran as follows:

Dear Ellen: Such a friendship as ours can bear the imposition with which I am about to tax you. You know the sad tale of this poor Indian girl, and how it lacerates all our hearts afresh, even to look upon her; and knowing this, you will do all those little kindnesses for her that we cannot, and which her situation requires. She sees that we *cannot* look upon her with complacency, and *now* she misinterprets it. God knows we wish to wreak no vengeance upon her for my poor brother's death. Do make her sensible of all this. You, my dear Ellen, that know so well how to compass these delicate offices so much better than any one else—do give her all the comfort the case admits of, and administer such consolation as her peculiar nature requires. Explain to her our feelings, and that they are the farthest in the world removed from unkindness Oh, Ellen, you know what a shock we have sustained, and will, I know, acquit us of any mawkish sensibility in the case. I trust her entirely to your kindness and discretion. My father has just stepped in, and anticipating my object, begged to see this note; and he now begs me to say to you, that Wingina must be closely watched, else her brother will contrive some subtle scheme to whisk her off again.

Dear Ellen, I love to turn to you in my distress, as you have often turned to me in like circumstances. May we ever lean upon each other with a confiding faith that knows no doubt.

Sincerely, your friend,   KATE.

This note was sealed and handed to Wingina, who was nothing loth to depart—in fact, she was more than half offended, and arrived at the Doctor's in rather a sullen mood. She found Ellen herself not in the most amiable state of calmness and repose. She, too, was beginning to be offended in another quarter. She had expected a visit from Hall, and was disappointed that he did not come. Her father made many excuses for him—mentioned the meeting at the capital among others, but they were not satisfactory. She had reasons of her own for wishing to see him previous to that very meeting, and he had reasons of his own why he wished to avoid it, until that meeting was over. Our readers will soon perceive that his were substantial ones. He was engaged during the remainder of the afternoon in one of the upper rooms of the Palace, before a large table entirely covered with printed and manuscript papers, from which, from time to time, he took notes, while others he tied up in a bundle, and marked for use. Occasionally he rose from his engrossing occupation and strode through the room under an excitement of feeling, which he strove in vain to calm. He was, in fact, laboring under the most painful suspense as to the result of his message to York. Could he have been assured that all was right in that quarter, he might have prepared himself for the coming contest more calmly. He knew that the crisis of his fate had arrived, and under his present want of recent information from Europe, he knew not what evidence might be brought against him for the share he had taken in the affair of Gen. Elliot. He knew not but his enemies might prove him an attainted rebel, and thus baffle one of the greatest desires of his life, (to bear an active part in the tramontane expedition,) as well as throw him out once more from the association of that circle which he loved so well.

His reasons for not presenting himself at the Doctor's house, were the farthest possibly removed from ingratitude. He thought of the interpretation which Miss Evylin and the Doctor might put upon his conduct, but he resolved to risk their present displeasure for their future approval. Such, indeed, was the whole constitution and character of his mind—he had ever sought future good by present sacrifices, and denied himself that others might be gratified.

It will be readily gathered from what has been said, and from what is already known of his past history, that he was in a poor state of preparation

for a defence of all that was dear in life to him.   He was about to throw off
a masquerading dress, which had been adopted at first from the sternest
necessity, and perhaps place himself thereby in defiance of the laws of his
country—those laws for which he had now come to feel an uncommon reverence.   Now, he knew what it was to attempt in the roisterous and thoughtless days of youth to revolutionize the whole current of society, according
to the immature views of that period—he knew that it was better to suffer
partial evils, in an otherwise wholesome and benign government, for the general
good, rather than that every mad youth should set himself up for lawgiver
and judge.   In short, his futile aims at unattainable perfections were put to
flight by the most profound consideration of the utter debasement of human
nature.   This is a point of knowledge not often attained in young life, without
bitter personal experience ; and he that comes into active life without this
experience, and after sailing always upon summer seas, is very apt to become
an amiable (but nevertheless) fool.

But, however much his spirit was grieved, and the immature notions of his
sanguine youth ground down, he had yet to suffer for the follies which they
had engendered.   Repentance, alone, will not always answer in this world—
there must be restitution, and retribution, as far as possible.   Hall's business
now was with the present, and not with the past.   He was now to chalk out
a new career for himself, but he had first to overcome the one great error of
his youth, and to which he could now distinctly trace all his subsequent misfortunes.   He reviewed hastily his past career—thought over the successive
difficulties in which he had been involved, and from the most important of
which he had just been delivered by a manifest interference of Providence.
This conviction nerved his heart for the contest, and all his late despondency
and want of confiding trust in a benign and overruling power vanished.   He
rose up from his papers re-invigorated, and thrusting his bundle into his pocket,
walked down stairs.   He had not been there long before he was called out
by a servant—he was met at the door by the messenger who had been despatched to York, who placed in his hands a large paper package, covered with tape and sealing wax, and a note of apparently more recent date.   He
tore open the latter, and read it by the light of the lamp, (for it was growing
dark.)   The old Governor had followed him, and was anxiously waiting to
hear the result of his message.   Hall did not appear to be aware of his presence, or if he was, forgot in the exultation of the moment.   He jumped
straight up from the floor, whirled himself round—kissed the letter, and then
ran out upon the green, where he walked rapidly among the trees for ten or
fifteen minutes talking away and gesticulating to himself in the strangest manner and performing antics, which not a little surprised if they did not amuse
the old veteran who was still eyeing him.   At length he became conscious of
the ridiculous figure which he was cutting, and walked back to the Palace and
met the Governor at the portico, and seizing his hand, wrung it warmly with
the simple exclamation, "It is all right, Sir,—all right—now, indeed, I am a
free man."

"I am none the less rejoiced," said his Excellency, "that I know not the
cause of your wild exultation, but I trust it bears upon the point we talked of
during the day."

"It does—it does—and right to the point—strikes the nail right upon the
head."

The Capitol bell was now pouring a merry peal over the town, and an-
nouncing to the young chivalry of the Colony, that the time appointed for their
meeting had arrived.   The carriage soon after drove up to the door, and not
many minutes had elapsed before Dr. Evylin's also drove up, to accompany
the party from the Palace.   Hall walked to the window, the blinds of which
had been let down, and shook hands with the Doctor, but Ellen did not extend

hers, contenting herself with a slight inclination of the head. The cause of this we will explain at another time, but our readers should not attach inconsistency to our favorite, from which, indeed, none of her sex was more free. The party from the Palace was soon made up, and as the carriages turned from the avenue into Gloucester street, they encountered many more pursuing the same route.

Seldom, since the foundation of the Colony, had there been a meeting which attracted so large a share of public attention. It was the last meeting of those who were to set out on the morrow for the mountains, an undertaking at that day quite as perilous as one in ours to the Rocky Mountains. Indeed the route was far less known, and had never been traversed at all by that Anglo-Saxon race which was and is destined to appropriate such a large portion of the Globe to themselves, and to disseminate their laws, their language, and their religion, over such countless millions. Grand and enthusiastic as were the conceptions of Sir Alexander Spotswood and his young followers, they had little idea that they were then about to commence a march which would be renewed from generation to generation, until, in the course of little more than a single century, it would transcend the Rio del Norte, and which perhaps in half that time may traverse the utmost boundaries of Mexico. But the sober old granddads of the Colony thought the Governor visionary enough in his present views, bounded as they were by the Apalachee and the Mississippi, and that he had led the youngsters of the Colony sufficiently astray already, without extending his prophetic vision to Texas and Mexico.

CHAPTER XIII.

MEETING OF THE TRAMONTANE ORDER.

THE Capitol was brilliantly lighted, and already crowded to excess, when our party arrived. The seats appropriated o the members of the expedition, were already pre-occupied by ladies, and the galleries were crowded to suffocation by many of the rank and file of the little army, who had crowded in to hear their leaders talk of the campaign. There was a feverish anxiety and restlessness already visible among the elite on the lower floor, and when Hall followed the Governor's party into the midst of them, there was a general cessation of the buz and hum of eager gossip, and all eyes were turned enquiringly towards him. It seemed as if the public mind had been prepared to expect a renewed encounter between him and his persecutors. Seats had been preserved for the Governor's party, just in front of the Speaker's chair, but Hall after waiting to see them all comfortably provided, did not assume so conspicuous a place himself—he walked to one of the farthest and most obscure corners of the room and seated himself, and rested his head upon his hand in a meek meditative mood, and so as to elude the painful gaze of the multitude. He had scarcely thus ensconced himself before the purient eyes of the people were attracted by the entrance of the well known champion of the opposite side—Mr. Henry Lee. He walked up the main vestibule, arm in arm with young Carter, and holding quite ostentatiously a bundle of papers under his arm. After he was seated near the centre of the room, and exactly in front of the Governor's party, he cast his haughty eye round the hall in search of his antagonist, but he was not successful in detecting his whereabouts, and he doubtless concluded that he had not yet arrived—consequently he kept his eye anxiously and eagerly upon the door. The room, however, was now as full as it could hold, and by general consent they were ready to proceed to busi-

ness. Dr. Blair rose up and said : " As this is a meeting for the purpose of
deciding the best means of advancing the cause of civilization and of carrying the cross of our blessed Redeemer into unknown heathen lands, I propose
that it be opened with prayer !"

As this was one of those propositions which none in those days though
unconstitutional, it was adopted *nem. con.* and the old prelate offered an
eloquent appeal to the throne of mercy, that the expedition might be crowned
with success and all its arrangements distinguished by that harmony and good
will to men, which should ever characterize missionary enterprises. After
the prayer was concluded he rose to his feet and addressed a few words to the
young gentry present, and distinctly characterized them as young missionaries about to herald the cross to heathen lands, and begged them to preserve
their characters and conduct pure and above reproach—that they might con-
sistently look to Heaven for its approbation upon their undertaking.

This proceding of the old Doctor took the sanguine and impatient youths
all aback. They had been dreaming of naught but military conquest, and
magnificent landed acquisitions, but this suddenly converting them all into
missionaries of the cross, was what they were not exactly prepared for.
Besides it seemed to awe into silence the turbulent passions which they had
expected to see burst into fierce and angry contention—it converted, as it
were, the arena of personal contention at once into a sacred place."

However, some one rose and nominated Governor Spotswood to the Chair.
The question was put and carried unanimously, and two of the young gentlemen escorted him to his seat. On assuming the chair, he stated that he
understood the meeting to consist only of the young gentry of the land who
intended to march on the morrow for the mountains—of such as had marched
their retainers or followers voluntarily to his standard—and that their object
was to adopt certain regulations and arrange preliminaries, so as best to
accomplish the noble ends of the enterprise, by such means as had been so
well set forth by his Reverend friend who had preceded him. He said he had
understood that it was to be proposed there, that none but those of gentle
blood should be admitted into this exclusive association. He hoped that no
such proposition would be offered. Let the noble objects of our ambition be
open to every gentleman of fair fame, and to all the *officers* of the Rangers.

Here he undertook to prove to them, that it was absolutely necessary for
the purposes of military discipline, that there should be but one order among
his subordinates in command, and therefore that the officers of the Rangers
must come into their association.

He sat down amidst no murmurs of applause ; on the contrary, there was
marked disapprobation of his views on more than one countenance. Of this
party, Carter became the spokesman. He said, after the draft of the constitution had been read, if the line already drawn by those appointed to that
duty was once broken down, there was no telling where it would stop—that
if they commenced with the officers of the Rangers, the non-commissioned
officers might come in under the same rule. He undertook also to rebut the
Governor's position as to military discipline—said that this was entirely a
private association of gentlemen, intended in no way to interfere with the
Governor's proper authority in the field or camp—that like all other chivalrous associations which had gone forth to do battle, either in the cause of
religion, humanity, or the more general purposes of righting the wronged,
they were desirous of purifying themselves ; and here he instanced the
prolonged fasts, vigils, and religious ceremonies preceding the outset of other
knightly bodies ; and " though," said he, " we may not yet have received the
acolade, who knows but our sovereign may honor many of these noble
youths here assembled upon our return. Like honors have often been
bestowed for less services."

Here there was a general smile among the ladies, and the speaker himself had a half serious half comic expression upon his face. He little knew then what those services and hardships were to be. His speech was well received by all the exclusives, those who were for confining the honors entirely among the young gentry of the Colony. There was a large party, however, of opposite views, and of these, Bernard Moore became the spokesman. He said, "that this discussion was what might be called, in military language, firing from a masked battery. That the gentlemen on the other side had certain objects to attain by all this machinery—certain persons to exclude. Now he could not see that they could attain more by one plan than the other. The Governor's rule would exclude every improper person from the Tramontane Order, and the other could do no more, while the latter was burdened with odious features—it put every gentleman upon his pedigree—a matter not at all times and places fit for public discussion and investigation. He called upon the opposite side to come out manfully and show their hands—to say at what they were aiming. He would not ask them to point out who it was they aimed at, but their objects, if praise-worthy and legitimate, could be attained by general regulations such as he before alluded to. He concluded by an earnest appeal to their patriotism, and called upon all the real friends of the enterprise and its distinguished author, to mark these initiatory proceedings by harmony; assuring them, that should they commence with heart-burning and discord, much of the pleasure which they all anticipated would be destroyed."

These remarks called up Henry Lee. He said that for his part he had nothing to conceal; that he wished to make the badge of the Tramontane Order not only a distinction to be sought after, but to elevate the requisitions for membership, so as to ensure its future honors. "If these rules and regulations be adopted," said he, "I predict that our order will be one that will live in the future history of the Colony, and to have been a member of it, will confer honors worthy of being transmitted to our descendants. The gentleman who has just taken his seat calls upon our side of the house to come out manfully, and show our hands. We are ready and willing to do so, as far as the nature of the case will admit. It has been currently reported that a certain individual who has now become quite notorious in the Colony will attempt to force himself upon us, and I acknowledge frankly, for one, that my design is to exclude him. I had hoped to have seen him present before I took the floor."

Here Hall rose—he said "not for the purpose of interrupting the gentleman, but to show him that he was present and ready to meet him."

Lee exclaimed, when Hall resumed his seat, "ah! I am glad of it, then we have not been misinformed. The issue is now made up, and there can be no more complaints of masked batteries. I leave the question with the meeting."

Moore made the attempt to take the floor, as well as several others on the same side, and the chairman became very restless, as if he too desired to take a hand in the game, but all gave way to Hall, as soon as they saw that he desired to speak. He said he had but few words to say—that he would not have intruded at all at this stage of the proceedings, if he had not been so pointedly alluded to, that he could not misunderstand it. He called upon his friends to cease their opposition and suffer the regulations to be adopted, that he was ready and willing to abide by them.

We have not given these regulations in detail, because we did not wish to fatigue our readers with the whole constitution of a society, in much of which they could feel no interest. The scope and object of it may be abundantly gathered by what has been and will be said. There seemed now no longer any necessity for opposition, though the friends of the last speaker could not tell what he was aiming at. They thought that by his easy acquiescence, he was voluntarily entering into a snare, set for him by his enemies, but they

could not very well hold out when he had yielded. The articles of association were now read *seriatim*, and adopted *nem. con.* The first of these, of
any interest to our readers, required the unanimous election of six out of the
whole number of names handed in as candidates for admission, This was a
very difficult thing to accomplish, and consumed considerable time. The
whole six were ballotted for at once, after having been put in nomination by
their friends. It will be perceived that this plan required that each candidate
should receive every vote. Bernard Moore obtained this distinction at the
first ballot. Carter at the second, and so on, until the board was complete.
Harry Lee, after running the gauntlet of every trial, was excluded by two
votes only, much to his chagrin and disappointment. It had nearly upset
the whole scheme which he had so ingeniously concocted.

The candidates for admission were now to advance singly to the clerk's
table and record their names, provided there was no dissenting voice of the six
censors. If there should be—then the case was postponed to the last, when
it was to be decided by a vote of the whole association—two-thirds being
required to effect an admission.

The Tramontane order was now rapidly filling up its ranks, and nought
further had occured to disturb the harmony of the meeting, until Hall rose
from his secluded corner, and walked to the table of the Secretary, took up
the pen to record his name. Carter immediately rose and objected, and the
candidate fell back to bide his time. The proceedings went on smoothly
enough again, until Henry Lee approached to record his name, which he
had half accomplished before he could fully comprehend that there was objection made. It was by Hall, of course, so that they stood as the challengers
of each other, in fact, for all understood who Carter's prompter was, and
were fairly pitted for the contest.

It was now incumbent on Lee to state his objections first, and make them
good. He rose, and stated to the meeting that he had objected, through his
friend, to the candidate, first, because of the general circumstances of mystery and suspicion which attached to him, and now pretty generally known
throughout the Colony. This, he presumed, would be sufficient of itself, but
he would not leave the matter even doubtful and, therefore, he would state his
second objection to be, that he stood before the meeting under an assumed
name, and that name adopted for dishonest and disreputable purposes. Thirdly, that he was an attainted rebel and an outlaw, with a price set upon his
head.

Hall rose up to answer to these grave charges, neither with an exulting nor
a desponding air, but quite calm and dignified. He repelled, indignantly, the
first charge, inasmuch as most of the suspicions which had been engendered
against him in the Colony, had been the coinage of his accuser's own brain—
on that very day he had, by an evident interposition of an all-wise and overruling Providence, been triumphantly freed from the meshes of one of the most
ingenious plots ever contrived to destroy an innocent man. Such, said he,
are all the gentleman's suspicious circumstances. As for the second and
third counts, he put him upon his proofs. Lee beckoned to some one in the
gallery to come down, and for a few moments the whole assemblage were left
in breathless suspense, for it had somehow been rumored that Lee was to confront Mr. Hall with the real personage whose name he had assumed. It was
not long before a young man, of elegant exterior and carriage, entered the
door of the lower floor, and walked up the passage towards the centre of the
room. Hall, so far from shrinking from the encounter, rose up also, and approached the table, to which all eyes were now attracted. The stranger was
not quite so tall as Mr. Hall, nor of so large a frame, but the hair and whiskers
were exactly of the same color, and there was, besides, a striking general resemblance in the two. Those on the back seats rose up, and those in front.

were pressed forward, and for an instant there was some confusion in the general rush to see the strange encounter. Still they approached each other, and many supposed they were bent only upon a rude and hostile encounter. But what was the surprise and astonishment of the people, and of Henry Lee, in particular, when the two rushed into each other's arms and embraced most cordially. Both the young men seemed much affected by the meeting, and each stood gazing upon the other, as if each waited for the other to speak. Henry Lee, who was standing upon his feet, exclaimed in a hoarse and agitated voice :

" Mr. President, this jugglery requires explanation !"

Hall waved his hand, and appealed by his looks for a moment's patience and silence in the crowd, that he might be heard. In the mean time many voices cried out, " which is the real Hall ? Which is the real Hall ?"

The President begged the members and the association to be seated, and suffer the young gentlemen to explain their own mystery—that it was impossible to hear amidst the present confusion. When order and silence were once more restored—Hall, or the young gentleman who had assumed that name, arose and taking the stranger by the hand, led him to the foot of the table, and said :

" Mr. President, and good people all, I take pleasure in introducing to you the real Henry Hall, whose name I have so long borne. The idea of first assuming it was suggested by the resemblance in our persons, having often been mistaken for each other. I took up another name because it had become dangerous for me to wear my own. My offence, I acknowledge frankly, was a grave one; but it was wholly political, and I am happy in being able, at the same time, that I resume my own, to state to this enlightened meeting, that it no longer rests under the proscription of our sovereign. I hold in my hand a free pardon, one of the first acts of clemency of our new King, for I am under the necessity of informing you at the same time, of the death of her gracious and most excellent Majesty, the late Queen Ann. She died on the first of last month."

There was a general exclamation of surprise and regret, which was followed by the buz and hum of conversation—carried on in an under tone throughout the room, and during which the speaker temporarily resumed his seat.

Silence being once more restored, the President reminded the gentleman last on the floor, that he had not yet completed his explanation. He resumed. " I have but few words more to utter, Mr. President, it only remains for me to resume a name once honored in this Colony—Francis Lee !" Here a deafening shout of applause shook the Capitol to its foundations, in the midst of which, both the spokesman, together with Harry Lee, were seen wildly gesticulating, but not a word could be heard for some moments from either. Frank, (as we shall henceforth call him,) seeing his brother's frantic gestures, ceased his own and stood back a moment to hear what it was he said. " I protest, Mr. President, against this new phase of this arch impostor's jugglery—I disclaim all kindred with him, and I call upon all those present who remember my brother, boy as he was, whether he had not light hair."

Frank stood forward, with a playful smile upon his countenance, and putting his hand deliberately to his head, in a single instant denuded it of its dark flowing locks, revealing at the same time a fine turned head, closely matted over with short light curls. The transformation was instantaneous, and many voices testified aloud, " it is Frank Lee ! it is Frank Lee !" Old Dr. Evylin rushed forward and seized his hand, but at the very same moment Ellen fell over into the arms of one of her female friends. Frank's eye had hardly ever for a moment been entirely removed from her eager and agitated countenance, and quick as thought, he flew to where she had fallen, and bore her out of the crowd in his arms.

CHAPTER XIV.

RETROSPECT.

WE must turn back, only for half a chapter, and we are sure our fair readers will forgive us, when they recollect it is the only indulgence of the kind we have asked—that we have spun the thread of our story straight forward, without turning to the right or the left. We stated in a former chapter that Ellen Evylin, when she drove up to the door of the Governor's mansion, was rather cold and distant to the young gentleman then called Hall, and for fear our fair readers might think her fickle and capricious, we will explain why it was so. It will be recollected that the Indian girl had expressly stated, that the young lady then in captivity, had sent a most urgent appeal to Mr. Hall in her behalf, and such an one as only a lady betrothed would send to her lover. Now, supposing that Miss Evylin had had for some time a shrewd suspicion who this Mr. Henry Hall really was—a sort of half doubting, half confident possession of his secret, how could she explain satisfactorily his equivocal position between herself and Miss Eugenia Elliot. She knew from the young gentleman's own statement, that this very young lady accompanied him across the ocean—that she was a party to the masking adventure; that her father had been involved in the same political troubles with himself; and she, moreover, remembered tha the was under the impression at the time of the voyage, that she (Miss Evylin) was either affianced or married to another. What more probable then, than that he should seek consolation from such a charming source. She most ingeniously tormented herself in imagining what an embarrassing position he had thus placed himself in, between two young ladies, and most innocently too, if her surmises were correct. Thus she accounted for much of the studied mystery and reserve of the young man; and our readers may readily imagine what was her resolution upon the painful subject—it was to surrender up all claims upon the instant.

So admirably, however, had Frank Lee (for we shall henceforth call him by his right name) mystified even his oldest and best friends, and so constantly had he worn his masquerading dress, and pertinaciously had he continued to carry out the delusion through trials and difficulties, that she was by no means certain that her suspicions as to his identity were correct. Nothing but this constantly harrassing doubt prevented her from sending for him at once and releasing him from his early engagement, which she had tortured herself with supposing, was now so embarrassing to him.

She was carried from the meeting of the members of " the Tramontane Order" by Frank Lee, it will be remembered, and that ardent and emancipated young gentleman seemed determined to make amends for his past losses, and let loose his long suppressed affections in a burst of endearments to his half dead mistress. How ardently he folded his lovely burden in his arms, and with what glowing animation he pressed his lips to her cold and clammy cheeks. We know of no restorative like it. The olfactories may be, and no doubt are, very sensitive, but a ladies sensorium is sooner reached through those thrilling thermometers of vitality, the lips. So it proved in the present instance; and by the time Frank had reached the green in front of the Capitol, Ellen was pleading, at first most eloquently, and at length indignantly, to be set down and left alone. And what sounded not less strange in his ears, she called him Mr. Lee. Now, it might have sounded strange to him, from the fact of his having so long suffered it to fall into disuse himself—that was not the idea here; however—there was a chilling and distant tone and manner in it, which he had never encountered but once, even as the poor adventurer Hall, and he was consequently taken all aback—he had anticipated a very different reception, and was utterly at a loss to account for it. His failure to present himself after his acquittal, was the only thing which he could in his rapid review of his conduct surmise as the cause, and he commenced his protestations accordingly, but it was all met by a çold wave of the hand, and an earnest supplication to be conducted to her father's carriage. Of course such an appeal, or rather demand, was not to be resisted, and he reluctantly escorted her to the carriage. Most wistfully did he gaze by the dim light to see if there was no relenting—no hint or look implying a desire for his company in her solitary ride home, but there was none, and his pride coming to his relief, he closed the door with a hasty good night, and strutted off in high disdain. He was marching thus, like a grenadier, with his nose in the wind, and gesticulating with great animation, when Moore walked up, and touched him on the arm. Frank gazed at him as if he had fallen from the moon, so completely had he forgotten his whereabouts.

" You are unanimously admitted into the Tramontane Order," said Moore, with a bright smile.

" Oh, the plague take the Tramontane Order," responded Frank, still striding on and Moore following' down Gloucester street.

" Your brother decamped from the meeting instanter."

" Well, I hope he may never return."

" Why, Frank ?" exclaimed Moore in surprise, " this in the first moment of your restoration and our mutual recognition ? You have not given up the mysteries yet, I see."

" Forgive me, Bernard," said he, suddenly wheeling round, and seizing his friend's hand. " Forgive me—the fact is, I have been thrown all out of sorts by an inexplicable piece of capriciousness in one whom I believed too far exalted above such little feminine arts."

" Hah ! a petticoat in the case is there ? I'll tell you a secret, my fine fellow—there's none of them above caprice—always except Kate."

" Bernard, an hour ago I would have thrown down my glove upon it, against all comers, that there was not such another model of constancy—ingenuousness—frankness—firmness—modesty—gentleness ; in short, my dear fellow, a very personification of all the female virtues, with many borrowed from ours. This has been my solace under every trial and difficulty ; and then to turn round in the very moment of my triumph, and descend to the little arts of her sex, and dash my brimming cup to the ground. Oh, it was too bad."

" Nay, nay, Frank—it was certainly a better chosen moment than the period of your adversity would have been—you must admit that ; but there is some mistake, you may depend upon it—I know her too well to suppose that she would indulge in any idle caprice at such a moment."

" I'll call at the Doctor's upon the spot, and demand an explanation. I cannot stand this cruel suspense, just upon the eve of what I supposed would be one of the happiest moments of my life—what I supposed would compensate me for a life of unexampled misfortunes."

" Do so, Frank—I am sure there is some misunderstanding—perhaps there is some charge which she has deferred preferring until you were entirely clear of all difficulties—i. e. if she really penetrated your disguise, as I am told many did, now that the *eclaircisement* is made. What wonderful sagacity the many-headed monster is blessed with ! But to return—the surmise that I ventured just now is the true solution—it is very much like her, depend upon it."

" No, no, Bernard—Ellen penetrated my mask at least, I am sure, and we played a sort of mutual masquerade, under which nearly every subject of personal interest or otherwise was discussed ; and oh, Moore, when she first began to peep behind my mask, and I to reproduce the shadow of her long lost lover, as his best friend, Henry Hall, what exquisite moments I enjoyed. Can it be possible that she designs now to revenge herself on me, for thus surreptitiously plundering her heart of its secrets ?"

" It is not in character, Frank, she has no revenge to accomplish—it is some higher object, real or imaginary, that she has in view—perhaps she fears a deadly encounter between your brother and yourself—that's it—that's it, Frank."

" But how could her snubbing me in this fashion prevent Harry and me from coming to high words, perhaps blows ?"

" Perhaps she caught a glimpse of him, eaves-dropping ?"

" No, no, Bernard. With all his malice and uncharitableness, he is not so mean as that ; but I will solve the riddle before I am an hour older. I will merely call at the Palace to deposit these papers, and then for a trial of my fate."

Together they proceeded on foot, when just as they entered the avenue leading to the Palace, they discovered the Doctor's carriage driving away, and Kate hastily retreating from the door. Now, as this avenue was always lighted at night, they could see that Ellen still sat alone upon the back seat, and that she was weeping. She also caught a glimpse of them, and drew herself up in the corner of the carriage, out of sight. This was all very strange and inexplicable to the young men, especially on such a night, and after all that had happened at the Capitol. It was just the reverse of what Frank had anticipated, but he proceeded on his course, none the less bent on clearing up the mystery from what he had just seen. He was destined to some farther experience in the matter, earlier than he expected; for no sooner had he entered the hall of the Palace, than a servant presented him with a message from Miss Kate—she desired to speak a few words with him. He followed and was led into one of the sitting rooms on the lower floor, where Kate awaited him with a bundle in her hand. She congratuated him upon his restoration to his proper name and station, and said she was sorry to be the bearer of unpleasant news at such a time, but her friend Ellen had charged her with the mission, and she was compelled to perform it. She said that Ellen had commissioned her to deliver into his hands that package and a miniature of himself, with a complete discharge from all engagements to her. Frank was speechless with astonishment—he seemed as if he would choke, so parched became his throat, and so vain his attempt at utterance. Kate seeing his pitiable condition, and that he still gazed at the things she held in her hand without taking them, and that his face was almost convulsed, so intense was the working of his troubled spirit, she handed him a chair, and begged him to be seated. Her efforts at consolation were at first not very success- ful, for her auditor seemed not to be listening to a word she said. His eyes were riveted upon the locket, the early memento of his youthful passion. What overwhelming recollections of days and joys gone by forever poured in upon his memory, with all their blended associations of sorrow and joy ; that picture, which he had not seen before that day, since he had plighted his faith, upon the occasion of its being given ? How vividly it brought back the bright morning of his youthful love—those halcyon days that have but one dawn, one bright morning, ere they are closed over forever by a long, and dark, and bitter night. The long years which had intervened, with their sad and blighting experience and bitter memories, were rolled back, and he stood before the youthful beauty in his mental vision, as he stood before her with her hand clasped in his, as when he had presented her with that picture. Was it any wonder that he spoke not ? Such memories have no voice.

Frank Lee had perhaps came as near acting out and preserving the first freshness of his early romantic love, as is ever permitted to mortal man, but his self-condemnation, upon the return of that picture, knew no sophistry or deception.   He stood abashed, in recollection of the bright purity and unwavering constancy of his mistress—of these, he had indubitable evidence—he was compelled, therefore, to make a hasty retrospect of his conduct towards her ; and though self-condemned in many respects, as we have said, for his life he could not divine in what he had offended towards the object of his early, undivided, and constant attachment, and he at length resolved to vindicate himself before his offended mistress. Scarcely was the resolution formed, ere he seized upon the package and the picture, and rushed from the house.

As he passed out, he had nearly upset the Governor, who, with his party, were just returned from the Capitol. The hardy old soldier turned round and looked after his retreating figure, with a dubious and amusing stare of astonishment.

" Gad," said he, " that fellow will die in a mystery," touching his forehead at the same time with his finger, as much as to express a fear that all was not right in that quarter.

Frank scarcely knew that he had passed, much less been rude, to any one. He soon found himself knocking at the Doctor's door. Now, as the old Doctor was one of those who accompanied the Governor, the coast was clear—there was nothing to prevent his having the interview and explanation he sought. Yet he trembled more when ushered into the presence of the little offended beauty, than when recently on trial for his life. And to say truth, the young lady herself was not in the most serene mood in the world. They stood before each other like two culprits. Frank, with the letters and the trinkets, like stolen goods, still in his hand. He made many efforts to speak, and nearly choked at the formality of calling her Miss Evylin, but at length burst through all embarrassments and restraint, and exclaimed, " Ellen, will you, can you, tell me what all this means?" pointing to the things he held in his hand.

She motioned him to be seated, and began, " Mr. Lee !"

But he held up his hand in a deprecating mood, and begged her, " For God's sake, no more of that—I shall die upon it !"

" Well, then, Frank," resumed she, " I have accidentally learned that you had most innocently, as I presume, engaged yourself to another and most excellent and beautiful lady. Nay, be not so impatient, I will conclude all I have to say in one moment."

" No," said he, hurriedly, and striding impatiently about the room, " not another word will I listen to of the sort—it is all an infamous falsehood, and the coinage of the same prolific brain which has devised so many disasters for me already."

" Indeed, indeed, Frank, you are mistaken," said Ellen, very much softened in her manner, however."

" Well, then, Ellen, go on until I see from whence the story came."

" Of that I can inform you in a moment. It came from the lady herself, Miss Eugenia Elliot, and you know that you gave me such a description of her, yourself, as none but a lover could give."

Frank was bewildered, he had stopped, and stood facing his partially appeased mistress. " You astonish me !" said he, " for I know that Eugenia Elliot is incapable of falsehood or deception." He was wrapped in a *deep* study for a moment, and then striking his forehead and capering about the room like one wild, cried out, " I have it ! I have it !"

Ellen was agitated, and began to think somewhat like the Governor, that his misfortunes had touched his brain, and she rose up from her seat, as if about to escape, but Frank caught her in his arms, and after imprinting sundry most extravagant kisses upon her forehead, cheeks and lips, seated her *nolens volens.*

" I have it, my Ellen! I have it! The mistake has originated in the confusion of the two Halls. It is the real Henry Hall who is engaged to Eugenia Elliot; fool that I was not to think of this, when that little Indian girl delivered the message, but of this you shall be certain within the half hour ;" and he put on his hat and was hurrying out, but Ellen, with a sweet smile of forgiveness on her face, called him back.

" It needs not, Frank," said she, as he returned into the room, " you see I have taken you at your word, and resumed those precious treasures of our childish days," and she held out her hand at the same time.

It may be readily imagined that Frank was not satisfied with a mere shake of the hand, or even carrying it to his lips, but over that evening we dare not venture to intrude the stranger's gaze. Their hearts and their memories poured forth their long pent up treasures without stint.

Happy, happy are they, who, after whatever trials and afflictions, maintain their first pure affections uncontaminated by the world. It is a god-send, and sufficient for most men, that the memory preserves these delicious dreams of youth, to be called up at pleasure to reinvest with their bright colors the otherwise sombre views of the present and the future. A large majority of mankind are only thus partially blest—it is enough to vibrate a single cord of the instrument, but with our now happy young couple, their whole hearts throbbed in perfect unison, not a jar was heard in the beautiful concord of sweet words.

Is it because such delicious hours so intoxicate the senses, that no durable record has ever been taken of these too fleeting joys ; or, is the impression so evanescent that no durable impression is left ? That it is not the latter, the heart and memory of every one can testify; the impression is more lasting than life; many a miserable sufferer in this world lives out his dreary pilgrimage upon the bare hope of living o'er all these scenes again in another stage of existence. The wish, the hope, is never perhaps embodied into language, but they nevertheless exist under grave visages, and quaint garbs and fashions of the world. The heart of every man, and especially of every woman, is a store-house of these hidden things, treasured up through every trial and vicissitude, where they lie buried along with the cherished memories of other youthful dreams, only to be revived once in a long time, by some sudden turn of circumstances or some unforeseen providential occurrence.

We could multiply instances and illustrations, were we disposed to digress, and show at the same time that " truth is stranger than fiction," but we leave the matter to be tested by the experience of each reader, and to be admitted or thrown aside, as to each may seem best.

Though we will not intrude upon that portion of their discourse which occupied a large part of the night, during this their delightful reunion, we must nevertheless touch upon the conclusion of their meeting, because it bears upon the subject of our narrative.

Frank had several times made an effort to tear himself away; he was at last conscious that the night was far spent, but then the approaching departure on the morrow furnished an admirable excuse. " Your father, too," said he, "is still at the Governor's, surely I may stay here as long as he stays there."

" I will sit up all night if you choose, Frank," replied Ellen, her hand clasped in that of her lover, and her eyes looking so bright that one would suppose that sleep never approached them, much less that they had lately been dimmed by sickness and suffering.

The fact was, the old Doctor was long ago comfortably stowed in bed—he had learned from the servant at the door that Mr. Lee was there, and supposing how the matter stood, very discreetly retired and left them to themselves.

" No, no," said Frank, " that would never do, it would dim your bright eyes to-morrow before their time, for you must know, my Ellen, that I flatter myself that you will not see me again depart upon an indefinite absence without a tear—just one little pearl."

"Oh, Frank, how can you talk lightly upon such a subject, after such an absence and such a return—bear with me, therefore, if I turn your gay thoughts for a moment to a serious matter."

"No, no, Ellen, no serious subjects to-night—I have resolved to be happy while I may. For the brief hours, nay, minutes, that are left us, let dull care be thrown aside."

"But, Frank," and she laid her hand imploringly upon his arm," your brother!"

He bounded to his feet in an instant, and strode through the room, and sawed his arm vehemently in the air, as if he would dispel a disagreeable spectre which she had conjured up, she following all the while, and her countenance wholly changed from its late happy, placid expression to one of anxiety and distress.

"Oh Ellen!" he at length exclaimed, "how could you obtrude that hated name at such a time?"

"Hated, Frank?"

"Aye, hated!"

"What! hate your own brother, Frank? How different your present feelings from your noble and magnanimous defence of him while in prison!"

"No, no, Ellen, hate is too strong a word, or, at all events, I will only hate his actions, while I commiserate the man."

"Ah, Frank! Frank! that is a nice distinction for so young a moralist—search your heart, and see how inseparable are the actions and the actor—it is a refinement, which I fear, Frank, is not only beyond your strength, but beyond human power."

"Well, my Ellen, what would you have me do? Must I profess to love him, and clasp the monster to my heart, while my whole nature revolts at the hypocrisy?"

"No! not that either, but forgive him, Frank, and do him justice."

"Do him justice! then I should become his executioner; I should dye my hands in his blood!"

Ellen shuddered at the ferocious expression of his countenance, which she had never seen before; all formed for gentle emotions, as it seemed to her, and ever ready to melt at a tale of sorrow and distress. She sat down and covered her face with her hands. Seeing which, he approached already softened and repentant.

"Forgive me, my Ellen—I have offended you?"

"No, not offended, Frank," said she, and looking up with a tear glistening in her eye, "but I confess to you that I am disappointed. I thought that your trials had wholly changed that ardent and impetuous nature of yours."

"Would you have my nature changed, Ellen?"

She returned his ardent and steady gaze for some moments, and then laying her hand affectionately in his, she said steadily and firmly, "Yes!"

He let her hand drop, as he said, "Now, Ellen, I in my turn am disappointed. I thought we knew each other thoroughly, and that in the language of the marriage ceremony, we had determined 'to take each other for better for worse,' that you loved me for myself—as I am, with all my faults."

"And so I do, Frank, and have said already—how often, I am ashamed to say, that I will be yours 'for better for worse' when you return, but——"

"Oh stop there, Ellen, and let me go now, let me depart to-morrow with those sweet words still ringing in my ears," and he imprinted a kiss upon her lips, and broke away.

An hour afterwards he returned, and gazed upon the now black and dreary looking house, wrapped in profound darkness. Well was it that he did so—

most providential was the prompting that led him to that spot at such a late hour of the night, or rather morning; for he had not stood there many moments ere he saw a light spring up in a wing of the Doctor's house, the lower part of which was the old physician's office, and the upper scarcely ever used. He watched it from the time it was no bigger than his hand, until the whole curtain was in a bright blaze, and he could no longer doubt. He sounded the alarm of fire, and running to the enclosure, laid his hand upon it and sprung lightly over. He was very much surprised to hear the tramp of several horses feet leaving the enclosure as he entered. If it were the old Doctor just setting out upon one of his nightly pilgrimages, why did he not return, at the alarm of fire? He repeated the cry still louder than before, and several voices in the street re-echoed it, and he could hear the people running in towards the front entrance, but still the flying horsemen seemed but to increase their speed. He found the back door of the wing, where he had seen the fire, wide open—he ran up stairs, the first to arrive there, and found the curtains of the window and those of the bed, from which some person seemed just to have escaped, all in a blaze. He tore down the fast consuming combustibles, and with such things as he could hastily find, thrust out the sashes and the burning fragments after them; and with the assistance of others, who now arrived on the spot, soon tumbled the burning bed-clothes and the curtains out of the window. In a shorter time than we have taken to relate it, the fire, except the burning things in the yard below, was entirely extinguished; and in a very few moments after, the old Doctor in his nightcap, and Ellen in her dishabille, entered. Their whole concern and anxiety were for Wingina, whom Ellen said she saw safely in bed herself not an hour before. Frank was as much surprised to see the old Doctor as *he* was to see Frank, the latter supposing the old Doctor cantering away upon an errand of life and death, while the Doctor thought Frank snugly in bed at the Palace. Diligent search was now made for Wingina. It was supposed, that frightened at the fire, she had run out into the grounds below, or perhaps into the street. Her outer garments were still hanging over the chair, where Ellen had seen her place them when she retired to bed.

While they were yet prosecuting the search in the court below, the garden and the shrubbery, several reports of fire-arms were heard in quick succession, which those present most conversant in such matters pronounced to be by the picket guards beyond the College. Our readers must know that the little army then encamped in and around the city, was already assuming that order and discipline for which the old chief in command was so noted. Notwithstanding this rigid military discipline, it now became pretty evident to Frank Lee and the Doctor, who were holding together anxious council on the subject, that those lines had been surreptitiously entered by the Indians, and Wingina spirited away by her brother. Such were their hasty surmises, and they were speedily confirmed by the reports which soon came in from the sentinels. It appeared that the horsemen, whose retreating figures Frank Lee had really seen, were those of a party of the dare devils headed by Chunoluskee—that he bore his sister on the horse before him, and that they had dashed through the line of sentinels without sustaining any material damage, though repeatedly fired at. It now became a matter of anxious inquiry, how they had obtained ingress; and when the business was investigated, it turned out that the footsteps of the Indians as usual were tracked in blood. A drowsy sentinel had been stolen upon and tomahawked before any alarm could be given, and thus they had found their way into the very heart of the city, and borne off the prize—hostage or victim, as the case might prove.

This daring deed, upon the eve of the march of the expedition, opened the eyes of the careless young cavaliers, upon whom mainly rested its fate. Many of them were carousing in their tents at the very hour when they had been stolen upon.

The novelty of a camp life, and some difficulty in procuring lodgings, had induced many of them thus early to spread their canvass upon the common, and some were sleeping, some drinking, and some singing and telling stories of adventure, when the report of fire-arms startled them' from their various attitudes. Some forty or fifty of them were speedily mounted, Frank Lee among the number, taking the road indicated by the sentinels, in pursuit. How well Frank remembered that road ! He had but recently travelled it—first flying from prison, and then returning to it again in irons. Dark as it was, he knew every foot of it. How gaily bounded his steed, and how elastic his spirits now, in comparison with what they were then. Even a night alarm and a recent murder scarcely threw a shadow across his bright visions of the future. It must be confessed, too, that his thoughts were scarcely, as they should have been, devoted solely to the enterprise in hand—they were still lingering in the capital. Yet he rode first of the band, spurring on his mettled charger. We pity the horse of a lover, for he is required to keep pace with the thoughts of his rider. Frank would have ridden, perhaps, till day-light, and never perceived that his companions had halted, had they not shouted after him. It was found, after several miles pursuit, to be a vain effort. The road had been examined several times, and the trail was already lost. Doubtless the marauders had taken to the woods, as soon as they left the capital. It was therefore determined to return to the city.

CHAPTER XV:

THE DAY OF DEPARTURE.

THE eventful day at length dawned upon the thronged capital of Virginia—that day pregnant with so many bright hopes—so long looked for, and so ardently desired, in particular by the chivalrous Governor of the Colony.

At the first peep of ay, the drums and trumpets were in requisition, and the young gentry were seen marshalling their little bands of followers in separate squads, over the common and in the by lanes and streets. Any one who has ever seen a militia training, or a "general muster," in Old Virginia, may form a pretty accurate idea of these raw troops and their manœuvres.

The Rangers, or regular troops, as they may be called, presented quite a different aspect. They were paraded in Gloucester street, in full uniform, well equipped and mounted. They had long been under the supervision of the old veteran their commander, and presented an array never before seen in Virginia, for they had never before paraded at the capital in one body.

In addition to this solid column of soldierly looking men, there was drawn up on the other side of the street a long line of sumpter mules, loaded with every kind of dried provisions, clothing, cooking utensils, tools and iron. Many carts and wagons were also in requisition, with the heavier baggage and provender. These were intended to go no farther than the frontier, when the tents and baggage would be transferred to the backs of the mules, and the wagons would return.

Even thus early in the morning, Gen. Spotswood was mounted upon his horse, and was busily superintending the delivery of arms from the round tower, to the militia, of whom we have already spoken. The old hero could scarce preserve his gravity, as he, one after the other, ordered up the militia in review before him. He had yet to learn, in actual service in the field, the worth of these hardy tatterdemalions. They were mostly dressed in hunting shirts and foraging caps, rudely put together, from the fur of every sort of wild animal—many of them still flourishing the tail which belonged to the animal. To any but the stern military eye of their camp drilled commander, their appearance would have been quite picturesque.

Such a parade, it may be readily believed, was not without interest to those who were not to be of the expedition—the ladies filled every window, balcony or cupola, and gaily fluttered their white handkerchiefs in the wind, as some well known young cavalier rode by with his troops.

Frank Lee and young Nathaniel Dandridge had been appointed aids to the Governor, and their occupations on this busy morning were arduous indeed. They were kept constantly on the gallop—bringing up one troop, and marching off another—both, doubtless, though glorying in their appointments, would have far preferred another occupation on this particular occasion. There remained a hundred unsaid things to their lady-loves, which they now recalled for the first time; but they did not yet despair of saying at least farewell, once again. Often they caught the beam of a bright eye upon them, as they rode through the streets. The Governor's two daughters already had their horses saddled at the court of the Palace, intending to accompany the expedition for some miles on the journey.

There was yet one solemn public ceremony which remained to be performed, after the distribution of arms and ammunition was completed. A platform had been erected in front of the new church, on Gloucester street, and here, it was understood, the Reverend Commissary would dismiss the little army, with an exhortation and solemn benediction.

After the morning meal was completed, the troops were set in motion towards this point. The open space, enclosed for a cemetery, was already filled with a crowd of spectators, and the troops now closely packed in front of the church and along the square, in front of the Palace, formed quite an imposing array. The bell had ceased its summons, and a solemn silence pervaded the assembly, when the Reverend Commissary, accompanied by the Rev. Hugh Jones, appeared in front of the church. Instantly every hat was doffed, and the clear voice of the good old prelate was heard in earnest exhortation. He approved decidedly of the enterprise, and urged them to go forward in the great march of civilization, and told them that thousands yet unborn would bless the hardy pioneers then about to set out upon the exploration of a new and unknown country. He told them that it was no idle military conquest, barren of all useful results—no pageant, to result in unmeaning and fruitless trophies, but emphatically an enterprise in behalf of their country—of the age—of the world. He trusted, he said, that their conquests would be bloodless ones, and their message to the benighted inhabitants of the regions to which they were bound, one of peace, and mercy, and good will—that the past conduct of his excellent friend, their commander, in behalf of the aborigines, was a sure guarantee of his future conduct towards them.

He said that his chief aid in the ministry, the Reverend Gentleman then present, would accompany them, and he trusted that they would continue to render homage to that Being, in whose hands was the success or defeat of their enterprise.

Every knee was then bowed, to supplicate the divine favor for the undertaking, in which they were all about to engage with so much enthusiasm. It was a solemn sight—to behold those gay young cavaliers and their rude followers, and the more disciplined Rangers, all kneeling beside their horses, and every tongue hushed to a solemn stillness, while the venerable prelate poured forth his honest and eloquent appeals in their behalf.

Then followed a scene of indescribable confusion—the leave taking. Wives rushing in among soldiers and horses, to have one more shake of' the hand, or one more parting word. Lassies taking a parting good by of their lovers, and fathers of their sons. Few old men joined the enterprise—the Governor himself was, perhaps, the oldest man of the little army. After a grand flourish of drums, something like order was once more resumed, and the troops began to deploy into line, preparatory to their final departure.

The old veteran rode along the line, with real pride and a martial glow mantling his cheeks, which had long lain dormant, for want of proper occasions for its display. Like most successful military leaders, he felt as confident of success on that day as he did on the day of his return, for he knew that he possessed the energy and the knowledge to ensure it. To us, at this distant day, with all the results before us, this does not seem strange or improbable ; but it was by no means so then. His grand hobby, as it was called by the elderly gentry, met with far more ridicule than support and countenance. As we have before said, many over prudent fathers opposed their sons accompanying him at all; and wiseacres were not wanting in abundance, who predicted its total failure, and that the final catastrophe would be an Indian massacre in some mountain defile. This last surmise had gained not a little ground, since the daring inroad of a band of the Indians during the night, into the very heart of the capital—garrisoned as it was by their whole army. And they reasoned not very unjustly, that if such things could be done with impunity there, what might not be done among their own mountain fastnesses, whose intricate defiles were known only to themselves ?

A white guide had been provided hastily in Chunoluskee's stead. He was a hunter, and had penetrated farther towards the mountains than any one known in the colonies. He was of tried metal, too, for he had fought the Indians in his day. His name was Jarvis—son of the old fisherman, whom we introduced to the reader, in the early part of our narrative. Joe Jarvis—commonly called Red Jarvis—was of a class which is fast gliding from notice in the older settlements of the States. They were called in that day, and indeed long afterwards, *scouts.*

The troops were now in motion, and the front lines were already passing the College square, the long line of sumpter mules and wagons bringing up the rear. The Governor and his suite had not yet left the city. They waited for the scout, who had gone on a farewell visit the night before to his father at Temple Farm. While the Governor and his aids, with many of the young gentry, sat upon their horses, near the round tower, in the market square, and while they were beginning to express doubts and misgivings of their second guide, the very man himself glided into their midst ; and such a man—so remarkable, and he performs such an important part in the grand expedition, that we must describe him. He was a tall specimen, in every sense of the word—six feet and more in his stockings, (if he ever wore any.) On the present occasion, his feet and legs were clad in buckskin leggings and moccasins fitting close to the members. His breeches were of homespun, and his hunting shirt of the same material, held together by a broad leather strap, into which were stuck various utensils of the woodman's craft, with others of a more warlike character, among which was a knife cased in a leather sheath, which, in a single-handed encounter, would be a most deadly weapon. His face expressed any thing but daring and decided character. Its principal characteristic was fun and frolic, but of a quiet and subdued sort. There was a constant inclination of' the head to one side, with one eye partially closed at the same time, and a quiet smile about the mouth. His excessive self-confidence would have given him the appearance of boldness and presumption, had it not been for the sly peculiarities we are attempting to describe. He had large red whiskers, extending under his throat, the only protection it had, and these were burnt and faded to a sandy or yellow shade, at their extremities, by long exposure to sun and rain. Hence his *soubriquet* of Red Jarvis. Upon his shoulder he carried a long gun, much longer than the pony upon which he was mounted. Thus accoutred, he rode into the midst of the gentry, who awaited so impatiently his arrival, followed by a large dog, which was just about as much used to such company as his master. There was this great difference between them, however, the dog slunk about the horses legs, quite confounded and abashed; while Joe rode into their midst, one eye cocked, with as quiet a leer as if he had rode to the front of his father's cabin. As he glanced around, his eye naturally fell upon the short carbines slung across the backs of the young gentlemen who sat on horseback around him, and then wandered along the huge thing which he carried himself. The result of the mental comparison was a sly inward chuckle, which, however, he subdued into his habitual cock of one eye, as it rested upon the Governor, who was surveying him, from the coonskin cap on his head to his feet, which almost touched the ground. The result of the Governor's examination was pretty much like Joe's survey of the young men's armaments, a laugh—he could not resist Joe's *outre* appearance.

" Well, Jarvis," said he, " how far do you expect to carry that pony ?"

" Jist as far as he'll carry me, your honor."

" Well said, but I fear that will not be far."

" *Hoses* is like men, Governor—it is not always the smoothest coats has the bravest hearts inside on 'em ;" and his half closed eye ranged again over the gaudy attire and gold lace around him, which gradually grew into an unsuppressed chuckle, the cause of which the Governor was induced to inquire.

" Why, I was thinkin', Sir, how all this gold and flummery would look the day we marched in again."

" True, true, Joe, these lads will be glad to have your hunting shirt and moccasins before they return, and so I have been telling them."

" There won't be a whole shirt, Sir, in the army, when we come back ; and for that reason, I left mine behind ;" and here he gave another quiet laugh, as he surveyed the magnificent lace ruffles and collars flowing about him.

Some of the young cavaliers had a curiosity to know what substitute *he* had in place of a shirt.

" Why here," said Joe, handling the red hair under his throat, as if he was bearding a lion, " is my ruffles ;" and pulling open his hunting shirt, he displayed a buckskin, tanned with the hair on, and corresponding so near in color to the ruffles of which he had just boasted, that it looked like part and parcel of the same animal. He enjoyed highly the stare of astonishment with which his garments were examined by the ball room soldiers, as he called them.

" But, Jarvis," said the Governor, " how comes it that you are so dilatory this first morning of the march—we thought you were the very soul of punctuality and promptitude."

Joe looked a little confused for a moment, and tugging at his coon skin cap, so as to place the tail exactly behind, and coughed and hemmed several times ere he answered :—" You see, your worship, as I was comin' to town this mornin' fore day, I heard the news of the *rupture* of the savages last night, and I jist tuck a turn or two through the woods on my own hook, to see if I could find the trail."

Here one of the young gentlemen bending over, whispered to the Governor that Joe had formerly been an admirer of Winginia.

" Aye, aye," said the old veteran, " I see ! well, did you fall upon their trail ?"

" Yes, Sir, I rather think I did. It would take a cunning Indian, and more 'specially a dozen of 'em, to march through these pines and leave no trail that I could'nt find. I *blazed* a couple of miles or so, and then turned back for fear you mought be awaitin' on me."

Blazing was performed in those days by the scouts, or pioneer, taking the lead in a new or untried route, by striking a chip off one side of a tree. They may be seen at night, if not very dark. New roads were laid off in the same primitive manner. Joe carried his tomahawk in his belt, ready for such service, not a little of which he was about to perform ; for the army once beyond the ruins of Germana, every foot of the route had to be marked out by him after the manner described.

The Governor, after some consultation with his aids and the scout, came to the conclusion that it was useless to follow the trail marked out by Joe, at present, as he assured them that they would fall upon it again before night, at such a distance from the settlement as would render pursuit more likely to result in success.

The last sumpter mules were now passing the suburbs of the city, and the little party round the military tower separated to bid a last farewell with those near and dear to them. The Governor's two daughters were already mounted, as likewise were little Bob, Dr. Blair, and several servants, intended as their return escort. The Governor, therefore, only dismounted for a moment, entered the Palace, folded his lady in one long embrace, and then mounted and galloped off, followed by his veteran life-guard, the bugles enlivening the scene by their martial airs. By the side of Kate, rode Bernard Moore; while Dorothea was escorted by young Dandridge, now quite proud at his elevation into the Governor's military family.

Whether Moore's rival knew that the Governor and suite were to be thus accompanied, or whether his military duties required him elsewhere, we know not ; but certain it is, none of the company regretted his absence. Indeed, Kate was quite offended with him for the part he had taken against Frank Lee, and perhaps, knowing this to be the case, he had voluntarily absented himself.

The lovers rode quite by themselves, and to have seen the earnestness and eagerness with which they conversed, one would have supposed that the whole success of the expedition depended upon their sapient conclusions. That they were looking far into futurity, no one will doubt who knows any thing of the proverbial impatience and imprudence of lovers. Moore had, despite of his jocular pledge to his rival, more than once pretty broadly hinted the state of his heart, and his hopes, and his aspirations, preceding the sad catastrophe which had so long (as he thought it) shut them up within the walls of the Palace. He had longed, above all things, for just such an opportunity as now presented itself, to complete the matter. Yet, when he glanced at the proud and brilliant beauty cantering at his side, looking still more beautiful and bright from the contrast of her sable riding habit, his heart almost misgave him. He dreaded more the bright beams of those eyes, that occasionally encountered his own, than the glare of an hundred hostile Indians. The precious moments were fast gliding by—never did time so gallop by a true-hearted lover. The fact is, that Kate coquetted just a little with him. She had hitherto succeeded in listening to his protestations without committing herself by any reply. It had so happened, that she was favored by circumstances in this respect. With feminine sagacity in these matters, she at once now penetrated the objects of her lover, and saw plainly his embarrassment and its cause, and instead of helping him out of his difficulty, or even remaining silent to afford him an opportunity, she rattled away in the most brilliant style, compelling him to answer. But such answers ! They were mere monosyllables—and more than half the time he said no, for yes ; and yes, for no. Kate was compelled to laugh, at length, and ask him " what was the matter ?"

" To tell you the truth, Kate, I feel sad—sad at leaving you ;" and his voice became husky.

Kate broke into the midst of this exordium—" What ! so sentimental Bernard ? Don't you know that papa ordered us to put on our brightest smiles, and that he hates a gloomy good-by !"

" I was going to say, Kate, that your wit is all lost upon me this morning, because my heart is not in the subject of your merriment. Let me intreat you to be serious for five minutes—my time is short, and you know that I have been banished from your presence by the sad accident which we all deplore so much."

Kate was as solemn as a judge in the twinkling of an eye, and replied, "Oh cruel, cruel Bernard, how could you dash all my bright morning's efforts by such an allusion !"

" Forgive me, dearest Kate, but it was accidental, and fell from my lips without reflection, and now let me banish the dreadful past by holding up a bright future. Oh, Kate, how bright, my imagination scarcely dares contemplate, if you will only consent to blend your hopes and destinies with mine."

He paused for a reply, but not a word escaped her now sealed lips.

He continued. " You have held me in probation a long, long time. You are sufficiently acquainted with all my habits, even of thought, to know by this time whether you can consent to place your future happiness in my keeping, and surely you will not suffer me to depart upon such a long journey without letting me know my fate—a journey, too, Kate, undertaken more through your influence than your father's. You have driven me into exile, and it is for you to say whether I shall return."

" Oh, Bernard, how can you say so ; I never urged you to go by word or sign of any sort—indeed I was opposed——" There she left the sentence unfinished.

" Go on, Kate, go on," said Moore eagerly. " Were you indeed loth to see me go."

Kate blushed, but finished not the sentence.

" Would you have me turn back now ?" eagerly inquired he.

" Oh, not for the world !" she exclaimed suddenly, " it would be disgrace in the eyes of my father."

" Oh, Kate, Kate," said Moore, after gazing at her thoughtfully for a moment, " you may as well confess that you take an interest in my movements, whether I go or stay. Say, then, should I return victorious with your father—for I hear we shall have some fighting—will you crown my young triumphs with that hand which I have so long and so devotedly sought ?"

Kate placed her hand in that of the eager youth, exclaiming suddenly, " there." And there we shall leave them cantering away on the road, having fallen far behind the cortege of the Governor. How the more youthful pair settled their *quarrels*, for every one said that Dandridge's and Dorothea's love-making was more like quarrelling than any thing else, we shall not venture to say, but certain it is, that Nat had his face slapped with her fan more than once during the ride. The Governor was in the habit of calling them his Catherine and Petruchio. But we must leave them to make the best of their way, while we turn back and see what has become of Frank Lee and he scout, both of whom were left in the city and still remained there.

Where they were, or where the principal was, will not be hard to imagine. Frank was at the Doctor's house, and his new attendant sat astride of his rugged little pony at the wicket gate, holding Frank's horse, and cracking his rough jokes upon his acquaintances that passed. It will be readily perceived from this, that Joe was not entirely disconsolate at the abduction of his lady-love—that he was by no means one of the sentimental sort. Whether he was aware of the ugly stories circulated through the town, to the great discredit of

her good name, we shall not undertake to say, nor to speculate upon his probable course, should it appear that he was fully aware of the whole scandal;
sufficient for our purpose to state, that he was fully determined to follow the
"bloody varmints" to the end of the world. Where that end of the world was,
Joe had very little thought or care. He was ripe for the tramontane expedition, and perhaps of all the number who that day set out in its accomplishment, he was the best informed of its hazards, and the best prepared to endure
its hardships. He had heard of Frank's late perils and adventures, and at
once taken a fancy to him; it was fully reciprocated by his more accomplished
friend, which will account for the present position of the parties. Frank told
him when he jumped off his horse and threw him the reins, that he would be
gone just five minutes. He had already been absent an hour, and Joe having
exhausted his jokes, was becoming rather impatient. He turned round to the
servant, who sat upon his horse at a respectful distance, and exclaimed, "I
say, you darkey, are your master's five minutes always like *this?*"

"Can't say," replied Cuffy, "I is just arrived from the plantation."

So we will give our readers a glance for themselves into that little
parlour, flanked by the aviary and green house, and which so captivated
Henry Lee's heart.

Frank and Ellen were seated side by side, talking as earnestly as if
poor Joe and his pony were over the mountains, while the old Doctor
promenaded the veranda rather impatiently.

"Oh, Frank!" said Ellen, "I cannot bear the thoughts of your leaving
me again, now that the parting moment has come, and yet I would not
have you stay."

"No indeed, my Ellen, I know you would not tempt me to desert my
excellent friend, the Governor, just upon the eve of accomplishing one of
the great designs of his life."

"And yet, Frank, when I think of our former parting and and all that
followed—how long I mourned you as dead—my woman's heart shrinks
from the trial."

"I would not part with the blessed certainty which I derived from
those trials and afflictions, of your devotedness, *for all* the suffering which
they brought. Besides, my Ellen, my name has been somewhat tarnished
as a rebel. I go forth now to redeem my good name."

"I care not a fig for worldly honors, Frank, and did hope that you too,
were weaned from such empty vanities."

"And so I am from all empty vanities. We are impelled by higher
motives, I assure you."

"Ah, Frank, Frank, you are still the same ardent, impetuous, sanguine fellow, that I knew you to be when a boy in my father's house."

"And to whom you pledged your young affections, children as we were.
Oh most nobly have you kept that pledge, my Ellen, and I but ask you
to pardon the unworthy truant for another short, short absence, and then—
and then. Oh such visions are death to the tramontane expedition. Farewell, Ellen—farewell."

"You will write to me, Frank, by every returning courier. I understand that the Governor will despatch messengers at stated intervals informing us of his progress. Send me a journal of every day, Frank."

"I will—I will."

Amidst such parting exclamations and sundry other little remembrances
too tedious to mention, he tore himself away, wrung the old Doctor's
hand—sprung upon his horse, and was soon on his way towards the
mountains. Joe was trotting at a murderous rate to keep by his side,
but all in vain, for the first mile or two; at length, however, he succeeded in arresting the attention of his companion; when he addressed

him after the following manner: "I say, Squire, is that black leather thing behind your nigger filled with ruffled shirts, like the rest on 'em ?"

"Why, Joe, to tell you the truth, there is some useless finery there, now that I think of it."

Joe laughed, and continued. "And not a pair of shoes or moccasins, not a flint, nor a powder-horn, nor ere a spoon, nor a fork, nor a screwer, nor a frying-pan ? Ha! ha! ha! Now, do tell me, what is in them, besides the ruffles and the spangles ?"

"Well, Joe, there are a dozen shirts, sundry inexpressibles, an extra coat, some writing paper, an ink-stand and drawing materials, and lastly, a pair of small pistols."

"Well, all I've got to say, is, that your black mail bag will come back filled with another sort of plunder, that's all."

CHAPTER XVI.

A GLIMPSE OF THE FUGITIVE.

FRANK LEE did not ride many miles further, before he met the return party of ladies. Kate was riding on ahead of the now melancholy little cortege, weeping quite bitterly, and her eyes were so blinded, and her thoughts so absorbed, that she did not perceive the horsemen approaching, until Frank reined up right along side of her.

A smile broke over her sunny face, as she perceived Frank shaking his finger threateningly at her.

"I will give a good account of those bright drops, some of these long nights, around our watch fires, and will guarantee that I find one interested auditor, at least."

Kate waved her hand in adieu, and putting whip to her horse, cantered off on her way, calling out after him, over her shoulder, "Filial tears, filial tears, Mr. Lee."

And thus the last link was severed between the daughters of the city and the mountain adventurers.

It must be remembered that the vast territories since claimed for Virginia, extending almost, if not quite, to the Pacific Ocean, owed their titles to the very expedition which we have been thus departing from the ancient capital. But it was quite different in those primitive days ; the whole population was contained in some twenty or thirty counties, and the present sites of some of our most populous cities were then actually on the frontier, so that our adventurers had to march but a short distance before they were beyond the reach of the thickly settled regions.

Our readers must cast their thoughts back to the days far anterior to Mc-Adamized roads, steamboats, and railroads, and imagine to themselves, if they can, a state of things in the Old Dominion, when sumpter mules and baggage wagons of a rude sort, performed all the offices now so rapidly accomplished by these modern inventions. Some idea may be realized of the primitive state of the country, and how completely the population was shut up within the tide water region, when we state, upon undoubted authority, that among the great number of horses employed in the enterprise which we have just seen under way, not one had ever been shod. Those persons living in the sandy regions of the United States will readily conceive this, but it will be almost incredible to those who now dwell in those favored vales, first discovered and appreciated by this very expedition. Such was the fact, as will be seen hereafter, by the remarkable circumstance from which our humble narrative takes its name.

For the first day, however, no inconvenience was inexperienced. Never did a happier or more jovial little army set out in search of adventures. The old military veteran, their commander, was so well pleased himself that his long desired scheme was really about to be accomplished, that he did not, for the present, quarrel with the rude gaiety of those around him. Those, however, who knew him well, knew, also, that this state of things would not last long—that, in a day or two's march, they would enter a country filled with savages.

With the route of the first few day's journey, the Governor was perfectly familiar. He had more than once passed over the ground, and had, as we have before stated, established Indian preparatory schools throughout the districts inhabited by the tributary Indians.

He was now quite anxious to see what influence Chunoluskee and his associates had been able to exercise over these, and he had it in contemplation to time the march, so as to arrive at the end of the sacred day at the first of these schools, lying within his proposed route.

Though we have seen the Governor permit a somewhat lax discipline to prevail upon emerging from the city, there were already symptoms that this state of things would not last long. He soon summoned his aids and the scout to his side, and was busily detailing to them his commands, as to the conduct of the men during the march and in camp—and consulting with the latter as to the route, forage, and subsistence. The latter subject gave him far more uneasiness than any apprehended danger from the savages ; and how hundreds of men, and as many horses and mules, were to be subsisted in an entirely new and uncultivated country, an unexplored wilderness in fact, was a subject of anxious reflection with him. He knew that the supplies contained in his baggage wagons and haversacks would scarcely last him beyond the extreme frontier settlements. Though he was a tried soldier from his very infancy, it must be recollected that his present adventure was as new to him in practice, as to the youthful aid by his side.

Our readers may think that he consulted strange counsel in the person of Red Jarvis, but so it was ; and of all that army, perhaps, he was the very man best calculated to give advice—in his own way, to be sure. He felt no doubts and misgivings like his superior—he felt as confident as he had done many a time before, when a hundred miles from the settlements, with no other protection and provision for the morrow except his trusty firelock. And as he had done, so he advised the whole army to do—literally to turn it into a great hunting party. The Governor was amused at the conceit, but he would not hear of the scheme for a moment. Nevertheless, the idea was serviceable, for it suggested the plan of detailing each day, parties for the purpose of killing game for the subsistence of the party.

He was pleased to find, as they emerged deeper into the forest, that the foliage became richer, and the grass more abundant. These were matters which now became of great moment, insignificant as they appear at the first glance, the whole success of the expedition in fact depending upon them.

Joe Jarvis was no sooner dismissed from the conference with the Governor, than he struck out into the woods, ahead of the troops, and began blazing away at the trees, as already described. He seemed to Frank Lee, who accompanied him, to know every foot of the ground, and likewise when game might be looked for, and when not. They had not travelled many miles through the wild and solitary forest, before Joe dismounted from his *tackey*, and handing the bundle to Frank, motioned with his hand for him to pause, and be silent. He moved stealthily through the bushes, examining his priming as he went, until he entirely disappeared from sight. In about fifteen minutes Frank heard the report of his gun, and as it appeared to him, but an instant after, a fine herd of deer came leaping over the tops of the bushes, and almost within pistol shot of where he sat upon his horse, his gun being unfortunately slung to his back. While he made a movement to bring it around, they all stopped and stared at him for a moment, and then bounded away like the wind. Joe had been a spectator of this scene, and emerged from the bushes, wiping his bloody knife, and laughing in his chuckling way, at Frank's discomfiture and chagrin.

"Now," said he, "you see the reason why I alway carry my gun in my hand. You asked me a while ago, and I promised to show you."

Frank immediately unstrapped his firelock, and wound up the leather straps and put them by, as if to show his teacher that he was determined to improve by his practical lessons.

"Well. Jarvis, what did you kill?"

"As fine a buck as ever you laid your eyes upon; you remember the Governor's talk, about the subsistence of the army?—you see, I'm going to show him the way we hunters provide for our daily wants."

By this time they had arrived at the head of a small stream, where Joe said the deer were in the habit of drinking, the water being a little brackish, of which they are very fond. He slung the fine animal, whose throat he had just cut, across his pony, and after securing it with thongs, and reloading his piece, proceeded by the side of Lee, talking all the while. He told him that more of the ruffle shirt gentry, as he loved to call them, would unsling their arms, before they had proceeded many days into the wilderness. Frank observed that Joe's attention was earnestly directed to each side of the path on which they were travelling, notwithstanding his constant stream of talk, and stopping every minute to blaze a tree. He saw that Jarvis stooped down and examined the bushes attentively every now and then, and when they came to the ford of the little stream upon whose banks they had been some travelling, Joe laid his hand upon the other's bridle rein, and then stooped down, and most attentively scanned some tracks of horses' hoofs, left in the soft mud of the opposite bank, and then carefully counted them. Frank asked him what was the meaning of all this, and if he had fallen upon the Indian trail?

"I rather suspicion I have," said Joe; "and more nor that, there is some one with them that would as soon be out of their clutches."

"How do you know, Jarvis?"

"Why, at every place where they have stopped, I find a twig bent down or broken. I reckon it is that little coquit, the interpreter's sister. She would be glad enough to see me now, I suppose."

"How long do you think it is since they forded the little stream, whose banks you have examined so carefully?

"Jist about daylight; and they were riding at a devil of a rate, you may be sure—look here," said the scout, and he placed his foot in one track and the butt of his gun in the other, to indicate the length of the leaps which the animal had taken.

"A slapping pace, indeed," said Frank, thoughtfully; "but tell me, Joe, how can you compute the time since they passed?"

"Why jist so; if they had jist now passed, you would see the splashing of the water around the tracks—if a little longer, you would see that all dried up, and the tracks themselves only moist—and longer still, the tracks would be entirely dry."

"Which latter is the case, is it?"

"Very near, very near—they mout a' passed a little arter daylight, but not much; we'll hear from 'em to-night—the red devils—depend upon it."

"Do you think so?"

"To be sure I do—I know the critters better nor the Governor and old parson Blair, with all their schooling and christianizing of the ungrateful varmints. An Ingin's an Ingin."

" What is there so absurd in the idea, Joe ?"

" Did you ever see a wolf tamed ?"

" No, I cannot say that I ever did, but I think it possible."

" Yes, I'll warrant; and so the Governor thinks of the red devils; but I saw a tamed wolf once, and he had a wonderful good *charecter* for a while. He was better behaved nor any sheep, and he would walk about among the flock as if he was bound to teach 'em good manners; but *bime by* the lambs began to be missed, and nearly every dog on the plantation was killed, on suspicion of being suspected. Still the lambs went, and after a while they laid a watch, and caught wolfy in the very act."

" And what then ?"

" Why they stretched his bloody neck, of course."

" And do you think this an analagous case to that of the interpreter and his associates ?"

" Exactly ! no good *kin* come out of an Ingin. I've hearn tell of all the grand talk about their native gifts, and all that, but if you will listen to my racket, you may build a college over every son of a gun of 'em, and clap a church on the tip top o' that, and after all, he will have a turkey buzzard's heart in him. God never made an Ingin for a human critter."

" Pooh, pooh, Joe, you have imbibed all the prejudices of the early hunters against the race. Do you know that our ancestors on the other side of the water, many hundred years ago, were quite as savage and barbarous as these poor red men ?"

" Bless my soul—you don't tell me so. Well, that beats all natur, I never hearn tell of that afore. I thought they were white, and came down Christians, along side of the Bible, the whole way."

" So they were always white, Joe; but what do you mean by coming down Christians, along side of the Bible ?"

" Why, you know that old Adam was a white man—you'll give that up, I reckon ?"

" I suppose I must, Joe."

" Well, that's what I mean; that we came down straight from old Adam, and brought the Bible all the way down with us."

" You are entirely mistaken, Joe; neither the Old nor the New Testament was given to our British ancestors. Even when our Saviour appeared upon the earth, they were as great savages as these very red men, against whom you are so prejudiced."

" Good, gracious Heavens ! you don't say so ! then we are not Christian born under the covenant, as my old dad used to say, after all ! Well, this puts a patching over any thing I hearn tell of; but you're making game of me, with all your book larnin."

" No, Joe, I am not; I've told you nothing but the plain truth."

" Well, then, how come we to be white, tell me that ?"

" A red skin and a savage nature are not always inseparable; all the learning and refinement of the world have been transmitted to us through dark skins."

" Oh ! you are a bamboozlin' of me, that's plain."

" No, I am not; but tell me, Joe, how is it that you are supposed to have a fancy for one of these red skins yourself."

" Oh, Squire, there you have flung me. I give it up now, you've clean got the upper side of me in the argument."

" But explain it, Joe—how could you fall in love with the daughter of a race you so thoroughly despise ?"

" Well, now, it does beat all natur', that's a fact. How it ever came about, was jist a little touch above my larnin'."

" You plead guilty to the charge, however ?"

" It's not worth the while to deny it, seeing every body seems to know it.

Even old dad got wind of it somehow; and he told me if ever I married an Ingin squaw, he would disinherit me. Poor old man, the only thing he ever had to leave me, I've got already."

" What's that ?"

" Why, his red head—and I believe it was this infernal red mop of mine that got me into the scrape, too."

" How was that ?"

" The Ingins, you know, have all sorts of a likin' for red heads, and blast my hind-sights if I don't think they're more nor half right. Don't every body fancy red birds and red feathers ? Look at the old Governor, when he gets on that velvet coat of hisen, all bespangled with gold lace. Look at the ladies, God bless 'em—they're never dressed without some red garment or other about 'em."

" A pretty forcible defence of your head, Joe, but it would be equally forcible in favor of red eyes."

This was a poser to Joe, and he scratched the debatable ground unmercifully for an answer, but nothing could be got out of it; seeing which, Frank gently led him back to the point from which he had digressed, his love for Wingina, or rather his passion.

" And so the interpreter's sister fell in love with your red hair first, did she ?"

" Yes, she axed me for a cut of it one day, and I was mighty proud of it, till I saw it floatin' in that everlastin' cap of her brother's, along side of the cock and eagle feathers."

" What ! did that queer faded tuft of hair grow upon your head ? I thought it had been some proud trophy of his prowess, perhaps the scalp of an enemy."

" By the long hollows, he's got as much of my *sculp* as he'll ever git ; and if he don't take care, I'll take my locks back, with interest—a piece of the hide stickin' to it."

" What, Joe, you would not scalp a man ?"

" No, I would'nt sculp a man, but I would sculp an Ingin, howsomever."

" And is not an Indian a man, with a soul and body like yourself?"

" No, no more nor that dog.   That stuff, now, you got from old parson Blair. We never heerd tell of the like in these parts 'till he got to preaching of it about, and putting the varmints to school—he and the Governor. Now, look what it's all come to—the Governor's got his son killed by the very man he helped most of 'em all ; and the interpreter would a' worn the parson's sculp at his girdle, if he had cotched him in such a place as he cotched Squire John."

" Ay, but Joe, you forget that John Spotswood is said to have deeply wronged his sister."

" Now, are you so green as to believe all them old wives' tales. What the devil does an Ingin keer for such wrongs as these, even supposing, for the sake of argument, it mout be so ?"

" Chunoluskee has been taught to feel the shame by associating with us. But what reason have you to doubt the common rumor on the subject ?"

" The very best in the world ; for I tried to sleeve her myself the very day she begged that tuft of hair of me, and she looked like one of them tragedy Queens that I saw on the stage down to Williamsburg."

" And still you loved her, notwithstanding such a rebuff?"

" Why, you see, Squire, I thought it was only a grand way she had picked up from the Governor's darters at second-hand, of sayin' that she was only to be had for the marryin'."

" And why did'nt you marry her, Joe, and thus have saved the Governor and his family this deep affliction, and the poor girl what was to her more than life ?"

" Why, in the first place, I never axed her consent; in the second, you know dad would a' disinherited me: and third and lastly, as Parson Blair says, this story of Squire Spotswood tuck me so by surprise, that I had'nt time. Now, you know the whole story. I rather reckon that I'll be at the truth of the business afore I'm done."

"So you have a settled purpose in going to the mountains of your own?"

"Yes, I've got a leetle speculation on my own hook. Don't you be surprised, Squire, if you see me stay up among them mountains, and hear afterwards of my bein' head chief among the Shawnese. I'm told they have a plague of a fancy for red hair up in them diggins."

"And so you calculate after all, upon making amends for the old man's disinheritance of that wonderful legacy of his, your red hair?"

"I don't see, Squire, why I should'nt make my fortune by my head as well as my betters. There's the two parsons, Dr. Blair and Parson Jones, they lives by their wits; and there's the Governor, the heaviest tool he ever handles is a sword; and there's Gen. Clayton and the other lawyers, they lives by their wits; and there's Dr. Evylin, he lives by his wits; and there's all them long gown fellers in the College, they lives by their wits; indeed, I don't see but the most on you here in our mountain company, lives by their wits. But I guess there'll be more nor head work afore they gets back. Well, as I was a sayin'—I don't see why my head should'nt make my fortune, too. To be sure, mine lies on the outside, and yours on the inside. It's all head work, any way you can fix it."

"It is true enough, Joe, I believe that the Indians have a peculiar veneration for a red head, but how are you going to take advantage of it? Suppose these ruinous stories to the discredit of your mistress should prove true—and I fear they are but too true—what will you do then? Will you still take her for better for worse?"

"By George, I never knowed what that better for worse in the marriage doins meant before; that's jist it, no doubt. As to what I will do in sich a case, why I hav'nt exactly considered of it yit, seein' as how I did'nt believe it. In sich a case she will be a sort of Ingin-in-law to the Governor, and a great bite for the likes of me. Could you tell me now, by your head mathew matticks, what kin I would be to the old Gineral?"

Frank turned away his head to indulge in a suppressed laugh ere he answered. "I suppose you would be step-father to his natural grandchild."

"Quite a natural thing, sure enough, but would there be any parquisites?"

"Oh, if you are in earnest, and really desire to bring about such a thing, I have no doubt but the Governor would favor your suit and give you some of the perquisites too, as you call them. It would be an arrangement to be desired, and far more than the girl has a right to expect, or indeed deserves. But tell me, how is it that you, professing such derogatory opinions of the Indians, are still willing to take a wife among them?"

"Oh, Squire, as to my opinions about their skin, that's my rael belief—well, my leanin' towards the gal, is rael too—now when a man's head pulls one way, and his feelin's another, it will be mighty apt to pull the haslets* out of a fellow; besides I'm a hunter by trade, and settlements have been crowding on me for some time, and this here mountain scheme of the Governor's—though the old codgers laugh at it—is going to make things a heap worse with me."

"As how, Joe?"

"Why it will extend the settlements to the mountains. There's scarce an elk or a buffalo to be found now this side of the hills, and he's a gwine to drive them all clean over the ridge."

"And so you are determined to emigrate with the game? Your head seems to be as full of schemes of your own as the Governor's."

"Yes, and I reckon that I have counted the costs a leetle better nor most of 'em he's got in his train, and mout be than he has himself. You'll see who's

---

* Liver and Lights.

the best man among us, when we get among the mountains, and when neither money nor larnin' can do much for a man. Them's the times to try what men's got in 'em."

They were now several miles ahead of the army, and Joe knew the privations of the forest well enough to call a halt at a fine spring, which threw its sparkling waters across their path. He unslung the deer from his poney's back, slipped the head stall over his neck, and turned him loose to graze among the bushes—advising Frank to do the same with his, showing him, at the same time, how to fix the halter, so as to impede his more impatient temper.

These arrangements being completed, he carefully examined the priming of his gun, and set it against a tree, within the reach of his hand, and then took a wallet, which he had removed from behind his saddle, and spread a cold collation before Frank; not a tempting one, it is true, to a dainty appetite, but substantial and tempting enough, to one who had been on horseback from early morning. Out of the same greasy looking receptacle, Joe next drew a bottle, and after wiping the neck carefully upon the sleeve of his coat, handed it to Frank. The latter declined the *aqua vitæ*, but turned in manfully upon the jerked beef and corn dodgers. Joe laughed in his sleeve at Frank's refusing the bottle, and then took a long and hearty draught himself. Drawing a long breath and smacking his lips, he said, "Every drop of this here liquor mought be sold for all the gold lace in the Governor's troop, afore we're among the mountains a week, and you, Squire, will not refuse it, when we come this near home again."

"Perhaps not—perhaps not, Joe, but sufficient for the day is the evil thereof."

"Yes, you may well say that, Squire, for evils there will be enough on 'em for every day after the provisions give out. Do you see that dog of mine hopping so frisky over the bushes yonder?"

"Yes."

"Well, I almost cried, as I looked at him comin' along the road this morning, when he kept jumping upon me and licking my hand."

"For what, I pray?"

"Why, to think that I should see the day when some of your young gentry would eat a fine dinner off of his carcass."

"Pooh! Joe, have done, you take away my appetite. You are only trying to choke me off from your jerked beef, upon which I have been making such inroads."

"Not I! not a bit of it. I tell you, Squire Lee, as sure as you're a settin' there, you'll see hard times afore we git back. That dainty Mr. Carter, that I heer'd a talking about pheasants and woodcocks, will be glad enough to git a mess of young kittins afore many weeks."

"Why, Joe, I cannot eat a morsel more if you talk thus. I did not know before, that you were such a croaker."

"No more am I, but I can't help seeing how out of fix, for a mountain jaunt, is all them ribbons, and ruffles, and gold lace, and silver and gold spurs, and swords made for parade. And look at the cattle, too! Every one of them horses is gwine to give out afore they reaches their journey's eend— and yours among the rest."

"Mine, Joe! why he's the best blood in the Colony."

"Oh, as to that, my pony's got blood in him too. How could the critter live without it? But I'm not talking of the blood, I'll show you what I'm driving at"—and with that he gave a whistle, and his pony came trotting through the bushes and ate a piece of corn bread from his hand. Joe then caught him and held up one of his feet for Frank's inspection. "Do you see them little iron shoes—well I put them on yesterday with my own hands— that's what I call preparation for the mountains. Now, among all the horses of the Governor's troops, there's not a shoe among them; they've been used to the sand of this here tide water region. The Governor and you young gents, seem to think that the mountains are made of sand too. I've seen enough of the rough hills, far, far this side, to know better nor that. Now, Squire, which is agoin' to be the best stand by, the blood in your horses' veins, or the shoes on mine's feet?"

"I confess, Joe, there's reason in what you say—I never thought of that part of the preparation before. I will speak to the Governor about it this very night."

"No, don't you! you'll spile sport if you do. Some of these mornings you will see the funniest army of cripples you ever laid eyes on."

"But it may be a fatal error, Joe, and it is my duty to speak out"

"Not a bit of it—not a bit of it. You can't mend the matter now, and I've seen already to providin' the materials, when the time comes. I put the Commissary up to providin' the materials to make shoes of—though he arn't in all the plans. He don't know what it's for, and no doubt thinks for trade with the Ingins."

Thus assured, Frank acquiesced in Joe's scheme to keep quiet until the emergency occurred. After conversing upon these matters for an hour or two, Joe caught the horses and slung his buck over the pony, and then saddled and readjusted the bridle of Frank's, ready for him to mount. The latter asked him why he prepared to resume their journey before the troops came up.

"Case," said Joe, "they're acomin' now, not more nor a mile off."

Frank looked down the long vista of blazed trees as far as his eye could penetrate, but he could not see even a bush shake, and seemed not a little surprised at Joe's confident assertion.

Joe chuckled as usual, and then threw himself on the ground, and beckoned to his companion to do likewise. Frank did so, and instantly perceived the tramp of cavalry upon the ground.

"You see," said Joe, "I'm agoin' to make a scout of you. You're a pickin' up my craft smart, I swear. I heard that ere sound when I was lying on the ground a quarter of an hour ago."

The advanced guard having at length hove in sight, and the bugles now being distinctly heard, our two adventurers resumed their journey, Joe blazing the trees as he went, and initiating Frank into the mysteries of a scout's life, his pony following quietly all the while, and bearing patiently his huge burden. Occasionally Lee dismounted and walked by his side for a mile or two, which not a little gratified Joe's pride.

<hr />

CHAPTER XVII.

A LETTER FROM THE CAMP.

THAT night the expedition arrived, (owing to the foresight of Joe) at the ruins of a deserted Indian village, with water, and a clearing suitable for a large encampment in the centre, and fine forage, of nature's providing, for the horses, around.

It was the first night in the forest, and not wanting in wild adventure and novelty for the amusement of the young gentry.

The white tents stretching out in picturesque lines against the fading green of the forest; the bright blaze of the camp fires, throwing fantastic shadows of the wagons and horses, and moving objects around; the merry laugh of those within; the rude jest; the recounting of the adventures of the day; the loud song of the old soldiers of the life guard; the measured tramp of the sentinels on duty; the neighing of the horses in the forest, the braying of the asses and mules; the lowing of cows, (for even this luxury had been provided,) altogether presented an enchanting scene amid the primeval forests of nature. About a hundred yards from the Governor's marquee, stood Frank Lee and Bernard Moore, leaning in the shadow of a tree, while old June sat nodding over a great log fire, where the Governor's venison was roasting on a rude spit, and at which old June with a watery mouth cast a wistful glance every now and then, as he rose and fell in the cadences of his song. Lee had called the attention of Moore to this effort of the old banjo-player, because he was evidently the hero of his story. He was celebrating his love for Miss Kate, and bemoaning the separation.

They had not stood there long amusing themselves with old June, before Jarvis touched Frank upon the arm, and beckoned him into the forest. As they passed the last camp fire, Joe seized a large lightwood knot, and holding it for a few moments in the burning coals, produced a bright light, with which he guided his companion some hundred yards beyond the sentinels. He stopped at a secluded nook among the bushes, where horses had evidently been picking around, and where several persons had recently been seated in the centre; for bones and pieces of bread were scattered about in all directions. Joe suffered Frank to satisfy himself about them, and then led him a few yards farther into the bushes, where a white pocket handkerchief of fine texture, was suspended to the top of a stick and leaned against a tree. Joe said he had not disturbed it since the discovery, as he wanted Frank to observe first, the cautious manner in which it had been placed behind the tree, so as to be out of view of those who sat around the fire. Frank took it down, and examining it carefully, discovered a name which it thrilled his heart to meet in that strange wild place. It was Ellen Evylin in full, and in her own handwriting. They readily imagined that it had been placed there by Winginia, that very day, and that it was intended to signify to them that she was borne away against her will. Joe pointed out to the young cavalier, also, several twigs, which had been snapped off, marking distinctly a pathway from the spot where the handkerchief had been found, to the spot where they had mounted their horses. He called his attention again to the slapping pace at which they rode, as evinced by signs before pointed out.

"Well, Joe," said he, "what more can we do for her deliverance than we are doing now; does anything suggest itself to you?"

"Yes, lots—lots. You see, Squire, these cunning varmints will jist play hide and seek with this great company of the Governor's, which he marches through the woods with flags a flyin' and trumpets a soundin' every now and then. He mout as well send me ahead to shout to these red devils, 'git out of the way you yaller varmints, the Governor's acoming!'"

"Well, Joe, how can we help it?"

"No, it's not well, it's very wrong. The old Gineral, he's used to fighten grand battles in an open field with white men like himself, but it's a very different game he's got to play now, and he ain't found it out yit, but take my word for it, he will afore long, if he don't take advice from them as has experience in Ingin fightin'. Now, if he would give you the command of about ten men, that I could pick out of them huntin' shirt boys, and let me be among 'em, we could push ahead, and I would jist like to show you, that there's more nor Ingins can play at the game of hide and seek."

Lee was quite taken with the proposition, and returned with Joe to the Governor's marquee, and sent in to request an audience. After waiting a short time, they were admitted. The Governor was sitting upon a camp stool, and busily pouring over his maps, and at his old employment of sticking pins along his contemplated route. On the ground near him, young Dandridge was seated, and drawing out, according to the Governor's instructions, from time to time, a diagram of the route they had already traversed. The

Governor listened with much interest to the discoveries which Joe had made and gave a respectful consideration to his scheme for cutting off the marauders, but at length shook his head as much as to say, that it would not do. He pondered upon it for some time, hastily walking about the marquee, but after a while seated himself again, and turning to Joe, said it was a good idea, but could not be adopted on account of its taking him from his present indispensable employment; and he told Frank that he would not trust him, as yet, with any other guide, because the savages would pick them off singly, and destroy the whole of them finally, without accomplishing any good. Joe did not want Frank to go unless he could himself be of the party, and therefore he readily acquiesced in the latter part of the Governor's argument. He went off with Frank, however, telling him that they would see what this fighting Indians on a grand parade, would come to.

Having left Joe to pursue his vocation, Frank folded up the handkerchief which had been discovered, and put it near his heart. The sight of that name and that handwriting, called up vividly the image of her who had so long engrossed his most ardent affections. He thought over all that she had said and done since his landing at York, and his early attachment drew new strength from the approbation which his maturer judgment stamped upon his youthful fancy. He was, experienced enough in life to know that this very seldom happens—that the " sweet hearts" of boyish days seldom stand the test of man's matured examination. If all is right as regards the object herself—interest and ambition find their way like the tempter into Eden, and destroy the first, and brightest, and purest emanations of the young heart. But Frank Lee was an independent man in every sense of the word. His fortune was ample, and his ambition, chastened as it was in the school of adversity, threw no impediments in the way. Had he been poor and friendless, it cannot be doubted that his decision would have been the same. He strolled at length into his tent, which he found empty, and taking out his writing tackle and spreading them upon a rude camp seat, sat himself down upon the ground to commune with his affianced wife after the following manner :

Camp Chick-a-hominy

DEAREST ELLEN :

I again resume my sweet correspondence with you, after an interval it seems to me of an age : computed by what I have (may I not say we have) suffered. But during all my unexampled difficulties and trials, one constant source of consolation remained to me. It was your steady constancy. It is true, that for a time, I was laboring under a delusion in regard to it, but even during that time, you were as unwavering as before. No portion of blame can attach to you, that I was led astray. You, my Ellen, have been like my evening and morning star—the last ray of serene comfort at night, and the brightest dawn of hope in the morning. From day to day, and from year to year, have you clung to the memory of the youth to whom you plighted your young affections—through good and through evil report—through life and in death, (as was supposed) you have without wavering or turning aside, cherished the first bright morning dream of youthful love. Do you know, my Ellen, that the world scarcely believes in the reality of such early attachments enduring to the end. The heartless throng know not, my sweet playmate, of the little romantic world we possess within ourselves. They have all gone astray after strange gods, and cannot believe that others will be more true and devoted than they have been. Especially has the odium of all such failures been laid to the charge of your sex, but I am sure unjustly. The first slight or unkindness nearly always proceeds from the other, and this slight or unkindness cannot be blazoned to the world—it is hidden within the recesses of the sufferer's heart, and pride (perhaps proper maidenly pride) prevents it from ever being known. How happy are we my Ellen, that not a shadow of distrust has fallen out between us—if indeed I except your momentary confounding me with the gentleman whose name I had assumed, and my temporary mistake about my brother's marriage with you. You see I have brought myself to write that name. While I am upon the subject of Miss Elliot's engagement, permit me to explain one thing which I omitted in the hurry of departure, and the confusion which attended all its exciting scenes. That young lady though present at the masking scene at the Governor's house, and knowing of my design to present myself in disguise, among my old associates, was not made acquainted with the name or occupation which I would assume. The resolution to adopt that name was seized upon after the departure of that young lady and her father. Hence her supposition, on hearing that Mr. Hall had arrived in the Colony, that it was her own Henry. I am led to think of these things, by seeing, so frequently, this young gentleman, with whom I was, and am, on the most intimate terms. His distress of mind is truly pitiable—he appears like one physically alive and well, and yet dead to all hope. Not absolutely dead to all hope either, for you should have seen how the blessed, but dormant, faculty flashed up for a moment or two, when I told him, a little while ago, that there was a prospect of an expedition being sent ahead of the troops, in pursuit of the assassins and robbers who murdered our old friend and stole his mistress. Oh, if he could be sent off upon such an expedition, what a blessed relief the activity and excitement of the pursuit would be to him. But the Governor, though sympathizing fully with him and me, would not consent to it, and I must say his reasons were to me, satisfactory ; not so, however, with my poor friend ; he is dissatisfied with the Governor on account of it, and if it were not for my restraining and urgent counsel, he would start off, single handed, in pursuit. The fact is, his apprehensions for the fate of the poor girl, *whether dead or alive*, are so desponding, that the madness and rashness of such an adventure, only add new charms to it, in his eyes, and I can only seduce him from such wild designs by dwelling upon the known clemency of the Indians to other females, who have for months and years remained captives with them. I have exhausted all my recollections of the kind, and I have put the scout, Jarvis, in possession of his dreadful secret, and commanded him to detail all his knowledge favorable to my views. At this very moment he is walking with Joe, among the tall pines, his melancholy eye wandering among the stars, while Joe is telling a long story of a Mrs. Thompson, who was taken prisoner by them and carried beyond the mountains. I at first suspected my new forest friend, of romancing in the wildest vein, and inventing as he went along, for the justifiable purpose, as it seemed to me, of plucking the rooted sorrow from the heart of my friend, but I am satisfied now that it is a true narrative, because he recounted several circumstances about the route to the mountains, which he had before told me he had procured from an old lady, who had been a prisoner among the Indians. Seeing that he was, for the time, so absorbed with the story of the scout, I have stolen away, my Ellen, to hold this sweet converse with you. If you had but known the charming girl, about whom my friend thus mourns, you would neither be surprised nor jealous that even I feel an anxious interest in her fate. Think too of her sad history,—the loss of her uncle by whom she was adopted, and upon whom she doted as a father, little less fond than the real one whom she has now lost, also. Think, too, of the dreadful manner of their two deaths —of her nearest and dearest kinsmen. Then bring before your mind the highly educated, delicate and sensitive girl herself—torn from the reeking body of her deceased parent; and borne a captive among a rude and wild people, not one word of whose language she understands. Oh its a dreadful fate for one like her. She is a most lovely girl in every sense of the word, and as good as she is beautiful ! I feel a double interest in her fate, because her sad lot is so much like my own. We were first wrecked by the same disastrous political storm—thrown upon the same shores, and among the same people for a time.

The Governor, you know, is her distant kinsman, and of course he feels as lively an interest in the pursuit of her captors as it is possible under the circumstances, but he is a stern old soldier, and will not risk the success of his expedition for any mere private feelings, however near home they may come.

Poor Hall! we are of the same mess, and of course our tent is to be a melancholy place, for he walks about like a troubled spirit. Many a time at midnight, I will turn to you for companionship, for though distant in body we are ever present I trust in spirit.

Before I close this scrawl, scratched upon a camp stool, as I sit upon the ground, I cannot help recurring to the last letter which I wrote to you. It was penned under circumstances scarcely more favorable to my caligraphy than this, for I was then propped up in my bed and wrote upon my portfolio. Little did I imagine then, my Ellen, that that letter would ever be productive of some of the most delightful moments of my life. It is almost impossible for you to conceive of the delight with which I surreptitiously stole away the treasured memories stored up in your heart. You thought then, my Ellen, did you not, that they were garnered up, never to be again gazed upon by mortal man upon this earth?—but by the talisman of that real letter I produced a key —one, it is true, crusted over with the deepest sorrows known to the human heart. Nor did you even then have a sly suspicion that your long lost lover had risen from the dead to be the bearer of his own last dying words. No, no, my own Ellen, your affliction was too real to have suffered any suspicion of the bearer to intrude—it was not until I began to unfold those habits of thought which touched upon old times, those dearest treasures of the heart, those associations linked in inseparably with the very fibres of our being, that you began to suspect me, Do you remember the walk we had by the little romantic brook where we were talking of the falling of the leaves—and I ventured upon the dangerous experiment of reproducing some of *our old* talk. Methinks I see your stare of astonishment now, and your startling turn of the head every now and then, as link by link I touched those dear old associations; every word gushing and teeming with meanings only known to ourselves? I expected every moment to hear your startled scream, but if you penetrated my disguise, your prudence triumphed, and you suffered me to wear my masquerading dress until such time as my own circumstances should point out the time of unmasking. I know that you must have been frightfully mystified just at that time, and until all doubt vanished. I sympathized fully in your distress, but I would not make you an accessory, even after the fact, to my treason. Had I failed in my application to my sovereign, I might have proposed to you to desert your venerable and excellent father, and your own dear and delightful home, for other and strange lands, but I had not fully come to the resolve, and would not have done so, until that application failed. Even then I could scarcely have had the heart to tear you away from all the endearments which now cluster around you. Do you know my own Ellen, that I love your home—your flowers—your books—your music—your pictures— your chairs—every thing that is yours. This little Testament of our Lord and Master, with your name written in it, which lies before me, looks like no other book. The very letters seem to be illuminated—the book actually has an appearance about it belonging to no other, and that with which it is invested, is far more vividly impressed upon those household objects which daily surround you. Could I have torn you away from all these? My memory wanders, even now among your books, and music, and flowers, and birds, and everything that goes to make up that dear home, which you have so inseparably stamped with your own identity. How vividly the charming domestic picture rises up before my fancy! Indeed, it is scarcely ever absent from my thoughts, sleeping or waking.

Even over these wild scenes into which we are penetrating each hour, deeper and farther, these blessed visions throw a softened and mellowed light. What a blessed thing is memory, *to all the virtuous creatures of the earth!*—

that magic store-house of the heart's treasures. It is surely the divinest of faculties, it penetrates the farthest back, and will last longest of them all, for it will constitute the connecting link between this and a higher and purer state of existence. It is the most distinguishing characteristic of our race, and above every thing else marks us out as immortals. Oh, what true wisdom and beneficence in that provision which confines its wondrous powers to man. Did you ever reflect what an awful thing, this truly blessed thing to us, would have been to the lower orders of creation? It would have made the earth to them a Hell, teeming and multiplying with horrors. That it has been given to us alone, is at once a testimony and a guarantee of our immortality. Do you know that I doubt the capacity of any one for enduring attachments, who doubts the immortality of the soul? The mere hope and belief elevates us above common sensuality, and refines and purifies our nature. *All good men desire and believe it.* You may smile at my thus founding, what is ordinarily called an effort of the understanding in the heart; but those who have observed human nature most, will be most ready to believe it.

The pure sentiment of love, though blended with passion, is very near kin to *the divine*, especially that sublimated phase of it, which you exhibited for your dead lover. Your trials of the heart, my Ellen, have been truly great, and I feel humbled in the comparison with you. Though I cannot approach your excellence and exaltation of character, I hope to blend my future existence so inseparably with yours, that I may catch a portion of its exaltation.

I have often heard you say, that if required, you could lay down your life with me, and that you would far rather do it than survive me, either married or unmarried. This is a test of which I solemnly believe many of your sex capable, but alas for ours, there is not one in ten thousand capable of it.— You were suprised at my shrinking from the question, my love, because you had not understood, and could not, thoroughly understand the characteristic difference of the sex. You were loth to believe that your lover was so earthly as to desire the earth for its own sake, and when all that bright halo which sentiment throws around its dreary paths, was blotted out; but you reasoned from within and not from without, from your own experience and not from the world's. Oh when the world is all thus purified and sublimated, then will the lion lie down with the lamb. Your heart has been purified by a high faith and a bright hope. God's holy spirit has poured its benign influence on your heart—already, more than commonly elevated above its kind—and most truly did you say that your affection for me was blended with all your holiest and highest aspirations; no wonder then that you could die a martyr in a double sense. I will strive, my own Ellen, to make myself worthy of an attachment so pure, so far above the dross of this earth. It might be a wise question for moralists, how such an attachment could hold to one so confessedly impure as your correspondent; one so weighed down with the grosser passions of selfishness in its thousand phases, and ambition with its earthly means. But I do not desire to perplex your sensitive mind with the question. I am sufficiently happy that my youthful fancy was *fated* to select one so every way worthy of my maturest approbation.

I will write to you daily. You see I have already renewed our old subjects of conversation. I cannot now exist without communing in the spirit with you. I cannot ask you to answer my letters, but should a courier be despatched after the army, for any purpose, I am sure I shall hear from you.

Yours, most affectionately,
FRANK LEE.

CHAPTER XVIII.

ADVENTURES ON THE ROUTE.

AFTER a somewhat rainy and stormy night, the morning broke brightly and beautifully clear. The air was fresh and invigorating, and a long and sound sleep after the fatigues of the day's march, left the luxurious young cavaliers with elastic and buoyant spirits. The brilliant songsters of the feathered tribes were startled from their first essay by the reveille from the martial instruments. The leaves of the trees were glittering with rain drops, and the autumnal forest flowers bursting into life and beauty with the heat of the morning sun. All nature looked calm and bright and beautiful, and mere existence seemed a pleasure, but it was a pleasure inviting to repose and contemplation.

The officer of the guard had some half hour gone upon his rounds to march the pickets in, when all at once the repose of the scene was disturbed by the idlers and followers of the camp running in a particular direction, as if something unusual had occurred there during the night. Frank Lee, and Dandridge, and Hall, mounted their horses and galloped to the scene. The officer of the guard had halted his men and was just about to despatch a messenger to the Governor, when his aids were discovered approaching. When the three young cavaliers rode up, they discovered the sentry who had been stationed there during the last relief, sitting against a tree, and most cruelly tomahawked. Joe Jarvis was stooping over him, examining the wound most critically; he looked up when he saw the officers approaching and laying his finger upon the wound, said to Frank, "Did'nt I tell the Governor that the varmints were not far off, he's warm yit, its been done since the rain;" and away he started through the woods to examine the trail.

When the three returned to make their report to the old chief, they found him breakfasting upon some of Joe's venison steaks. He was startled by the daring atrocity of the act, but pronounced at once that the man must have slept upon his post. Jarvis was sent for, and soon made his appearance, scratching his red mop as he entered. He had the same cunning squint of the eye, and waggish leer as when before presented in the same presence.

"Well, Joe, I understand, you say that this thing was done since the rain; you have, doubtless, then, been able to fall upon the trail, and can tell us how many of them ventured into the camp, and what they came for."

"It is true enough, your honor, I did say so, and I stick to it, but as to the trail and all that, it would bother an older scout nor me. The critters are a growin' cunninger Sir, every day of their lives. There's not the print of so much as a man's hand round the premises, much less of a moccasined foot."

"You don't mean to insinuate, scout, that this man has been murdered by one of our own men?"

"Not I, Sir, no such thing, he was tomahawked from behind the tree by an Ingin."

"And yet there are no footsteps in the soft mud behind that tree, and leading to it? Why how have they contrived to obliterate them?"

"That's just it, you've struck the nail right on the head; how did they contrive it? I'll tell you how they did it. They borrowed the legs of other varmints."

"What! they did not approach on horseback."

"No, Sir, but they come whole-hog fashion. If your honor will jist condescend to ride down there, I will shew you that there is not the print of a living creter's foot 'scept an old sows, any where about."

The Governor and Lee followed Joe to the spot and there, sure enough, were the distinct prints of a hog's feet, on a straight line to the tree, leading from a small stream, on the banks of which, many of the horses and mules were yet tied.

"Now, sir," said Joe triumphantly, "did you ever see a dumb brute walk a straight line like that?"

"True enough, Joe, swine do not gather mast thus, but how in the name of Heaven did they manage it?"

"Nothing easier, sir; they jist take a hog's shanks into their hands, and makes crutches on 'em. You see 'em here, Sir, to the water's edge, and then they mounted and rode off. But, Sir, this was'nt all for nothin', it was'nt all unmeaning deviltry; there's a meaning in it. They're not College-larned for nothin', depend upon it."

The Governor did not like this thrust, and wheeled his horse and rode away, first leaving orders to have the man decently interred.

Joe sat about investigating the cause of the strange visit, and he first observed that the sentinel's arms had been stolen, next that a sumpter mule had been led through the water some distance up the stream, for he followed it upon his poney until he discovered the place where they had emerged. He then came back and had the Commissary summoned, and requested him to have the mules counted; and sure enough one of them was missing. Still Joe persevered—he said he was determined to find out what else they had stolen. At first, it could not be ascertained that any thing more was missing. The provisions were all safe, and the arms were out of their reach, or rather too near the grasp of those who were full ready and willing to use them. Joe continued to rummage among the wagons and mules, until at length he lit upon the ammunition, when it was found they had carried off several canisters. Joe went straightway to the Governor's marquee, and there meeting the Aids-de-camp, he related to them his discovery.

"Did you ever see sich cunning brutes? how in the name of old scratch they found out where the things lay, beats me all to flinders; but this convinces me, Squire, that what I told you before is true, that these varmints mean to keep us from the mountains if they kin. Howsomdever, they didn't know that Red Jarvis was to be of the party. The Interpreter is laughing in his sleeve now, to think how you're all bamboozled with them hog-tracks, and he thinks moreover, that the powder will never be missed—that you'll all be so taken up with the onaccountable death of yon poor fellow—and that ain't all, they mean to try it agin, or they would'ent a taken so much pains to cover up their deviltry."

"Well Joe," said Lee "what do you aim at by the pains which you are taking to ferret out their cunning."

"Why, you see Squire, they're not comin' back to-night, but to-morrow night they'll think we're sound enough asleep. I guess there'll be one wide enough awake for 'em. Do you jist give the Commissary his orders that I'm to sleep in that there ammunition wagon—that's all."

The troops were again in motion, and in an hour after their departure, all traces of the gloom and melancholy of the funeral had disappeared even from the mess of the buried soldier. Such is miliary life. The soldier seems to take pride in marching from his comrade's grave to a lively air and with buoyant step, and we suppose it will always be so, while men organize themselves to slay each other.

The route up to this time had been nearly in a straight line to the mountains, for the river along the banks of which they mainly marched, lay fortunately in that direction; but it became necessary now to diverge to the east, in order to take Germana in their way. It was fully a day's march, or more, out of their route, but such were the Governor's orders, and all obeyed with alacrity.

This day they began to exchange the monotonous pine barrens for forests more genial to the eye. The country, although nearly in a state of nature, was rich in all that pleases the eye, and enlivens the heart. For the first time, regular parties were detailed to precede the main body of the troops, and skirt their flanks on each side, for the purpose of hunting. One of them accompanied the scout immediately in front, and it was the Governor's orders that each, in succession, should be under the direction of the veteran woodsman. As Joe predicted, however, they had but poor luck, a single herd of deer was encountered, and they, after a hot pursuit, only lost two of their number. Jarvis told the Governor's aids, at night, that "them everlasting trumpets would have to be spiked, else they would all starve when the provisions gave out."

That night they encamped among the head waters of the Mattapony river, having left the beautiful banks of the Pamunky far in their rear, and accomplished, during the day, even a better journey than on the previous one. All were now in fine spirits, notwithstanding the fortune of the hunting parties, upon which in a short time, not only the fate of the enterprise, but their very lives were to depend. As yet, however, provisions were abundant, without even trenching upon the stores of jerked beef, and hard bread and parched corn laid up in their wagons, and on the backs of their mules. With the young, and the gay, and the thoughtless, sufficient for the day were the evils thereof.

The camp fires were enlivened with many a song and story, and to tell the truth, the sparkling wine cup was not wanting to enliven the festivities of the gay young cavaliers. The novelty of the scene around them had not yet worn off, and bright hope painted to their mental vision more enrapturing beauties and brighter landscapes beyond. The Governor failed not to encourage their glowing anticipations, from his own store of imaginary pictures. It is true, he had ceased to quote Chunoluskee as authority, but nevertheless he retailed many of *his* stories under new titles and editions. , In fact he believed them himself, and far more than had ever been told. He was a very imaginative man, but regulated by a sound judgment, and great military experience. He had, however, so long suffered his fancy to well upon the El Dorado beyond the mountains, that he had come to look upon those imaginary scenes almost as certainties, which were in fact very far from the truth. Not that he overrated the country, to which he was bound, but that he had erroneous conceptions of it, and still more erroneous views of the difficulties to be encountered to get to it. The poor scout, ignorant as he was, had a far truer conception of both, but the time had not yet come, to consult such counsels on any material point. Though Joe was required to blaze the route, the Governor was himself on foot, a greater part of the time, compass in hand, with young Dandridge by his side, taking notes of his observations. As they crossed the river they came to an Indian village, on an island, one of the loveliest spots in nature. The young gentry were in raptures with the beauty of the site. Not so with their old chief. He was pained to observe that the Indians even here had been induced to desert their homes and were retreating before the march of his little army. Every indication, thus far, tended to confirm the suspicion that his enterprise was looked upon with fear and distrust by the Indians. He knew, full well, from what source all this came, but how they had all been moved, by one accord in so incredibly short a time, confounded all his calculations. He could only settle the difficulty by supposing his late hostages and beneficiaries treacherous; far antecedent to the time of their desertion. He was loth to believe all this, for he was a true friend to the race and as genuine a philanthropist as ever lived. But here was one of the locations of his primary schools, and every inhabitant of the village was gone, with all their stores and plunder, and the schoolmaster was perhaps murdered. Of that, however, they had no evidence. He might have been carried off a prisoner, beyond the mountains.

Poor Hall! for hours he detained his friend Lee, wandering among the deserted wigwams, long after the sound of the trumpets and the tramp of the horses had ceased. He had looked forward with eagerness to their arrival at this spot, he had expected here to see some of that race in whose possession was all that he prized on this earth—he had expected to be re-assured of her safety, and had even hoped to procure a runner to send on after his lost Eugenia to assure her of his speedy approach. To him the deserted wigwams looked like her funeral pile. His heart sank within him as he beheld this new evidence of the old hostility still subsisting between the races. The fires of the ancient feud had only been smothered for a time. During the three years of Governor Spotswood's stewardship he had succeeded in making them believe that he was their true friend, because he had never committed any aggressions upon them, but now he was about to outstrip all his predecessors in the daring strides of his adventurous spirit. Hall would have lingered on among the tenantless wigwams of the deserted village, but his friend Lee almost forced him upon his horse.

That night. although encamped in a beautiful country, and general joy and hiliarity pervaded the camp, he sat in one corner of his tent, and leaned his head upon his hands in the most listless attitude imaginable. He took no notice of the entrance and departure of any one, and really performed the routine of his military duties in such a dead and alive manner, that Frank had to apply to the Governor to have him invalided. So deeply absorbed was he with his brooding sorrow that he scarcely noticed this change. Though cards and wine and songs and revelry resounded all around him, and made the old woods merry again with the dissipation and the wild mirth of the mad young cavaliers, it passed all unheeded by poor Hall.

The same night Frank Lee, Nat. Dandridge, Hall and Moore, being invited to the Governor's marquee, Jarvis asked permission of the former to write a letter in his tent, and to furnish him with the materials.

"What! can you write, Joe?" inquired Lee, with surprise.

"No, not much Squire, but I can turn the pot-hooks and hangers into some sort of signs that the man'll understand I'm goin' to write too.'

"And who may that be, pray?"

"An old croney o'mine, Squire, and as his readin' aint no better nor my writin' it'll be a dead match."

"The worse you write Joe, the better he should read."

"Oh, that's his business, so here goes "

Frank stood for a few moments on the eve of his departure, and laughed immoderately at the awful faces which Joe made, as he turned his pen in its travail. 'That's harder work than fighting Indians, Joe!"

"Aye, Squire, you may say that—I reckon I could make a round O on one of 'em in a leetle shorter time than I can fetch up one of these, but do you go Squire, you put me out a lookin' at me." Frank departed accordingly, dragging poor Hall with him, and leaving Joe already bathed in a profuse perspiration.

The Governor had kindly invited his young friends in hopes to cheer up the stranger whose unfortunate story he had hitherto been prevented from listening to with that attention which he desired, on account of his engrossing engagements. He felt a deep interest in this young man, partly because of his connexion with Frank's strange adventures, and the mystery which he had hitherto thrown around his name, and partly on account of his known engagement to his unfortunate young kinswoman. Indeed the interest felt on account of the latter, extended to many of the young gentry, who had heard Frank's description of the ill fated but charming girl. In that day such a captivity was not at all uncommon with the wives and daughters of the humbler farmers, and we have seen individuals of the gentler sex in ours, who had spent years in captivity among the aborigines; but seldom within the knowledge of the young men had one so beautiful, so highly connected and so gently nurtured, been carried off. Her misfortunes excited a profound interest among all such, and not a little added to their eager desire to come up with their enemies—for enemies they were now acknowledged to be even by the Governor.

But we will leave Hall to drag out his weary game of whist among his kindly disposed friends, while we take a glance at Joe's epistle to his friend.

Camp Nigger-foot.

'To BILLY BIVINS :

Well Bill, I'm dad shamed if I don't bust if I don't write to you a spell—the fact is Bill, I've kept company with these here gold laced gentry so long that I'm gettin' spiled—fact! I rubbed myself all over last night head and ears with salt for fear on't. Yes, and if you and Charley and Ikey don't take keer, I'll cut you when I come back. But without any joke at all about it, I've got into the greatest mess that ever the likes of you clapped eyes on. There's that Mr. Hall—the real genuine Mr. Hall, the one as come last ; O Lord if you could only see how he takes on—dash my flint, if I don't think he's a leetle teched in the upper story. All day long he rides that black horse—(and he's dressed in black you know) and looks as if he was a goin' to his grandmother's funeral. Poor lad, they say he's got cause enough, the yaller niggers have run away with his sweet heart, but you don't know nothin' about them sort of tender things, Bill, its only a throwin' of pearls before swine to tell you of 'em, else I would tell you that Mr. Hall and me is exactly in the same fix. Yes, you and Charley may laugh, confound you, if so be you ever spell this out. We're exactly in the same situation—the yaller niggers has run away with my sweet heart too. You know the little Ingin gal that asked me for that lock 'o hair, but you know al about it and what's the use of swettin' over agin. Well, Squire Lee, that Mr. Hall was tried for killin' the Governor's son; well, he says she's a ruined gal, and to hear him talk, you'd think that she was dead and buried and he a sayin' of the funeral service over her. I tell you Bill, these gentry are queerish folks, they don't know nothin' of human nature. He says he wants to know if I would take another man's cast off mistress. Now, Bill, ain't her lover dead, and could'nt I make an honest woman of her, by a marryin' of her, I'd like to know that. But the best part of the story is to come yit. The Governor's been axed about it, and he's all agreed, and says moreover, that he'll settle fifty pounds a year on me, if the gal will have me. So you see, Bill , she's a fortune. Did'nt I tell you that I was a goin to seek my fortune, and that you had better come along. But I've talked about myself long enough, now let me tell you something of our betters. The old Governor, I tell you what, he's a tip top old feller, in the field. He don't know nothing about fightin' Ingins yit, but I'll tell you, he'll catch it mighty quick ; he makes every one stand up to the rack, and as for running away from an enemy, it ain't in his dictionary. I am told he drinks gunpowder every mornin' in his bitters, and as for shootin,' he's tip top at that, too. He thinks nothin' of takin' off a wild turkeys' head with them there pistols of his'n. You may'nt believe the story about the gunpowder, but I got from old June, his shoe black, who sleeps behind his tent, and I reckon he ought to know, if any body does. He rides a hoss as if he rammed down the gunpowder with half a dozen ramrods. You ought to see him a ridin' a review of a mornin'. I swang if his cocked hat don't look like a pictur', and I'm told he's all riddled with bullets too, and that he sometimes picks the lead out of his teeth yit. He's a a whole team, Bill ; set that down in your books. The next man o the Governor is Mr. Frank, that I told you of a while ago ; he belongs to the gunpowder breed too he's got an eye like a eagle, and, Bill when they made a gintleman of him they spiled one of the best scouts in all these parts. If there's any fightin' you take my word for it, he'll have his share. Some of the men do say that he was for upsettin' the Queen when he was to England, and that's the reason he came over in disguise. One thing I know, he's got no *airs* about him ; he talks to me just as he does to the Governor, and this present writin', as the lawyers say, is writ on his camp stool and with his pen and paper. I guess he'll find his pen druv up to the stump. Well, I suppose you want to know what I call this camp nigger foot for. I'll tell you, for I christened it myself. I was a follow-in' of a fresh trail as hard as one of the Governor's hounds arter a buck—when what should we light upon, but the track of of a big nigger's foot in the mud here among em—fact! I told the Governor afore I seed the print of the nigger's foot that they had had some spy or another at Williamsburg, else they would'nt a know'd the waggons as had the powder in 'em. Oh, I forgot to tell you that the yaller raskels killed one of the sentinels, and stole a heap of powder and lead. Yes, and they had the wagon tops marked with red paint.

I hav'nt told the Governor about the mark yet, and I don't mean to, till I sleep there a night or so. You know, Bill, how I'll sleep there! I'll skin my eye open as tight as an old weasel in a hen roost. But Brag's a good dog you say, and Hold-fast's a better. Well, well, Bill, the proof of the puddin' is in chewin' of the bag; so let that stand over till next time. Howsomdever, you know I'm good enough for twice my weight of the yaller raskels any day, and call that no braggin' either. Oh, Bill, all I want now is one of you fellows here for company to make this one of the greatest turn outs thats happened in our time. This Trimountain expedition is agoin to be the makin of me. The Governor's offered a reward for the Interpreter— yes, a hundred pounds for him, dead or alive. Whew! my stars, I would'nt give that for all the Ingins this side of the mountains, nor tother, neither. That's neither here nor there, but I'm agoin to set a trap for the College bred rascal; but I won't bait him with one of Dr. Blair's sermons. Howsomdever, you'll hear of that all in good time. If you see old dad tell him I'm alive and a kickin,' and that I've got that red sculp of mine all sound yit, and with the help of God, mean to keep it. Oh! I like to forgot to tell you that we are agoin to take Germana in our way, which I told the Governor was clear out of the route; but it seems that's the place where the yonng lady, Miss Elliot, was carried off, and her father sculped. Now, I would like to know what's the use of goin to look at the hawk's nest when the old ones and young ones have all flew away. They may pick up some of the feathers of the innocent creters they've killed but, what's the use? I say. The Governor thinks, I expect, that as that's near the front of the frontiers—the jumpin' off place as I may say—that the Ingins may give him a little brush there. The fact is, the old gentleman's appetite for a fresh smell of gunpowder, is gittin' stronger and stronger every day. I'm deuced affraid he'll kill the Interpreter with his own hand if we come up with them. Kase he killed his son, you know. Whenever any one talks of that College bred raskel, the old soldier's eye flashes jist like my gun when she burns primin'. Did you ever see a wild cat's eye away down in a dark hole? Well, that's just the way he looks then; I suppose it all comes of that gunpowder he drinks afore breakfast. I would like to see him cuttin' and slashin' about a dozen Ingins when sich a fit is on him; if it was only to drive them Ingin schools and colleges out of his head. He wants to give his stomach a thump of that kind afore we comes plump into one of their ambus-cades. Take care of my dogs and remember me to Dad and Charley and Ikey.

Your's till death,   JOE JARVIS.

CHAPTER XIX.

ADVENTURES IN CAMP.

THE next day's trail varied but little from the preceding one, except that it was shorter, owing to the necessary fatigue of man and beast. At night the scout, having received permission from the Commissary, quietly took his berth in the wagon which had been before robbed, and which he stated had been marked. Truth to say, however, the said mark looked very much like a dozen other stains upon the cover, from the red clay which had soiled it by the splashing of the wheels. The scout, however, was an important character, and displayed so much more knowledge of the country and the habits of the Indians, than had been anticipated, that he was suffered to have his own way, in those things not pertaining to military discipline. The early part of the evening was spent by the Governor and his associates, very much as the previous ones had been, except that the latter began now to seek their rude pallets much earlier than at first. Nothing occurred to disturb the solemn tramp of the sentinels, and the more selemn cry of the whippoorwill, as they resounded through the silent forests at midnight. Scarcely a soul stirred in all that little city of canvass, except poor Hall, who walked about on the outskirts of the camp, like some disturbed spirit. The melancholy flickering of the camp fires, as they died away, and the solemn moaning of the tree-tops seemed more in unison with his depressed spirits, than the revelry of his companions. He had just taken a walk within the line of sentries, and was standing in front of his tent and gazing at the clear cold moon—its silvery tints falling over tree and shrub, and flower, when he was startled by a stealthy tread. He drew himself within the shadow of a large tree, which stood near, and watched and listened for a renewal of the sounds which had alarmed him. But a few moments had elapsed before he heard a sharp ringing sound like the springing of machinery, followed by a most hideous and unearthly screech, and the next moment Joe's merry laughter was ringing through the woods. He followed the sound toward the baggage wagons, and beheld, what he then supposed, to be an enormous dog, with his forefoot fastened in a wolf-trap and cutting the strangest antics on his hind legs, he had ever seen a quadruped perform. Joe had sprung upon the ground and was performing others very little less extravagant, and exclaiming "I told you I would trap the varmints, I told you I would trap the varmints!" By this time several of the nearest sentinels also came running in to see the cause of alarm. To these Joe consigned his prisoner, and darted off into the woods in the direction of the river, which was some fifty yards off.

The dog turned out to be a young Indian, enveloped in the skin of the animal, and he had passed the sentinel on all fours, doubtless, as they all averred that no biped had crossed their walks. Lee, with many others of the young officers had, by this time, gathered around, and the former ordered the young rascal to be released from his agonizing position, which he was increasing every moment, by his vain efforts to work himself loose. The wolf-trap was made of parallel steel bars, without teeth, but clasping together with great force. Nothing but the thick dog's hide had prevented it from crushing the bones of the prisoner's wrist. He was now standing on his legs, and before the bright pine torches at midnight, presented one of the strangest sights imaginable. His very writhings and tortures from the pain of the steel-trap, produced merriment among the soldiers, as he looked through his canine mask, and whisked his tail about. While the crowd gathered around the young Indian, each indulging his curiosity or his merriment according to the taste of the new comer, the report of Joe's gun was heard, but a short distance off, immediately followed by that startling sound to all civilized ears, the war-whoop.

The captive was quickly deserted by all except the two soldiers who had him immediately in charge. When the party arrived at the bank of the river they beheld, by the light of the moon, Joe in a truly perilous position. He was standing in a canoe in the middle of the stream, and defending himself most manfully against four stalwart warriors, and a negro, each scarcely inferior in size to the scout himself. He had what appeared to be a handspike in his hand, with which he was laying about him at a tremendous rate, while his foes each in a separate canoe, (with the exception of the negro who sculled for one of the party,) attempted to surround him at first, but when they discovered what a formidable giant they had to deal with at close quarters, they changed their method of attack and attempted to drown him. The anxious spectators on shore could render no assistance, for there was not a canoe or plank to float upon, along the shore. Frank Lee dashed down the banks with frantic speed in search of some such thing, but to no purpose. The savages had been careful enough to leave only one for the escape of the young rogue who had been caught in the steel-trap. By this time, Joe had reduced the numbers of his antagonists to the warrior in the canoe with the negro, but the others were in the water and would speedily swamp his canoe. He saw them approaching, and knew that his scouting days were ended if they once got *round* him, and he was powerless as to all direction of the frail thing in which he stood. At this stage of the desperate rencounter, young Hall threw off his outer garments and would have thrown himself into the stream, had he not been forcibly detained by Lee. At the same time Joe made a *coup de grace* worthy of a more veteran scout. At one bound he sprang into the enemies' canoe and lit right upon the negro sculling with a paddle in the stern. Down went Indian, scout and negro.; but in less time than we have taken to relate it, Joe rose to the surface, dragging the negro by the hair with one hand, while he struck for the shore with the other. Fortunately the negro came up with his back towards him, and whenever he made an effort to change his position, Joe submerged his nose until he completely cooled his courage. The Indians made an attempt to follow, but the scout in a few yards touched bottom, and then the crowd from the shore rushed in pell mell to his rescue. As soon as he was completely separated from his antagonists, the bullets began to whistle and skip over the water among the swimming heads, while the savages dived like ducks. They tried hard to save their canoes, but so hot became the shower of lead around them, that they were glad to escape with the broken crowns which the scout had given three of them.

"Why Cæsar," exclaimed Lee, " is it possible ?" " Why Cæsar," repeated many voices. He was but lately a servant near the person of Harry Lee. Every one from the capital knew him at once. Joe shook off the water from his mane like a lion, and then gave a snort to blow it from his pipes, which if it had been on the ocean might have been mistaken for a whale's.

The Governor was roused by the first report from the scout's gun, and by the time the party from the river returned, he was dressed and met them on the way. "Old times you see a coming back, Governor, with the Ingins—they, hav'nt all gone to Heaven yit."

" No Jarvis, and I am afraid you will not teach them the way there soon."

" I don't know that Governor, if you had seen some of the hard knocks I give some of their knowledge boxes jist now, you would 'a sworn I was in a fair way to send one or two on 'em to the happy huntin' ground."

At this moment the Governor cast a scrutinizing glance at the shrinking negro, whom the scout still continued to drag by the hair.

"Why Cæsar !" exclaimed he also; but in a moment after, a dark suspicion seemed to cross his mind, and he turned to one side and led Frank by the arm a few yards distant, and then they talked and gesticulated with great earnestness for a quarter of an hour, when they resumed their walk towards head quarters, Frank expostulating and the Governor insisting upon some measure which he had proposed.

" Well, well, Lee," said the latter at length, "I will send the rascal back to the capital in irons, and we can investigate the matter privately when we return."

" No privacy on my account your Excellency—tuck him up now, and learn the extent of the treachery at once; it may be important to the success of our expedition."

" Impossible—impossible, it requires a laborious and pains-taking investigation to get at the bottom of such affairs. As for the treachery, I think the scout has pretty well blown their present schemes of annoyance. One thing I want to know of him—here Jarvis! Was the interpreter in that cut-throat gang?"

"I'll tell you how it was your Excellency—when I tuck yon young varmint in the steel trap, (here he had to stop and indulge in one of his heartsome chuckles,) when I tuck the varmint in the trap," he was compelled to give way in a loud guffaw.

"Why, what is there so amusing in it, Jarvis?—it seems to me quite a serious business."

"You know Governor, the first day out, you snubbed me off short about callin' of 'em *varmints*, and said they had souls as much as we had. Well jist step here and look if this is'nt a varmint I've tuck in my wolf trap?" Saying which he walked up to the wagon where the guard held the young rogue a close prisoner, and taking him by the throat led him into the presence of the old chief. Governor Spotswood started back as the strange animal stood before him, apparently on its hind legs.

"Now," said Joe, "do you see this here wolf in sheep's clothin'—if that is'nt a varmint, I don't know what is?"

"Well," said the Governor, "I give it up for the present—go on with your account of this affair."

"Jist so—as I was a sayin', when I saw this here dog's hide, I know'd it in a minute, the yaller niggers ai'nt got no such dog among 'em, and thinkin' of the nigger track we saw on the trail last night, I jist popped out of the wagon, give this here *thing* to the guard, and made chase. When I came to the bank of the river, it was swelled monstrous with the rains, and not a thing in sight but a leetle bark canoe. In I jumped, determined to scout along the banks, and catch the nigger if I could. You see I thought it was that ere snow ball all the time, kase I know'd his dog, or the varmints would'nt a caught me nappin' as they did. Well, when I got into the canoe, there was nothin' to paddle with but a club which this son of a bitch left in it."

"Fie, fie, Jarvis, remember in whose presence you speak."

"I beg ten thousand pardons; but I thought if ever so mout be I could use the word at all, now's the time, seein' he's made a dog of himself! But that's neither here nor there. When I had got some twenty yards or more from shore, I hearn a sort of snake in the grass, and when I looks round, what should I see but four canoes stealin' out of the bushes from round a point of land, and cutting me completely off. I soon seed how the cat jumped; there was five on 'em to me one. So I ups with old Sally Wagoner (his gun,) and let fly at the biggest lookin' of 'em; they did'nt know I had her a layin' asleep in the bottom."

"Did you kill him?"

"I'm ashamed to say I did'nt, but I commenced a sculpin of him, which I'll finish some day, please God."

"Scalping him?—why how did you commence scalping him?"

"I sent a bullet, your Excellency, a scoutin' right along the top of his knowledge box, for I seed the blood a tricklin' down his face, arter the water had washed all the paint off."

"You have not yet answered one of my questions, Jarvis?"

"Oh, I ax your pardon, Sir; but I can't say whether the interpreter was one on 'em or not. The one I shot is exactly his size; but if so be it's him, he's changed all them ere red cloaks, and gold lace, and grand feathers, he used to wear down to Temple Farm. If it was him, I guess he smel't hell."

"Jarvis, Jarvis, this sort of disrespectful language will never do—for tho' not belonging to the regular command, your example breeds disrespect and insubordination among those who are;" saying which, he walked off in such an offended manner, that Joe was alarmed, and appealed in a whisper to Frank Lee, to know if he was really angry.

"It will all blow over, Joe, by morning, especially when he remembers the timely and excellent services which you have rendered to-night."

The Governor did not proceed far, before he stopped and called Nat. Dandridge to him, and told him to have the dog's hide taken from the young rogue, and to put handcuffs upon Cæsar, and have them carefully guarded till daylight

"Egad! I think Cæsar had an idea of imitating his great patronymic," said Carter to Moore, as they turned away to seek their tents again.

"Yes," replied Moore, "if we may take the poetical license of naming this stream the Rubicon."

"It's a far nobler one, I assure you, but poor Cæsar looks very little like the hero now."

The same dark suspicions crossed Moore's thoughts as he was thus forcibly reminded who Cæsar's master was, and of all the other suspicious circumstances of the case, and knowing Carter's friendship for Harry Lee, and not wishing to provoke a quarrel by giving utterance to them, he changed the subject, and they soon after separated for the night.

CHAPTER XX.

THE CAPTIVES.

CÆSAR, the captive negro, was, as we have before represented him, not only a family servant, brought up about the house, but he was a personal attendant upon the younger Lee. As soon as Frank heard the exclamations of surprise from those who knew the negro, he at once drew back in the crowd, and did not again present himself before him, until complete quiet was restored in the camp. Then he sought the solitary quarters of his father's old servant, and it may readily be imagined that it was a painful meeting on both sides. Frank had not seen Cæsar before, since he left College, and the first sight of such a living memento of by-gone years, would under any circumstances call up painful reflections, but when he thought of the old negro's equivocal position, and the suspicion which others entertained as well as himself, that he was not there of his own accord, he could have wept over the deep degradation and mortification of the African. Cæsar looked as if he could have fallen down at his young master's feet and wept too, and yet he did not dare to approach him. Frank, on his part, was in fully as painful a position towards the old servant—he felt for him, on account of the considerations before mentioned, but he could not accept the negro's atonement, through the inculpation of his only brother.

"I will tell you all—de whole trut, 'fore God, Mass Frank," exclaimed the poor penitent.

"Not a single word to me, Cæsar—I will not hear it. You are to be sent back to the capital to-morrow, and it will be time enough to make your disclosures when the Governor returns; but even then he will not listen to you, unless you have white testimony to corroborate your statements. You see, therefore, unless you produce that testimony, you are likely to suffer in your own person. Nay, do not answer me. I understand all you would say, and it is with the hope of saving you from punishment, that I have called to see you. I will endeavor so to explain the matter to the Governor, that he will make your punishment at all events light, if not remit it altogether; but it can only be brought about by your master and yourself leaving the country. I will write to him this night, or rather this morning, and point out to him his proper course. I did purpose, likewise, to ask you many questions about the old place, but I had not anticipated how painful the sight of you thus would be. I will, therefore, defer it to a more fitting opportunity. By that time, I trust you will be far from scenes that may bring back to your recollection this degradation. Little did I think when last I saw you, as one of the time honored servants of my father, ever to look upon you in chains as a criminal. I am as much mortified as if you had been one of my own kinsmen. Farewell, Cæsar!"

The old fellow stretched out his hand, amidst a plentiful shower of tears, and could only exclaim, between his agonizing sobs, " Oh ! Mass Frank, God bless you !"

Frank returned at once to write the promised letter, for it may be readily imagined that he felt little disposed to sleep. It was short, but to the point.

Camp Negro Foot.

To Henry Lee, Esq.:

The ink would blister the paper, could I be guilty of the hypocrisy of commencing a letter to you with an endearing epithet, after all that is past and gone. Indeed, it was my intention never to have addressed you again in any manner this side of the grave. I thought you had done your worst towards me and mine, and I was resolved, if I could not forgive, that I would at least bear it in silence. But I was mistaken, you had not done your worst, as this night's experience teaches me. I find that my heart yearns towards every thing connected with the happy days of our infancy. Over many of these you have power, and through these you can wound me grievously. I do not, and will not, charge you with suborning one of our father's faithful servants, to his own ruin and disgrace. I leave it entirely with you and your God.— But if even innocent, (which I trust in God you are,) yet you are responsible for their conduct. Nay, the world, even your old associates here, hold you now as the accessory before the fact, to this poor fellow's crime. Oh, Henry, how have your passions led you on, from step to step, to this degradation ! Can you be the proud boy that I once knew as an affectionate brother ? But I will not be weak ; my object in writing is merely a matter of business. I have a proposition to make to you—it is that you abandon your home and country forever. Start not, but listen to me. You know that you will be largely indebted to me for the yearly proceeds of my property, every cent of which you have drawn, and which I understand you will not be able to repay, without sacrificing your own property. Now, I propose to give you a clear quittance for the whole of it, if you will sail for Europe before my return, and take poor Cæsar with you. I know that you can find means to liberate him— indeed, I do not think the Governor himself will be much displeased to find this scheme carried into effect upon his return. Reflect well upon it, and may God forgive you for your past errors. I shall never cease to pray not only for that, but that I may myself learn to grant you that free and full forgiveness which I daily ask him for myself.

Your brother,　FRANK LEE.

While Lee thus communed with his father's once faithful servant, and afterwards with his brother in writing, the Governor held a very different dialogue with the other captive. In this emergency, the scout was found to be a real treasure ; for besides his woodman's craft, he could converse so as to be understood by the young rogue whom his own ingenuity had taken prisoner. Having ascertained this, the Governor ordered Joe and his captive into his marquee. We will not take the reader through the tedious process of the double questions and answers, but give Joe's version of the old chief's talk and the young savage's replies, at least so far as they are pertinent to our narrative. And thus he rendered his patron's exordium. " Do you know, you d———d young rascal, that the great Father of all the white folks between the herring pond and sun-down, is a goin' to stretch your wind-pipe ?" Here there was a pause—after which, the captive made one or two short guttural exclamations.

"What does he say, Jarvis?" exclaimed His Excellency impatiently.

"Why, Sir, he says he does not understand a word of your talk, nor what I mean in his own lingo by a stretchin' of his wind-pipe. I reckon he never seed the operation performed. As you've got to hang the *snow-ball* any how down yonder, would'nt it be as well jist to let me tuck him up before this young varmint? I guess he'd understand that, and then you could jist make what you please out of him."

"Pshaw, pshaw, Jarvis, don't make yourself out more brutal than you really are. You would be the first man to rescue even that poor negro from a watery grave."

"You may say that, your Excellency, seein' I pulled him out of the water no very long time ago; but to speak the truth and shame the devil, it was kase I hated to see the gallows cheated out of its due."

"Well, well, have your own way, but make this fellow understand that he has fairly forfeited his life."

"Look here, stranger, (in the Indian language,) you've got to pull hemp, a standin' on nothin'."

"Ugh!" a sort of note of interrogation from the captive.

"Oh! you don't know what hemp is, don't you? Well, it's a weed that grows plenty in this Colony, one of the wholesomest bitters as grows, but howsomdever it kills lots of people. What! you don't understand that neither. Well, may be you'll understand this."—(and he took a cord laying in one corner of the tent, and making a running noose, slipt it over the lad's head, and began to tighten it apace.) "You understand that, don't you? Oh, I thought so—well, the Governor wants to know if you are willing to save your neck by bein' of use to him?"

To this he replied in the affirmative. The Governor then asked him through Joe, if he had ever been over the mountains. He said he had often. When asked if he would pilot the expedition over—he said he would. This matter being arranged, he was next interrogated as to his agency in the massacre and burning of Germana. He stoutly denied that he had been there at all, but acknowledged that his father and brother had. He was next asked if he knew anything of the young lady (Eugenia Elliot) who had been abducted from that place. He said that he had not seen her, but he had heard that she had been taken over the mountains, with the people from the Indian villages, who had fled before the Governor's troops. After many other inquiries as to their treatment of female captives—their customs with regard to the marriage of such persons to native chiefs, the nature of the country beyond the mountains, &c., &c., he was remanded to the care of the guard on duty. These latter replies were of such a consolatory nature, that the Governor, as soon as the day had dawned, threw himself in the way of young Hall, to cheer him also with the news. He stated to him (upon the authority of his captive) that his people were in the habit of disposing of female captives to the nearest relations of those who had fallen in the battle where such captives were taken. But as no lives were lost in the sacking of Germana, he had understood that the young lady (pale faced squaw) was to be given to the young Chief for whom Wingina was originally intended, and that that very Chief had been Joe's formidable antagonist last night.

All this was truly heart-cheering to poor Hall, especially that part which assured him that the Chief for whom his Eugenia was intended, was still hovering upon their outskirts, and was likely to be, until the expedition was triumphantly completed, or abandoned in despair. He knew Gov. Spotswood's character too well, to believe for one moment that he would ever abandon the poor girl to her fate. There was one point that he interceded hard for, and that was that the Governor would permit him to take the captive as his own, set him free and go with him over the mountains, ahead of the troops. To this, of course, the Governor would not listen for a moment.

It was a gallant sight to behold that bright and joyous band of cavaliers, in their plumes and brilliant dresses and fluttering banners, not yet soiled by the dust and toil of travel, as they wound through the green vistas fresh from the hands of nature, and their prancing steeds still elastic and buoyant with high blood and breeding. It cheered the heart of the veteran warrior, their commander, to see the columns file off before him as he sat upon his horse and received their salutes. The expedition numbered in its ranks some of the most hopeful scions of the old aristocratic stock of Virginia, some, whose descendants were destined to make imperishable names in the future history of their country, and many whose descendants still figure honorably in the highest trusts of the republic.

The route to Germana was little varied by adventures or mishaps of any kind; but the country through which they passed was hourly becoming more bold and picturesque, and the scenery more grand and imposing. The land commenced to be what, in the language of the country, is called rolling. It was broken into long wavy or undulating lines, scarcely amounting to a hill, and yet relieving the eye, in a great measure, from the monotony of the dead level tide water country. The romantic and excited youths who surrounded the Governor, were already expressing themselves in raptures at the new views every moment bursting upon their vision. Many of them had never in their lives beheld any thing so lovely. At these raptures the old chief would smile, and sometimes encourage their enthusiasm, but always foretelling them of the Apalachian wonders which they would behold. Indeed, being a native of a bold and mountainous country himself, he longed as much as any of them to feast his eye on the top of a crag, from which he could behold a horizon with mountains piled upon mountains, one behind another, reaching, as it were, to meet the clouds.

Sometimes he would descant upon these mountain wonders, and tell of his own boyish adventures in his native land, until his moist eye told of his still clinging affections to that glorious land, rich in whatever delights the heart of the patriot, and richer above all, in a border minstrelsy and traditionary treasures, now consecrated to everlasting love and remembrance, with the name of him who has made them familiar as household words in every civilized family, from the rising to the setting sun. We thank God that we have lived in the days when those tales of witchery and romance were sent forth from Abbotsford, to cheer the desponding hearts of thousands, and tens of thousands. He not only threw a romantic charm around the scenes of his stories, but he has actually made the world we live in more lovely in our eyes. The visions which his magic wand created before our youthful eyes, rise up in every hill and vale in our own bright and favored land. Who is there that has not, ere now, found his imagination clothing some lass, as she burst upon his view from a mountain defile in full canter, with the imperishable vestments of *Die Vernon?*

Gov. Spotswood was by no means singular in his ardent attachment to his native hills. It has often been remarked how ardent is the attachment to home of every mountaineer, and as this homely feeling is the basis of all true patriotism, it is a feeling to be admired and cherished. Philosophers may wonder why it is that the natives of these cloud capped regions should be more devotedly attached to them, than the tide-landers are to their ocean-washed homes, and they may endeavor to fathom the why and the wherefore, with no more success than hitherto. We simply state the fact from personal experience. It has been our fate to exchange a home, combining the grandest and the loveliest extremes of nature—the green valley and the rugged mountain cliff—the serenest pictures of domestic comfort, in juxtaposition with the wildest ravines and most towering precipices—for one within the reach of old Neptune's everlasting roar—and our heart still yearns towards our native mountains.

Germana, was alas! in ruins. The mill, which benevolence, more than any hope of gain, had induced the Governor to have erected there, was a mere shell, its stone walls black and disfigured with smoke. The water wheel was still in perpetual revolution to a fruitless end, set in motion, no doubt, by the wanton wickedness of the savages. But these things, seen from a distance, were soon displaced by one of horror, which arrested their attention upon the halt of the army at the ruins of the old stockade. The dead bodies of their friends lay unburied and half consumed by wild beasts and birds of prey or partially blackened and disfigured by fire.

As Frank Lee walked away in melancholy reverie from this disgusting sight, his footsteps were followed by the scout, whom he heard muttering every now and then, " I'm glad of it! I am glad of it!"

Lee wheeled upon him, almost fiercely, and demanded what there was to rejoice him in such a sight?

" Oh! I beg your pardon, Squire, I'm not glad the poor fellers were sculped! by no manner o' means ; I only meant to say, I was glad the Governor had seen it.   Now, he'll know how we scouts come to hate the yaller niggers as we do.   This will cure him of all the love he ever had for the etarnal critters, and when we come to meet 'em face to face, if so be that ever is, why then he'll let us go at them with a will."

" Is that all, well here's my hand upon it, Jarvis—you are right—for it has produced exactly the effect on me, which you have predicted of our comman der."

" I know the critters, Squire, like a book, and a great deal better."

~~~~~~~~~~~~~~~~

CHAPTER XXI.

FORE-SHADOWING OF THE HORSE-SHOE.

Notwithstanding the horrors of the massacre at Germana, many of the remains of which stared our adventurers in the face, upon their arrival there the night was spent pretty much as the others had been, by the young gentry, viz. over their wine and cards. Carter and some of his friends were thus engaged during the evening, when Moore and Lee entered with the hope of dissipating the melancholy feelings engendered by the ghastly sights which still haunted them. As they entered, the former could not help but observe that he had been the subject of conversation, for an embarrassing silence ensued, some meaning smiles might have been detected, and one young gentleman unable well to control his risible faculties, burst into a loud laugh. Moore, being a frank and straight-forward fellow, told them that he saw that he had been the subject of their conversation, and begged to be informed of its cause. To this appeal Carter was compelled to respond, for the eyes of all his companions turned to him at once.

" Why, Moore," said he, " I was only telling my messmates of the bargain which you and I made in jest, about not prosecuting our suits with Kate until our return, and how handsomely I had stolen a march upon you, before our departure from the city."

" Oh!" said Moore, with a sly but bitter smile, " and so you violated the compact, and met with a rebuff for your pains ?"

" I plead guilty to the first charge, Moore, but I have not spoken as to the second count "

" Then, I suppose, we are to understand that you were successful, by the cheerful manner in which you relate it ?"

Carter made no reply, but plied his cards busily, and Moore continued,

"Silence is one sort of affirmation; am I so to understand you, Carter?"
Still no reply, but renewed attention to the game. He evidently designed only
to annoy Moore, and amuse his friends with him. But placed as the latter
was, (as the reader has already been informed,) he felt bound to rescue the
fair name of his lady-love from the imputation of double dealing. In that light
he knew her conduct would appear to Lee, to whom he had confidentially
communicated her gracious answer to his proposal. Accordingly, he renewed
the attack pertinaciously and with some warmth. "I insist, Carter, that you
give me an answer; now that you have carried the matter thus far, I demand
it as a right!"

"The devil you do!" said Carter, dropping his cards, "then I shall not give
any other answer than I have already given."

Moore rose to leave the tent in anger, but Lee begged him to stay a moment. "Gentlemen," said he, "remember your positions, and think well of
whom you are about to quarrel—no less than the daughter of our commander. If it comes to the light, which it will do if you prosecute it farther, it
must annoy the Governor excessively, and throw a damp over our whole
enterprise."

Carter was excited with wine, and had been losing heavily at the game,
and was not in the most placid humor imaginable. True, he had been con-
soling himself with a laugh at his adversary, but that, too, was now turned to
bitterness, and he sat sullen and without a word of reply to Lee's appeal.
Truth to say, he liked not the source from which it came. The other gentlemen present, however, seeing the force of Lee's view of the case, interfered
and argued the matter with both belligerents, until they prevailed upon them
to drop it, at all events until their return to the capital. This armistice having
been thus concluded, Lee and Moore continued their walk, and the latter remarked as they went, "did I not tell you that Carter would never resign his
pretensions without seeking a cause of quarrel? He betrayed me into a
hasty acknowledgment of my rights, purposely. It was a settled and premeditated design, and not accidental, as it seemed."

"But how could he know that we were coming to his tent?"

"Oh, that as well as the subject of discourse at the moment of our entrance,
was accidental, but the turn given after that to the conversation, was in furtherance of a preconceived design."

"Well, well, Moore, let us drop the subject now, as you have agreed to
adjourn the point for a long time; meanwhile he will grow sober, and I hope
less bellicose."

The sentinels were placed this night with unusual care, as the Governor
had a suspicion that the Indians would make a combined attack upon him here,
this having been for some time the centre of their operations. But the night
passed with unusual quiet, and though the scout and his band were out most
of the time, no fresh signs were discovered. Young Hall accompanied them,
in the hope of discovering some trace of his lost Eugenia. Jarvis assured
him that she was already beating hominy and carrying water for the old
squaw—the mother of her intended husband. Joe did not perceive that he was
every now and then thrusting a dagger into the heart of his new friend, by his
free and unbridled discourse, for the poor youth writhed in secret. The rude
scout was no sentimentalist, and had not the slightest conception of such sorrows as were weighing down his silent and moody companion. The reader
has seen how he bore his own troubles of the same sort, and he imagined that
there was a remarkable congeniality and fellow feeling between them, owing
to the similarity of their misfortunes. Every effort at consolation, however,
only made the matter worse, as will be perceived by the following portion of
their dialogue:

"How is it, Jarvis, when a young woman is thus set apart for the wife of a
chief? Is her will nothing, or is she forced to compliance?"

" Why, Squire, the will of a woman does'nt pass for much among 'em, but to tell you the truth and shame the devil, I believes they do sort o' ax their consent at first, for they carries corn and hominy, and skins, and other plunder, to the wigwam of the gal's father, and if she takes 'em, then he carries her off some night, by force."

" And have they no rites—no marriage ceremony ?"

" Oh, as to that, they may jump the broom stick, or the likes o' that, but cuss me if I think they're even so much christenated as that comes to. As to this gal of yourn, you see she's got no father among 'em to cozen with the skins and plunder, and as she's already in the wigwam of that he rascal that I knocked on the head tother night, what's the use of rites and ceremonies, as you call 'em ? When he gets to home, if ever he does—consarn him—he'll no doubt consider her as his'en already." Here a groan from his auditor averted the flow of his discourse for a moment, but he speedily resumed, " I'll tell you what you've got to do, Squire Hall, you've got to slit his wind-pipe."

" Oh, Scout, if I could only meet him in any sort of an encounter, however unequal, how gladly would I seize the opportunity ?"

" That's talking like a man, now ! jist throw away them blue devils and stick to that, and I'll bring you up with the rascals before we're clean over the mountains. There's no need for you to take on so, any how, kase we've to give them an etarnal thrashing afore they'll let us over the mountains, or they will sculp us, in which case, you know, you won't want the gal."

Leaving Germana, the course of the expedition was directed for several days in a diagonal line towards the direct route to the mountains. That time brought our adventurers into a region of country such as many of them had never seen before. The land was thickly strewn with rocks, and stones, and pebbles. These were a subject of curiosity and admiration at first, but soon turned to one of annoyance, as will be seen as we progress with our narrative.

Several spurs of mountains stretching in broken lines from the main chain of the Blue Ridge, already presented their formidable barriers before them, and being able to grasp an extended view from their base, they thought that they had already arrived at the long desired point of their journey. Eager were the emulous young cavaliers in their struggles to see who should first lead their followers to the top of these heights, but, alas! they were only destined to meet disappointment, for the same interminable view of broken and rolling country met the view beyond, bounded still by that dim blue outline in the back ground, and seeming rather to recede as they advanced. Hearty was the laughter of the Scout—in which even the Governor joined—as they stood upon the highest summit of the first of them, and surveyed with dismay the mountains piled upon mountains beyond.

Governor Spotswood now, for the first time, began to have clear conceptions of the vast region which lay before him—the difficulties of the undertaking, and the hardships which would have to be endured before he accomplished his design. Already the hunting department had been greatly enlarged, and as they progressed farther into the wilderness, game became more abundant. Several buffalo had been encountered and taken, after a severe chase and many hair breadth escapes. Still they encountered not their great adversaries—the combined savage forces, those who had sworn that they should never cross the mountains alive. But a new difficulty, wholly unanticipated, began now, for the first time, to present itself. The baggage wagons had been left at Germana, and of course the burdens of the sumpter mules and the supernumerary horses required to be doubled. These were nearly all lame already. The first day the lame animals were relieved by others taken from the soldiers, while the latter were required to walk. But the substitutes in their turn became lame. Small as the difficulty at first seemed, not many days elapsed ere the whole expedition was brought to a complete stand-still, and what added not a little to their discomfiture, their saddle horses began to share the same fate, insomuch that the stragglers, with their crippled animals, strewed the route for miles. The experienced judgment of the commander quickly perceived that this was exposing them to the hazard of a murderous attack from the Indians, and a general halt was ordered for several day's encampment, to recruit the cavalry. The encampment was pitched upon a beautiful plain, in that region of country now called Albermarle, one of the most charming spots in America. The mountains were distinctly in view, on more sides than one, but the dark blue boundaries of the horizon in the West, were apparently as far off as ever.

So badly were many of the horses lamed, that some of the stragglers did not arrive until after midnight, and even then some of them had not made their appearance. The Governor became alarmed, lest they might have been cut off by the ever watchful enemy, and he ordered the scout and twenty followers, with the soundest horses to return and bring them in, while large fires were kindled to show the position of the encampment. Lee and Moore determined to be of the party—partly to amuse themselves and partly on account of Moore's uneasiness about old June, who was among the missing. Indeed Kate had specially charged her lover to have an eye to the safety of the faithful old fellow.

They found the wearied soldiers, some tugging along leading their limping chargers, with loud and bitter curses, while others, less persevering, were sitting in despair by the way side, and the worn out animals were lying down to die, as it seemed.

For miles along their route, they encountered nothing but lame horses and worn out soldiers. Many of the latter having lost the blazed track, were shouting despairingly to their companions from remote distances in the forest. Some cried lustily for help, their horses having laid down in utter helplessness. The darkness of the night only served to render their accumulating disasters more annoying to the soldiers.

Lee, seeing how much this state of things could be remedied by keeping the soldiers together, ordered those in the lead to halt until their lost companions were found, and until those in the rear should come up. At the same time he directed pine torches to be kindled and held aloft as a guide to the poor stragglers. The whole scene resembled a defeated army during a retreat, and the feeble minded and the wavering were already sunk in gloomy despair at the prospect of such a termination of their enterprise. The distant mountains in view, only seemed to render their despair more hopeless, for they seemed rather to recede as the expedition advanced, and such glimpses as had been caught from the tops of the highest spurs which they had yet ascended, presented one continued pile of mountains behind mountains, seemingly interminable in their breadth. These things it must be confessed, were very disheartening to the timid, but not so to the old veteran, who commanded the expedition. All day he marched on foot in the front ranks, cheering those around him and carrying his instruments and his arms upon his person, while his noble war-horse, as yet but slightly lamed, was given to a sick soldier. The reader's particular acquaintances "of the order"—Lee, Dandrige, Moore, and Carter, followed the Governor's example, and cheered up the drooping spirits of the weary and despairing.

The former especially, now shone out in his true colours. He was every inch a soldier, and the Governor relied on him now, with unreserved confidence—twitting him the while, notwithstanding, concerning his vagaries at the capital.

Lee and his friends pursued their backward route for some miles and until the soldiers with their lame horses were becoming few and far between, and yet no tidings were heard of poor old June. He had not been seen since the noon meal, and the last straggler declared that he had not heard a single voice in his rear. Still they pursued their route, determined to persevere until day light, rather than give up the old banjo player. When they had passed the last horseman, some five or six miles, and were just coming to the conclusion that they would find him at the lunch ground, still some four miles off, Moore halted abruptly behind a projecting point of hill, descending to a creek which they were just about to ford, and laid his hand upon the bridle of Lee's horse. The latter drew his pistol upon the instant, and placed himself so as to be ready for action, but presently his ear caught a well known sound, which induced him to return his weapon to its holster, while he could scarcely suppress a laugh, so strange did old June's voice and banjo sound in the still and solitary forest. They moved as close as possible, so as to catch a glimpse of the old fellow and yet not to be seen. He was leaning against the saddle and portmanteau, his horse lying dead by his side, while he chaunted the following words to one of his most melancholy airs,

> Farewell old Beginny,
> I lebe you now may be f orebber,
> Im gwine to lebe de Chesapeake,
> I lebe you crab, you prawn, you oyster,—
>   Way down in Old Beginny.
>
> My fishing smak, my net and tackle,
> I lebe you by de riber side,
> I gwine to lebe de swamp and woods,
> Where de coon and possum sleep—
>   Way down in Old Beginny.
>
> All my friends I lebe behind me—
> Ben, Harry, Bill and old aunt Dinah,
> Maum, Mary and te Sarah child,
> And my young misses, I blige to lebe you —
>   Way down in Old Beginny.
>
> De rattle snake, de deer, de turkey,
> He got dis country all to eself—
> He high like steeple, and deep like well,
> No like de shore I lebe behind me—
>   Way down in Old Beginny
>
> A long farewell. my old Beginny,
> I gwine fight bloody Ingin now,
> He sculp old June, he broke he banjo,
> He no more sing to he young missus—
>   Way down in Old Beginny.
>
> The chimney corner' is all dark now,
> No banjo da to make him merry,
> A long farewell to my old missus—
> A long farewell to my old missus
>   Way down in Old Beginny.

" Why June," exclaimed Moore, " has every one deserted you ?"

" Oh, Mass Bernard, I glad to see you for true. I tought de Governor left old June for good and all."

" But your horse,—could you not get him along at all ?"

" Oh, Mass Bernard, he settle all he account in dis world—he dead as a makeral, and June glad ob it too."

" Glad ! why what are you glad for."

" Case he grunt so solemcoly, go right trough June's heart like a funeral sarmon."

Moore mounted the old fellow on behind his servant, proposing to leave the saddle, portmanteau, and even the banjo, until he could send back for them, but to the latter part of the proposition, June stoutly objected, and they were fair to take him, banjo and all, as it was getting to be late.

Before day dawned, all the stragglers with most of their horses were brought safely into camp without the Indians having discovered their helpless condition, if indeed they still watched the movements of the troops. Jarvis and those most conversant with their habits argued from this circumstance, that they no longer hovered upon the outskirts of the army.

CHAPTER XXII.

HORSE-SHOE ENCAMPMENT.

STRANGE that neither the Governor or any of his subordinates in command had yet discovered the true reason of the disastrous condition of their cavalry ; but they had so long dwelt along the sandy shores of the Chesapeake and the alluvial soil of the rivers, that they were not aware of the effects of the hard, stony ground upon their horses' feet. A general council of " the order," was summoned after breakfast to take into consideration the condition of the army and what it behooved them to do, under the circumstances. Various opinions were expressed. Some were for abandoning the horses altogether, and continuing their route on foot, and some were for remaining in their present encampment until their horses could be sufficiently recruited to prosecute the journey. To this latter opinion the Governor was inclined. Lee, who had been in consultation with his staunch friend and counsellor Jarvis, stated that the latter had predicted this very state of things in his hearing, and he attributed it entirely to the want of shoes upon their horses' feet, to protect them from the pebbles and small stones, which made them sore by the constant wear and friction of travel. Jarvis was summoned and required to explain the matter. Several of the lame horses were led up before the marquee, where they were assembled, and Joe, taking up one of the poor animal's feet, commenced quite an erudite lecture upon the complicated structure of that admirably contrived apparatus. True, the scout indulged in no high sounding technicalities, nor was he acquainted with the *art* of farriery, as laid down in books, but he understood the true philosophy of the subject, upon which he had undertaken to enlarge. By way of enforcing his views he brought his own pony which he had shod himself, and holding up his foot to the astonished young gentlemen pointed out to them how well he could stand the pressure of his knife handle rudely thrust against the frog, and from which all the other animals had shrunk with pain. It now became a subject of anxious deliberation, *what they were to do?* Any one could now see that little would be gained by rest alone, for no sooner would they have recommenced the journey, than the same difficulty would occur again with ten fold aggravation as the route yet to be traversed was of course more stony and precipitous. Besides they were every day approaching nearer and nearer to the country of the hostile Indians, where the Governor's peaceful tributary and missionary systems had scarcely penetrated.

The only alternatives left seemed either to abandon the expedition and go home, or to abandon their horses and pursue the route on foot. In their secret hearts many preferred the former and hoped it would be forced upon the old chief, whether he would or not, but no one dared to make such a proposition. He must, however, have discovered their secret leaning that way, for he told them that any one who was home-sick, or who felt disheartened by such obstacles as they had already encountered might return ; as for himself he intended to scale the mountain if he left his bones bleeching on the top. *All* responded to his hardy perseverance, whatever some of them may have felt, while the scout could scarcely refrain from raising his coon skin in triumph over those of his comrades, who had confidently predicted to him their speedy return.

What was to be done? That was the question ; and one which, small as it may appear at this distant day of graduated and McAdamized roads, was of vital interest to them. To shoe several hundred horses, without the proper artificers to do the work seemed such a chimera of the brain, that when the Governor proposed it, he was answered by a general shout of laughter, in which he joined as heartily as the youngest of them. Nevertheless, he said be would show them that it could be done, and that he would set the example himself. Accordingly, he ordered a shed to be immediately erected for a blacksmith shop—into which the scout was installed as chief artificer. Joe said that his father had once bound him apprentice to the trade of a blacksmith, but that he was always mending old gun locks and pistols on his own hook, for which his master licked him so often, that he ran away before his time was half out. He expressed his sorrow, that he could not foresee at the time, that he would have the Governor and all the young gentry, one day under him as apprentices, in which case he would have acted very differently. However, he went manfully to work, and really turned out horse-shoes, which would have been creditable to his old master.

During the first day, most of the youngsters stood around and watched Jarvis teaching the Governor of Virginia, the art of horse-shoeing. Frequently he required the assistance of the sledge hammer, which the old veteran would suffer no one to wield but himself, and most gallantly did the old hero of many battles bare his brawny arms to wield the ponderous instrument. More than once Joe had to let go his read hot iron, and fall back against his rude forge, and laugh out right. He said he had never expected to see the day when the Governor would be striker to him.

" My old master," continued he, " used to tell me that the devil would make me striker to him when he cotch'd me, but I reckon he missed the figure."

By the second day, the Governor could make a very passable horseshoe, and Jarvis nailed a set of his own making upon his old war-horse. When the job was completed, the Governor mounted him and cantered round the encampment, his whole face flushed with the double effects of his triumph and his work at the forge. The young men were no longer sceptical, but turned in, each one to shoe his own charger. Some were not gifted with mechanical tact and ingenuity, while others fully equalled the Governor in skill. The former were allowed to hire Jarvis, and such ingenious soldiers as he had pressed into his service, to do the work for them, by which operation the scout lined his pockets handsomely. He declared to Frank Lee that he had never possessed as much money in all his life, as he made in that one week—but we anticipate. A new difficulty now presented itself, for all the iron, which the foresight of the scout had provided, had given out, and great numbers of horses remained yet to be shod. In this emergency, some one luckily remembered the wagons left at Germana, and a detachment was immediately despatched with the horses already provided, to bring the tire from off the wheels, and such other pieces of the metal as they could gather from them.

This expedient furnished an abundant supply, and the army was rapidly recruiting its strength and spirits, while the horses were as fresh as the day they left the capital. Game was found in great abundance, and the tables of our adventurers smoked each day of their unwonted labors with haunches of venison, which their sovereign might have envied, and truth to say, they did not render tardy justice to the good things set before them. Celebrated as the Cavaliers of Virginia were for their love of good eating, the members of the Tramontane Order surpassed all the feats of their forefathers ; never were such trencher men seen ; venison steaks and buffalo humps disappeared with marvellous rapidity. Nor was the convivial glass wanting—a few bottles here and there had been preserved from their previous wassail, which were generously produced on these now joyful evenings. Songs and toasts once more enlivened the festive board.

On the last night but one of the horse shoe encampment, the Governor invited the whole of the order to sup with him, and as his stock of wines were known to be almost untouched, most cheerfully was the summons answered. Long tables—rude, it is true—were set out under a fine grove of oaks, from the branches of which were hung such lamps as could be found through the camp.

About eight o'clock the Governor gave the signal for the onslaught, taking the head of the table himself, and assigning the second post of honor to Frank Lee. On the right hand of the giver of the feast, sat the Rev. Hugh Jones, "Chaplain to the General Assembly of His Majesty's Colony in Virginia," as he styles himself in the work which he has left behind him, and in which he gives a short account of the "Tramontane Expedition," though the work was professedly written for other purposes.*

The old hero felt that he had achieved a greater triumph over surrounding obstacles, than when he led the charge at Blenheim, and he was consequently neither chary of his wine nor his wit. After the saddles of venison, wild turkeys, and pheasants, had all disappeared, the Governor led the way to the festivities of the evening by his standing toast, as in duty bound, now altered of course by the ascension of a male Sovereign to the throne. It was varied also by the services which he supposed himself to be rendering to his royal master. Every one rose up with him, as he filled his glass and gave, " *Our new Sovereign!* may the 'Tramontane Order' push the boundaries of his empire in America to the banks of the Mississippi."†

It was drunk with three times three. It must be recollected by our readers, however, that they supposed the Mississippi to be just beyond the mountains before them.

Strange enough, that both Columbus and Spotswood, the one the pioneer across the ocean, and the other across the mountains, should have both been led on to their grand achievements by a geographical illusion—the one, in search of the Indies, discovering America—and the other, in search of the Mississippi, discovering the fairest portion of what is now the United States. The discoveries of the latter may fairly claim that much, for he was in reality the great pioneer, who first led the chivalrous youths of the Old Dominion upon those tramontane pilgrimages, which have already been so gloriously commemorated upon the plains of San Jacinto, by one of the same peripatetic race, and which we confidently predict will never rest this side of the gates of Mexico. Never was there an individual so chiefly instrumental in the great onward movements, which have since so distinguished our country and our countrymen, and whose memory has been suffered to fall into such utter forgetfulness, as the far-sighted soldier and statesman, to whose name we have attempted to offer an humble tribute. How vast were the results of this expedition! While we write, the Congress of the United States is endeavoring to distribute those very lands to which his hardy enterprise and indomitable gallantry first led the way. We hear of Daniel Boon, and other hardy western pioneers of a later day, but the name of the real first conqueror and disoverer of that vast and almost boundless country is never mentioned, except by historians, and by them, in the most meagre and unsatisfactory manner.

It is well that the old chief could not foresee the ingratitude which awaited him even in his life-time, and doubly fortunate that he could not see that to which we have alluded, else the festivities of the evening might have been marred. As it was, every thing went on swimmingly, toast succeeded toast in rapid succession, and the conversation began now to grasp the objects of the enterprise, as something almost within their reach. The Governor told them that he intended to offer a brilliant prize to the gentleman who should first plant the British standard upon the summit of the great Apalachee. This was the first faint adumbration of the Golden Horse Shoe which we can discover. It was received with glowing enthusiasm, and every youth professed himself ready to die in the attempt. The old tactician knew well how to fire the ardor of the gallant youths under his command, and having brought their

---

* There is a copy of this rare work in the old Franklin Library, Phil., and another at Cambridge University, and perhaps others. A short account of the expedition may also be found in Oldmixon's British Empire in America—one copy of which is now in possession of the Georgia Historical Society.

† The Governor was too modest by half—he ought to have said to Mexico.

spirits and their emulation to that point which he desired, and for which the feast was given, he retired with his reverend friend, and left the youngsters to their unrestrained merriment.

After the veteran had withdrawn, his health was drunk with great enthusiasm, but it is doubtful whether the toast would have gone down so unanimously on the night of their arrival at the "horse-shoe encampment," so disheartened were many of the young cavaliers, and so fickle is popular opinion. A toast to the lasses they had left behind them, was received and drunk with much feeling. As the Chairman (Frank Lee) resumed his seat, he discovered the scout leaning against a tree near, with his bare and brawny arms folded, while they, as well as his face, were black with the smoke of his smithy, which he had just deserted for the sounds of merriment in his near neighborhood. Lee led him forward, and placed a flagon of undiluted spirits in his hand, which he would have quaffed without much preface, but that many youths gathered around him, and sang out for a toast. "A toast from the scout!—A toast from the scout!" was carried by acclamation. Joe scratched "his inheritance," as he called his red flock, and advanced one foot, but his ideas did not seem to flow so readily under the process, as the sparks from under his herculean hammer. At length, however, his eye was seen to sparkle, and his fingers to cease the cultivation of "his inheritance," at which demonstration the chairman thumped the table with his knife for silence and attention. "Gents," said Joe, "as you've drunk to the gals you have left behind you, here's to the gals we have got before us," slapping poor Hall upon the back, who was just sitting before him, leaning his head upon his hand. Hall could not resist such an appeal, especially when urged by all the company to join the scout in a bumper. Thus passed the evening, or rather the night, for they kept up the revelry until a late hour, and then separated in a good humor with themselves and all the world.

CHAPTER XXIII.

OLD FASHIONED LOVE LETTERS.

During the lengthened encampment of the horsemen, a courier arrived from the Capitol, bringing letters for the Governor, and for many of the young gentry who were with him. Numerous were the epistles of the anxious mothers and not less solicitous fathers, beseeching their sons to caution and prudence in the hazardous enterprise in which they were embarked; but with these we have no immediate business. We hope, however, that the following epistle may possess some interest for our readers:

Williamsburg, 1714.

To Francis Lee, Esq.

Dear Frank.—But a few days have elapsed since your departure, yet it seems an age. Short as the time is, however, I must write now in compliance with my promise, or lose all opportunity of writing, until the expedition is on its return. The courier who takes this, it is hoped, will overtake you near the foot of the mountains. First and foremost, then, I must be selfish enough to begin at home. Out of the fullness of the heart the mouth speaketh, and I suppose the pen writeth. You will, I am sure, be surprised to learn that my father seems to miss your society even more than I. After your departure, he would sit up for hours, wrapped up in his own thoughts. At first I did not heed this particularly, because he often does so, when any of his patients are sick unto death; but I soon found that my caresses—a successful remedy generally—were entirely unheeded; and once I saw a tear stealing down his dear and venerable face. I could submit tacitly no longer, but begged him to tell me what disturbed him. He said he was beginning to find out my value just as he was about to lose me. "Dear father," said I "I will never, never leave you. We have been too long all in all to each other!" Was I not right, Frank, in giving him this assurance, and will you not doubly assure him, when you come back? I know you will. "How can you make any such promise, my child," he asked, "when you have given your whole heart and soul to another?" Now, was not this a strange speech for the good old man to make? Do you not discover a little—just a little—jealousy in it? I thought I did, and I laughed at the idea, though the tears were coursing each other down his cheeks faster than ever; and I taxed him with the strange manifestation. "Well," said he, "have you not been wife, and daughter, and companion, and comforter, and nurse, and every thing to me—and how can I live, when all that gives life and cheerfulness to my house is gone? It will be putting out the light of mine eyes—for my Ellen, all is dark and dreary, when your shadow does not fall within the range of these fast failing orbs."

I again and again renewed the assurance that we would live with him. "Pooh, pooh," said he, "I have thought of all that. Frank has a large landed estate and negroes to look after, and when you are married, you will have corresponding duties as a wealthy planter's wife. How, then, can either of you remain here?" "Then," said I, "you can go and live with us in the country." "No, no," said he, "never, never will I leave this spot. There is a silent history in these walls, my Ellen, which you know not, for you were too young to know her whose sweet presence still lingers around every chair, and table, and wainscot, and wall, which you see." Little did he remember, Frank, that those very inanimate objects had so long been telling me a sweet tale of my own, but I disturbed not his hallowed memories. Oh, Frank, are there many such husbands in the world? Your sex is sadly belied, if there are. My poor father is a lover yet, though his head is silvered o'er with age and sorrow. Dear Frank, will you thus cherish the homely household remembrances which I may leave behind me? Yes, I have as full faith in you as I have in my own father, and I declare to you that I would not entrust my happiness with one in whom I had less. But we have not the hazards and uncertainties of other people, for we know each other's every thought and sentiment. My father went on in the same strain for a long time, until finally I succeeded in imbuing him with some of my own trust and confidence, that you would make any pecuniary sacrifice rather than separate us. An old man's life, or rather the enjoyments of that life, are made up, in a great measure, of the past—of these recollections of by-gone years—and one of the first duties of his children is to see that they are not rudely shocked. You know that I studied to have the arrangements even of the furniture, so that my excellent father should see no change from " old times," as he loves to call them. I have shocked him with no innovations or modern improvements in any thing that pertains to his own personal comfort. His cocked hat hangs upon the very peg in the hall on which he was accustomed to hang it in my mother's time, and I make it my business to take it down and brush it regularly every morning before he goes out. I knit his woollen stockings and gloves as exactly like the last made by my mother's hands as possible, and I have endeavored, in all things, to let him feel his loss as little as may be. Strange that he should, since your return, first begin to notice all these little things. It is the prospect of losing me, that has now brought them conspicuously before him, for I have studied to make them minister almost unconsciously to his comforts. There is another thing which I have observed since you went away. You know, that since his eye-sight began to fail, I have read the family prayers—at which, all the servants are present. The other night he rose from his knees, with his face suffused in tears, and told the servants to remain; it was Sunday night. I had before observed the same evidence of recent emotion. He said to the servants—"you had better lay these religious exercises to heart, for the time will soon come when you will hear no more from your young mistress. That old organ will soon be removed to a new home. True," said he, seeming to recollect himself, "many of you will go along; of course, you will prefer to accompany your young mistress." Is'nt he getting almost childish—I fear this bodes no good."

After he had said a good deal more of the same sort, I suffered them to depart, and then begged him to be assured that I would never permit the instrument to be removed, even if I should go away myself, and that I would not suffer one of the servants to leave him, except my own maid.

You see, dear Frank, that I make no apology for telling you of these things—gossip it may be—nevertheless, it is very near the heart. I think I know you too well to suppose that you will be indifferent to them before marriage, and far, far less afterwards. You will see, also, that I suffer no mawkish delicacy to prevent me from talking to you as unreservedly as I would to my father. Are you not shortly to be my husband? and ought that confidence to begin in an instant of time? Can it be?—does it ever so begin? Nay, does not life often end without establishing it, when the parties have begun by a false move in the first instance? I rejoice that I can repose this unreserved confidence in you, even thus early. To you I know my little domestic records will have the same interest as if you had thought and acted them yourself. Kate has just been here. You see I am making for you a sort of diary of my letter, and to tell the truth it has been written at several sittings. Well, as I just told you, Kate has been here, and has made confidents of you and me. The saucy baggage said she knew it was just the same thing as telling it to you. You must know that she has promised her hand, where her heart has long been given, to your friend Moore. Your friend will find Kate a more charming girl than even he imagines. I know him to be amiable and accomplished, as the polite world view these things, but I fear he lacks the highest finish to be the true gentleman. What can make us such *gentle*-men or *gentle*-women as that spirit within us which ever prompts us to love our neigbors as ourselves? This germ of the christian doctrine, if properly cultivated, will expand into an universal philanthropy. How different is this from your code of honor, which has one conscience for its followers, and another for the world! The conscience of a gentleman of honor substitutes what others think of us for that unerring monitor within our own bosoms. Indeed, the conventional conscience often silences the still, small voice of the inward man, and this, too, often in supposed deference to the opinions of *our* sex.

Now, I wish to set you and Mr. Moore both right on this point. *No lady whose opinion is worth having, ever sides with these laws of honor.* True, there are fashionable females, who *pretend* to applaud all the vaunting and vain glorious chivalry of the world, but even they, in their secret hearts, love to see men who dare to erect higher standards of excellence and morality. Kate and I, at least, have the unfashionable ambition to see our lovers repudiate the false standard which the world has established. All this prating has been brought upon your head, by some servants' news which has come to Kate's ears. Do not throw down my letter—she could not help it. Some of Mr. Carter's servants have told her maid, that their master would never suffer Mr. Moore to triumph over him in his love. Now, do not laugh at our woman's fears, but attend to what we say. For myself, I think it would be a very good test for Kate to submit her beau to—this ordeal of the true monitor against the false one. So many of the cavaliers emigrated to Virginia, during the old troubles at home, that they established here, in undisputed sway, this false and corrupt standard. I am very sure you would not follow it—would you, dear Frank? No one could be more gratified at any honorable distinction of another, than I would be at yours, but I could never *accept that hand in marriage*, which had been previously stained by the blood of a fellow-being—shed in single combat, and in cold blood. Heigh ho. I find I have commenced a lecture to your friend, or rather about your friend, and brought it all down at last upon your own head. Forgive me, dear Frank. You were brought up in the same school that I was—taught to pray, kneeling at the same family altar. Oh, may we long kneel at the same holy shrine! To return to our mutual friends—as I said before, there has been no unreserved confidence between them. He will write to Kate I know—indeed, I suppose his letters (with your own) are already on the way,—but you can very well imagine what a lover's first epistle will be, or what they generally are, always excepting yours, dear Frank. Now, could you not open his eyes?—above all, could you not guard him against falling an easy prey to Mr. Carter's designs, if any such he has? Do watch over him, Frank, as you would over a younger brother.

And now, dear Frank, I have little more to say, than how much I want to see you, and how I do hope that you will return, before there is any *greater* change in my dear father—(shall I say our father, Frank?) Farewell. Take care of Mr. Moore, Kate says, and of old June—and I say, above all, take care of yourself.   YOUR OWN ELLEN.

It would have been quite amusing to a disinterested spectator to have sat at the same camp-table, and watched Frank Lee and Bernard Moore reading their several epistles. There was *a* spectator in the tent, and disinterested enough in all conscience—Jarvis the scout. He was sitting upon a portmanteau in one corner, availing himself of the light, to fix an old gun lock, which had lost some of its proper functions. From time to time he ceased his filing and screwing, and turned his blackened and greasy face towards the young men, at first with an inquiring glance, as much as to say, "why do you read those letters over again, when you have already read every line?" But when they both, as if moved by one impulse, and wholly regardless of each other, turned them over and over again, and read and re-read them, he could hold in no longer, and burst out into a laugh. Both of them started as if roused from one of the sweetest dreams imaginable, and laying their hands upon the table, still holding the epistles, stared at Joe in turn. Their movements and the expression of their countenances were so exactly alike, that Joe went off again "half cocked," as he called it, in the rude apology which he attempted in his own justification.

"Well well," said Lee, " now that we are all attention, will you be so good as to enlighten us as to the cause of your merriment?"

" Why, Squire, you and Mr. Moore put me so plagidly in mind of the time when I used to go to school a gittin' my lessons over and over agin, that for the life of me I could'nt a help'd larfin. Then Mr. Moore, he worked his mouth and waved his hand so grand like, that he looked exactly like the player men down to Williamsburg. I guess you're a goin to have some play actin' here in camp some of these nights, aint you?—or is them real ginuine letters, sure enough?

" As true letters, Joe," replied Lee, after the young men had indulged in their laugh, both at their own ludicrous behavior and the impressions it made upon their rude friend ; " as true letters, Joe, as ever were written—at least I can vouch for mine, and I think for Moore's, with safety. But how comes it, Joe, that every one received letters by the courier but you? It strikes me you have a correspondent. Were you not writing to some one but recently?"

" O aye, and the Governor gin me a letter too, out of the letter bag, from the same feller I was a writing to—one William Bivins—we calls him Billy, for short." And Joe drew out of his shot pouch lying on the ground beside him, a blackened and disfigured letter, which already looked worn enough to take the heart of an antiquarian. But we will not detain the reader with Joe's correspondence, as it in no way related to the interests of the expedition, nor to the development of our story. In its stead, we will transcribe the other letter alluded to. It was from Kate, of course.

Williamsburg, 1714.

Dear Bernard :—

According to promise, you see I have begun to write you a letter—and one dozen have I commenced before, but tore them up, because I did not know exactly what word to prefix to your name. First I tried plain Bernard—that looked too cold and abrupt ; and then Mr. Moore—and that appeared too business like and formal ; and then I began without any prefix at all. At last, I went to Ellen in my distress, and she rated me roundly for being ashamed to salute with an endearing epithet a man to whom I had promised my hand, and given my heart. Nor was that all—she took me to task for still wrapping myself up in that reserve which the world compels us to wear, instead of endeavoring, as is *my duty*, (you know I call her Mrs. Duty,) to establish an unreserved confidence between us, and to learn and *betray* at the same time all those peculiarities of thought and feeling which go to make up our identity. As I told her, that is the very thing which I dread.

I am not so pure and holy in my thoughts, that I may, like her, lay them open to the gaze even of a *conditionally accepted lover*. Nevertheless, she has frightened me so, with the dread of future matrimonial unhappiness, that I have resolved to make a clean breast of it, or at least to make the effort. And so to begin fairly, I asked my demure friend to tell me honestly and candidly, what she thought was my besetting sin ? And what do you think she said ? Why, " love of admiration !" Just think of that. Now, is it so, Bernard ? Can you, in your heart, accuse me of that heartless thing, coquetry, except just a little harmless flirting, with which the sages of our country allow us to arm ourselves. Is it any thing more, Bernard ? But stop—I must answer that myself, on my conscience ; and though I almost quarrelled with Ellen at her own house about it, I had scarcely seated myself in the carriage, on my return home, before the silent monitor likewise began to accuse me. I cried bitterly about it, and then sat myself down to make a true and honest confession. You must be aware though, Bernard, that the position of the Governor's eldest daughter is a little different from that of other young ladies, even among the gentry. Alas ! poor me ! what am I saying ? Attempting a defence of the very thing which I promised to amend ! No, no, the daughter of His Majesty's representative is more bound, than any other young lady, to present a model even more blameless than common, inasmuch as her example is looked up to and followed by those, who are beneath her in rank and position. Ellen says, that even the tradesmen's daughters are already imitating my dress and manners, carricatured though they may be. Then I do confess, (as I suppose I must,) that I have rather been pleased with the insidious flattery, but I do assure you that it was unconsciously—that I never knew it, until I was induced to make a rigid self-examination. To know it, is to amend it, for, since I have analyzed the passion, I am heartily disgusted at its grossness. I am disgusted at myself, that I ever sought promiscuous admiration. The player-women on the stage seek the same thing, and have a better excuse for it, for it is to them a means of subsistence. Oh! Bernard, the bare contemplation of what it leads to, if once it obtains the mastery, fills me with the most profound self-abasement. I am sure, at least I hope, you will find me a very different girl on your return.

There, now, if that is not as pretty a confession of a coquet, as could be desired by "Mrs. Duty" herself? · But tell me, dear Bernard, are you willing to marry a coquette. Do answer your anxious and too repentant   KATE.

It is not consistent with our allotted limits to ransack the mail bag any further at this time, though we may again present such of the correspondence of the parties on the other side as relates to their adventures, or the progress of the great enterprise. Preparations were now busily making to break up the celebrated encampment of the "horse-shoe." Nearly the whole cavalry had recovered their feet, and an abundance of jerked venison, and dried buffalo and tongues, &c., had been also provided, so that they were prepared to set out with renewed strength and spirits. The murmurs of the discontented had now nearly ceased, and the young soldiers began to relish the rude, but exciting life of the camp. The old chief at their head was in his glory. He had gained in health, and strength, and spirits, with every day's journey, though he had performed as great a share of it on foot as the meanest soldier in his ranks.

The scout, too, was in his true element, and besides, was now in high favor with His Excellency, to the success of whose grand enterprise he was found so indispensable an auxiliary. Many times a day the Governor would exclaim, what a god-send it was that he had exchanged his promised guide for the one he had picked up at the eleventh hour. He now saw that the wary Indian had purposely deceived him from the beginning, and especially with regard to the face of the country. He was now, too, fully persuaded that the young chiefs recently in College, had been preparing to dispute his passage across the mountains, exactly as he advanced in his preparations to effect that object. Already more than one had been seen and encountered, who had never been at the College, a positive proof that far more were concerned than the pupils. Then the desertion of the village, and the retreat of its inhabitants before him towards the mountains, all showed that they either intended to abandon the country wholly before the march of his troops, or else to dispute the mountain passes with him, hand to hand. He knew too well to suppose the former for a moment, and their constant annoyance of his outskirts was proof enough, if any additional had been wanting, that they entertained no such design.

Little information as to the movements of his people was gained from the captive, though each night he had been brought to the Governor's marquee to be interrogated, and though Jarvis repeated more than once the hempen admonition before administered. It is very questionable whether Joe's feelings of philanthropy and benevolence were not such, that he would willingly have extended that admonition, had the Governor permitted it. He assured the old chief that the young rascal would tell every thing, if he would only permit him (Jarvis) to hang him a little—just a little; but the Governor had seen too much of the scout's tender mercies towards the race, to trust the captive in his hands.

* * * * *

CHAPTER XXIV.

FIRE IN THE MOUNTAINS.

At length the army was again in motion—the horses having recovered the use of their legs, and the riders their spirits. They were now passing thro' a country wholly new, even to the scout, and one of surpassing magnificence and beauty. The forest crowned hills, and the bright sparkling streams tumbling over their rocky beds, succeeded each other with astonishing rapidity, exhibiting some of the finest landscapes in nature.

The general course of the expedition was along the banks of these water courses—supposed to have their rise near or beyond the mountains—but their devious windings were not pursued—so that they often crossed the same stream some twenty times a day, in pursuance of the more direct compass line of the old chief.

Towards night of the first day's march after leaving the "horse-shoe," some twenty miles, the great range of mountains began to appear distinctly in view, so that it was confidently predicted that another day's journey would bring them up to the base.

How gloriously the blue mountains loomed up in the distance to the astonished and delighted gaze of the young Cavaliers, who supposed themselves just ready to grasp the magnificent prize for which they had so long toiled! But as the next day's march drew towards its close, they were very much surprised to find the mountains still apparently as far off, as though they pursued an *ignis fatuus*—so delusive were the distances to eyes accustomed so long to view objects on a dead level. These daily disappointments and vexations at length, however, began to revive the Governor's youthful experience and recollection of such things. Still that experience was not exactly in point, because here, the towering heights were clothed in dense forests, over which the changing seasons were now throwing the gorgeous drapery of their autumnal hues, so that he was nearly as much at fault as his juniors.

In enthusiastic admiration of the matchless succession of panoramas which hourly greeted his sight, he was not a whit behind any of them. Often would he halt his suite, as they preceded the main body over some high hill, and all, with one voice, would burst out in admiration at the new scenes presented, sometimes stretching far away into green secluded valleys, and then towering up from their very borders into the most majestic and precipitous heights. As they advanced nearer and nearer to the mountains, these characteristics gradually thickened upon them, until now the army was often closed up entirely between surrounding hills, and at other times the front ranks of the imposing array would be ascending one hill, while the rear guard was descending another. Often, too, were the echoes of the mountains awakened by the martial music of the trumpets and bugles, notwithstanding the oft repeated remonstrances of the scout. Any one who has not heard a bugle among the mountains, can form but a faint idea of the charming effect, produced by the reverberation resounding from hill to valley, and from valley to hill. For the greater part of the journey, it was more like a triumphal procession, than an army marching to new conquests through an unknown country.

On one of the last nights spent on the eastern side of the mountains, after the usual bustle of pitching tents and building fires had somewhat subsided, when soldiers and officers were lying about in lazy attitudes, seeking that repose made so necessary by the fatigue of a long day's march, powerfully induced, likewise, by one of those delightful Virginia autumnal twilights—Lee and Moore were resting themselves on the grass and exchanging congratulations upon their prosperous journey, thus far, and the fine prospects of the morrow, when they observed the scout, instead of seeking that repose in which so many of his superiors were indulging, bustling about at a great rate. Our two adventurers soon discovered that something more than common was in hand, and they called the scout to them and inquired what new scheme against the "varmints" he was now plotting?

"Oh, Gents," replied Joe, "its another sort of cattle I'm arter now—rare sport a comin' Gents, but its a secret."

"No, no, Jarvis," replied Lee, as they both rose from their recumbent position, "no secrets from us, that is against our compact."

"Well then," said Joe, "we are to have a grand fight to night."

"What! to night?" exclaimed both with one accord, springing to their feet, "where, and with whom?"

"Ha! ha! ha!" not so fast, not so fast, its not with the yaller niggers."

They both turned away disappointed, and as they walked off, Joe called after them. "It's a grand cock fight, Gents."

Both turned again almost as eagerly as before, and enquired of the scout how, in the name of all the wonders, the game cocks had been brought so far from home. Joe told them that the servants of some of the young gentry had brought them by their master's orders, and as they found it impossible to carry them farther, they were determined to have one fight out of them, before they were abandoned to their fate. "To tell you the truth" continued the scout, "I thought the critters would 'a been made into cock broth afore now along with that dog 'o mine, Squire Lee," and he indulged again in a sort of inward chuckle, at the idea of eating the tough fowls, and dining from his dog's carcass, to which he still persisted in saying, they were to come, before they reached their journey's end. As the walked toward the hastily arranged cock pit, he went on to tell them what the Governor had said, when he (Jarvis) had made the prediction to him, that they would at last have to return for want of forage and provisions. "The Governor said, says he to me, do you see those military boots, scout?" "Yes Sir," says I. "Well," says he, "when I have supped upon them, and dined upon my saddle, then we may talk about going back without crossing the mountains. That's the sort of commander for me, there is no back out in his breed, depend upon it. They do say among the messes of the old life guard that he's eat his boots afore now, and June swears he had a bull frog cooked the other night, and that he eat him up. Now I reckon that's the next thing to eating tanned leather."

By this time they arrived at the place already designated, by many torches and a crowd gathered round a rope fastened to stakes driven in a circle of considerable extent, on the borders of the encampment. A couple of cocks, belonging to some of the soldiers, were already engaged by way of prelude, while they waited the arrival of the young gentry. They fought without gaffs;—nevertheless it was a bloody encounter, and one of them was soon gasping in the death struggle.*

When the rest of the young gentry had arrived and the cocks were pitted, how eagerly were the bets offered and taken!—how excited became every eye! The rope was bent almost to the ground, with the eager pressing forward of the excited men. The exclamations flew round "ten to one on the red and white"—"done!"—"an even bet on the brindle,"—"hurra! that was a home thrust!" &c., &c.

Now it so happened, that the tents of the encampment were pitched just under one of those spurs of the mountains, which they were daily encountering and which had more than once deceived them with the idea that they had at last arrived at the foot of the real Apalachee. Whether this was the real Blue Ridge, (for the Blue Ridge and the Alleganies were then all confounded together,) they had not yet ascertained, but an incident now occurred which induced them to believe, that they had at last arrived at the base of the true mountains. While so many were crowded round the cock pits absorbed in the national amusement, an astounding crash was heard, like a avalanche coming down the mountains. Some huge object seemed to be coming directly toward them, bending and crashing the trees, and tracking its course in parks of fire. Some thought a volcanic irruption had occurred—while

---

*We trust that our countrymen of this day will not find fault with us for giving a true picture of the amusements of our ancestors. The cock fight was then almost a national game.

others supposed it to be an avalanche; but in far less time, than we have taken to record it, a huge fragment of rock, weighing several tons, and carrying before it a shower of lesser bodies of the same sort came leaping and bounding toward the very spot where the cock pit was located. Fortunately a large tree stood directly between the crowd and the track of the fragment, or hundreds would have been instantly killed. As it was, several were badly hurt by the bursting of the rock and the scattering of its fragments. Jarvis shouted at once, that it was the Indians, and in a few moments his sagacity was verified, for the whole side of the mountain seemed suddenly belted with a ribbon of fire. Appalling as the salutation had been, the young cavaliers stood lost in admiration at the grand and novel sight, which now saluted their wondering eyes, until roused from their dangerous trance, by the loud and commanding voice of Lee, who was already on horse-back, and calling his comrades to arm, by the command of the Governor. When he had drawn them sufficiently away from their dangerous propinquity to the base of the mountains, and while they were speedily mounting, a thought occurred to him, which was productive of the happiest results. He had ordered the camp fires extinguished, but suddenly countermanded the order and directed them to be furnished with fresh fuel, while he galloped off, to communicate his scheme to the Governor.

He found the veteran already in the saddle, and eager for the contest, which he supposed about to ensue. His first order was to remove the tents and horses away from the base of the mountain, and out of reach of the new sort of artillery with which they were threatened. This was executed with alacrity and promptitude—the opposite side of the plain or valley furnishing an equally commodious site for the encampment and sure protection against the enemy. The next was to extinguish the fires, as before ordered at first, by Frank Lee, but here the latter interposed, and suggested to the Governor to have them burning, and to avoid all signs of the kind at the new camp ground. Scarcely were the tents and horses removed, before the wisdom of this course was made manifest—for the thundering missiles were again heard crashing down the mountain.

Frank also suggested, that a body of volunteers should be sent round the spur or projection from the main body of the mountain, and thus out-flank the enemy, while they were engaged in loosing and hurling down the huge fragments of rock. He expressed his belief that such a force, might ascend on foot, before daylight, and either get above them, or hold them in check, while the main body ascended more leisurely with the baggage.

The Governor listened with attention to his scheme and proposed that they should ascend the eminence behind them on the other side of the valley and reconnoitre, and suggested that then they could form a more accurate idea of the position of the enemy and the feasibility of the plan. Accordingly he took his aids-de-camp and those in whose sagacity he had confidence, and ascended the eminence. By the time they had attained the desired elevation, however, the whole scene on the opposite mountain had changed its appearance. The wind, which had been sometime blowing a moderate breeze from the north-west, suddenly chopped round to the north-east and blew almost a gale, sweeping the belt or cordon of fire with which the savages had surrounded themselves on three sides, into magnificent eddies, and curling and sweeping over the mountains with a rapidity inconceivable to those who have never witnessed such a scene. For some moments, the Governor and his party were lost in admiration at the grandeur of the spectacle, and the army, the threatened battle, and every thing else, but the sight before them, were forgotten for the moment. The towering objects around, threw fantastic and collossal shadows over the sides of the mountain, and sometimes the entranced officers imagined that they could see spires, and domes, and huge edifices, encircled with the flames, when suddenly these fairy creations of the furious element would vanish and leave nothing behind but a cluster of pine trees, with the curling flames encircling their now livid trunks, and occasionally pouring in one continuous sheet from their centres, presenting again an almost exact resemblance to the stock of some huge furnace, burned white hot with the ungovernable fury of its own fires. Sometimes too, they imagined they saw a fearful array of grim warriors marshalled behind the long line of fire, but as the fury of the latter would become exhausted for lack of new combustibles in the course of the wind, or by the interposition of a ledge of rock, the warriors would dwindle into the trunks of black jacks, and mountain laurels and other products of the soil. The leaves were hung with magnificent festoons of crimson and purple, constantly changing its hues like the dying dolphin, as the fire burnt out over one track, and pursued its resistless career to another.

Every one saw now, that they had indeed arrived at the veritable Blue Ridge, for the fire that had commenced in the spur beneath which the army had encamped, had by this time, swept around its base, and entered upon the wider field of the main mountain, revealing what the Governor had been so fearful of not being able to find, the gap of the mountains. This was a depression made by nature, as if on purpose to afford a passage for man. The buffalo first make their path along the winding track of these, and the Indians with true savage sagacity, are sure to follow in their foot-steps. While one party on the hill were expressing their delight at this discovery, the scout was heard, ascending just beneath them on foot, singing in loud and joyous tones, the old song beginning:

"Run boys, run boys, fire in the mountains," &c., &c.

*   *   *   *   *

When Jarvis had attained to the same level, the Governor suffered him to run his eye over the scene, before he addressed him. The sagacious woodsman saw into the whole geography of the scene before him at a single survey, and no sooner had he done so than he seized his old coon skin cap, and tossed it into the air with boyish delight, exclaiming with the action, "we've caught 'em in there own trap! we've caught 'em in their own trap!"

The Governor rode round to his side, and asked him if he thought it possible to convey the horses and baggage over the gap!"

"Sartin, sure, your honor," replied Joe without the least hesitation, "haven't they gone over before us, and is'nt there a buffalo path all the way over, beginning at the hollow!"—(a ravine which separated the spur from the main mountain,) and with his finger he traced out, along the sides of the mountain, the probable course of the winding path. He was then told of Lee's scheme of ascending with a picket company on the other side of the spur, and getting behind the savages.

" The very thing itself," said Joe, "the very *idee*, I was going to propose to you, and I'll tell you what it is, Governor, as fine a scout was spiled when Squire Frank was made a gentlemen of, as ever wore a moccasin."

At this regret of Joe's, all the young cavaliers laughed.

It was evident enough to the veteran leader, that here the savages had concentrated their whole force to make one last and desperate effort against the encroachment of the whites. They were evidently determined to dispute the passage of the mountains.

CHAPTER XXV.

THE ENROLLMENT

WHEN the Governor and his suite had descended once more into the valley, then about ten o'clock at night, all the young gentry and the officers of the Rangers were summoned to the Governor's presence. It was a solemn conclave in the open forest, without any other lights than those afforded by the starry firmament above, and the fantastic reflections from the fires in the mountains, which latter seemed sometimes to hang almost over them. Every now and then, as they gravely deliberated upon the subjects before mentioned, they were startled by the ponderous fragments of stone, leaping and plunging against some old time-honored king of the forest, which would stagger and quiver for a moment, and then plunge into the dark chaos beneath, sending up a shower of sparks and fragments of burning branches and living coals, until the whole scene beneath was as light as day for an instant, and then covered with a pitchy darkness from the contrast.

The characteristic exclamations of Joe at these occasional interruptions, as he sat smoking upon an old dead tree near by, would almost upset the more youthful of the counsellors. Such as "Oh the yaller rascals—old *Saatan* never had better journeymen nor them, and the intarpreter he's boss."

"Oh, if Dr. Blair could only 'a seed this here night's work, he'd never preach another sarmint to the varmints—no, never—never." Then he would break out into his old song again, "Run boys, run boys, fire in the mountains, &c., &c., &c. Meanwhile the deliberations proceeded. The Governor laid the case before his youthful counsellors, pointing out to them, with his sword, the probable route the Indians had taken—where they would be likely to make a stand—and the difficulties to be encountered. He then unfolded to them Lee's scheme, and told them that he approved of it highly, after having maturely examined its feasibility. At the same time he did not disguise its difficulties, telling them that it would have to be undertaken on foot, until they joined the main force. He placed Lee's claims to the command, on the ground of his being the author of the plan. With most of them this appeared reasonable enough, but there were others who were manifestly reluctant to march under his orders, and others, perhaps, who preferred the easier route along the beaten path. The old veteran assured them, that in his opinion they would have fighting to their heart's content on either route. The difficulty was soon settled, however, suffering the new scheme to be a voluntary thing with them. Such as chose to be of the expedition were invited to step to one side, while those who preferred to remain under his immediate command, filed to the other. Lee's party happening to place themselves near the old log where Joe was entertaining Nat Dandridge with his songs and stories, the scout immediately stood upon the log, intimating thereby that he, too, intended to accompany the more desperate adventure.

The new expedition was to start within the hour; consequently, all of them were soon in motion, filling their knapsacks with provisions, and replenishing their stock of ammunition. Moore gave Lee one hearty grasp of the hand, ere he entered the Governor's tent for his last instructions.

"Farewell, Lee," said he, "you, it seems, are going to make an attempt to outflank the enemy, we will meet you, my fine fellow, more than half way."

By the time that Lee had received his commander's parting orders, the whole of the adventurous band was drawn up immediately in front of the latter's quarters. The old veteran stepped out, bare headed, and told them that he knew perfectly well that they required no incentive to daring deeds from him; that his object in having a few parting words was to charge them on the contrary to caution and prudence in dealing with the wily enemy "Remember," continued he, "that you are all young, and comparatively inexperienced, and that young blood is proverbially hot. I feel deeply my responsibility to your parents and friends, now more especially when I am about to trust you to your own guidance for a short time. Do nothing to shake the confidence which I have placed in you, or to bring our expedition into discredit. Twenty-four hours will decide whether we are to become laughing stocks to the whole Colony, or whether we are to earn glorious names, which shall live long after these mountains are traversed with the king's high way. I have only to add that I have the highest confidence, in the cool courage and judgment of your commander; remember that there is no such thing as success in any military enterprise, without discipline, and consequently without one recognized source of command. I am the more particular in enforcing this, because each of you is a gentleman born, and perhaps capable of taking the lead in his own person. I have designated to your leader his successors in their order, should he unfortunately fall, or be disabled. May the God of battles watch over you."

After this each of the young adventurers were permitted to stop in rotation and shake the old veteran by the hand. Following close in their wake came Joe, who doffed his coon skin and even took his pipe out of his mouth. The Governor, unreservedly held out his hand to him too, which Jarvis seized eagerly, and wrung with the gripe of a vice, and would have passed on then, but the Governor called out, " Hark ye, Scout, remember these lads are now greatly dependant for their success on the manner in which you pilot them!"

" Aye, aye, your honor, I'll lead 'em right on the tip-top of yon yaller camp, depend upon it; they shall have their bellies full of fightin' for once in their lives, or you may call Joe Jarvis a liar at sight."

" I shall draw no such drafts on you, Scout. I depend upon you fully."

Only picked men, of course, were taken by each of the young gentlemen who had volunteered, because if each had taken his fifty men, the party would have been entirely too unwieldy—besides weakening too much the main body upon whom, in any event, much the heaviest part of the fighting would in all probability fall. They numbered something less than a hundred and fifty, all told. The foremost of these were already ascending, by a winding path, the spur beneath which the main army were encamped, and in an opposite direction, as it seemed, to that route in which the Governor contemplated marching at daylight. Simply, one party purposed marching up the ravine on one side of the mountain, and the other party were to encircle it until they should meet the first, near the head of the gap. To one accustomed to the mountains, in our day, this would seem no very difficult undertaking, but it must be remembered that this sort of travelling was wholly new to every one, except the scout, and even he had never been tried upon such a gigantic scale. Any one who has ascended a mountain for the first time, through a trackless forest, may form some idea of the excessive toil and fatigue which our luxurious youths endured that night. Often and often did Lee and his inseparable companion, the scout, seat themselves upon some flat rock, or piece of table land, and wait for their wearied and straggling companions. For more than half a mile beneath, they could distinguish the sounds of the rolling stones, as they were precipitated beneath the tread of their followers, and every now and then the shrill whistle of some straggler, who had wandered from the main body. This last device was one of Jarvis's suggesting, in order to exclude the possibility of alarming the savage camp on the other face of the mountain, or, perchance of arresting the attention of some straggling party of hunters, who might be out on that side, for the purpose of supplying the camp. The latter danger was the scout's whole dread, and therefore he pushed so far ahead of the main body. His gun he kept constantly ready for use, not for game, for every one had been charged not to fire upon any sort of animal short of a two legged one, as Joe expressed it, and even the noise of this he deprecated, if the flight of such an one could be arrested by any other means.

When they had ascended about half way up the mountain, (on the opposite side from the encampment,*) about the first hour after midnight, the scout (who was now some hundred or two yards ahead even of Lee,) suddenly

---

* Often when we speak of the different sides, we mean only the several faces presented by the huge angles of the spurs.

pounced upon a fire between two projecting rocks, and before the bright red coals of which some fine venison steaks were even then broiling, suspended upon sharpened sticks, after the Indian fashion. The fine buck, from whose loins the meat had been taken, was also found neatly suspended on a stick in the crotch of a small tree. The scout was very much alarmed at these indubitable signs of the near neighborhood of an Indian hunting party, not that he feared anything such a party could do of themselves—but he feared that the whole plan of the attack would be blown by the hunter's running in and sounding the alarm, and thus bring down the whole force of the savages upon their small party. Joe's dog immediately commenced running about and whining, and snuffing the ground in the most unusual manner, until at length he struck a trail and followed it to the foot of a large and thickly leaved black jack. There he commenced barking furiously until the scout was compelled to choke him off, and even then he would return to the charge. Jarvis took up his station at this tree, and here also Lee followed him with many others, when they arrived at the same level. The young commander now despatched his fleetest men up the sides of the mountain, to intercept any of the hunters who might have escaped.

"As for this varmint," said Joe, "I guess he's treed as snug as any coon."

And yet no one could see him except the scout, and Lee even doubted whether the scout and his dog had not both been mistaken. Joe rose up from the stone on which he had seated himself, with his gun cocked and ready to fire in case the savage should make a spring, and poking the end of it among the leaves pulling them to one side, "There Capting, don't you see his red breeches now?"

"Yes," said Lee, "I see what you mean, but they are no breeches, Joe."

"Well, the old coon's there any how, and if his breeches aint long, his leggins makes up for 'em. We've got the longest end of ours fastened to our waistbands, and he's got his'n fastened to his moccasins. I reckon if he could get out of this tree, he would run leggins and breeches and all off, to let the yaller niggers on tother side of the mountains know we're a commin."

The scout now addressed him in one of the aboriginal languages and ordered him down, but he either would not or could not understand, more probably, the latter. "You don't understand that, hey? Well, here's talk I reckon's as good Shawnese as 'tis English," and with that he unslung an axe from his back and commenced cutting down the tree. He had not made a dozen strokes, however, before the savage commenced sliding down like a bear. "Ho! ho! ho! ha! ha! ha!" screeched Joe, "there's no mistakin' that ere kind of talk. Oh, Squire, if we had nothin' else to do, what fun we mout a had a smokin' of this feller down." The scout, after he was down, again attempted to make him understand, but he received nothing but guttural answers unintelligible to him. The parties which had been sent up the mountain now returned without any tidings of others of the hunting party, if such there had been, and the scout was of opinion, after a careful examination of the sticks of meat, the foot marks, or the trail, as Joe expressed it more technically, that he was alone. He was, therefore, speedily bound, with his hands behind him, and marched immediately in front. Too much time had already been lost with this unexpected interruption. However the scout was now in fine spirits, as he supposed they had encountered the only difficulty of that sort which they were likely to meet. They were drawing towards the summit of the first half of the gap. We say first half, for they discovered, even before the dawn of day, that there was an intervening piece of table land, between the spur and the mountain, and upon this the savages had encamped. The fires could occasionally be seen by our company, as they wound round the mountain. It was, therefore, necessary for Lee and his party to make a detour still farther round this table land, in order to be above the Indians, as agreed upon with the old chief. This was accomplished with as much secrecy and celerity as possible. Joe took the precaution, however, of gagging his prisoner, while they were circumventing the hostile encampment. A single war-whoop, or the accidental discharge of a gun, would have been instant destruction. The whole of the little band of adventurers now trod as lightly as veteran scouts, for each one could see for himself the hazard. For more than an hour they were winding round the hostile encampment, and every moment dreading some momentary surprise. Jarvis even tied a withe round his faithful dog's throat and held it in his hand, so that by a single twist he could throttle him and stop his wind. He said he had two dogs in his charge and both on 'em gagged, but that the four legged one was much the more to be depended on of the two. Several times he raised the glittering blade of his huge knife, and made a sign of drawing it across the Indian's windpipe, and pointing at the same time to his mouth, as much as to say that if he so much as screeched through the gag, he would stop his war whoop forever. It was a truly trying and perilous undertaking to conduct so many men almost entirely round and above an Indian encampment, and within rifle shot, sometimes, and not rouse those ever watchful sons of the forest. They could see the smouldering fire beneath them, now that they were ascending the main mountain, and occasionally the parties engaged in hurling stones upon the white encampment beneath. It was fortunate for our party that the Indians were so engaged, else they might not have passed so easily. By the dawn of day the whole party was snugly stowed away behind projecting rocks, trees, and undergrowth, so that not a glimpse of them could be obtained by any eye in the savage encampment. Indeed the Indians seemed wholly engrossed with the movements of the Governor's party below, which Lee judged to be already in motion, from the great stir among their enemies. The latter were, all hands, engaged with renewed energy hurling fragments down the mountain. This, Lee and the scout, could distinctly see from their well chosen retreat. The latter had placed a sentinel over the captive and the dog, while his services were in requisition by his youthful commander.

As soon as Lee discovered the exact position of the enemy's encampment he had despatched a trusty messenger to the Governor, informing him of every important particular.

By the time this messenger reached the foot of the mountain, the Governor's party was already under way, threading their tedious and winding path, far remote from the buffalo track across which the savages were hurling their missiles ; but the old veteran very soon perceived that it would be entirely impracticable to convey his horses and sumpter mules by this route, in time to co-operate with his aid. By the time, therefore, that Lee's messenger overtook him, he had already called a halt, and was detailing a small party to return with the horses, mules and baggage, back to their late encampment. He was delighted to hear of the admirable manner in which his youthful adjunct had thus far conducted his secret and dangerous adventure, and not less so to hear of the exact position of the enemy. This last information enabled him to lay down his own route definitely. He determined to abandon the path entirely, and to strike higher up the mountain, still winding round it, so as to avoid the point, where the savages were hurling their new and formidable artillery. We shall leave them to plod their way up the sides of the mountain, and in the next chapter relate the result of the adventure.

CHAPTER XXVI.

THE BATTLE.

ABOUT two hours after meridian, the Governor let fly the signal agreed upon with his reserve, which was nothing less than a volley of musketry upon the astounded enemy, who were still engaged in hurling stones and firing the mountains along the supposed route of those who so unexpectedly presented themselves upon their flank, and, rather above them. The Governor's fire was answered by a sound, which made the hair of many a gallant youth stand erect—it was the war-whoop from fifteen hundred savage throats at once—a thing once heard, never to be forgotten while memory lasts. The Governor himself, veteran as he was, dropped his compass, and seized his arms. The very trees of the forest seemed to have become moved by the unearthly discord. The enemy, though completely taken by surprise and disconcerted for the moment, were not long inactive. As if moved by one common impulse, each warrior seized his arms and took to a tree or log, so that, in a few moments, they seemed to have disappeared as if by magic, and except for the 'stealthy fire, which they now commenced, the field might have been supposed entirely abandoned. If any labored under this delusion, they were ere long undeceived. Never had Gen. Spotswood been placed in such a position before. He and his little army seemed stationed upon the mountain side, only as targets for his unseen enemy. He was just beginning to wonder what had become of his adjunct, when the reserve came 'swooping down behind the enemy like an avalanche—Lee and Jarvis seeming to vie with each other in their eagerness to spring first to the deadly encounter. At the same instant, the Governor's party advanced to the charge, so as to assail the enemy at the very moment he was dislodged by the party in the rear.

Such was the impetuosity of the charge, however, on both sides of the field, that whites and Indians were very soon indiscriminately mingled in one general melee, fighting hand to hand, in many instances—while in others, one of each party fired from behind neighboring trees. Jarvis had early in the engagement thus ensconced himself, and was loading and firing with the greatest coolness and deliberation, picking off here and there the most conspicuous of their leaders. He had been for some time thus engaged, when, as if by a sudden impulse, he rushed from behind his hiding place, and closed in deadly encounter with a warrior, his swarthy visage, naturally frightful, rendered still more hideous, by the ghastly effect of the paint with which it was besmeared. The encounter between them was long doubtful, but, as is generally the case in such struggles, the scout was triumphant. He was not content with a mere nominal victory ; for he tied his prisoner, and immediately regained his arms and commenced firing from the very tree, behind which his late antagonist had hid himself. The slaughter of the savages was dreadful, for more than half of them were only armed with bows, and arrows, and the tomahawk. Nor would they have maintained their ground as long as they did, but for the precipitate manner in which the two parties of whites rushed to the encounter—thus giving their enemies a chance to use their deadly knives and tomahawks. As soon as the Governor became certain that victory perched upon his standard, he issued orders to his troops to deal in mercy with the enemy.

While the main body of both parties were thus engaged, in a hand to hand conflict for the most part, on the very ground of the late Indian encampment, other portions of the field presented different aspects of the battle. Lee and a large part of his force had swept down the mountain side with such impetuousity, that they were borne far past the table land, on which the general battle raged—carrying with them an equal number of the enemy. These were engaged in a straggling sort of warfare far down the defile, so that the whole side of the mountain presented one great battle-field—stretching, in some instances, for half a mile from the encampment. Long after that portion of the enemy with which the Governor and his command were engaged, was entirely vanquished or captured, straggling shots were heard down the mountain, as if parties still pursued the retreating enemy. In vain the

Governor ordered his bugles to call in the scattered troops. Many of them lay bleeding and helpless on their rocky beds. As Lee and his party returned from the pursuit, most of his men were ordered by him to the assistance of the wounded—in many instances, four or five being required to carry one man up the steep acclivity. When that young officer returned to the presence of his commander, he fell prostrate, with exhaustion and loss of blood. The Governor ordered his outer garments to be stripped off, and proceeded in person to examine his wounds. Luckily they were not found to be mortal. The old veteran dressed them and bound them up with his own hands, and had him carried to his tent. Here a new difficulty presented itself. No surgeon had been provided for the expedition, and many of the troops were wounded with poisoned arrows, and were suffering great pain. In this emergency, it was remembered that a student of Dr. Evylin, who had made considerable progress in his studies, belonged to the expedition. He was speedily required to doff his military gear, and resume his instruments. Never had the poor fellow seen such a day of surgery; for the old chief required the wounded Indians, as well as his own wounded, to be ministered to.

These behests of mercy all attended to, the Governor assembled the young gentry and the officers of rangers around him, to witness the interesting ceremony of planting the British standard upon the highest peak of the Blue Ridge, in the name of his sovereign. They still, however, called it under the general term of Apalachee, under the mistaken impression with which they set out, that there was but one chain of mountains.

After a toilsome struggle from the table land before described, and upon which the battle had been fought, they at length found themselves on the real summit of the long sought eminence, and the Governor planted the British standard upon the highest rock, with due form, and in the name of his royal master.

It was a bleak and barren spot, made up wholly of huge fragments of rock, piled up one upon the other, as if in some far remote age, they had been cast there by a violent convulsion of nature. It was fortunate, however, that it was thus barren of vegetation in one respect—for it gave them an uninterrupted view of what has since been called the VALLEY OF VIRGINIA! What a panorama there burst upon the enraptured vision of the assembled young chivalry of Virginia! Never did the eye of mortal man rest upon a more magnificent scene! The vale beneath looked like a great sea of vegetation in the moon-light, rising and falling in undulating and picturesque lines, as far as the eye could reach towards the north-east and south-west; but their vision was interrupted on the opposite side by the Alleghanies. For hours the old veteran chief stood on the identical spot which he first occupied, drinking in rapture from the vision which he beheld. Few words were spoken by any one, after the first exclamations of surprise and enthusiasm were over. The scene was too overpowering—the grand solitudes, the sublime stillness, gave rise to profound emotions which found no utterance. Nearly every one wandered off and seated himself upon some towering crag, and then held communion with the silent spirit of the place. There lay the valley of Virginia, that garden spot of the earth, in its first freshness and purity, as it came from the hands of its Maker. Not a white man had ever trod that virgin soil, from the beginning of the world. What a solemn and sublime temple of nature was there—and who could look upon it, as it spread far out to the east and west, until it was lost in the dim and hazy horizon, and not feel deeply impressed with the majesty of its Author.

Governor Spotswood carried his thoughts into the future, and imagined the fine country which he beheld, peopled and glowing under the hands of the husbandman, and all his bright anticipations were more than realized.

At length he turned to Moore, who sat near him not less entranced, and said, " They call me a visionary, but what imagination ever conjured up a vision like that ? Oh ! 'tis a magnificent panorama ; but tell me do you not see smoke curling up there among the trees like a blue thread ?"

The young officer rose instantly, and gazed into the leafy world below, and after a long and searching inspection, confirmed the Governor's suspicion.

" It is doubtless the camp of the Indian women and children, waiting for their warriors, whom they suppose still engaged with us on the east side of the mountain.   It is a happy discovery—haste Mr. Moore, and call our young men together, and ascertain who is willing to bear a flag of truce to them.   Now is the time to rescue Miss Elliot, before they hear the disastrous news respecting their own party from other lips."

" It requires no prophet to tell who will go, even without summoning them," replied Moore.

"You mean Hall ! true, true—but would it be prudent, think you, to suffer him to set out upon such an errand ?"

" I do not know, Sir, but Lee says that he fought like a lion, and behaved in every way in the most prudent as well as gallant manner."

" Then bring him here, with the scout."

In the course of little more than an hour, young Hall stood before the Governor, with the scout by his side.

" Are you willing to carry a flag of truce to the enemy's camp or village, as the case may be ?" enquired His Excellency.

" I desire that privilege of all things, Sir, and am ready to set out."

The Governor then turned to Jarvis, but started back, and said, " Why, who the d———l have you got there ?"

" This is one of the yaller niggers, your honor—I fout him myself, and hearin' that you was a goin' to send this young gent with me to the Ingin village, I thought it best to take him along, 'case he can tell his folks that we've got lots more of 'em up here, and that your honor will hang one on 'em for every hair in Mr. Hall's head that they meddle with—for your Excellency knows that they've got quite a curious way of medlin' with people's hair sometimes."

" A good idea, Jarvis; but I did hear that you had captured the interpreter, Chunoluskee—is it so ?"

" Sartin sure, but I am too old a coon to take him down yonder.   He's the best card we've got in our pack, and you know, Governor, it aint always the best plan to lead off with your trumps, unless you've got a desperate bad hand, which aint the case with us, by no manner o' means."

Without farther parley, the Governor instructed Hall to go with Jarvis, and search out the spot from which the smoke rose, and if he found out the encampment or village, to offer ten of their best warriors among the prisoners for the release of Miss Elliot—indeed, to go to any extent in like offers, if necessary, besides promising them valuable presents, " which," said he, " we will ratify when we descend to the mountain.   Should they, however, turn a deaf ear to all your overtures, and break up the encampment and move off, kindle fires on their trail, Jarvis, and we will station parties ready to cut off their retreat in either direction."

The Governor then returned to his own encampment, and our adventurers commenced their perilous enterprise.

CHAPTER XXVII

A RESCUE

HALL and the scout, with their captured warrior, proceeded down the mountain, guided by the smoke from the Indian wigwams, Jarvis beguiling the way, as usual, with his rude humor, and every now and then making the woods ring with his merriment, but a more inattentive auditor he could not have selected from the entire encampment. Hall's whole mind and soul was absorbed with the intensely interesting business on hand—with the hope, the near prospect of soon beholding and releasing the youthful idol of his heart. Before they had near descended into the valley, however, night was approaching; still they pursued their way, invigorated by what Jarvis drew from the captive warrior, viz: that they would find the pale-faced squaw in the very encampment to which they were bound. Hall was no longer oppressed with lethargy. He bounded over the rocks and précipices, as if he would annihilate both time and space. After several hours of such running and leaping, our adventurers found themselves at sun-set in a beautiful valley, watered by one of those sparkling mountain streams, which gathered its waters from the ravines of the mountain itself—here receiving a tributary, tumbling in beautiful cascades over its rocky bed, and there taking up some quiet little brook, which bubbled along its course in more modest guise. On the banks of the main stream, about half a mile distant, they could plainly perceive the fires of the savages' encampment. And here they called a halt, while the scout should reconnoitre the enemy's position. He was gone about half an hour, which seemed to Hall an age, so impatient was he to hear tidings of Eugenia. The scout came back quite chop-fallen, and proposed their instant retreat up the mountain.

The very first piece of information which he communicated, (and Hall would listen to nothing else until he heard that,) determined the young officer to proceed at all hazards to himself. It was, that the scout had seen with his own eyes the object of their search. He stated, moreover, that the stragglers who had escaped from the battle were pouring into the encampment, and that the squaws and relations of the slain were already setting up their hideous lamentations, which indeed they could hear from where they stood.

Jarvis told him that it would be certain death, and perhaps torture, to present themselves under such circumstances, and while they were smarting under defeat and the loss of their kindred. Hall pointed with a confident air to the white handkerchief, which he was busily fastening to its staff.

"They won't mind it, Squire, to the *vally* of this," said the scout, tossing out of his mouth a huge chew of tobacco.

"Well," said Hall, "you may return, with or without the prisoner, scout, but as for me I go forward with this flag of truce, if I were certain that they would tear me to pieces the next moment with red hot pincers."

Jarvis seemed irresolute what to do. He did not like to suffer the young man to go forward by himself, and yet he knew, if he accompanied him, he would thereby render himself powerless as to all assistance, in case of Hall's being detained. Besides, he considered the young man, though his superior officer, as really under his guidance. He scratched his head for full a quarter of an hour, and thought maturely of all the perilous circumstances surrounding them. In fact, he considered the responsibility of the adventure upon his own shoulders. At length he seemed to have formed his plans, and taking Hall a little distance from his bound captive, still keeping his beagle eye on him, however, whispered to the young man that he (Hall) had better take the warrior, and go on to the camp alone; that in case they should detain him, then he (Jarvis) could make the signal agreed upon with the Governor, and be at hand moreover to attempt his release, in case they should practice any of their bloody experiments upon him, before a party could come to the rescue.

This plan, although putting Hall forward into the post of immediate danger, was by no means desired by the scout, in order to avoid any such thing himself, but because he knew that it was impracticable to leave his companion to wait patiently while he should venture into the camp. He knew that Hall was not in a proper state of mind for such a thing, and was besides ignorant of that stealthy and wary mode of watching, necessary to avoid the Indians and accomplish any thing, in case of the worst. He adopted his plan, therefore, with a single eye to Hall's ultimate safety, and without the slightest consideration of self. When the time came for the trial, he walked along with Hall, as if he intended to bear him company all the way, but soon left him, carefully concealing his whereabouts from the wary and sly old warrior, who kept his stealthy eye always upon their movements, as much as he could without attracting attention.

After the scout had left the young man, the latter bethought him of a difficulty which had not before occurred to him, and that was how he was to communicate with the enemy. He was in a state of mind, however, not to be deterred from his purpose by even greater difficulties than this, and he moved steadily forward, keeping the captive immediately in front—the stream on one side, and the foot of the mountain but a few yards distant, on the other—until they arrived immediately opposite the encampment, and separated from it only by the small creek, upon the surface of which were reflected the Indian fires and wigwams. He could see the groups of savages as they sat, and lounged, and stood around the various fires—and the frantic gestures of those who had lost husbands and sons in the late battle. It was but a few moments that he took to examine the various attitudes of those with whom he would so soon have to deal, or who might so soon have to deal with him. He was nothing daunted by all those sinister portents which had alarmed the more experienced scout, but loosing his prisoner, pointed across the stream, an intimation that he was at liberty. He did not require a second telling, but bounded across the narrow stream like a deer, and soon stood in the midst of his friends. His arrival was received with many demonstrations of joy; but when he had exchanged a few words with them, and pointing and gesticulating all the while in the direction where Hall stood, and where they had left Jarvis, such a hideous yell as they sent up might well have appalled a stouter heart than Hall's. The savages immediately seized their weapons, and some score of them dashed down the stream, where the scout had been last seen.

Hall saw that now was the time to approach, if at all, and he walked deliberately across the stream, bearing his flag of truce aloft. Never was joy, exultation and malignity more manifest than it was in the countenances of the demoniacs who now crowded around the bearer of that flag, not excepting even the women and children. Not that they were ignorant of the meaning attached to a flag of truce. Hall was bewildered—his faculties already weakened—he was lost in the whirl and excitement of the moment, and he stood like a statue in the midst of his enemies. His face was pale, but his eye bright. He made a faint effort to speak at first, but seeing that he was not understood, and that his late captive was still haranguing his people—gesticulating all the while, and pointing to him and the flag, and the spot where he had left the scout, he remained a passive prisoner in their hands. That he might consider himself a prisoner, he did not doubt for a moment.

When his late prisoner had got through with his harangue or narrative or whatever it might be, one of the oldest warriors took the flag from his hand and then calling to a hideous old parchment faced hag placed it in her hands amidst the peculiar merriment of Indian women and children. He then proceeded to disarm the young man, and to strip him of his garments. While these preperations were going forward others of more fearful portent were also under way. Armsfull of finely split pine wood were thrown in a pile and some of the squaws and children were already building them into the peculiar shape required for the immolation of a victim. Luckily Hall was not familiar with the horrid details of their barbarities and he was, therefore spared the dreadful anticipation. When they had stripped him to a state of nudity, and during a calm and quiet moment, which had succeeded to the late strong exhibitions of triumph—the wild and solemn scene was disturbed by a scream which might have waked the dead. Scarcely had its echoes died away among the solemn forest ere a youthful and beautiful creature, dressed something after the Indian fashion came bounding like a deer through the bushes, dropping one of the rude earthen vessels of the Indians, as she ran, and clasped the captive in her arms. There she clung like a vine which had grown to a sturdy oak, but Hall could return no corresponding endearments, for his hands were already tied behind him. Once or twice she turned her head partially around and caught glimpses, first, of the grim warriors around, and next of the fearful pile in the course of construction, and then she would bury her head in his bosom as if she would seek protection there, exclaiming in agonized sobs, "Oh Harry, your efforts to save me have destroyed you—they are going to put you to the torture. Why, oh why, did you come alone?"

Hall, in a whisper, informed her that he had borne a flag of truce from the Governor and that the scout could not be far off, as he had accompanied him within sight of the camp. While they thus exchanged a few hurried explanations, a sudden thought seemed to strike the distressed maiden, and she ran off toward the spring, to which she had been when Hall first made his appearance. In a few moments she returned, dragging along with feeble steps our old acquaintance, Wingina. When she had brought her face to face with the chiefs, she, with the energy and eloquence of despair, bid Wingina inform her cruel kinsmen of the sacred nature of a flag of truce, and what signal vengeance the Governor would take upon them if they violated it. To all this the same old chief before pointed out, answered that before the Governor was done his breakfast, they would be half way across the valley, and hence their hasty preparations for the torture. Eugenia clasped her hands and wrung them in frantic despair, alternately praying, and wailing in the most distracted and heart-rending appeals. But it all fell powerless upon the strong hearts of the grim savages who surrounded her.

While they were in the very act of dragging poor Hall to the spot appointed for his last agonies, a bright light burst upon the scene, followed by another, and another, encircling the camp at the distance of a quarter of a mile, with a complete belt; and so rapidly were they kindled that the Indians supposed themselves surrounded, and stood upon their arms. Poor Eugenia fell upon her knees and alternately calling upon her earthly friends for help and returning thanks to her God for the prospect of deliverance. The horrors of Germana were still rising up vividly before her mental vision with renewed terrors.

The Indians knew not what to do. They were afraid to move in any direction, for their enemies seemed to be all around them. Yet the death-like stillness of the forest was uninterrupted, except by the wailing of the white maiden, and she was soon effectually silenced by the threatened attitude of a warrior with uplifted tomahawk. There stood the savages, each warrior behind a tree—stealthily peeping out every now and then, in the direction of the fires, and the women and children flat upon the ground, behind logs, if they could find them, but all as far as possible from their own fires, so that they did not approach too near the light of those that surrounded them. After remaining in this position for some twenty minutes, the savages began to wonder why their enemies did not close in upon them as they at first apprehended they would. Then one warrior was seen to steal to the hiding place of another, until they were soon broken into little groups again, still keeping within the shadows of the trees, and without the light of the fires. Hall, Eugenia and Wingina, were in bright relief, surrounded with all these dark and stealthy figures, and for somes minutes the two latter had been consulting together, the result of which was made manifest in an attempt of Wingina to put out the fire, and Eugenia to loose her lover. The latter movement, was, alas, discovered instantly, by their enemies, and one of them occupying a tree nearest to them came out from his hiding place, threw the blazing faggots again into a heap, and approached with uplifted tomahawk to make short work with the punishment of Hall and effectually prevent his escape. The glittering blade was suspended almost over his head, when a deadly messenger arrested the murderous arm. It was shot from the mountain side. In that direction there were no fires. Every Indian again darted to his hiding place and the squaws and papooses who had risen to their knees to see the savage sport fell prostrate again, and all was as quiet as the grave. Nothing was heard, but the solemn moaning of the majestic forest, swayed by the night breeze, as they bent their towering heads to the majesty of the winds. 'Twas just before dawn—the moon having gone down and a night to make a savage, even, superstitious, and the mysterious circumstances surrounding them, added not a little to their terror; for whatever may have been said or sung to the contrary the aborigines of this country are superstitious to the last degree. After waiting another half hour, again the attempt was made to approach the group near the middle of the original encampment and with the same unerring result, only that the shot came from a different direction. Hall, Engenia and Wingina, now began to wonder, themselves, why their friends did not close in upon their enemies, when the former seemed to have the latter so completely in their power. The same solemn and mysterious calm again reigned throughout the forest, and this time it lasted until the suspense to our three sufferers became almost unsupportable. The savages maintained their position, and the squaws even put their papooses to sleep as they lay, but they were destined to a fearful wakening. The measured tramp of troops, apparently at some little distance, was now distinctly heard, and this again mystified the savages, as well as their captives. Were they approaching or departing? It was not long left doubtful. Nearer and nearer approached the glad and welcome harbingers to the prisoners. The former only waited to ascertain from which direction the sounds proceeded, when they simultaneously burst from their hiding places, dodging from tree to tree, as they ran. More than one attempted to wreak his vengeance upon the captive, before they departed, but the same unerring aim seemed to be pointed always ready to pick them off. When the whole body of savages had approached near to the fires in the opposite direction from that whence the tramp of troops had been heard, they were unexpectedly saluted with a volley or carbines. Such as escaped the deadly weapons ran back in the opposite direction, and there met the same welcome. Many of them escaped, nevertheless, and for many hours, even after daylight, the woods rang with the report of fire arms, that sort of stealthy warfare peculiar to the American savage, having been kept up.

No sooner was the original encampment cleared, however, than Jarvis stood beside the bound captive, and with one stroke of his knife severed the thongs which pinioned him in his painful position. In the very act of freeing his late companion and fellow-adventurer, the same low guttural chuckle was heard. "You may think it strange," said he, "that I larf at such a thing as this, but by the long chase I cant help it, just to think that I, one, by myself one, surrounded a whole camp of the yaller niggers. Let no body tell me arter to night, that they ain't cowards, and fools to boot."

"You dont mean to say," enquired Hall, in surprise, "that you were alone?"

"I am dad shamed if I dont mean to say jist that same thing. For two long hours I sot yonder on the hill and popped off the rascals as they started up at you. I kindled the fires you know, 'case that was the signal agreed upon with the Governor, and as we were to mark the route they took by the fires, I thought like as not if I kindled one all round, even the old codger would know what it meant, and sure enough he did too, know more than I thought for, 'case he must a started the boys long before he seed these fires from the top of the mountain. Lord, Mr. Hall, with a leetle, jist a leetle more practice, he'd be the very devil among these *Ingins*. He suspicioned 'em, he did. He *warnt* a going to trust you and that *dilicate* young thing there with nothing but a flag o' truce over your heads. He knowed a devilish sight better nor that. A flag o' truce to an *Ingin*!! Why, Mr. Hall, you mout as well whistle jigs to a mile stone, or sing psalms to a dead horse. But mercy on us, do jist see how that little sweet-heart of you'rn is a takin on when the danger's all over—she'll cry her eyes out. What! larfin and cryin at the same time? Well, I'm smoked up a holler tree if that aint woman all over. I have seed a man—even a man, cry in my time, but I never seed a man cry and larf too at the same time. It looks exactly like rain when the sun's a shinin'. Come go to her Squire, I guess she's about the prettiest squaw you ever seed with moccasins and leggins on, while I have a word or too with this tother one, and she's a real squaw sure enough. No larfin and cryin' there Squire." Saying which, the scout snubbed Wingina with his thumb, by way of a friendly salutation.

We will leave him to advance his suit as best he might, and Hall to resume his clothes, while we inform our readers of Eugenia Elliot's costume and how she looked in it.

She was dressed partly in the Indian and partly in the European style. She wore the leggins and moccasins of the former, while the remainder of her dress was made up of such articles as she had preserved from Indian cupidity. About her person was an old riding dress—the skirts cut short, while her hair floated in natural ringlets, about her neck. Every ornament, with which she was wont to confine it, had been either purloined or given by her as peace offerings to her captors. As long as none but savage eyes rested upon her, she felt neither shame nor embarrassment, but no sooner did she find herself alone with her lover, even in that strange wild scene, than all her conventional feelings returned.

It may be conceived how interesting was the conversation between the lovers—how much they had to tell—yet she every now and then cast her eyes over her strange appearance, and then covered her face with her hands.

On the horrors of the massacre at Germana, and her father's cruel murder, and her own subsequent sufferings, Hall would not suffer her to dwell. He barely listened to a short and abbreviated narrative, because he saw that it was necessary for her to disburden her distracted thoughts. Then he led her gently to more hopeful themes—to the bright prospect which was still left to them. He told her of Lee's free pardon, the news of which he had the happiness to be the first to bring over. After two hours of conversation upon such interesting matters, he succeeded in restoring her to something like hope and composure. Her fitful moods of crying and laughing—which had excited Jarvis's special wonder—were now supplanted by a gentle and winning melancholy. She walked about the encampment, her hand clasped in her lover's, with the fondness of a child. She seemed to dread the separation of a moment, and was even yet startled at the continued but distant report of fire-arms.

At the suggestion of Hall, she took Wingina as a guide, and went about among the tents to collect such pieces of her wardrobe as the squaws had left in the hurry of their flight, and of which they had previously robbed her. They found Jarvis seated on the ground beside the Indian girl, apparently not having made much progress in his suit, fer they were conversing in a sharp and rather angry mood. The fact was, Wingina had been rather effectually spoiled for Jarvis's purpose—in other words, her notions were too high for the poor scout, and he could not exactly comprehend it. The home-thrusts which he gave her towards the conclusion of their conversation, about her loss of caste, and all that, it would not be exactly proper for us to repeat in his homely and rude phraseology. Suffice it to say, that when they were separated by the approach of Hall and Eugenia, they were thoroughly angered with each other.

Eugenia was compelled to forego the protection of her lover's hand for a time, while she and Wingina rummaged the tents, and while Hall turned his attention once more to his military duties.

He soon found, however, that one superior in command to himself had headed the party to whose timely interference he owed his life, and the rescue of his mistress. Bernard Moore met them as they were making the rounds of the camp, and the three proceeded on together, to call in the scattered troops. Jarvis's tongue was in no measure silenced by the presence of the commander of the scouting party. He had been too much exasperated and disappointed for that. While Moore and Hall conversed together upon other matters, the scout would break out into a soliloquy, after the following fashion :

" The pampered heifer, to turn up her yaller nose at an honest man's son like me. I reckon there's as good fish in the sea as ever was cotched. And she to tell me—the likes of her—to tell me, that she was the daughter of a King ! I reckon she wants for to come for to go to marry Mr. Lee, or Mr. Moore, or Mr. Hall, at the very least."

" What's that, scout ?" said both, as they turned round, upon hearing their names mentioned.

" Oh, it's nothin' worth talking about gents—I was only arguin' the matter betwixt that *sassy* little yaller baggage and me. She curls up her royal nose so high at me, that you would a thought I had just come in from a skunk huntin'. I reckon an honest white man's as good as an Ingin—whew—fal, lal de liddle"—and here he cut a few fandangoes to his own music, and snapped his fingers ; after which, he continued :—" I reckon I am as well out of the scrape as she is—if it war'nt for Bill, and Ikey, and them fellers to Williamsburg, a larfin at me, I would'nt care a chew tabacco. What a fool I was to go and blab the thing beforehand."

The troops were by this time dropping in from pursuit of the enemy, and such as had been wounded or killed in the skirmish were borne into camp, upon rude litters. Moore's attention was now required to his military duties, and Hall, being relieved, he returned once more to the presence of her whom he had followed to the wilderness. She clung to him like a frightened bird, and all night long they sat by the camp-fire and conversed of the past, and sometimes, too, of the brighter future. Truth to say, however, her young life had suffered a blight in its first morning bloom, which was not to be dispelled in an hour, even by one who was now all in all to her. There was a shade of melancholy cast over her most cheerful glimpses of the future, and there was that constant looking forward to, and dread of, some new horror, about to be enacted, so common to those who have suffered appalling disasters.

CHAPTER XXVIII.

ENTRANCE INTO THE VALLEY.

As the morning dawned, the main body of the Governor's force was perceived coming down the mountain. The shouts of the soldiers could be heard from time to time. These were led by one of the younger officers. The old chief himself was detained by two causes—first, to bring up the horses and mules left behind ; and secondly, lay out a wide military road from the gap down the western side of the mountain. Some days after this a similar one was cut on its eastern side.

Every one was now in the highest spirits—the main objects of the expedition were already attained. They had cut their way across the mountains—defeated the savages, who had sworn they should never penetrate beyond the mountains, except over their dead bodies—and they had discovered that long looked for El Dorado, so ardently desired by the Governor and his friends. True, they nowhere discovered the sources of the Mississippi, but that was now sufficiently explained, by the towering barriers which every where presented themselves along the western horizon, verifying exactly the descriptions which Chunoluskee had given to the Governor, as detailed in the early part of our narrative. They had, however, discovered a beautiful and extensive country between the mountains, and they were satisfied for the present. Towards evening the Governor, with the horses and wounded, joined the main force, and pitched his encampment upon the very ground lately occupied by his enemies, and where Hall had so nearly lost his life. The first person who presented himself at the Governor's quarters was the scout. He had left a captive on the other side, about whom he was very solicitous.

"Well, scout," said the Governor, "so you have come to claim your reward, I suppose, for capturing the traitor and murderer, Chunoluskee; but why did you not bring him to me immediately after the battle?"

"To tell you the truth, Governor, I was afeer'ed you would exchange him, as he would be a big bate among his people, but I hope you have made sure of the yaller rascal."

"Aye, certainly; but you had no design to propitiate his sister, by retaining this captive upon your own account?"

"What! me, your honor? none in the world! the deuce take his sister, I say; she turns up her royal nose at your honor's scout, as if she would'nt let me touch her with a ten foot pole."

"So, then, you have met with a rebuff already! What reason did she give for her refusal of such an advantageous offer?"

"None, Sir, none—except that it was the woodpecker seeking to mate with the eagle!"

The Governor laughed, and so did Joe—nothing discomfited, apparently, by his recent rejection. He seemed already to have forgotten almost that such a scheme had ever entered his head. In fact, he was at the time at which we have arrived, upon a very different errand—he was waiting to receive his reward for capturing the interpreter. And while we are upon the subject of the traitor, we may as well despatch it at once. Some days after, he was summoned before a court-martial, tried, found guilty, and condemned to death. He was, however, never executed—the Governor was so much elated with the success of his grand enterprise, that before his departure from the valley, he set all the captives free, and fully pardoned the murderer of his own son. He required but one condition to his clemency, and that was, that they and their people were to abandon the valley at once and forever. He charged them that if ever they were found this side of the western ridge, that they would be shot down like wild beasts. All this was done to the utter horror of the scout and all his class. It is true, the former was somewhat mollified, by seeing that the Governor no longer attempted to put in force his christianizing and tributary systems.

He was heard to declare, "that the licking which the Governor had given them on the other side of the mountains, had done more to humanize 'em, than all the book larnin' they had ever got to Williamsburg, and at schools among the nations."

On the second day of the encampment in the valley, the usual notice was posted up, that the Governor would the next morning despatch a courier for the capital. Many letters were written on the joyful occasion, some of which we will give to our readers.

To the Rev. Dr. Blair :—   *Valley of Virginia*, 1714.

My *Dear Sir*—At length we have scaled the Blue Mountains, but not without a sharp skirmish with the savages, and many of them, I am sorry to say, were of those who so lately received our bounty, and were besides objects of such deep solicitude to us.   All our labors, my dear Sir, towards civilizing and christianizing even the tributaries, have been worse than thrown away.   Mr. Boyle's splendid scheme of philanthropy is a failure, and we, his humble agents, have no other consolation left, but a consciousness of having done our duty, with a perseverance which neither scorn nor scepticism could not turn aside.   Let it not be said hereafter, that no effort was made in Virginia to treat the Aborigines with the same spirit of clemency and mildness which was so successful in Pennsylvania.   Far greater efforts have been made by us, than was ever made in that favored colony.   The difference in the result is no doubt owing to the fact, that the subjects with whom we have had to deal were irretrievably spoiled before they came under our charge—not so with those of Pennsylvania.   I mention these things to you, because you know that it was my determination when I sat out, to cross the mountains, peaceably if I could, and forcibly if I must.   The latter has been the alternative forced upon me.   From almost the very moment of setting out, our steps have been dogged, and our flanks harrassed by these lawless men, and more than one murder has been committed upon our sentries.   But of these things we can converse when we meet.   I suppose you are anxious to hear something of the country, which I have so long desired to see with my own eyes.   Well, Sir, the descriptions given to us at Temple Farm by the interpreter were not at all exaggerated, and were, besides, wonderfully accurate in a geographical point of view.   It is indeed true enough that there are double ranges of mountains, and that the sources of the Mississippi do not rise here.   We are now in a valley between these ranges, with the western mountains distinctly in view, and the eastern ones immediately in our rear. This valley seems to extend for hundreds of miles to the northeast and southwest, and may be some fifty or sixty broad.   I learn from my prisoners that it has been mostly kept sacred by the Indians as a choice hunting ground, and has not been the permanent residence of any of them, but that they came and squatted during the hunting season.   All this the interpreter kept (very wisely, as he thought, no doubt) to himself.   We have not yet seen the miraculous boiling and medicinal springs, nor the bridge across the mountains ; but parties of exploration are daily going out, and such extravagant accounts as they give of the game, and the country, and the rivers, and the magnificent prospects, beggar my pen to describe.   I can see enough, my dear Sir, from the heights in my near neighborhood, to know that it is one of the most charming retreats in the world.   I do not hesitate to predict that a second Virginia will grow up here, which will rival the famed shores of the Chesapeake; but the products will be different, and the people must be different ; for it is a colder region.   We have already had nipping frosts, and some ice upon the borders of the streams.

The Indian prisoners tell me that the springs before mentioned are beyond the second range of mountains, and that there also are to be found the sources of the Mississippi—the French settlements and many other of the objects for which we set out.   They must now be left for another campaign.   In the meantime, the frontiers of the Colony must be speedily pushed hitherward.   This country will suit admirably for our Scotch and Irish emigrants, and inducements must be held out to them to venture into the wilderness, while we see to making roads for them and affording them protection.   I am delighted with my adventure so far, and only one subject of disappointment remains.   I cannot have a brush with our ancient enemies. These captives tell me that the French and the six nations have uninterrupted intercourse from the lakes to the Mississippi. This great tramontane highway must be broken up at all hazards, else all that magnificent western country slips from our grasp, and besides we will be constantly subject to be harrassed by these disagreeable neighbors. In short, my dear Sir, the boundaries of Virginia must be pushed to the banks of the Mississippi. I know you will say that my towering military ambition is running away with me, but I feel very sure that I can submit such representations to the council, as will induce them to unite with me in an earnest appeal to the ministry at home for aid in the magnificent conquest. You will readily perceive from what I have already said, that I consider our enterprise but half accomplished, and that another far more extensive will be prepared as soon as we can hear from the other side of the water.* My young men have behaved most gallantly. Young Lee will make a fine soldier, his daring bravery is among the least of his qualifications. He has rendered me most important services, so indeed have Moore, and Carter, and Hall, and even my protege Dandridge. I send you a list of others of the young gentry who distinguished themselves. I wish you to have a Golden Horse-Shoe made for each of them to wear upon the breast, as a distinction for meritorious services : with the motto on one side, " *Sic juvat transcendere montes*," and on the other, " *The Tramontane Order*." Have them ready if possible by our return, which you may now expect in a few weeks. I shall despatch letters for my own family— I have only therefore, farther to say, that I remain your friend,

A. Spotswood.

Valley Camp, 1714.

Dear Ellen :

I am once more writing from a couch of some pain and suffering, but thank God not like the last from which I addressed you that dismal letter, which I then supposed would be my last. I have no such apprehensions now. My wounds are in a fair way, and I am even permitted to walk about this large tent—(the Governor's marquee) and above all, I am permitted to write to you.

Our camp is now pitched near to a rising knoll at the western base of the mountains, commanding a magnificent view of one of the most charming valleys that ever blessed the vision of enthusiasts. And I am told by the parties which nightly come in from exploring expeditions, that I have not seen half of its beauties. You never heard such enthusiastic accounts of a country, and the Governor is not a whit behind the youngest of them in admiration of its charms. But I must postpone my raptures about the country until I tell you something of your friend's young kinswoman, who has been so long in captivity. I am sure that this time you will not be jealous, if I tell you a great deal about that charming creature. First, then, we have recovered her, but nearly at the expense of Hall's life. Nothing prevented such a catastrophe but the foresight of our experienced chief, and the admirable presence of mind of our chief scout, Joe Jarvis—but of these things we can converse more fully when we meet face to face—I trust to part no more.

When Eugenia first made her appearance in camp, she was less strange in her appearance than was her state of mind. She was dressed something as you have seen Wingina, half in the European and half in the Indian costume, and to tell the truth, she looked exceedingly pretty : but, alas ! there was a wild vacancy about her eyes and countenance generally, which alarmed me. It was more perceptible to me, because I had known her in her better days

---

*We have every reason to suppose that this was the very subject upon which the Governor subsequently quarrelled with the ministry. They attempted to retrace their steps at an immense loss of blood and treasure afterwards, at the celebrated defeat of Braddock.

and under more favorable circumstances. This, as I expected and feared, terminated in sickness, and she has been lying ever since in an ample tent, almost touching ours. She has been constantly attended by Hall, and by a young man who was formerly a pupil of your excellent father. Since I have been permitted to move about, I have visited her almost every hour. Her case would have furnished a curious study for some one more philosophically disposed, than any one we can boast of in our ranks. Her disease seemed like Ophelia's, a rooted sorrow from which no mere mortal physician could pluck the sting. Even her mental faculties seemed in a sort of eclipse—not that she wandered, as it is called, or was at all frantic, but she appeared imbecile and childish. This was succeeded by such a load of oppression, that I, who knew her, feared her heart would break : but good old mother nature always came to her relief in the shape of a plentiful shower of hysterical tears, mingled sometimes with frightful laughter. The latter ugly concomitant has been gradually subsiding, and true and genuine tears have taken their place. At first they forbid her to talk upon the melancholy particulars of the sad affair at Germana, but I saw that this was all wrong, and I at length persuaded the Governor to let me try the opposite plan; I am happy to say it has succeeded beyond my most sanguine expectations. She now loves to talk over her melancholy story, and I left her but a few moments ago, talking and crying with poor Hall. Her sensibility is evidently returning, and with it her mental strength. By the time she reaches Williamsburg, you will see that she is worthy of all the commendations I have bestowed upon her. I have not and will not say that she has attained to that excellence which my Ellen has aimed at, but she possesses all the native materials to work upon, and will doubtless attain, as she grows in experience and knowledge of the world, to a point worthy of moving in your delightful circle. You must recollect that she early lost her mother. True, you were equally unfortunate, but then her place was supplied to you by such a father as seldom blesses the orphan female in this world. You must recollect, too, that the lamented uncle who adopted her was a purely military character, and how poorly calculated were his daily associates to refine and model the forming character of our young friend. It was the brightness with which she shone under such disadvantageous circumstances, which first attracted my attention. I thought then what a charming creature she would be if she could only possess the advantages which you possessed. Dreadful has been her experience—the hand of affliction has been laid heavily upon her, and I regret of all things, that she cannot be at this very moment under your care as well as that of your father.

You would like to hear something doubtless of your former protege Wingina. I have been loth to say any thing about her, because I could not say any thing that would be pleasing to you. She, I fear, brought nothing away from civilized life, but its evils. Jarvis, the scout, seems to have a rude sort of a passion for her, but she treats him with scorn and detestation ; and to tell you the truth, I am rejoiced at it, on account of both. He is almost as much a savage as one of her race, but there is this difference—the scout has a substratum (if I may be allowed the expression) in his character, which promises better things than any which he now exhibits, while the Indian, I fear, is just the reverse.

I have learned to feel something like an attachment for the scout. The native soil is a good one, and with judicious attention and skilful guidance, he might be made a useful man in his sphere. I have proposed to him to go home with me, when we return, and live upon my land, but he declares that he means to live in this valley. Time will show whether he is to be moved from his purpose.

The Governor's benevolent views towards the Indians have received a terrible shock with his Tramontane experience, and I suspect that we shall hear little of Mr. Boyle's plans in future, and less of his own tributary schools.

Why, what a love letter is this, that Frank has written to me, you will say. Think of it again, my dear Ellen, and you will consider it a compliment to your understanding, as well as to your heart. Certainly I feel proud that I can already discourse of such reasonable matters to my promised wife.

I will fulfil all your promises to your dear and venerable father, with interest, my Ellen. Is he not mine also?—has he not been more than a father to me, and how much more than father will he be, when he entrusts to my keeping such a daughter? We will consult his prejudices, and should he have even whims in old age, his second childhood shall be as sacred to me, as my first was to him. God evidently looks with peculiar benignity upon those children who lead the steps of the aged (even in senility) with tender care and affection. Trust me, my Ellen, that the very peg upon which his cocked hat hangs, shall be as sacred in my eyes, as it is in those of his dutiful and affectionate daughter. Every pledge of filial affection which you make to your venerable parent, I cherish as guarantees of the excellencies of my future wife. That the worthy object of them may long live to bless our lives, is the sincere prayer of your own   FRANK.

CHAPTER XXIX.

LIFE IN THE WILDERNESS.

Two delightful weeks were spent in the valley of Virginia by the Governor and his followers, during which time the magnificent forests of that region underwent a daily transmutation. At first, the leaves began to wither, and then fade to a sickly green—before they assumed their gorgeous autumnal dress. The tenderest and earliest of their kind had already fallen and strewed the ground with a carpet little less rich than the canopy over head. The migratory birds were already on their passage southward, sometimes making *their* encampments in the near and dangerous neighborhood of their human contemporaries. The tops of the highest mountains were already covered with snow, and though the days were of a delightful temperature, the nights were bitter cold to our thinly clad adventurers. All these signs and changes admonished the Governor that it was time to turn his face homeward. He was reluctant to leave the country which he had discovered and conquered.* Gladly would he have pitched his tent there for life, but his responsible position at the head of his Majesty's Colony, required that he should be elsewhere, and orders were accordingly issued for striking the tents and recrossing the mountains. Nearly all his followers obeyed the summons with alacrity. The wounded and the sick (many suffering with cold) were sufficiently recovered to travel on horseback. Lee, looked pale and wan, but his eye was bright, his countenance cheerful, and his spirits elastic as ever. A sort of side-saddle had benn constructed out of one of the dragoon saddles for Eugenia, and she professed herself fully able to undertake the journey. The Governor had her carried across the mountain in a litter, over his new military road, which, by the by, was nothing but an enlargement and widening of the Indian and buffalo paths. Even in its improved state, it would have made McAdam laugh. Wingina, professed herself desirous of returning to her civilized friends. Whether this determination, so different from the instincts of the native savage—was produced by fear of her now liberated brother, or by delicate considerations of another nature, it is not for us to determine. She was

*This is the region which ought to have been called Spotsylvania.

also mounted on horse-back, and formed one of the Governor's own immedi-ate party. Though there was this general willingness and alacrity to com-mence the return march, there was one exception to it. The Governor had his foot in the stirrup, when the Scout approached with his coon skin in hand, and unusually polite.

"Well Jarvis," said the Governor, casting his eye to the Indian girl at the same time, "what's your will now? Do you wish to form one of our escort?"

The Scout saw the direction of the Governor's eye and readily understood his meaning, and he replied accordingly, "Not I, your Excellency, a wood-pecker would make but a sorry show a flying along side of an eagle;" and he chuckled as he looked up at the scornful Indian beauty, seated upon her high horse in more senses of the word than one.

"What. then, is it, Jarvis?—you have but to ask any thing reasonable, at our hands, to have it granted forthwith."

"I'm mighty glad to hear your Honor say so, 'case I am come to ask a whop-pin' big thing—It's a plantation!"

"A plantation, Jarvis? why, are you going to retire to the shades of private life?"

"Jist exactly the very words Governor, only they wer'nt no where in my dictionary. You've struck the very trail. I want to retire to the shades of private life, and I guess you'll call this private life, and them shades enough down here in this valley."

The Governor laughed at the conceits of the woodsman ere he replied: "Certainly, Jarvis, you have fully earned your plantation, and I think I may guarantee that a grant* will be made out for you in due time, but you have no idea of remaining here at present."

"Yes, but I have though, got that very idea in my head, and if your Excel-lency will just let me collect about fifty recruits from these hunting shirt boys, we'll fall to work out of hand, and by the time you come back, you will see log cabins a plenty sprinkled about these woods."

The Governor meditated upon this strange proposition a few moments, and then replied; "Not now, Jarvis—not now—I want you to return with us to the Capital. It will be time enough next spring. Then your fifty shall be increased to a thousand."†

Jarvis knew that it was useless to talk farther on the subject, when the Governor had once made up his mind. He was, nevertheless, disappointed for the moment. No one would have found it out, however, two hours after, when his merry voice was heard on the mountain side. His unsuccessful love-making soon became bruited about among his boon companions, and it may readily be imagined with what avidity they showered their jeers and jibes upon one so ready to crack his jokes upon others. He bore it all patiently for a while, but his naturally pugnacious temperament, broke forth at last, and as he said, "when they gave him mustard he sent them back pepper."

Poor Wingina came in for not a few of his sallies. Not that he durst offer her any indignity in the Governor's presence, but as she would appear occasion-ally, in windings of the mountain defile, he would let fly a few shafts at the eagle in her lofty flights.

It is not our intention to follow the party step by step on its return, over the same ground which we have once already conducted it. Suffice it then to say, that in due time the Governor and his followers encamped within a day's march of the Capital, and the same night a courier was despatched to

---

*Whether the present Joe Jarvis, who still inhabits the mountain side, and with whom we have had many a merry drive, is a lineal descendant of Old Joe, we leave to those curious in such matters to ascertain.

†We believe that it was more than ten years afterwards before any effectual settlements were made in the valley. Our own ancestors were among the pioneers.

the senior councillor, Dr. Blair, informing him that he had arrived safe so far on his return.

Great was the rejoicing next day at Williamsburg—and the expected arrival of the Governor of the Colony was announced early in the morning by the discharge of cannon, bon-fires, and ringing of bells. Large parties of ladies and gentlemen were all day leaving the city to escort the mountain adventurers home; so that toward evening when they came once more in sight of the Capital, their numbers were greatly increased.

As Lee rode along side of Ellen Evylin, the old Doctor being on the other, the Scout came cantering up on his poney, and hailed the former loudly. So absorbed, however, was that young gentleman with the interesting conversation, that Jarvis had almost to shout in his ear before he could command his attention.

"What is it Jarvis?" said he almost petulantly.

"I didn't know, Squire, that you were so much engaged, but as I was a ridin' along the ranks jist now I couldn't help a wonderin' what had become of all the gold lace and ruffles that travelled over this road a few weeks ago."

This remark of the Scout induced Lee to cast his eye over his own outward man, and to remove his now slouched (instead of cocked) hat from his head. The result was a hearty laugh from the whole party, including the Scout of course.

Seldom had such a way-worn, dusty and ragged army made their appearance in any city, since the days of Jack Falstaff. It was hard to imagine the contrast which they presented to their former selves on the day of their departure, at which time they literally glittered with finery. But if their outward man was shabby and ragged—their inward man was in a corresponding ratio, bright and joyous.

Ellen at first looked with apprehension at the pale and emaciated features of her lover, but when she heard once more that joyous laugh which had made her father's house merry in the days of their infancy, she was satisfied. Her heart was full, she did little as she rode by Frank's side but to listen to the narration of their tramontane adventures.

Eugenia Elliot was seized upon and monopolized by Kate and Dorothea, her cousins, much to the discomfiture of poor Moore. He might well have been called the Knight of the rueful countenance. He ought, however, to have been satisfied, for Kate was doing nothing but her duty, and besides, if lovers were not the most unreasonable creatures in the world, he would have been fully compensated by the glances of pride and affection which the now subdued beauty cast upon him. If he had had more reason and less passion about him, he would have seen a visible improvement in Kate at a single glance. The very shake of her hand was more hearty, frank and confidential than it had ever been before, and even her countenance had undergone a change. There was before almost a boldness in her free and easy carriage, but now this was softened down into the most winning grace— a little arch, sometimes, perhaps, as she could not resist the really absurd and ludicrous deportment of Moore.

There was one keen and close observer of all these things, not far off, and he was abundantly gratified. It was Carter. He was not enough behind the curtain to understand all this by-play, but he saw enough to know that his rival was discomfited and mortified. The Governor rode into the city in the highest spirits imaginable. The sun was just sinking behind the western horizon as the troops defiled own Gloucester street, and arrived in front of the Church. There stood the same platform which had been erected a few weeks ago, and upon it the good old Doctor in his canonicals, and his prayer-book in his hand. The Governor took the hint, and the troops were formed as before, and the adventurous band kneeled down to return thanks to Almighty God for their safe return. Thus did our chivalrous ancestors; let their children go and do likewise.

CHAPTER XXX.

THE KNIGHTS OF THE HORSE-SHOE.

WE do not know why it is (and always has been) that winter is described in gloomy colors. It may be that the hoar frosts, and the glittering icicles, and the snow clad fields and the leafless trees and plants, convey such impressions to a majority of mankind, but it is not so with all. There is something bracing and invigorating in a snow storm to some, (we speak not of the bleak and extreme north,) one of those old fashioned steady falls of large flat flakes, which sometimes herald in the Christmas Holidays. Such a day was the twenty-fifth of December, seventeen hundred and fourteen. There was little wind, the cold was not intense, and the merry lads let loose from school, and the negroes freed from labor were making merry with the snow balls in the ancient city. But beside the usual gaiety and freedom from care of the festive season, there were indications abroad that this day had been set apart for some extraordinary ceremony other than those incident to the season.

Martial music was heard in various directions, and soldiers almost blinded by the snow—the same troops who but a few weeks ago presented such a tatterdemalion appearance—were threading their way towards the capital. The bells, too, were pouring a merry peal over the town, and carriages and horses lined the way from the church in Gloucester street to the aforementioned edifice. Many of the ladies, occupying the vehicles, had just come from attending the usual church service on that day, but now the altars and the church hung with mistletoe, were deserted even by the Rev. Prelate* who stately officiated there. He was still robed in his canonicals, and occupied a seat in one of the carriages. When the Hall of the House of Burgesses was thrown open, the Governor was presented to the people, occupying the elevated seat usually filled by the speaker. On his right hand sat the chaplain to the General Assembly, the Rev. Hugh Jones, in his sacred robes, and round them in a semi-circle sat the members of "the Tramontane order." After the usual solemn opening of the meeting by the chaplain, the Governor stepped down the small flight of steps which led to a platform still elevated above the people. He was dressed in full court costume, wig—crimson velvet coat—ruffles at the throat and wrist. Before him was placed a table on which were spread out various ornaments of jewelry, many of them studded with gems and precious stones, but all of them wrought into the shape of horse shoes. He took one of them in his hand and read the inscription on one side, " The Tramontane Order," and turning it over, read also the motto on the other, " *Sic juvat transcendere montes.*" Here a great clapping of hands and waving of ladies' handkerchiefs in the gallery arrested its progress for a moment, during which time a happy and benignant smile played over the noble old man's features. He was evidently well pleased, but struggling with his emotions, for his eye glistened unwontedly. Whether he was thinking at the moment of other important ceremonies which were soon to be performed and in which those near and dear to him were deeply interested—or whether he was thinking of the separation which was about to take place between him and his young associates in arms, and some of them perhaps, forever, we know not. His address was brief, and something like the following : "Friends and mem-

---

* He was truly a Bishop in every thing but the name.

bers of the order. I hold in my hand a simple and unostentatious ornament, designed for the purpose of perpetuating the remembrance of one of the most glorious achievements of our lives. I am sure it is of mine (which has been longer and more eventful than that of any of my late associates in arms) and I would fain hope it is so considered by them. [Applause.] I knew that you would dearly cherish the remembrance of our mountain expedition, and it is my wish that you may continue to do so through whatever may be your future adventures. From a military experience now somewhat extended, I am proud to say, that I never yet was in command of a nobler little army. Your conduct, gentlemen, one and all, during the trying scenes through which we have passed, met with my most hearty approbation. Such a commencement of your martial career is a sure guarantee, that should our Sovereign again require the aid of your arms, no second call will be necessary to bring you forth again from your peaceful and happy homes. Some of you I learn are about to embark for the shores of our father-land in pursuit of a wider and more extended field of observation—and in furtherance of a laudable ambition to improve your understanding by examining the institutions of the old world. These insignia which I am about to present to you, will be new to the chivalry of that time-honored country, but I trust not unrecognized. I am sure when you bear these to the presence of Majesty itself, and when you inform our gracious Sovereign what a new and glorious empire you have added to'his dominions, he will recognize you as a part of the chivalry of the empire—of that glorious band of Knights and gentlemen who surround his throne like a bulwark. [Applause.]

I have only now to say farther, that I have been authorized by his Majesty's council to invest each of the following named young gentlemen with one of these badges.

Francis Lee, Ralph Wormley, Mann Page, John Randolph, Dudley Diggs, John Peyton, Thomas Bray, Theodoric Bland, Wm. Beverley, Benjamin Harrison, Oliver Yelverton, Peyton Skipwith, Peter Berkly, William Byrd, Charles Ludwell, John Fitzhugh, Thomas Fairfax, Bernard Moore, Nathaniel Dandridge, Kit Carter, Francis Brooke, John Washington, Hugh Taylor, Alexander Nott, Charles Mercer, Edward Saunders, William Moseley, Edmund Pendleton, George Hay, George Wythe, John Munroe.

May you wear them gentlemen through long and happy lives, and when you descend honored and lamented to your graves, may they descend as heirlooms to your children. When the wilderness which you have discovered and conquered shall blossom as the rose,—as most assuredly it will—these badges may be sought after by the antiquarians of a future age, as honored mementos of the first pioniers of their happy and favored country. Let them be religiously preserved then, I charge you. The simple words which form the inscription, may some day reveal the history of a portion of our country and its honored founders, when the revolutions of empires and the passing away of generations, may have submerged every other record.

Your own names, gentlemen, honored and distinguished as they now are, by illustrious ancestry, may by the mutations and instability of human greatness, be yet rescued from oblivion by these simple memorials.

The members of the order then kneeled down and were invested in due form with the insignia of the " Knights of the Horse-Shoe."*

After which the assembly dispersed, the Knights to dine with the master and founder of their order, and the people to join in the festivities of the season.

---

* Whether they received the acolade after the established custom of investing a Knight, and whether the Governor of a colony was authorized to confer such a distinction, are questions with which we have not ventured to meddle. We have only stated what we know to be true, of which some evidence will be offered to the reader.

CONCLUSION.

During the same Christmas holidays, when the cheerful fires burned bright, and the serene and happy faces around them beamed brighter still, and when the snow storm had blown over and the sun poured his cheerful rays over the bright winter scene—on such a day, a plain but elegant carriage and four stood before the modest and vine-clad dwelling of Dr. Evylin; and sundry other vehicles of different kinds, were packed with travelling trunks—and servants, male and female, were marshalled in the rear. The one first described was, as yet empty, and various groups of idlers stood round the gate to catch a glimpse of those whom madam rumor assigned as its intended occupants.

As the hour hand pointed to a certain figure on the dial plate, and the last tones of the bell died away, the Old Doctor and his daughter rose simultaneously and were locked in each other's embrace. Lee stood by, and any one, (if not by his dress, at least by his bright face,) might have told that he was *the* happy man. Ellen shed tears, as she saw the gittering drops falling fast from her father's eyes, and as she felt his trembling frame locked in the last embrace. Lee brought the old gentleman's cocked hat, and handed him his gloves, and assisted him in wrapping up his feeble frame in a fur-lined cloak, after which all three entered the carriage and drove to the church.

When they arrived at the door two more bridal parties already awaited their arrival. We need scarcely say that they consisted of Moore and Kate, and Hall and Eugenia. There was a serene melancholy upon the faces of most of those present—especially on those of the brides. Even Kate looked subdued and rather apprehensive, not that she doubted the man at all, to whom she was about to plight her faith, but the ceremony was so solemn—the change so important—the new relations about to be assumed for weal, or wo, so enduring. These were far more oppressive to her at the altar, than to Ellen, because the latter had longer and more maturely deliberated upon them. Eugenia was the most melancholy of the three, but it was pleasing, and had more relation to things past, than to those future. As Ellen walked up the aisle, hand in hand with her lover, and her father immediately in the rear, she really looked charming in her simple white dress, and her slightly flushed cheeks. Some one in the gallery uttered a sort of exclamation of applause. Lee looked over his shoulder and discovered Jarvis screwed up into one corner near the organ, and making a feint with his coon-skin cap, as much as to say that he would wave it over his head and shout if he dared. Lee placed his finger on his lip to enjoin silence, which the scout answered by placing his hand over his mouth. Few observed these things but the actors.

Kate's toilet had been more elaborately and expensively made than Ellen's, but it was still elegantly simple. A single necklace was the only costly ornament of jewelry which she wore, and it her mother had worn before her on a similar occasion. The Rev. Dr. Blair was already at the altar with his book open before him; all the parties, except Eugenia and Hall, were more to him like his own children than ordinary parishioners, and the good old man's eye betrayed his deep sympathy with the parties, and his solemn appreciation of the importance of the change which was about to pass over so many of his former pupils. The Governor gave away his own daughter as well as his young kinswoman, and the old Doctor gave away Ellen.

The bridal ceremony concluded, the whole party drove to the palace where a cold collation was served up for them preparatory to their departure to their several places of destination. Lee and Hall with their brides, were to spend the Chrismas holidays at the country establishment of the former, and old Doctor Evylin had been persuaded to accompany them for the visit only.

Kate and Moore determined to spend their honey-moon at Temple Farm, partly because their happiest days of courtship had been spent there, and partly because it would give such unmeasured delight to their humble depen- dants, old June among the number. The old fellow was now—since his mountain adventures—quite a hero in the kitchen chimney corner, and Kate had presented him with a new banjo, which, together with his new materials of song, had quite set him up in business.

Time and death have both set their seals upon these marriages, and contra- ry to what is usual at the announcement of such events, we can look forward at once to their results. We know that they were eminently happy, that the parties lived long in as much felicity as is ever vouchsafed to mortals on this earth. With the descendants of Gen. Bernard Moore and Catherine Ann Spotswood, we have long been intimate, and we can pronounce from a knowl- edge so attained, that many of their fine qualities still adorn the lives and characters of those who fill their places.

Ellen and Frank lived with the old Doctor, and fulfilled together to the utmost those filial duties which the former had made so much the business and pleasure of her days of single blessedness. The old man lived to fondle on his knee several of the descendants of his happy children, and was at last, full of honors and full of years, buried beneath the stones of that Church, which he had helped to build, and in which he had so long been a devout and faithful worshipper. A tablet to his memory, erected by Gov. Spotswood, and stating on its face the grief of his Excellency at the death of the old man, still adorns one of the niches of the Church at Williamsburg; at least it did but a few years ago.

Jarvis moved to the valley of Virginia and built a log cabin on the side, where he had first fallen in love with that beautiful country. Whether he married a Squaw or not we have no means of knowing. Those of the same name inhabiting the same region to this day, have, however, a slight bronze tinge to their complexion.

Governor Spotswood ruled over the affairs of Virginia for six years from the date of the Tramontane Expedition, and after his surrendering the Guberna- torial chair, was appointed Post Master General of His Majesty's Colonies, and subsequently Commander-in-Chief of an expedition against the Spaniards in Florida. He, however, died at Annapolis, Maryland, on his way to assume that command. His mortal remains lie there to this day, unhonored we be- lieve, even by a tablet.

And now our story is told, and as in duty bound, we would most respectfully make our bow to those kind readers who have followed us thus far. Before, however, we bid them farewell, we would gossip with them a little longer— we would fain prolong our pleasant evening talks by the fire-side, and discourse still farther of the cocked hat gentry in the old dominion. And were we to consult our own feelings alone, most assuredly they would be prolonged, and our story should have engrafted upon it a sequel, or another concerning the same old time-honored gentry, but when we cast our thoughts back over the time of our kind readers, which we have already engrossed, we are admonish- ed that it is indeed time to bring our story to a close. We have now only to offer some evidence that our story was indeed founded upon the traditions which have descended to our times. The venerable jurist from whom the following letter was received has so long adorned the highest judicial tribunals in Virginia, and is, therefore, so extensively known, that it would be useless to multiply testimony upon the point to which he alludes; if it were, we could do so, to any reasonable extent. Many are the persons still living in Virginia, who have seen with their own eyes these Golden Horse-Shoes. Indeed we were some time upon the trace of one of the curious relics itself, and were only prevented from pursuing our researches to a successful issue, by the want

of time and the distance of our present residence, from the scene of the celebrated adventure.

To the descendants of Governor Spotswood and General Bernard Moore, we
are under many obligations for the materials with which they have so kindly
furnished us. To Colonel Spotswood of Indiana, and Charles Campbell, Esq.
editor of the Petersburg Statesman, in particular, we are greatly indebted, and
we return them our hearty thanks, and only regret that we have not been able to
do greater and more merited justice to the character of their common ancestors.

Western Virginia should erect some enduring monument to the memory of
the far-sighted statesman and gallant soldier who first discovered that noble
country.

The following is a copy of Judge Brooke's letter to the Author:

ST. JULIEN, (near Fredericksburg,) Va., February 25th, 1841.

To Dr. Wm. A. Caruthers:

My Dear Sir: I have received your letter of the 5th inst., and in reply to it,
can only say what I some years past said to my friend George W. Summers,*
on the subject of your letter. I said to him, that I had seen in the possession
of the eldest branch of my family, a Golden Horse-Shoe set with garnets,
and having inscribed on it the motto : " *Sic juvat transcendere montes,*" which
from tradition, I always understood was presented by Governor Spotswood, to
my Grandfather, as one of many gentlemen who acompanied him across the
mountains.

With great respect, yours,

FRANCIS BROOKE.

* The Hon. Geo. W. Summers, the present representative in Congress, from the Kenawha District, in Virginia.